C000142922

Legacy

by David Lingard

Edited by Denise Boorman

A note from the author

I just wanted to say here, thank you, whoever you are for however you have arrived at this book and my story. It makes a big difference to authors like me, who like to feel as though their hard work and dedication is appreciated when our work is read.

Your investment of your own time and money is as always, well appreciated. It takes a long time and a lot of effort to write, edit and release a book, so please, I ask that you **rate** and **review** everything that you read – and not just this book, so that lesser known authors can grow their audience and gain the credibility that they deserve.

Also, I have a website that is usually kept up to date with current works, reviews and a few extra little bits. You'll find it at: www.davidlingard.com

Prologue

Fifteen years ago, Intergalactic Council meeting, starship Contessa.

"What do we do with them?" the first speaker asked the council members around the table, each representing a different sentient race.

"We must destroy them," a second replied.

"All of them?"

The second speaker and advocate of destruction nodded slowly. He was from a race of beings that had learnt harsh lessons about leaving potential threats to grow for too long. Jorell of the Ascara was over three hundred years old himself and had witnessed first hand the rise and fall of races who'd gained power all too quickly, taking others along with them in their inevitable downfall.

The Ascara were respected around the table of Intergalactic Council, though it was a democracy and not a dictatorship so although the humanoid – albeit with four arms and yellowish skin – spoke with authority, his decision wouldn't be final without a majority vote.

The first speaker was a member of the Intari, a smaller, gnome-like race whose constitution was far less inclined to start (or finish) wars, as they very much preferred to follow a policy of non-interference wherever it was possible. Of course, the Intari had never had to deal with the fallout from allowing a powerful race to grow within their own sectors of the galaxy as the Ascara had, so their opinion on the matter was somewhat less informed.

The room was slightly darkened so as to not offend some of the races that were used to living underground or on planets where the central sun was distant or dimming due to its age. Be it young or old, though, it was a happy compromise for the meeting that was taking place to determine what should be done with the humans of planet earth.

Never before had Jorell witnessed a race so intent on destroying itself from within, as though human beings were a cancer that was causing the planet they called home to implode; the only way that the humans had decided they could survive was the idiotic notion that they should wipe themselves out. The logic made no sense to him – the humans had been waging wars with each other for centuries, millennia even, but up until this very moment their methods of war had been somewhat lacking and focussed on their set objectives. Even Jorell could appreciate military action when it was necessary – of course the Ascara hadn't been without their own issues, wars and near-planetary destruction events, but the humans seemed just so focussed on their own destruction.

The council had been called as a matter of urgency once it was apparent that the humans of earth had travelled along a course of evolution that they were calling 'nuclear weapons.' Many of the races around the table had had their own close calls with such technologies, though its use was universally frowned upon due to its long-term and totally destructive nature. Nuclear weapons were not manufactured to destroy targets with precision, rather they were made to threaten, scare and inevitably cause wide-ranging, indiscriminate destruction.

Nuclear weapons had been called by a great number of names across the inhabited worlds across all of the systems of the council, and generally it was assumed that once a world had researched such destructive technologies, they were almost always evolved enough to understand that they should never be used, threatened to be used, or manufactured in any large quantities. It was a gateway power to bigger and better things, such as fission, or plasma-based technologies that could benefit the given race with immeasurable energy considerations. Humans, however, had apparently reached nuclear weapons and stopped right there. And that made them extremely dangerous. A race that saw such terrible and destructive power and rubbed its hands together at the thought was one to be very wary of.

"Why don't we help them out instead? Teach them the better ways?" The Intari offered, though the suggestion seemed somewhat half-hearted and Jorell hardly even nodded his head in understanding. Every member of the council had a voice though so it was customary for him to acknowledge the speaker.

"And do what with them then? Jorell replied. They seem unable to comprehend the gravity of the destruction that they threaten, which in itself is enough reason for destruction. If we were to help this race through to the next stage in their evolutionary path, why would you not think that they'd become a larger threat to us all in the long run?" Jorell made his counter argument for destruction and around the table gestures of acknowledgement and agreement were returned.

"Because I think they are useful," another voice came in reply. It was higher pitched than Jorell's and the Intari's, though held no less weight as the council regarded all of its members as equal, no matter their military might or racial perceptions. It was part of what made the council so effective.

The room fell deathly silent allowing the new speaker to submit his own statement.

"Speak your mind, Kron. What is it you are proposing that these humans are useful for, if not destruction?" Jorell replied clearly.

"Forgive me, but I believe that that is exactly what they are useful for. This race has something that we have never seen within our combined alliances before. The humans are a warring race, as you have said. When they can't find someone to fight against they fight amongst themselves. They create hardships for each other and covet their resources over human-made borders rather than share and grow as is the logical path. These people pride themselves on diplomacy but ultimately it has failed them every single time. We know as a council that we lack a force with which to deter our enemies as one, but I believe that no race around this table would be forthcoming in providing a military for the council to call its own. With the threats that we are currently facing in the border sectors and the lack of military might we are able to amass between us, my proposal is..." the creature named Kron spoke and was interrupted by a chorus of agreement in his statement, for they all knew what he was about to suggest.

Eventually the choruses died down to a mere murmur and Jorell spoke again. "Then it shall go to a vote, which as always must be in favour of the proposal at fifty percent or more," he announced. "The human beings of earth will be used as the military might of the Intergalactic Council, to represent and fight for the interests of every race together at this table now. My own proposal is that we give this offer to the humans in a slightly condensed form. It must be seen as a good idea for them to join us in such a way, though they must not learn that we are a weakened military force. We have all grown through communications, alliances and technological advancement. We do not favour war and as such we have forgotten many of the ways of our ancestors. As with a cornered creature, we must not display our weaknesses, for it could ultimately be our downfall."

This was how the vote was cast to use human beings as the frontline soldiers of the Intergalactic Council, and the singular decision that would save earth – and humanity – from immediate destruction. Earth would be contacted and accepted as a potential member to a council that they had never known existed, consisting of alien races they had never known the universe contained.

The races that all formed the council had not always been so diplomatic, many of them evolving from creatures that had survived through war and could have even been thought of as predatory, but they all had one thing in common. Each race had grown, evolved and advanced technologically to a level universally known as the 'Information Age,' where information and communications were globally available to all citizens of the given race at all times without prejudice or bias. Then, they'd been able to move past their internal differences and achieve a state of peace that meant they were able to forget their war-like ancestors, for the most part at least. The irony of the fact was that individually they were weak though they all had the ability to appear strong as a collective.

As one the council knew that they needed to portray this strength to the humans, otherwise this whole gambit could turn out to backfire horrifically, and with the threats of the far reaches of the galaxy beginning to present themselves to their full extent, another enemy was not something they would be able to deal with.

Chapter 1

Charlie Sinclair was orphaned when he was just three years old and had been bouncing around care facilities, foster families, orphanages and the occasional jail cell ever since the day that his parents had died tragically in a car accident. The accident was nobody's fault – that was the finding of the investigations into the incident – but it'd left Charlie bitter and wanting to blame somebody- anybody - for the life that he'd been handed.

He knew he probably wasn't the easiest three year old to raise, though he often wondered just what he could've done for the universe to shit on him in such a monumental way, to deal him the dead man's hand without a single hope of achieving anything in his future other than the four concrete walls of the inside of a jail cell, as so many on his path before him had walked. Now he was just twelve years old on the cusp of puberty, and though he didn't know it just yet, his life was about to change dramatically on the back end of a decision made by an alien race, many many light years away.

Charlie was staying with the latest in a string of foster families, this one calling themselves the 'Browns', who had structured their entire being around the idea of a single child household. It was a nice change not to have to deal with an annoying foster brother or sister, but somewhere deep down Charlie felt lonely without that constant voice telling him to 'watch this' or 'why are you doing that.'

This night was not unlike any other in the Browns' house. Dinner was a three course affair in the dining room, followed by a forced game of Uno in front of an open fire. It was forced because although the Browns seemed so engrossed in making the entire ordeal pleasurable for everyone involved, Charlie felt as though it was a giant waste of time, and certainly didn't find it 'fun' to say the least.

Charlie was just thinking about how not fun this particular game of Uno was, when his vision started to blur and he had to blink a few times to keep his concentration. Had he been this tired all night or was it the heat that was making his eyes feel heavier than usual? A few seconds passed after he blinked away the fatigue and he felt a little better. The next thing he knew he was falling to his side, his head hitting the floor and his vision fading to an unwelcome and ominous black.

Charlie's eyes refocused as he was awakened by the annoyance of lights flashing overhead. He was on his back but the entire ceiling above him was moving quickly. He could feel a numbness in both of his arms and a sharp pain at the back of his neck. He tried to look down but his head wouldn't comply with his request and when he came to his senses he realised that it wasn't the ceiling moving, rather he was on his back on a hospital trolley being rushed through corridor after corridor.

He could hear people talking now, his foster parents and what must've been doctors and nurses giving their words of encouragement – like 'it'll be OK,' and 'don't you worry,' but how could he not? He couldn't move a muscle from the neck down and it terrified him.

"Please…" he whimpered as he regained his ability to speak, though his ability to create tears that rolled down his cheeks seemed unimpaired.

"Don't let me die.." he continued weakly. "I don't want…to die."

His usually strong bravado was replaced in a moment with begging and pleading for his life and he didn't know what had changed. He was scared and all that he could think of was: *was this how my parents felt when they died?"*

"Don't worry Charlie, everything will be OK, you're in the hospital and these nice doctors are going to do everything they can to make you better again, OK? You've had a fall and you've hit your head but everything's going to be OK, I promise…" Mr Brown's round red face came into view above Charlie as he spoke and to his surprise the familiarity of the man did seem to help calm him down slightly, until another and deeper, harsher male voice entered the conversation.

"You're going to have to wait out here I'm afraid," this person said. "We've got work to do and having you around isn't going to make that any easier. You can wait out here but it'll be hours before we know anything more and God knows how long after that until the anaesthetic wears off."

Mr and Mrs Brown then apparently disappeared after telling Charlie that they 'loved him,' and that they would 'see him in no time at all' but he knew that the gesture was empty – there was no way that this new family loved him any more than the last – but did he really care at this point? He felt as though he wanted to die, and for a twelve year old, that wasn't a very nice feeling.

Charlie was led through from the last pair of doors on his rolling bed to a small room in which he could just see the top of some cupboards, the ceiling, and most of a clock hung on the wall. Everything was white and it smelt like cleaning products... and it tasted like... pennies? He wasn't entirely sure but he felt as though his mouth was full of blood.

"We're going to put you under for a moment," the voice came once again from the stern doctor who was apparently tasked with making him feel better. "You won't feel anything, and when you wake up you're going to feel a bit dizzy and you'll probably be sick. That's normal,' he stated.

Charlie tried to nod slightly but his muscles wouldn't allow it. He didn't even feel the anaesthetic needle and drip enter into the back of his hand either, though as he watched the clock he felt his right arm freeze in place from some internal coldness. He saw the second hand tick a few long seconds before his vision doubled, then faded to black once again.

Whilst under anaesthetic, everyone experiences their unconscious state in different ways and Charlie was no exception. He had the dream where you were flying through the clouds with rainbows in the background and not a care in the world. His body was free, and flying was like a second nature. That would all come to an end though, once the anaesthetic wore off.

The doctor and one of his assistants hadn't yet changed from their scrubs, which did have some traces of blood still on them, though most of it would've been on the gloves which had thankfully been removed and discarded. They were ready to break the news to the Browns who'd been waiting outside the operating theatre for more than seven hours whilst the medical professionals did their work. At first the Browns were unable to rest due to their anxiety and worry for Charlie, but eventually the length of the day and fatigue had caught up with them and they'd both fallen asleep right there on their chairs.

"We did everything we could for the boy, but the next few hours are going to be crucial to his survival. My best estimates are that he's going to require long-term care and a whole lot of rehabilitation after what's happened to him." He sighed as he spoke as though the news was dire, though all the Browns heard was the fact that this doctor actually had hope that Charlie would be OK, and more importantly would be going home eventually.

It was determined that Charlie had suffered from an aphasia caused by excess pressure on his brain from a mass that had been slowly growing throughout his entire life. The irony of his situation was that had he not have blacked out, fainted and cracked his skull open on the edge of a wooden chair, he never would've had the scan that revealed the tumour that needed cutting out immediately to save him from certain death within the following few months or so. The downside was of course that by removing this tumour, he would possibly be left in a vegetative state, paralysed and unable to live without constant care for the rest of his life. Charlie didn't know any of this yet though, he was still flying through the clouds – and possibly happy for the very last time in his life.

Charlie awoke to the gentle pressure of a nurse clutching his wrist with a genuine smile on her face. She had long blond hair and blue eyes and her voice sounded as though it was far away, but Charlie could hear her clearly.

"You've just had surgery, you're OK and the anaesthetic will be wearing off now. Don't try to move just yet. Everyone is here for you and everything is OK." she said.

Charlie didn't try to make a move. All he knew was that his head felt huge and it panicked him a little that he felt no pain anywhere despite what he thought he knew about having surgery – the logic was that it should've hurt, and a lot.

Almost immediately after he was placed more upright than laying down in his curtain-walled room, he was given a platter of sandwiches and drinks ranging from orange juice to a pot of tea by a troupe of nurses and assistants. He didn't feel like taking advantage of any of it, and the food and drink were left sitting over his lap on a tray with the aromas teasing his nostrils and taste buds.

Eventually, due to a combination of both anaesthetic and anxiety wearing off, Charlie decided that he actually was hungry and that everything he had been offered looked both delicious and satiating. The only problem was that when he tried to move his arm to pick up the closest sandwich – prawn mayo – his arm didn't obey his command.

"Charlie?" Mr Brown's voice came from the far side of the curtain just at that moment and his smiling face appeared once it was parted.

Both of Charlie's foster parents came straight into the room and fawned over the boy with little regard for embarrassment as they both told him how 'special' and 'strong' he was for being so brave, and that they were so proud of him. While all this was happening all Charlie could think of was how hungry he was and how much he wanted that damned sandwich.

Eventually Mr. Brown caught both Charlie's gaze and look of desperation and realised what was happening.

"You hungry?' he asked in a happy tone.

Charlie didn't respond.

Mr. Brown picked up the sandwich and offered it to Charlie, who still couldn't move to take it. After a moment the man realised what was happening and changed the sandwich-trajectory to bring it up to Charlie's mouth, who in turn took a large bite and chewed it frantically.

Charlie chewed, then swallowed. Though when he tried to get the food to travel down his throat as it normally would, he realised that it simply wasn't working and within a moment he began choking viciously. Alarms started ringing from the machinery next to the bed and two nurses ran into the room, shooed the Browns out of the way and essentially tapped and rubbed Charlie's back and throat until the food had got to where it was supposed to be. The first – the blonde nurse again – then offered Charlie some orange juice and helped him to swallow the cool sweet liquid until it was apparent that he'd calmed down and felt a lot better about the whole situation.

"What...what happened?" Mrs. Brown asked once the second nurse left and the blonde one was about to leave as well.

"Well..." she started but it was obvious that she was having trouble delivering the bad news. Charlie could tell too. Though he was only twelve years old he knew when something needed to be said that was going to be a difficult conversation - he'd been there all too many times already. He kept his mouth tightly shut though.

Finally the nurse shrugged her shoulders and continued. "Charlie has... had a... tumour in his brain and when it was removed it was necessary to remove the connecting tissues that were mutating and feeding into it..." She stopped herself, deciding that the scientific approach probably wasn't the best way to go, particularly as she was still in front of Charlie. "At the moment, Charlie can't move anything from the neck down and unfortunately that includes the muscles that he needs to swallow food and drink.

"But that'll wear off right? That's just the anaesthetic isn't it?" Mrs. Brown asked with a half-hearted and worried smile.

"We...uh...I... we don't really know. It isn't the anaesthetic causing the paralysation paralysis? Though. We think that with determination..." she smiled at Charlie as she spoke "...and a little bit of hard work, he'll get right back to normal in no time at all!"

Was that a lie? Charlie thought to himself as he saw completely through the faked smile the nurse was offering and he immediately tried to move his arms, legs - anything at all - again but with absolutely no success. This was bad, very bad and he knew it.

Over the next few hours the after effects of the anaesthetic wore off and it left Charlie with the worst headache that he'd ever experienced in his life. In addition, he'd thrown up a couple of times and the back of his head where it'd been hit on the way down to the floor stung as if the headache wasn't enough. Mr and Mrs. Brown had also told him that when he was able to use the toilet, they'd be able to leave him alone to rest, something to do with the anaesthetic passing through and out of his system. He didn't care – all he did was to try his best to muster up a pee so that he could be left alone in peace.

Charlie spent some time checking his mental faculties to see if he was all still there after having his brain messed with. He was too young to appreciate the science behind what'd happened although old enough to know that when you mess with the brain it usually has more long lasting consequences than just going to hospital and getting all better. It was a bit of a misnomer though, as how could one possibly check their own internal faculties – would he know if he'd forgotten anything? What if he'd forgotten the word for 'apple' and simply forgot that he didn't know it? It was all too difficult a task to work through on his own, so in that moment he decided to call upon the one support network that he'd been gifted and opened his mouth.

"Mrs...Mrs Brown?" he said in a questioning tone. The woman looked up and smiled warmly at her fostered son.

"Yes dear, what is it?" she replied and in that moment Charlie realised the mistake he'd been making over the last number of years, the pushing people away and guarding himself to make any emotional pain feel like it wasn't there. The families he'd run away from and the harm he'd caused through fighting and stealing whenever he could. He knew these people had *chosen* to look after him regardless of his past and he felt as though a weight was lifted from his shoulders as he burst into floods of tears.

The Browns instantly leapt to their feet and surrounded Charlie carefully with their arms, they didn't need to say anything but in that very moment Charlie felt love and warmth unlike anything he could remember, and he sat and sobbed until nothing more would come out.

Chapter 2

Charlie spent a month in the hospital for observations and the beginnings of what the nurses called 'rehab,' though he found it entirely pointless as each time they asked if he could move his fingers or toes he had to respond that he couldn't, and each time it made him feel useless. He'd gotten better at swallowing food and drink though, as rather the technique was something to be perfected over the paralysation of whatever muscles in his throat were tasked with that function. The nurses helped a lot too, they were all so attentive, so caring, and Charlie felt as though he was always embarrassed by the things he'd done and thought in the past.

The Browns came twice a day to visit Charlie and push his wheelchair around the hospital grounds. He liked the routine of their visits and the conversations they had, which were admittedly one way – from them to him – but he made the effort to make the right noises in return and tried to offer up responses wherever he could. It was just difficult when all you saw all day were the same four walls and the same five or so people.

Charlie's demeanour had softened somewhat since he'd been in the hospital and he began to see how people cared for other people unconditionally. They weren't out to trick others or steal from them, they were just all so nice, and after a couple of weeks he'd made the internal decision to be a better kid, a better person and give more people the benefit of the doubt.

When he arrived back at the Browns' house after being discharged in his wheelchair having made no progress at all with rehab, Charlie rolled up the new wooden ramp into the tall townhouse and wondered idly just how he was going to get up and down the two flights of stairs the property consisted of., The first thing he saw, though, when he crossed the threshold into the house, was a brand new wheelchair-sized stair lift attached to the bottom staircase. There was also a banner across the dining room entrance that read 'Welcome home!' and he felt gratitude build up in his chest; although he had no physical feeling in his body, his emotional responses were still there.

Immediately Charlie felt tears starting to well in his eyes but before he could even take a moment to sniff them back into his tear ducts, his foster parents smothered him in a hunched over hug. Again Charlie didn't feel it physically, but the emotion was there, and he was happy.

A few months had gone by in the flash of an eye. Charlie didn't need to go back to school yet because of his additional needs, and in order to help fulfil those, Mrs. Brown had decided to take a sabbatical from her work as a primary school teacher. She would care for Charlie and ensure that his educational needs were met, as well as feed, bathe and clothe him, and every single day without fail she'd try to encourage him to use every ounce of energy he had in his body to try to move something, anything, from the waist down.

Although Charlie had tried his best to keep his spirits up and try as hard as he could whenever he could, he could tell that it was no use. In addition, he could also see that his muscles were starting to waste as they were not being used or taxed as they should be and what was already a rather small twelve year old, was starting to look scrawny and malnourished. He wished on a daily basis that he could just be a normal kid once again – he wanted to play football, to run and jump, to hug his foster parents back, even just once.

One day a knock had come at the door and Mrs Brown had paused her lesson on sedimentary rock formations to open it. Charlie could tell from the deep voice that a man had entered the house, though it was rather hushed when he spoke. He couldn't see the man from the dining room-cum-classroom, though in the reflection of the window he could see a tall dark man in a fancy military uniform holding a hat of some kind under his arm.

"Did you receive the letters we've been sending you?" the man asked. It was obvious that they didn't want Charlie to overhear, but being quiet and unmoving for the last few months had given him a somewhat increased sense of hearing.

"All we read was that you want to take him away and do some experiments on him. It's not going to happen," Mrs. Brown replied. " What do you think gives you the right to just ask that of a family?"

"Listen ma'am, you've got this all wrong. We don't want to take him away and do experiments on him. As the letter explained..." the man tried to speak but was interrupted.

"I don't care what you call it, he needs his family around him right now and the last thing he needs is to be filled with false hope..."

"I'd like to try something new," Charlie couldn't help but speak up. Both his foster mum and the military man seemed startled that he had overheard their conversation, but both walked over to him and into his line of sight, Mrs. Brown lowering herself to his wheelchair level.

"You don't understand, Charlie. They want to take you away and try some experimental treatment or something – you won't be allowed to come home and they'll keep you locked away – even if it works." She was practically begging Charlie not to make the wrong decision, but behind her eyes, Charlie could see the pain that he'd been causing her.

All of the sacrifices that she'd made for him, her career, her time and love, her care... he owed her so much and each and every day he stole one of hers just to live. He had to do something to put a stop to the rot that he was to her existence, and that thing was almost certainly recovering from his horrific predicament.

"I... what do you want me to do?" Charlie asked the military man.

"Charlie!" The man smiled as he spoke. "My name is Colonel Miles Hardman, and I have some good news for you!"

Mrs. Brown practically snarled at him. "Just tell him the details, don't sugar coat it like that." Charlie could tell that she meant business, though he'd never seen this side of his foster mother before.

"OK, listen," Hardman tried again. "We have a deal of sorts that has come with certain technological advances. Essentially – and facts only here – we've been assured that your condition is entirely curable. It's not easy, but we think..."

Charlie interrupted the Colonel – which seemed to be wearing thin with him. "I'll do it," his answer was so quick that both the adults in the room practically jumped backwards.

"Now it's not...uh....that simple,' the Colonel replied. "There's a thing, well.... you'd have to agree to sign up with us for a period of no less than ten years – but only if it works, otherwise you'll be free to come right back home, no strings attached." He winced slightly at his own words but Charlie didn't see the downside. It was either get healed or come home – the classic win-win situation, right?

Mrs. Brown didn't know what to say, though she tried her best through tear-filled eyes. "We want you to get better, but on your own – we don't want you to become some kind of lab rat. We love you, you know that, and we'll do anything to help you. I know it seems like it's been a long time and nothing is happening but please just give it some time. We'll miss you," she added in a tiny voice at the end of her statement and it made a guilt-lump form in Charlie's throat – which was quite the sensation for the paralysed boy.

"I…I want to go, I don't want you to have to put yourself out so much for me. I've ruined both of your lives so let me do this one thing for you. I can go away and get better and you won't have to look after me anymore." Tears had already begun to stream down Charlie's cheeks and Mrs. Brown instinctively wiped them away with a tissue. She was a mother through and through.

"When do we go?" Charlie asked quietly before his words conjured a reply from the quietly sobbing woman.

"It's…it's not… well,' the Colonel looked at Mrs. Brown and Charlie saw the compassion in the man's eyes. Through everything he'd learnt to read the unspoken emotions that adults shared when they wanted to speak without him knowing the tone of the conversation. "I'll let you talk with your family, and if you still want to do this, then we'll come back in a week," he said. Charlie saw the thankful tiny nod from Mrs. Brown to the Colonel, then the military man stood to attention, put his hat back on and made his exit. Both Charlie and his foster mother remained silent for what felt like forever, until Mrs. Brown managed to pull herself back together and continue the lesson on rock formations. Charlie knew this was not the time to be talking about this.

Over dinner that night, Mr and Mrs. Brown were uncharacteristically forlorn and Charlie suspected that they'd had the conversation about the experimental treatment he'd been offered. Knowing that it was definitely a conversation that needed to happen, he decided he would be the one to broach the subject.

"The Colonel said that he was sure he could cure me," he chose to dive right in as though they both knew what he was talking about, "and if they can't, I get to come back home – so it's not a big deal really, is it?" he asked.

Mr. Brown looked at his wife quickly before he spoke, "Listen, Charlie…these deals with the devil are never all they're cracked up to be. You say you get to come home if you aren't cured but what do you think happens in that scenario? Do you think you'd be in exactly the state you are in now? What if the experimentation is painful, or makes your condition worse? And let's look at it from the other point of view – what if it does work and you're cured - do you really want to spend the next ten years going through medical examinations and tests every single day? I know it all sounds so good right now, but sometimes it's better the devil you know, you know?"

Charlie really hadn't thought about it from that point of view, but really what could be worse than this existence? Being a burden to everyone he actually cared about, them having to live their lives around him and his needs? And what was ten years anyway? He'd barely be a man and then he'd have his body back up and running, it all just seemed so worth it.

"I think... I'd still like to give it a go," he said slowly. He wanted to show to them both that he was actually thinking this through and not just running straight toward the light at the end of the tunnel.

Mr. Brown's face began to turn red and his expression turned to that of a scowl. "Now listen here..." he started but Mrs. Brown placed her hand on his wrist and he stopped, the scowl fading and the blood dissipating from his face. Charlie knew though that his foster father was upset and not angry.

"If this is what you want," Mrs. Brown said quietly, "then I'll call the Colonel and tell him you've made up your mind, OK?"

Charlie thought for a moment. Really thought. He knew that they wanted him to stay, that they were prepared to alter their lives for him as long as it would take and that they'd never stop trying, but he didn't want that for them. Of course, he wanted the chance to get better but the fact that he felt like he was such a burden just added to that desire to take the Colonel up on his offer. He nodded at his foster parents. "I'd like to go," he said shortly. "I want to get better."

The following week went by without another mention of the Colonel and getting cured and Charlie felt that it was because the Browns didn't want to think of the impending deadline, so he didn't bring it up either. He continued his studies as well as he could, all the while in the back of his mind the day coming when he would be able to go and get his body back.

It was dinner time again, the evening before the deadline day, when Charlie thought it would be best to bring up the Colonel again along with his firm belief that this was the right thing to do.

"Have you... have you heard anything from the Colonel about what I've got to do?" Charlie asked slowly as the Browns ate their lasagna. It didn't escape him that this was his favourite meal, and he wondered if it was like a goodbye kind of thing, or perhaps a reason to stay.

Mrs Brown spoke first. "We have... but we wanted to ask you to reconsider again, We know you feel like you have to do this to get better, but there are other ways, the physiotherapy…"

"It's not working!" Charlie blurted out interrupting Mrs Brown and he felt his cheeks beginning to redden. "I try and I try and nothing works. Every day I wish that I could move just one little toe but it never works," Tears began streaming down his red cheeks and he was surprised at just how loud and emotive his statement had been. It was the first time he'd acknowledged the fact out loud and it hurt.

"Charlie, listen…" Mr Brown started to speak, but stopped for some reason Charlie didn't understand.

Charlie could see both of his foster parents' mouths moving but no sound coming from them, then they both abruptly stood up and begun clutching his shoulders, they looked terrified.

Charlie's vision blurred slightly, then faded, though he could still see the outlines of the Browns as he slipped slowly into unconsciousness. Unbeknownst to Charlie, this would be the last time he would see the Browns for a very, very long time.

Chapter 3

Charlie awoke slowly, feeling groggy as though he'd been asleep for far too long. Looking around he could see that he was in some kind of metal-walled room that was set out much like a dentist's office. There were cupboards and various metal implements, a sink with a plastic cup but there were no windows and what looked like just a single plain door. The bed that he was laying on wasn't uncomfortable, though it was hard and made a scrunching sound when he moved his head to look around, as though it was covered in cheap scratchy paper towels.

Directly above his head, a glass panel hung facing him as though it was some kind of floating window. Inspecting it with a fair amount of interest, the thing suddenly became opaque, and a picture of Colonel Hardman appeared on the panel.

Charlie watched to see if anything else was going to happen, but to his surprise, the picture started moving and speaking.

"Charlie! It's good to see you again," the Colonel said with a smile.

Charlie blinked but didn't say anything.

"Uh... can you hear me?" The Colonel said.

It took a moment, but Charlie eventually realised that this was a live video link between him and the Colonel.

"Where am I?' Charlie asked quietly once he realised he could actually talk back to the Colonel.

"It's good to see you Charlie!" he repeated now that he was sure that Charlie could hear him. "You had a bit of a thing happen so we came to collect you a little early. I hope you don't mind."

Charlie thought for a moment before he replied. "Am I cured?" he asked hopefully, trying enthusiastically to move his arm. To his dismay though, it didn't budge.

"Well, no... not yet anyway Charlie. It would appear that your tumour had grown back somewhat – so we picked you up and carried out the same surgery that you had before. It would seem like that little lump of yours isn't so easy to get rid of is it? But don't worry," he added quickly, "you're OK now, back to where you were before – no tumour but also sadly not cured of your paralysis just yet either."

"The Browns..." Charlie said slowly with a pang of guilt. "Are they OK?" It was one of the first times that he'd actually ever thought of anyone other than himself, and the thought brought tears to his eyes.

"Yes, they know what's happening," the Colonel replied, "but aren't you curious as to how you're going to be cured? This is what you wanted, isn't it?"

"It is," Charlie confirmed to the Colonel, "I just wish they could've come with me... or I could've at least said goodbye or something..." He trailed off as the guilt still panged and eventually he just closed his mouth without finishing his thought.

"Oh, they couldn't come with you even if they wanted to Charlie," the Colonel replied, "and that's because, well, you aren't on earth any more."

Charlie thought he'd misheard the man on the screen, so didn't say anything in reply.

"Did you hear me?" the Colonel said after a few moments and realising that the boy wasn't going to reply to his grand statement any time soon. "You aren't on earth any more."

"Then where am I?" Charlie asked. He wasn't quite sure of the gravitas of that very statement, though the Colonel seemed to be waiting for the question.

"You're on board a starship Charlie, a big one," the Colonel explained. "I'm speaking with you from a military base back on earth and I wanted to be the one to tell you this because, well... the owners of the ship you are on are a race of alien beings called the Kanaan..."

"Aliens?" Charlie blurted out then looked around himself conspiratorially as though they were in the room and perhaps invisible.

"Aliens Charlie, but these are the good kind; these are the beings with the technology to help you, to make you better again. I wanted to be the one to prepare you for this because we didn't want you to freak out about it. These aliens are our friends, so you have nothing to worry about, OK?"

Charlie was panicking now though and he thought that if two major brain surgeries hadn't managed to kill him, at least now they'd sent in the big guns, but just as Charlie was beginning to hyperventilate, the door opened and in walked a Kanaan alien.

The lizard-like creature walked on two legs like humans did, had two arms and legs but had yellow scaled skin – like a reptile – and his eyes were also bright yellow with a small central pupil. Charlie could see that it had pointed teeth like a dinosaur and instead of a nose, it had two small slits that he assumed the thing used to breathe. He also noted that it was wearing what seemed to be a white lab coat, with a stethoscope wrapped around its neck.

"Charlie, I want you to meet Doctor Kono, of the Kanaan," the Colonel spoke from the screen.

"Hello Charlie," the creature said in the most regular middle-class human doctor kind of accent, which totally threw Charlie off guard. "Tell me, do you feel anything from the neck down?"

Charlie didn't reply but shook his head ever so slightly from side to side.

"Ah, I do love these little human gestures," Dr. Kono said with a slight inflection of his mouth that Charlie guessed was an attempt at a smile. "What about this?" The lizard asked as he tapped Charlie's knee with a tiny plastic hammer.

"N... no," Charlie managed to force out his words.

The Colonel then raised his hand to gain Charlie's attention. "I can see you have a lot to do, so I'm going to leave you to it for now if that's OK with you Charlie, but if you need me you can ask Dr. Kono here to call me, OK?"

Charlie nodded slowly. He wanted to say so many things and above all else he wanted the Colonel to stay with him and not to leave him with the lizard-like creature, but he just couldn't get the words to come out. The Colonel waved, then the screen abruptly turned back to transparent glass.

"So you've had a few surgeries already Charlie?" Dr. Kono asked the question but it was clearly rhetorical, "That must be hard on someone your age."

Charlie didn't respond to the question, now fully in shock.

Dr. Kono waited for an answer, but when Charlie didn't give one he tapped the side of his head round about where his ear-hole should've been, and muttered quietly to himself, which Charlie managed to understand was: "Is this translator not working properly?"

"I... it is," Charlie stammered. "Sorry."

"Ah that's good," Dr. Kono said with a sigh, "I don't want you to be scared though Charlie. I want you to know that I have the means to cure you entirely, and also to make you something *more*."

Charlie's eyes went wide at the statement. "You aren't going to turn me into a lizard are you?"

Dr Kono stopped moving for a second, then a grating, rasping noise came directly from his throat and after a long moment Charlie realised that the doctor was laughing. For some reason, it made him smile too, the gesture was so disarming and so human that he simply couldn't help himself.

"No, no Charlie,' Dr. Kono said as the chuckles dissipated, "You'll still be one hundred percent human, don't you worry! All we have to do is a little repair work, some gene modifications and you'll be right back on your feet and stronger than ever."

Of course, Charlie didn't understand what 'gene modifications' were, but he did like the sound of getting back up on his feet. "What do I need to do?" he asked.

"Actually, nothing," Dr. Kono said. Whilst I was clearing your brain tumour, I took the liberty of inserting a piece of bio electric machinery which actually includes the translation module that allows us to talk as we are right now. This machinery will also allow me to insert a code directly into both your DNA and RNA, that your earth military has named the Genetic Advancement and Progression Program. That is to say, Charlie, welcome to the GAP program. Are you OK for me to start right now?"

Charlie didn't exactly know what 'starting now' was going to entail, though if the doctor required his permission to do it, he hardly thought it was going to be painless. He simply nodded, knowing that this was the only way that anything was ever going to get done around here.

The lizard doctor moved to a second glass terminal screen and started twisting virtual dials and typing lines of code onto the screen with a virtual keyboard, though from where he was lying down Charlie couldn't actually make out any of the letters let alone the words they formed. Eventually, the doctor finished typing and pressed a very obvious start button on the terminal. Charlie's legs immediately went cold.

The sensation that Charlie began to feel was not painful, though it was somewhat unpleasant. Charlie felt as though someone was filling his veins with extra blood from his head downwards, through his spine and stomach, along his arms and legs and into his hands and feet. It felt as if he was going to explode until he realised: this was the first time in as long as he could remember, that he could feel his body. He had sensations everywhere! And then it started to hurt.

"Charlie, I have to tell you," Dr. Kono said without turning to face the boy, "repairing your nervous system isn't going to be a pleasant experience for you, but I need you to remain conscious for me for the time being. I suggest that you try to lie still as much as you can and know that the pain will eventually be over."

Charlie certainly didn't like the sound of that, but before he could make any moves to object, he felt his spine erupt in a fireball of pain. It was unlike anything he'd ever experienced before, and with the immediate arching of his back from the medical table, a primal violent scream erupted from his mouth.

The screaming didn't stop for one second over the next hour or so and Charlie's voice was broken by the time the pain had subsided enough for him to reduce his volume to a mild whimper. Eventually it did stop and he was grateful, exhausted and in floods of tears. He just wanted to go home and be back with his family.

"Charlie, can you hear me?" Dr. Kono asked as Charlie's eyes began to close, exhaustion and trauma having set in immediately upon the ebb of his adrenaline response. "It doesn't matter, you need to rest now," the doctor said quietly as he pulled a sheet over Charlie all the way up to his neck. "You have a lot to do when you wake up."

Charlie woke up several hours later although it wasn't like the times he'd awoken after anaesthetic – those had been quite pleasant, nice dreams followed by nurses and refreshments, whereas this time he woke up to an all-over dull ache in his body.

Charlie was now in a new room. It was metal walled, as the medical bay had been but it was a much more homely affair. It seemed like he'd been given his own room to stay in aboard the ship, though he didn't know if this was to be a permanent engagement or just a room to recover in. There was a metal desk and a wooden chair, a metal locker and a single bed. What Charlie didn't realise immediately was the fact that in looking around the room, he was able to raise his chest upward slightly to be able to appraise it a little easier. It was subtle, but it was definite: he could move.

He had a headache again but he didn't care in the least because as far as Charlie was concerned, this was the single best thing to happen to him in a very long time, and he wasn't going to let a little headache spoil that fact.

He tried moving his arms and they responded, although they felt heavy and hardly moved a full inch, but they were certainly moving. He tried his legs with the same result. He felt like he was gaining back some control over his own body, though it was a little like the aftermath of pins and needles - heavy appendages that somewhat did what they were told, but would otherwise just hang there. Charlie smiled, he knew that this kind of progress in such a short time meant seriously good news, and made a note to thank Dr. Kono when he next got the chance.

The chance, coincidentally, came almost immediately. He hadn't seen it before but a glass panel sat atop the desk in the room. It had illuminated and the good doctor was now filling the screen, grinning – well Charlie assumed it was a grin - it was hard to tell with the lizardesque doctor.

"Charlie," the doctor announced almost nonchalantly. "How are you feeling?"

"My head hurts, but I'm starting to be able to move some parts of my body. It's slow and difficult but it's more than I've moved in months," Charlie replied with an air of glee in his words.

"That's good to hear and very much expected. Your muscles have atrophied over the time you haven't been able to use them and you have suffered a significant amount of wastage. According to our records, your body mass is more than thirty percent below average for a male human of your age and height. It looks like you're going to have some catching up to do," the doctor replied levelly.

Charlie was a little disappointed that the doctor wasn't as excited as he was with his breakthrough, but when he stopped to think about it for a moment, he couldn't be sure if this was just another day at the office for the alien doctor.

Dr. Kono continued speaking when Charlie didn't offer another response, "I'll give you a quick rundown of the changes we have made to your body, and what you can expect because of those changes. First, I have removed your tumours – yes there were more than one that your human doctors had missed. Then I have implanted into your brain, just behind your ear, a small device that is used first to translate many known languages within the universe and that is how we are talking now." Charlie instinctively wanted to feel for it but his arm barely moved, instead he imagined the implant sat behind his ear so vehemently that he could almost feel it there. "This device is also the transceiver that my systems use to send and receive genetic coding and instructions directly to your brain. We effectively edit your genetic code and upload the changes so that your human body can effect most of the cell replication for itself. Are you following?" he asked.

Charlie nodded slowly. "So you just send updates to me like a computer system?" he asked.

"Yes, exactly," Dr. Kono replied, not phased by the understanding coming from a twelve year old boy. "The process can be slow, taking years for some to gain full acceptance of the module – this is called the user's Perceived Intervention Percentage – or PIP level. This level ranges from zero percent, or no integration, all the way up to one hundred percent, or full integration. Your PIP level is currently one percent before you ask, meaning that your body has begun to accept the changes from the module, though it's at a level that is almost impossible to detect."

"So at what percentage will I be able to walk again?" Charlie asked enthusiastically, ignoring the rest of the changes that'd been made to his body.

"That is not an easy question to answer, Charlie," the doctor replied. "Other humans your age had had the use of their limbs before implantation, but remain at zero or one percent as well, so it is not a measure that we are particularly familiar with. It will not be directly linked to your PIP level, though, as with all others the higher your level, the stronger, and *better* your body will become."

"OK, then how do I increase my PIP level?" Charlie asked.

"It is a combination of training, learning and time, though it is different for every single human subject I have worked with," the doctor replied.

"Wait - how many humans have these PIP levels?" Charlie asked as he realised what Dr. Kono had actually said.

The doctor smiled. "You are clever and you ask the right questions. Currently the subjects are in groups of three hundred, who have been implanted with the technology. Their PIP levels right now range from zero to five percent, though not all subjects will be able to reach their full potential of one hundred percent as the program has included some level locks as a safeguard in this first round of experimentation."

"Groups of three hundred?" Charlie gasped. "Where are they? Are they all paralysed?"

"No, as I have said, others were fully able to use their body at the time of their implementation. You are a special case Charlie, and that's why you are being transported alone to your final destination."

Charlie was used to being called a 'special case' though it usually was meant in a derogatory way. The way the doctor had said it though, didn't sound like a bad thing at all.

"What makes me so special?" Charlie asked with a slight tone of worry creeping into his voice.

"Two reasons," Dr. Kono replied. "One: you were entirely paralysed when you joined the program, which meant that the PIP implant was able to reconnect your nervous system in a way that it deemed more beneficial to your personal growth. And two: you are the only subject without a lock on your PIP level. You are able to grow without a defined terminus for the implant, though I suggest you keep that information to yourself, as not a single other subject knows what their PIP level lock is, until they reach it that is." Dr. Kono smiled again before signing off with a "just rest now Charlie, we'll be there in no time." Charlie wouldn't rest though - all he wanted to do was see how far he could move his fingers, toes, arms and legs, and wonder where it was exactly that he was going.

Chapter 4

Charlie found that he could control the glass panel in his room by speaking commands out loud. It was after saying: "how do I turn the TV on?" in frustration that he discovered this delicious little fact, and to his delight he was able to navigate the menus for the TV much as he'd done in the past on his own various TV models. Eventually he settled for watching some cartoons – he was still a kid after all.

A few hours passed before he began to feel the pangs of hunger that his body produced to remind him that he needed fuel to survive, and almost immediately there was a clattering noise at his door, as though his thoughts had been telegraphed to the ship.

He wondered if he should shout 'come in' or try to get up to answer the noise, though after a moment, a small section of the bottom of the door slid back and a small motorised metal trolley rolled itself into his room.

Charlie watched as the trolley came to a stop about a metre away from him and he frowned. It was just out of his reach but something smelled delicious – whatever food stuffs were inside the little unit were obscured by its outer frame, but he wanted them *badly*.

Charlie waited for a minute to see if it would come any closer but to his annoyance it didn't. Then he tried whistling to it and cooing it as if it was a dog, which didn't work either. He even tried asking it to come closer in case it was voice controlled like the terminal was, but again it remained steadfast in its positioning, as though it was silently mocking him.

Eventually, Charlie realised the thing wasn't going to move, and if he wanted whatever was inside it to eat, he was going to have to do this all by himself. For the first time in just less than a year, Charlie rolled his own body from his front to his side and the feeling was magical, and pure elation.

'*I've done it!*' his mind raced at his latest accomplishment. Then without warning, his body kept rolling over to his front – which would've been OK if he wasn't lying on a small single bed. He rolled *off* of the bed and hit the floor with an almighty 'oof'. The impact winded him and he wondered if he'd actually hurt himself anywhere, used to the idea that he could actually be bleeding without knowing it, though after a moment of mental investigation, he decided that he was probably OK, other than his bruised pride of course.

The food robot was mere inches away from his face now, and with all of his mental capacity he willed his arm to move his hand towards the mouth watering aroma. To Charlie's shock and delight and probably somewhat thanks to his year-long physio efforts, his arm moved slowly, slowly toward the machine, but it was steady and not as difficult as he remembered from the few hours previous. He smiled as the movement became less alien, feeling more normal, and then it happened - his hand made contact with the food robot and the thing immediately split at the top, falling open to reveal a single, large round hot pizza.

It had everything on it that Charlie would've asked for: Tomato sauce, cheese, pepperoni and meatballs. It had been so long since he'd actually eaten such a delight and the smell – *oh God* did it smell good.

When Charlie had tried to eat a pizza before, he'd been surrounded by the Browns who would cut it into teeny tiny pieces then massage his throat to help him swallow. It was embarrassing at first, but what was worse was that it just didn't taste right, and by the half-way point of the meal, it was completely cold anyway. This one was hot though, and there was no one around to stop him simply going for it – choking hazard be damned!

Charlie's hand practically shook as he slid it under a slice of the pizza; he didn't want to try to use his grip as that wasn't yet something he'd tested and this was far too important to mess up now. He brought his arm and the pizza slice to his face, stopped for a moment to inhale the aroma, then opened his mouth and bit down on the slice. Charlie's eyes closed as his mouth filled with the most heavenly pizza he'd ever tasted in his entire life. It was pure pleasure, though he knew what needed to come next, and he didn't have his support network around him to help him swallow the damn thing. He was on his own with this one.

He took longer than usual to chew the pizza, partly because it was so good and partly because of the anxiety of possibly choking on it when the muscles in his throat didn't work as they should. Eventually, he knew he'd have to either spit it out of go for it. In a moment, he went for it.

The muscles in his throat, to his relief and happiness, worked as they should, constricting and expanding to allow the pizza to slide right down and toward his stomach. This was it, this was the moment that Charlie felt he would become whole again – he could eat by himself, he didn't need anybody else ever again.

Charlie savoured every single bite of the pizza and made the effort to try to taste each individual flavour that it offered. He knew he had the time to do so and that it was also the right thing to do, given his situation. He did want to thank whoever it was that cooked it though, because it was going to be the meal he thought he'd remember for the rest of his life. A glass of water accompanied the pizza, which he also drank and was again thankful that he didn't immediately choke on.

Eventually, Charlie did what everyone does when they eat pizza – he ate too much of it and had to lie still on the floor for a bit as the carb-bloat ran its course and absorbed all of the water he'd drunk. This in turn led to Charlie falling asleep on the floor, as he wasn't yet strong enough to pull himself back up onto the bed, although he did try, but failed miserably.

He wasn't sure how long he'd been asleep for, when Charlie was awoken sometime later by the annoying wail of a repeating siren. When he opened his eyes to investigate, he saw that the room he was in was bathed in an angry red glow – the lights apparently matching the alarm noise. What's more, he noticed that his door was open and he could see into the hallway outside.

Charlie's heart beat quicker at the change in his environment. He didn't know what the issue was, but instinctively he knew something bad was happening. He tried to look around the room to see if anything else had changed, but thankfully everything was right where he'd left it – including his own body, which was still prone on the floor.

Then he heard voices. He couldn't really make out what they were saying, but there was definitely some shouting, as if there was a struggle or a fight going on, and he could definitely make out three, no four, differing voices outside his room and in the corridor.

Just as Charlie was trying his best to hear the finer details of the commotion, a hand appeared grasping at the doorframe to his room. It looked human although it was covered in blood, and Charlie held his breath to try to remain unnoticed in the room. It was no use though, because following the bloodied hand was an exhausted looking face.

It was a woman, which surprised Charlie though he wasn't exactly sure why. She had long blond hair, which was soaked in deep red blood, and striking blue eyes.

"Are you here for the program?" the woman panted as she made panicked eye contact with Charlie.

Stunned, Charlie didn't respond.

The woman moved herself fully into the doorway and it was obvious that she was hurt. She hunched over slightly and kept a hand on her stomach that was apparently the source of all of the bleeding.

"I don't have... time anyway, here," she said as she threw a heavy looking black handgun onto the floor next to Charlie's head. Then she used both her hands to put pressure on her wound. "We've been boarded," she said looking very panicked.

"I... I... uh," Charlie stammered but couldn't form a coherent sentence; this all just seemed like it was too much for him. What he wanted to say was that he was unable to pick up the weapon, let alone use it.

"Pick it up, they're coming!" The woman said, then followed it up with a shouted "NOW!" before moving partly out of sight, apparently struggling with some unseen monster.

Charlie listened to the fight, wondering exactly how he'd gotten himself into this predicament, but it wasn't something he could make too much sense of. There were the grunts of effort, then a scream, a single gunshot, and then silence. Charlie held his breath again.

After a moment, the woman appeared in the doorway again.

"My name is Dawn," her voice was sweet and melodic, though if not still a little panicked. "I need you to get your shit together if we're going to make it out of this. Snap. Out. Of. It," she articulated.

It wasn't going to make the highlight of his day, but Charlie managed to pick up the handgun with a monumental amount of effort. Then he turned onto his front, placed both his hands on the floor in front of him and attempted to push his own body weight up and off of the floor. His arms shook and the effort started to give him a headache, but it was no use, he simply couldn't lift himself up and he fell back down to the ground face first.

Then the figure of a lizard-like creature appeared behind this 'Dawn' and Charlie's breath caught in his chest. It was clearly the shape of Dr. Kono – that was unless all of these creatures looked exactly the same – though the unique pattern of the markings on the doctor made him think that he was correct in his first assessment.

The doctor grabbed hold of Dawn around the waist and she screamed almost a little too dramatically for Charlie's liking, then the lizard man revealed a long, sharp claw which he proceeded to hold against Dawn's throat menacingly.

"Help... me..." Dawn almost whispered the words and the world seemed to stand still for Charlie and his decision-making process.

So many things didn't add up all at once and he was sure that there was something in his mind telling him to do a *better job* at analysing his surroundings. First, the doctor shouldn't have been making such an effort to portray being the big bad alien – he'd already taken the time to cure Charlie, or at least had made moves in that direction, so why waste the time? Then, this Dawn character was a new addition, so why hadn't she introduced herself before? And then there was the gunshot that seemed to have had no effect on the situation whatsoever. Why did she say we had been boarded when the doctor was clearly a member of the crew? And why make it look as though the doctor was holding Dawn hostage, when he could have just killed her? No, there were too many things that weren't adding up and Charlie knew there was something else going on.

Charlie raised a hand with a fair amount of effort and dropped the gun he held in the other. "This is a test, isn't it?" he asked calmly.

"What, NO! Do something!" Dawn begged, although after a few moments, the doctor released his grip from around her waist and she brushed herself off, clearly not plagued by her wound any more.

Dawn smiled. "That was... unexpected," she said. "I'm sorry we had to do that Charlie, but our testing has shown that PIP levels can be increased at times of emotional hardship. We thought we might have been able to speed your recovery up a little by subjecting you to a position where it was either going to be move or die. It is surprising that you saw through the deception though. How did you know?"

Charlie reeled off the list of things that he'd noticed in the confrontation, though even to him his observations had seemed a little too farfetched and when he finished both the doctor and Dawn remained silent for a few seconds to digest what he had said.

"Charlie," the doctor spoke now and Charlie was glad he wasn't playing a bloodthirsty alien any more. "The things that you noticed, these are things that you should not have done so in your heightened state. You must understand, that a normal person might have chosen to act more rashly in your situation."

"I did try to stand and fight, to help..." Charlie said slowly, "but I couldn't lift myself up off the ground." He felt embarrassed about saying it, but really it wasn't anything new to him.

Both the doctor and Dawn then realised that Charlie was *still* on the ground and *still* unable to right himself, so they each took an arm and lifted him onto his feet.

Although nothing to the two adults in the room, the moment may as well have been accompanied by trumpets and banners for Charlie. He was standing – and on his own two feet! Granted the pair still had a hold of his arms, but they were barely taking any of his weight. Charlie could feel the pressure on the soles of his feet, his knee joints, and the pain in his lower back as his spine compressed due to the physical effort of staying upright. Charlie was whole again, he could feel it.

Then Dawn and the doctor let go of their grip of Charlie's arms, and he wobbled and fell to his knees with a thud. Still, being able to stay on his knees was a massive deal and although he was upset that standing wasn't yet on the cards, kneeling upright was a step in the right direction, figuratively speaking.

After helping Charlie get back into his bed, Dawn had vanished and the doctor told him that his journey would be coming to an end in a matter of hours, so he should 'prepare' for their arrival on what the human military had designated EP1, or 'earth-like planet one'. It seemed like a bit of a rubbish name to Charlie, he would've thought up some amazing alien name like Xenos or Callatia, to name the first couple that came to his mind, but military people were always like this - boring and predictable.

The rest of the journey went by in a flash – mainly because it lasted only a couple of hours as he'd been told, but also partly because of, well, TV. Charlie didn't really feel up to pushing himself too hard after the little test that the doctor and Dawn had put him through, though he did think about what had happened to him during that time over and over as he watched the screen. Had he always been so perceptive, or was this a new part of his PIP level, or the GAP program or whatever it was he was a part of right now? Either way, he made the mental note to investigate further, and also the fact that the doctor had said that with heightened emotional responses, could come increases in his physical abilities. These were the things that Charlie would remember of his journey from earth to EP1, as he had the distinct feeling he was going to need all the help he could get in the coming weeks, days, months and years.

Chapter 5

Charlie felt the deceleration of the ship and the entry into the planet's atmosphere; of course, he wasn't sure that's what it was, but the feeling was pretty unmistakable. Eventually, he was sure that he had come to a full stop though and his door opened by itself to allow him to exit, although nobody seemed to be coming to his aid in any kind of hurry. He did try to lift himself from the bed again, though it was still no good, he was simply not yet strong enough to lift his own body weight.

Dr. Kono entered after a short while with a rather old-fashioned looking wheelchair in tow. Charlie was pretty shocked at the sight of it and a part of him wondered why there wasn't some new-fangled, alien contraption that drove itself around or something. When he thought about it a little longer though, he came to the realisation that if they could cure paralysis – which he was sure they would do completely (eventually) - then why would they have any need for wheelchairs?

Dr. Kono was joined by Dawn just a few moments later and both of them stood behind Charlie's wheelchair once they'd bundled him into it, careful to ensure he was comfortable. Charlie appreciated that - just because he had had no feelings before didn't mean his feelings couldn't be hurt. Charlie appreciated that - just because he had had no feelings before didn't mean his feelings couldn't be hurt.

"Charlie, listen to me closely," the doctor said in his ear. It was evident that he must have been bending over him to speak without being overheard because Charlie could feel the hot lizard-breath on his earlobe. "There is something you must know… you can't tell anyone about your

PIP level, there were limitations set by the Council that…"

The doctor was interrupted by the arrival of another person entering the ship, the sound of doors sliding open just out of sight.

"You can't tell anyone," he reiterated quickly. "It is a matter of life and death, do you understand?"

Charlie nodded silently.

"Oh and another thing," Dawn's voice came sweetly to Charlie's left ear this time. "From now on, my name is instructor Shepherd. Best not to tell anyone about the rather lacklustre acting earlier either, OK?"

Charlie smiled this time and nodded again, though he was excited to see just what role this 'instructor Shepherd' was going to play in this new location he was set to call home for a while.

The person who entered the ship turned out to be a middle aged man in army gear who didn't seem to need to introduce himself to the doctor or the instructor, and he barely even seemed to notice Charlie. The three were then led out of the ship – which turned out to be just a small shuttle and not a large warship – and into bright sunlight. Charlie remained in his wheelchair as he took in the sight of the desert-like planetscape - hot, humid air and mountainous peaks in the distance. Nowhere could he see any signs of houses and he wondered where exactly he was going to be living.

What was less alien to him, though, was the sight of the three hundred kids, all about his age, though some were noticeably larger, and not a single other in a wheelchair standing about in a huddle without much idea of what they were supposed to be doing. Charlie hadn't noticed it, but his two chaperones had disappeared and that effectively had left him stranded on the outskirts of the huddle.

Nearly all of the kids looked terrified, though there were a few that apparently hadn't yet got the memo and they were chatting about how they'd arrived on the planet, the TV that they'd managed to get to show cartoons, or the fact that their parents had volunteered them for this program. It appeared to Charlie ,when looking out across the sea of faces, that the kids actually represented a good cross section of humanity, with an equal number of males, females, black, white, Asian and everything in between. It made sense - not that the kids would know it yet - but to get the best of the best for their latest experiment, it was important that no dominant or recessive traits would be missed, as one simple oversight could mean the difference between a useful soldier, and a smoking pile of gore.

Charlie jumped when he felt a hand on his shoulder.

"I... um... I'm Laura," a small voice came from the girl who had startled him. She was pretty short, even for a twelve year old and had straight black hair covering much of her dark brown eyes and skin. "Laura Giardini," and she held out a hand for Charlie to shake but looked embarrassed when he made no moves to grasp it.

"I... Charlie," he managed to respond and he looked at her still outstretched hand. He decided to do his best to grasp it and shake it, though the motion took uncomfortably long and he could tell it had pained Laura.

Laura looked at Charlie as he feebly shook her hand and she seemed to come to the correct conclusion. "I'm sorry, but you don't move very well, do you?" she asked.

"I move just fine," Charlie blurted out. "It's everyone else that moves too fast!" He couldn't help himself, but thankfully Laura let out a little chuckle at his statement. He could already tell he was going to like this girl.

The group of kids was eventually called to attention by a booming voice somewhere at the front of the crowd and everyone took notice of it. Silence rippled through the kids and Charlie craned his neck slightly to try to see through the mass of bodies, though to his annoyance they were simply too dense and he was simply too short in his chair.

"My name is Marcus Cesari," the voice carried almost effortlessly through the crowd to Charlie's ears, "and I am your chief instructor here on EP1. You all have come from different backgrounds, for different reasons and are at different stages of your physical abilities and I am here to tell you right now, that none of that matters. To me you are all equal and to me you are all here to learn and grow. Disobedience will not be tolerated. Lack of effort will not be tolerated. Violence, unless instructed, will not be tolerated. Do you understand?"

Nobody replied.

"From this moment on, when I ask a question, you will answer with three words and three words only. Those words are: 'yes chief instructor,' do you understand?"

There was a murmur from the crowd of kids that resembled a 'yes chief instructor,' but it was half-hearted and clearly the man didn't appreciate the lack of effort.

"I said IS THAT CLEAR?" His tone made Charlie's back snap up to attention almost immediately and as one the children's brigade replied with a loud 'YES CHIEF INSTRUCTOR!'

"Better," the chief instructor's voice came in reply. "Now we have a short hike to the facility that you will be calling home for the foreseeable future. This is a good test of your endurance and physical stature. We will be travelling eight miles on foot in that direction," Charlie assumed the man had pointed to somewhere, though he still couldn't see. "Do not fall behind. Do not give less than one hundred percent and by God do not moan or complain or you will be punished."

Charlie's legs went cold. If there was one thing he knew he wouldn't be good at, it was hiking. Rolling he could probably do as the ground was hard and dry, but as his chair wasn't motorised and his arms were about as useful as over-boiled spaghetti, he had the feeling the only person falling behind right from the get-go was going to be him.

The crowd of kids began to slowly filter away to Charlie's left and he felt as though he should call out for help. Before he did so however, Laura appeared by his side and began pushing him and his chair behind the other kids. A few moments went by, then another pair of hands took his back too.

"This is Mauro," Laura said quietly from behind Charlie. I met him just before you."

"Mauro Latori," the boy said. He seemed bigger than a lot of the other kids, though not fat, just all round larger as though he was a year or two older. Having him help push would definitely speed things up, Charlie thought.

"You don't have to do this, guys," Charlie said aloud, though if he was being totally honest with them and himself, they totally did need to do this and he would be eternally grateful for it.

"Don't you worry, we got this, you just sit there all comfortable like and we'll do all the heavy lifting," Mauro replied, though Charlie' could tell he was smiling whilst he said it.

"Let's see if you're still smiling in eight miles," Charlie replied with a smile of his own and made a very animated effort to make himself comfortable.

Eight miles at a walking (or rolling) pace, took three hours and four minutes and by the end of it, the climate and additional load of Charlie plus the wheelchair had led to Laura and Mauro being drenched in sweat and panting by the time the journey was complete. They'd finally made it though, even if it was at the back of the group by quite some stretch.

Awaiting the three, the remainder of the group stood before a large concrete wall with closed metal gates big enough for at least two buses to fit through long-ways. It stood between two high cliff faces that rolled away into the distance and Charlie could tell that his new home was positioned in the valley beneath; it made sense to him - easily defensible, no need to build high walls everywhere, just slap a gate on the thing and be done with it. It was clever, really.

To the side of the group, Charlie could see a man in very posh looking military gear, insignia on his shoulders and a black peaked cap on his head covering his jet black hair. Instinctively, Charlie knew that this was the chief instructor.

"It is so nice of you to join us," the instructor called as the three approached. "Have you ever heard the expression that a chain is only as strong as its weakest link?" his voice carried across the gap between them for all to hear. "If you don't think my time is valuable enough, or that you think you can take your own time when given a task then I have some news for you, and news for all of you. Your rewards and/or punishments will be given based upon your performance within your classes – which you will discover later. Your class group is as poor as your weakest member and this is going to be your first lesson: Mr. Schumacher here was behind you all and as such your time has been recorded as his. Congratulations, you're all slow as shit, I hope you all enjoy porridge." He smiled as he announced his punishment and Charlie took an instant dislike to the man; was it really necessary to call him out like that? It really wasn't his fault that he needed a wheelchair to get around.

The kids in the crowd had all turned to face Charlie and some of the faces were sympathetic, some were indifferent and some looked outright pissed. He knew that he would need to do better, a lot better if he didn't want everyone to eventually despise him.

"Don't worry Charlie," Laura whispered into his ear, "It's not your fault, you'll get it next time." Her words made him feel slightly better, though he wondered how many chances he was going to get to 'do better next time'.

The gates before them slowly started to move, curving outwards from the middle and as they passed, Charlie noticed that they were at least three feet thick of solid concrete. Behind them though, in contrast to the arid desert that they'd traversed to get here from the landing site, the complex looked almost pleasant. Green grass was bisected by cobblestone pathways that led on the left to battleship-grey painted shipping containers, and on the right to what looked like firing ranges. Further back were other containers that varied in size though they were all painted in the dull grey. To Charlie, it looked like it was an army camp, though constructed of pre-fab units that'd simply been dropped into place. The camp went back further than he could see, though the valley was wide and very, very long so there didn't seem to be much of a limit to its size.

"Welcome to your home, recruits," chief instructor Marcus Cesari stated. "We call it 'Camp Rebirth'. You're going to fucking hate it."

Charlie felt a surge of pride at the name, not because he was some army-loving type with delusions of servitude, rather the feeling that he knew he was going to do his best to make this camp live up to its name.

The group then followed the chief instructor through the gates and along a straight path into a container-building that was at least five times bigger than the ones they'd passed along the way. Inside were seven long rows of metallic tables with a buffet-style canteen at one end. Charlie couldn't decide if it was more like a prison arrangement or a school lunch hall, though either way it didn't matter, the result was the same.

The crowd all took seats although being unsure if they were pre-allocated they mostly just took whatever they could get. Charlie was lucky for once in this respect, because he already had a seat so he didn't have to fight for one. Not that space was an issue of course, it was more the fact that nobody seemed to want to be on the outer edges of the tables in case they stood out and were called upon.

"Now," Cesari started, though he stopped once his eyes fell upon Charlie who was sitting in his chair between tables.

"Ah, Sinclair. Once again you have gained my attention. Tell me, is this something you are trying to do or is it simply poor luck? Do you think you are better than the rest of the recruits? Are these benches not comfortable enough for your high standards or do you simply feel that you are better than sharing a table with the rest of these lower beings?"

Charlie opened his mouth but no words came out, just a series of stutters. He'd been shocked to be called by his surname but the challenge afterwards left him feeling blindsided.

"As I have already made clear, and will continue to do so over your time here at Rebirth, you are all the same to me. You will all be treated as equals no matter your physical stature or abilities. Though this may sound like some utopian bliss to some, I can assure you it is quite the opposite. You are, as I have said before and will say again, as weak as your weakest link so will one of you God damn lazy pieces of meat pick up this sack of potatoes and put him on a GOD DAMNED BENCH?!" Visible spittle accompanied the instructor's shouting and immediately both Laura and Mauro stood from their seats and raised and lowered Charlie onto the bench between them.

"Ms. Giardini, Mr. Latori, thank-you. Now, if I have your permission, I'd like to move on." Cesari said at a more sociable volume.

Charlie's head hung in shame, partly so he didn't have to see if everyone was staring daggers again and partly because he felt once again that he was a burden to others. Deep down he knew that by helping him, Laura and Mauro had effectively let everyone know that they were with him – and that was never going to be a good thing to do.

"Welcome to Camp Rebirth," chief instructor Cesari said with his hands open in the universal gesture of welcoming. "To give you some history to this facility, well – it's new. It seemed that a benevolent group of alien races in their infinite wisdom – yes they exist, don't start – decided that we humans were lacking in our ability to play a part in the universe at large, and again in their infinite wisdom, together with the big brains on earth, devised the program of which you are now a part of - the GAP program. Before you ask, you are the first real participants in the program at this scale, so you'll want to make a good impression.

The GAP program is a military program that is designed to train the new recruits – that's you boys and girls – in the ways of wars that are fought on a universal scale. It has also been designed to alter your physiology so that your bodies can cope with the lives that you have signed up to be a part of. In short, you are to be the best of the best, the strongest of the strong and the fastest of the fast." Cesari's eyes fell upon Charlie again as he said these last words. "It is beyond my reasoning as to why some of you are here, though I can only assume that the study will require control groups and therefore there will be a clear disparity in your abilities that will become much clearer over the next few weeks and months. My advice to you right now, is to encourage those around you in order to grow with your team mates, otherwise it will be detrimental to *all* of you."

Charlie swallowed hard. As if he didn't have enough issues around thinking he was a burden, already he'd been told on three occasions that everyone here would suffer because of him. He felt so small all over again and he couldn't think of any way he could overcome it.

"Now you are all to be assessed for your physical abilities and placed in a corresponding specialisation. These are as follows: Heavy arms - subcategories: Berserker, Artillery. Scout - subcategories: Sniper, Recon. Assault - subcategories: Blitz, Cover. Support - subcategories: Tech, Medic. Special Ops - subcategories: Alpha, Communications."

Listening to the overview of specialisations, Charlie initially felt as though he would make a good sniper, he wouldn't have to move much and would be able to stay well clear of any real fighting, though once he thought about it he realised how much of a sitting duck he would be in that situation. His mind then turned to communications – that sounded much safer again away from the fighting just relaying information and pointing the real soldiers where they needed to go.

"Your specialisation is final," the chief instructor continued with his announcement. "And will be chosen for you after your initial assessments, which are to begin in fifteen minutes. Do not disappoint me."

Chapter 6

"Initial assessment, strength. Begin." The words were spoken by chief instructor Cesari, as he was not just in charge of the camp in its entirety, but also of the strength training portion of the kids' development. The assessment was a pretty simple affair, it was essentially a narrow runway with weighted walls in vertical sliders to prevent the person who was taking the assessment making it through to the next. The person taking the assessment would have to lift the walls over their head in turn to pass each section. Outdoors in the heat of the planet, it looked pretty difficult to begin with, though next to a number from one to twenty on each of the blocks was their weight. Number one was just five kilos, then each block increased first by five until level six, then by ten all the way up to one hundred and seventy kilos at number twenty. The participant would have to lift the block over their head and pass through the sliders to be able to say they passed that particular challenge. Charlie was certainly not looking forward to this one.

The kids, who had all been given what were essentially shorts and t-shirts to wear for their assessments, all formed into ten rows of thirty with Charlie right at the back in his wheelchair. He couldn't see his two helper-friends anymore, but he knew they'd be within the masses somewhere.

Charlie was just wishing there was a way out of all this when Cesari's voice boomed again.

"Wood, Marsh, Cooper, you're up," he called, and three girls approached the start of the runway apprehensively. All three had long dark brown hair and looked slightly dishevelled – an eight-mile hike in humid conditions tended to have that effect on long hair. The three lined up in what Charlie assumed was the order of their names being called, and at the sound of a piercing whistle, Wood made her move and darted toward the first wall with a determined look plastered across her face. She seemed delighted when she found that it was easy to lift, and she practically threw it over her head with hardly any effort at all. Then the same happened at number two and three. Wall number four at twenty kilos still wasn't particularly heavy, but fatigue had started to play a factor in the girl's progress. She heaved the wall over her head and stepped through to be faced with the twenty-five-kilo wall number five. This one was almost her downfall and she had to rest the wall on her shoulders to slowly manoeuvre herself underneath its weight with a tremendous amount of effort. It was no surprise then, that it was a step too far to try to lift the next, thirty-kilogram wall, and she bowed out with a score of five.

"Well done, Wood, very nice for a first attempt," Cesari shouted and Wood practically skipped away from the course win elation. "Marsh, you're up!"

The next two girls both reached level four and were told by Cesari to 'put a little more effort in next time'.

When the boys started filtering into the course, one of them named Matty Henderson actually managed to make it all the way to level eight, lifting the forty-kilo wall right above his head and stepping through cockily. He didn't even try the next wall though which led to the chief instructor shouting at the boy to not be so arrogant in future – although he did say during his tirade that the feat was 'impressive'.

All in all, Henderson's score wasn't to be beaten as all the rest of the two hundred and ninety-eight kids scored between a four and a seven on the course. That was all about to change, however, when the only one left to participate in the initial assessment, was Charlie, still a distance away from the start of the course, and still sitting quietly in his wheelchair.

"We're waiting Sinclair!" the chief instructor called as the rest of the kids stared silently at him, waiting for him to make some sort of move.

Charlie raised his hands slowly and rested them on the wheels of his chair as he let a look of determination wash across his face. Then, he willed his muscles to move just this one time so that he could at least wheel himself to the start of the course – the rest didn't matter, he just needed to make it there. Laura made to take a step out of line to come to Charlie's aid, but Cesari immediately shouted for her to stay in line, stating that Charlie was to do this for himself.

Charlie's body shook with effort, and he felt a bead of sweat forming on his forehead as he fought against his annoyingly uncooperative muscles, though when he heard Cesari starting to count down loudly from five, he knew he was never going to be able to even make it to the starting line, let alone participate in the task. Eventually, Charlie simply gritted his teeth and let his hands hang loosely to his sides.

"SINCLAIR!" The booming voice came from the instructor. "Never did I ever think that I'd have to mark any recruit down as a negative, simply because they couldn't actually make it to the *start* of the assessment. You are a disgrace and as such the rest of your classmates will suffer. Know that this is to get everyone used to the fact that when an individual fails, then the whole unit fails. TEN PUSHUPS NOW!" he barked. The instructor's face had turned red during his tirade and immediately, Charlie felt ashamed.

Charlie wondered if the instructor was being serious, surely he knew Charlie wouldn't be able to do a pushup, though when Charlie made no moves to even attempt it, the chief instructor shouted again. "THAT'S EVERYONE! NOW!"

All of the kids groaned loudly as they fell to the floor apprehensively and did their best to pay the push-up debt. Charlie simply sat in his chair and watched. There was nothing else he could do or say.

"Your classmates will pay for your shortcomings, Sinclair. Get better and get better quickly or you'll soon be making enemies of your own peers," Cesari stated, though it didn't sound as harsh as it could've done. It wasn't news to Charlie either; he knew the consequences of repeatedly causing everyone else hardship – after all he'd been living that life for almost a year already.

The second assessment was the speed and agility test. This one was designed not only to see just how fast the recruits could move, but also included changes in direction and would test their balance and co-ordination too. The test was to be overseen by instructor Salvatori, a middle-aged man with long brown hair plaited tightly behind his back. He wasn't muscular like the chief instructor, though Salvatori looked in great shape and his body seemed to be in perfect proportions for a rock climber, or yoga teacher.

Speed and agility was essentially an obstacle course made of wooden beams, metal platforms and hanging bars and hoops from overhead scaffold-like apparatus that the participant was expected to use to get from one end to the other. The idea was to complete the course as fast as possible but also, if it was possible and for the more expert climbers of the group, the participant could collect small rings that could be placed over their arms like bracelets for what was described as 'extra points'. It did seem to Charlie though, that if anybody wanted to actually collect any of these bracelets, it would mean taking more perilous paths over obstacles and ultimately that could lead to failure of the course overall – which he assumed was probably worse than not collecting any of the additional points.

The other members of the group carried out their assessment without much hassle as they'd done before and most actually finished the course, although their times weren't anything to write home about. They all seemed apprehensive, and no-one went for the extra-credit bracelets regardless of how cocky they seemed initially. Even Matty Henderson didn't try to overcomplicate anything, although he was notably quicker than many of the others.

Once again Charlie had the feeling that he was going to let everyone down and be berated for it, though once he was left as the last one to attempt the course, Salvatori clapped his hands once and announced to the recruits that they were all dismissed from the assessment.

"Can I talk to you for a moment?" the instructor asked once he was alone with Charlie at the start of the obstacle course. His tone was much more caring and sincere than he'd become used to from the chief instructor.

"Uh... sure?" Charlie answered slowly, not exactly sure what there was going to be to talk about.

"I wasn't sure if you wanted to give the course a go, but please know that it is open to you to practice on it anytime you like. I know the chief can be a little harsh in the way he does things, but I can assure you that he has his reasons and they aren't malicious. Would you like to have a go on the course now that everyone has left?"

Charlie was shocked at the man's statement and simply shook his head, unable to reply immediately.

"That's OK Sinclair. I'll have to mark you down as a zero, but I won't be punishing the rest of them for it. You let me know when you're ready, and we can try again."

Charlie wanted to thank the instructor, but before he knew it the man was gone, and Charlie was alone again. It took him a minute to realise though, that being alone right there meant that he had no way to get to the next test. He thought about calling for Salvatori to help him before he had gone too far away but Charlie felt as though he'd already been too much of a burden as it was.

Charlie placed his hands on the wheels on either side of his chair and bit his bottom lip in renewed anticipation. He *knew* that his body was recovering and he *knew* that if he simply tried hard enough he'd be able to do this.

He willed the muscles in his arms to do the work that he knew they could and his hands turned white as the effort reached his knuckles. Then the wheels, as slow as he could've ever imagined, started to turn. It was painfully slow at first and almost unnoticeable, but then he could feel the whole chair moving. He was moving himself and he knew that this was just the beginning.

With renewed confidence, momentum and the firm belief that he was getting stronger by the very second, Charlie slowly rolled himself to where the rest of the recruits had gone, to a firing range in the distance. As he made his approach, he could both see and hear that the tests had already begun.

Bang, Bang, Bang. Three shots rang out from the Lee-Enfield bolt action rifles from three recruits who were currently taking the test. Charlie recognised the rifles from old movies though he'd never actually fired any sort of gun before.

The firing range was very simple; three shooters would fire at five targets that were at progressively further distances away and would be scored based on the number they hit within the rings on the target. The three recruits currently firing had all hit the first target fairly well, one had hit the outer ring of the second target, though nobody had managed to hit anything beyond that.

Charlie wheeled himself over the threshold to the firing range and awaited further instruction at the back of the line. The instructor this time though, a short woman with blonde hair cut to shoulder length, beckoned him forward with a smile.

Instructor Rosewood introduced herself and told Charlie to take the next available space for the test and he felt acutely aware that by doing so, everyone would be watching him. He did have his renewed confidence though, as well as a growing strength in his arms that seemed to be pretty consistent since his last operation, so he was more optimistic about this task than he had been about any previous.

The instructor placed the rifle on Charlie's lap and told him to take his position behind a concrete wall that was about hip height for a normal recruit and Charlie realised what that meant for him. Sitting in his chair, he was able to rest the muzzle of the rifle on the concrete and he was in much more of a stable firing position than any of the others – and he didn't even have to put any effort into holding the rifle up!

Charlie's heart beat quickly at the anxiety of everyone watching him now and he breathed slowly to try to rid himself of the noxious chemicals that came along with it. He looked down the iron sights of the rifle and held his breath for just a moment before squeezing the trigger for the first time. It took more effort than he would have guessed but the rifle fired, and the first paper target let out a loud popping sound as his shot hit true.

"Bullseye," Rosewood announced with a smile, though you wouldn't have heard it from her voice, which remained completely professional.

Charlie was stunned at his shot, but he knew what he needed to do next. He pulled the bolt back on the rifle and reloaded it with some difficulty for his next shot. He readied the rifle, took a deep breath and squeezed the trigger again. This time, the second paper target made the popping sound.

"Again, bullseye, Rosewood said aloud for everyone to hear.

The recruits behind Charlie now turned deathly silent; The boy in the wheelchair had been the first to hit bullseye anyway, but two in a row! He reloaded and steadied the rifle for his third shot and took it quickly. The third target popped.

"Not quite... but still the target has been hit in the six zone," Rosewood said as Charlie let out his breath. Three in a row really would've been too much to ask for.

Nobody had even hit the fourth target yet, but Charlie had that one in his sights both literally and metaphorically now. He looked through the iron sights, took a deep breath then stopped. Whilst he was looking at the target it seemed to be growing, filling his field of view. Everything was just so clear and as he watched he could see just where the next bullet would strike. Dumbfounded, he lined up the sights with the bullseye and pulled the trigger.

"Bullseye," Rosewood announced this time and Charlie smiled. He knew it was going to be the perfect shot because that was just how he'd aimed it.

"And what about target number five, Mr. Oswald?" Rosewood asked of Charlie, who immediately got the reference to JFK's sharpshooter killer.

Buoyed by his success and the ease of the last target, Charlie readied the rifle and concentrated once more. This target was much, much further away but as he concentrated it too grew and became more focussed. He was astounded again by just how easy this seemed to be for him. He could see the paper of the target clearly and even each thin ink ring that separated the target zones. He concentrated, held his breath and fired once his shot was perfectly lined up.

The paper didn't move.

"That one was a miss," Rosewood announced, walking next to, then taking the rifle from Charlie.

"What happened? I was sure I was on target," Charlie said, clearly upset with the shot.

"Did you account for wind resistance, the parabola of the bullet due to the distance? These things you will learn with time, though what you have done so far has been very impressive Mr. Sinclair and you should be proud."

He didn't feel proud though, he felt annoyed that he wasn't able to hit the last target, though when he turned to see the faces that had been watching him it was clear that both Laura and Mauro were proud and smiling, though the rest of the recruits were scowling, some faces even contorted into angry snarls. Charlie couldn't think what he might have done to deserve such a reception, but he slowly wheeled himself back to the side of the crowd and out of the way of the assessment.

He heard a quiet voice from the crowd once the next recruits had taken their firing positions for the assessment. "Fucking cheater."

The final initial assessment was to be the unarmed combat test and another one that Charlie knew that he wouldn't be partaking in, after all, he could barely move his own body let alone defend himself.

This time this instructor was a very large man with dark skin and standing right beside him was chief instructor Cesari. Charlie knew that this surely wasn't going to be good.

"Giardini, Wu," Cesari called once the kids had all formed up before the two instructors. Behind them was a large, flat, sand covered square which Charlie immediately assumed was there specifically for fighting on.

Laura and the boy named Wu stepped forward and faced the chief instructor, who then addressed the cadets all as one.

"You will step onto the sands behind me. You will face one another and wait until my signal to fight. The fight will be over when one of you surrenders – this is signified by either holding a flat palm up in the air like so," he held an arm up in the air to demonstrate. "Being rendered unconscious, or if you are unable to raise your arm in the air you may surrender verbally. Do you understand?"

"Yes chief instructor," a *better* chorus responded to his question though it still wasn't perfect.

"Take your positions and... FIGHT!" Cesari shouted and moved out of the way of the pair to begin the bout.

Charlie had the distinct feeling that Cesari had chosen Laura to fight first because of her association to him, though he kept his mouth shut in case it caused any more trouble. He could see from both of the cadet's postures that they'd at least done some kind of fighting before, the boy named Wu, who was smaller than Laura, standing in a very boxing-like stance with his fists clenched and placed either side of his head. Laura though kept her hands open with her arms outstretched, looking as though she'd prefer to grapple over striking.

Wu lunged at Laura and Charlie gasped as Laura dropped her leading knee to duck under the strike that the boy threw, aimed remorselessly at her face. Then she wrapped her arms around the boy's waist and forced him back and to the ground. Quickly, she leapt atop him and pinned his arms under her knees, freeing both of her own hands to place the boy at her mercy. Laura waited motionless, looking down at her opponent for a moment, and eventually he caught her meaning. There was nothing he could do – he had lost.

"I... I surrender..." Wu called clearly, and Laura immediately stood up, releasing him from beneath her.

Cesari huffed but didn't comment on the fight. Either he had expected Laura to be taught a lesson, or perhaps he was annoyed at the verbal surrender.

"Latori, Torolev," Cesari called, confirming that the two people who'd helped Charlie were now firmly in the chief instructor's crosshairs.

This time, neither boy seemed as though they were used to fighting and although Mauro was quite a bit bigger than his opponent, without skill there didn't seem as if there was much to do. Eventually after a series of awkward grapples and half-punches, Mauro got the better of Torolev and placed him in a headlock. Not knowing what to do next though, he simply walked Torolev around the sands until the boy eventually had no choice but to blurt out his own surrender. Cesari snorted audibly.

"Henderson," the chief instructor called for the larger, stronger boy in the group. "And... Sinclair." Charlie's mouth went dry. Had he seriously called on him to fight? And against *that?*

Charlie looked at the second instructor pleadingly, though he didn't seem to be having any issues with the prescribed match. Charlie wheeled his chair onto the sands with some effort, the wheels sinking slightly making them difficult to turn. He sat ready in his chair, arms raised facing his much, much stronger and larger opponent, who was smirking.

"FIGHT!" Came the instruction and Henderson apparently didn't need to be told twice. He was across the short distance between them in a flash with his fist cocked back and ready to strike. That was when everything seemed to slow to a crawling pace. Charlie watched the larger boy floating through the air as he leapt toward him, the faces of the crowd, some angry at him still and some cheering for Henderson to teach him a lesson, and he saw the expression on Henderson's face, pure hatred for him. Then the world resumed as it should, and Charlie felt the force of a brick hitting him square in the nose.

A loud crack telegraphed the fact that something had definitely broken on the impact and Charlie felt hot blood streaming from his nostrils. His eyes watered, blurring his vision but as his opponent had mounted he and his chair, he only had to endure two more strikes – one to his broken nose and a second to his jaw, which turned his vision to black.

Chapter 7

Intergalactic Council space, Omnis Station.

"Do you still think that this is the correct course of action, council member?" asked Sorin, a member of a race called the Baccus.

Jorell of the Ascara scratched his chin thoughtfully. It was a habit that he'd picked up when watching and dealing with the human race over a number of years, and one that he didn't particularly enjoy, although he couldn't seem to stop himself from doing it. Two of his arms lay by his side and his yellowish skin was covered by a deep red sash that hinted at a high degree of muscle definition beneath.

In contrast, Sorin was thin and had very little muscle tone. His blueish skin was translucent to the point of showing his entire network of veins beneath it, and he too wore a sash, though blue with a gold trim that covered a good portion of his person.

The pair had met as old friends on Omnis station on the outskirts of Intergalactic Council members' space. It was the closest station to what was being called EP1, which was no accident. Sorin had wanted to hear more about the human project that the council had embarked upon and that was his ulterior motive for the meet-up.

"This was never my idea, it was passed by the council as a democracy, Sorin. The wisdom of collective decision-making should never be questioned." Although the words that Jorell had spoken were correct, it sounded to Sorin as though he didn't fully believe them himself, which was a good thing, especially with what Sorin was planning.

"Jorell, my friend, I know you well and you seem to speak with thought, though the words seem to be lacking heart. Tell me, what is happening with this project that you are unhappy with?" Sorin spoke sincerely to his friend, and he saw immediately that Jorell was uncomfortable at his own position.

"Sorin, these are not words that are to be spoken where one could be overheard, though I do feel that we are somewhat safe here in this station," Jorell cautiously looked about them both. "Very well. Your assessment is correct. My own thoughts on the situation were that the human race of earth could not be trusted to look after themselves, let alone be entrusted with advanced gene editing and advancement. I feel that by making these beings stronger, we are creating a threat to our own sovereignty in the long term, and as you know that is something that I have some experience in." Jorell spoke in a hushed tone and Sorin felt as though he was peeking under the lid of the larger being's true self. He nodded for Jorell to continue.

"The humans are strong and determined and pride themselves on their competitiveness. They fight and posture constantly to make their peers feel smaller and once they meet something they are unfamiliar with, they attempt to dominate it. I feel that if they are advanced to the level of some of the smaller races of the Council, they will try to form their own alliances with machinations towards war and domination. This is, after all, what we are helping them do with this project."

Jorell had spoken way too much and he and Sorin both knew it, but Sorin knew that it was the information that he wanted to hear.

"Jorell, old friend, this was a Council decision and not something that you are required to harass yourself over," Sorin began to comfort his counterpart. "Besides, there is always the option to remove the project should things take an unexpected turn, right?"

Jorell nodded slowly. There are ways to end the project, though without full agreement from the Council, these options would not be explored."

"Then let me offer you a new alternative my friend," Sorin had steered the conversation expertly and was ready to deal the killing blow. "If such an event were to occur that the project was to be deemed no longer savoury, let me take the modified humans of earth away with my fleet and we will expand the Council's reach into parts unknown. Instead of a defensive, police-like force, these humans could be used to overthrow, to wage war without thoughts of casualties on either side, and I am willing to take on this burden should the need arise. These humans could be the first blow to our enemies and the best part is that the Council and its members would never need to waste a soldier!"

Jorell thought about what Sorin was saying. He could tell that his friend was only asking these things in the eventuality that the project was to be scrapped, which he didn't really see happening any time soon anyway. He could also see that having an army of strong, genetically modified human soldiers at his beck and call could make Sorin a very powerful being, and he worried that this was what Sorin had been planning all along.

"Sorin, I hear what you are saying," Jorell spoke slowly and quietly still, "and I agree that it would be a waste if the project were to be scrapped, to just remove these humans from existence following all of our efforts. Though their ownership would most likely be voted on by the Council, I do not have the ear of every member and I would not be able to guarantee that your scenario would come to fruition."

Sorin had been expecting this answer and as usual had prepared one of his own. "Of course not, as in all democratic situations, the future of the humans would need to be voted upon. What I ask, though, is that you present this as an option, and offer your backing should the idea be accepted by the Council. Though I must press to remind you, and all of the Council members, that by sending this army off into the far reaches of space, there would be two benefits to our Council. Firstly, we would gain the firepower that they should afford us as stated, and secondly, these beings would be far, far from the centre of our sovereign space."

"That does sound acceptable to me, my friend," Jorell said as he rose from his seat, "though I can make no assurances or promises, and I must say that I do not see the project coming to an end any time soon. I will speak with you again soon, however, I am sure." And with that, Jorell left Sorin to sit on his own.

Sorin had been expecting all of this to happen. He knew that he could not simply gain the human soldiers *if* and *when* they were deemed unnecessary by the Council, though only he knew that it was his seed of an idea in the very first place that had led the Council to begin on this journey. The Baccus had always prided himself on his ability to seed his ideas into others and make them believe they were their own. He'd steered negotiations, debates and meetings to conclusions that he alone had intended, and nobody had ever seemed to figure out why or how he was doing it.

The cunning Baccus had now both seeded the idea of using humans as an army in the very first place, as well as the idea that if they couldn't be controlled, they would be used as an invading force. The beauty of his plans, however, was that there would be no downside to any of the other

Council members or their respective races, and therefore no reason to deny his request, for he had offered them all a way out. The cherry on top was of course that if they simply wanted to wash their hands of the humans at any time, he was the perfect solution – palm them off and forget about it.

The plans that the Baccus had for the human race, however, would remain Sorin's own secret for the time being. It was true that they would become an invading force to grow and expand the Intergalactic Council, but he knew that eventually those goals would be well behind him, and he had something much, much bigger in mind to use these belligerent humans for.

~ Twelve years prior ~

Sorin was the Talchiar – or captain - aboard the Baccus science vessel that had been commissioned into the outer reaches of the Intergalactic Council to search for life or evidence thereof. He had always been ambitious of course, though from early in his career he knew his place well and when to lower his gaze so as to not rise up above the rest and be quashed. He kept his mouth shut and his hands busy almost all of the time, though he could never quite shake the feeling that there was something bigger, something better out there for him. His steadfast determination and work ethic had eventually paid off and offered him this command, which he took although he wasn't excited about the prospect of a long mission in space that wasn't going to be particularly eventful.

The vessel he'd been given was small and pretty insignificant in the grand scheme of things, though that was often the way the cards fell into the hands of fate as this vessel in particular would be the one to discover the planet Earth, the humans, and their relatively newfound nuclear technologies.

The Baccus spent two years observing the humans from a distance and generating a dossier on the human race to be presented to the Council before they would leave for home and Sorin took particular note of the human race's ways of war and conflict, noting that they were unlike anything he'd ever seen within the Council members before. They were steadfast, strong, determined and confident to the point of overconfidence on so many occasions.

Since the first moment of his first captaincy, Sorin knew that he wanted to be a Grand Talchiar, a title afforded to a captain with multiple starships under their control - a fleet. He was well aware though, that going from Talchiar of a small insignificant science vessel to a militaristic Grand

Talchiar was not something that a Baccus of his station would be able to achieve without some kind of divine intervention. To Sorin, the human race provided an answer to that quandary.

Sorin proceeded over the following months to report on how the human race was simultaneously warlike, barbaric, highly skilled at fighting with each other, belligerent and technologically inferior. Above all, though, they had great and almost limitless potential. It was a difficult line to walk for Sorin, as if he presented that the humans were too skilled at war, it could've led to their immediate destruction, and if they weren't skilled enough then his ultimate goals for them would be dismissed.

From the moment he'd seen just how effective the humans were at killing, Sorin knew that they were his ticket upwards. With a fleet of vessels either manned by or carrying these creatures, his power would be both unknown and unmatched, which together would be a seriously dangerous combination.

The Council – fed with Sorin's seeds of forethought – had acted so predictably and exactly how he had wanted. Human soldiers were to be taken to a Council planet, and enhanced then trained to become an effective fighting force. He knew eventually that the Council would become afraid of them – they always did - and with sites all across the planet full of recruits, Sorin would have no shortage of soldiers once the time came.

Chapter 8

Charlie was awoken by a splitting headache, and not for the first or even second time. Instinctively he raised a hand to his head and groaned, not caring who was around to hear or witness it.

"Hey, Charlie," he heard Laura's voice from behind his closed eyes. "How are you feeling?"

The question should've been answered by his groan, though he thought that if this wasn't sufficient, he was actually going to have to say some words – and it was going to hurt his head.

Charlie opened his eyes slowly. He was clearly in a small medical room, metal walls all around, desks etc. again – in fact, it was much like the last one he'd woken up in and he sighed in relief.

"He didn't kill me then?" he asked as he noticed both Laura and Mauro in the room with him, but no one else.

Mauro let out a snort. "Nope, but it wasn't for the want of trying!" Charlie thought it was strange that Mauro was smiling as he said the words, as though he was enjoying this whole ordeal.

"What happened?" Charlie asked.

"You got your ass kicked!" Mauro was the first to answer, though Laura gave him a look that Charlie presumed told him to shut his big mouth – which he did. Then Laura spoke.

"You took a bit of a beating. Henderson is so much bigger than the rest of us and much stronger too. I thought that first punch was going to tip your wheelchair right over. After you passed out, he managed to get a few more hits in," she winced as she spoke, "until Cesari called an end to the fight.

"What's with that guy?" Charlie asked. "He's a fucking lunatic, right?"

Both Laura and Mauro exchanged a worried glance before speaking again. It was clear that they knew something – or thought they did – that Charlie didn't and didn't want to speak negatively about their chief instructor.

"He does seem to pick on you a little more than anyone else," Laura said. "Maybe it's to see if he pushes you harder then you'll step up? Not that I think you need to step up or anything... and that's nothing to do with your..." she turned bright red and placed a hand on her forehead. Charlie caught Mauro's eye and both of them burst into laughter at Laura's floundering. Truth be told Charlie really needed to have a good laugh and if that meant laughing at what he was coming to think of as one of his only two friends here, he was taking the opportunity.

"So how long have I been out, what's been happening?" Charlie asked. "Did I miss pizza night?"

"Pizza night?" Mauro cut in quickly, very interested in what Charlie had to say on the matter. "The best I've had is porridge with a bit of honey in it. Are you telling me you had pizza?"

Charlie hadn't meant to start something, but he did realise that he was pretty hungry and he remembered eating that pizza very clearly. How it tasted, how it felt as he chewed it. Then he remembered his unanswered question and asked again. "How long have I been out?"

Laura cringed slightly when she replied. "To you it's the next day. We all finished our assessments, received our ranks and had dinner before bed. By the way, you getting to sleep in your own bed... that was a touch of genius you know that?"

Charlie smiled, "It's what I did it for... though you didn't have to all sleep on the floor or anything, did you? Because that would be hilarious."

"No, actually we were all given suites that overlooked the valley with whirlpool baths and personal butlers if you must know. I was just trying to make you feel better about it," Laura joked. "Though yeah, we kind of all had to sleep in the mess hall because we hadn't yet been sorted into our classes. Apparently, we are to be assigned specialisations, then will be given dorms and gear from there. For one I'm pretty happy about that – you lot stink!"

"Hey!" Mauro interjected looking fake-hurt at Laura's words. "It takes a long time to work up this musk, don't you oppress me!"

Charlie smiled again although it fell once he remembered the events of the day before. "Where did you learn to fight like that?" he asked Laura.

"You kicked ass out there."

Laura turned red and it was her turn to look sheepish at the answer. "Back home my parents had me doing Brazilian Jiu-Jitsu since I was like four. It's pretty fun really but I never thought it was actually going to be this effective in the real world. I have to say right now I'm pretty thankful to them for that."

"Your parents?" Charlie asked. "Aren't you from the system, like…" he trailed off before finishing his question. He really didn't need any more embarrassment right now.

"My parents work hard, but I could see how hard it was to keep looking after me. They sent me here once they were approached with what I thought was a pretty good offer," she explained.

"A good offer? They sold you?" Charlie said loudly as though he couldn't believe his ears.

"No!" Laura could've laughed but refrained. "The offer was for me, stupid. They were thinking about sending me off to boarding school anyway to 'broaden my horizons,'" she air quoted the words. "But the military said that they would do the same here, plus fast track me through some specialised training – you know the usual spiel they give. Well, my parents fell for it and so did I. You'll find a lot of volunteers here actually, not just the ones who were sent by their parents as a last resort."

Charlie looked at Mauro questioningly. "Was it the same for you?" he asked.

"Ha. Volunteer? No. I'm not that stupid. They said I could be like superman! I begged my parents to let me go and here I am," Mauro smiled and Charlie held back a laugh.

"And are you like superman?" Charlie asked. "No wait, I think you are. You're on an alien planet amongst strangers and you don't know where your spaceship is!"

"And I have a bald arch-nemesis too!" Mauro chimed in, though the expression on Charlie's face betrayed his confusion at the statement. "Umm, looked in a mirror lately?" he added.

Laura shyly picked up a small handheld mirror from one of the metal work tables and turned it for Charlie to see his reflection. He almost recoiled in horror at what he saw.

Both of his eyes were dark purple where his nose had been broken, which itself was covered in bandages, but the thing Charlie hadn't really thought about in a long time was that atop his head he didn't have a single hair.

Charlie blinked slowly then looked away from his own reflection, it was all too much to deal with right now and he was happier not knowing what he looked like.

"S... sorry Charlie," Mauro said slowly.

"No, it's OK," Charlie replied and did his best to smile at the boy, after all he was sure they were friends by now and the last thing he wanted to do was blow it. "I'll be your Lex Luther."

"That's enough excitement for now," a voice came from an open doorway leading into the room and Charlie recognised it immediately.

"Dr. Kono?" he asked, though there was no need for verification as the lizard-man walked briskly into the room and shooed the two friends back out. "And eat something, you look small and weak," he added as the pair made their exit.

"You know you shouldn't speak so brashly about your superior officers. The walls have ears, to borrow an expression from the people of earth," Kono said as he pointed a thin, scaled finger at the ceiling.

Charlie narrowed his eyes but didn't argue the point.

"I know you're keen to make an impression Charlie, but it will take a few days for our modifications to affect your system. Until then you shouldn't go around picking fights with the other recruits." Dr. Kono said without even a hint of sarcasm.

"Picking fights?" Charlie said loudly, outraged. "It was that maniac, Cesari. He's hell bent on having me killed!"

Dr. Kono pointed to the ceiling again and Charlie immediately shut his mouth, remembering the doctor's warning about bad-mouthing the staff.

"I can assure you that the chief instructor is not trying to get you killed. I believe it is quite to the contrary." The doctor replied.

"He's trying... to save my life?" Charlie offered.

The doctor looked at Charlie for a moment then realised that his statement had been taken literally and smiled. "Not precisely, but close. The chief instructor is a very talented man and I believe that you should do exactly what he says, whenever he says it," Kono replied.

"Right, but does everything he say have to involve me getting embarrassed in front of everyone? Or beaten up?" Charlie asked sincerely.

Dr. Kono shrugged his shoulders as though deciding something internally and concluded with 'what's the worst that can happen'? "Cesari was a special operations soldier back on earth. He was highly trained for most of his life to carry out missions that required a top-level degree of precision and expertise. When the earth military forces were approached in the beginnings of contact with the Intergalactic Council, volunteers were requested to travel to distant worlds with the Council members so that they could better understand each other and Cesari was one of those volunteers. For years, he fought alongside a race known as the Baccus on the far reaches of Council-controlled space on a planet entrenched by an enemy warring race and for two years the chief instructor fought every single day until his last waking moment.

He killed countless enemy insurgents, suffered terrible wounds of which he still carries the scars today, and saved the lives of countless allied soldiers. Cesari is by all accounts the most famous human being and known to all Council members across controlled space. I assure you that no matter what you think or feel right now, Marcus Cesari is the very best man to lead all of the recruits on this base into the lives that you are expected to follow, and you are luckier than the others to have him here."

Charlie's internal ears pricked up at the doctor's last statement. "What do you mean *others*? Are there other camps with recruits on? And why kids? And how did the governments let them just take us away?" His questions kept over spilling as he asked them and Dr. Kono looked a little taken aback by the barrage.

"Charlie, I cannot answer all of your questions right now, though you will learn the answers soon. There are other camps carrying out the same work we are here though, and they are all on this very planet although spread very far apart. As for why pre-adolescent humans are chosen? It is because you have not yet grown to your potential, so the editing we can do to your genetic code is less restricted than if you were an adult. Essentially at your age, you are malleable, and that is what we need."

Charlie took in the dump of information like a sponge. He listened intently to every word the doctor said and noted everything down mentally in case he needed to recall any of the information at a later date.

"So... when can I go?" Charlie asked once he was sure the doctor wasn't going to reveal any more information to him at this time.

"Haven't you realised Charlie?" Kono said with a knowing smile and waited for the penny to drop.

Charlie looked down at his body and turned his hands over and over a few times before it struck him. "I... I lifted myself up, didn't I," he said slowly.

Kono nodded.

Charlie then placed both of his hands on the hard bed, one on either side of him, turned his legs to the side and held his breath until he felt the soles of his bare feet make contact with the cold metal floor.

Tears filled his eyes and when he looked to see if the doctor was still watching him in this new and amazing feat of strength, Charlie saw that he was, and he was making notes on a glass terminal that he held in his hands. Dr. Kono waited to see if Charlie was going to make any more moves.

Charlie knew what he had to do next, though his mind simply didn't accept that it was going to happen right here, right now. He had always imagined simply waking up one day and being able to stand – and walk again, though the day had never come, yet here he was holding up his own weight as he sat.

Kono had stopped making notes to watch Charlie's next moves intently and as they both remained silent, Charlie allowed his feet to take his full weight, then his legs and his knees, his hips, back and neck. All of Charlie's body felt the battle between gravity trying to pull him downwards and his own muscles struggling to prevent it from happening. But to his amazement, Charlie remained standing despite all the odds.

The doctor silently made a few more notes on his tablet, and then waited to see if Charlie would make any more leaps and bounds in his recovery.

Totally amazed at himself, Charlie had all but forgotten that simply standing up was not the extent of his ambitions. If he really wanted to make waves, he needed to take a step forward. To walk for himself had been such a dream and had seemed so distant a goal that again he was shocked that he stood – literally – on the precipice of such a monumental task.

Remembering precisely what he needed to do, Charlie lifted his left foot from the floor and his entire body wobbled slightly. It was difficult to balance on one leg, the muscles groaning at the effort they hadn't had to endure for so long – then he moved his left leg forwards about six inches and placed it back on the floor.

Then he immediately crumpled and collapsed into a heap on the floor.

Kono rushed to pick him up, but Charlie shooed his helping hand away and lifted himself back up and onto his feet. This was his moment and he knew that there was only one person to help him through this, and that was himself.

The stand-up-fall-down routine went on for longer than Charlie would have liked to admit, though he did feel like he was getting closer to taking his first step with every failing attempt and the doctor never failed to make notes each time Charlie's body crumpled down to the ground. Eventually, the doctor said that it was time for Charlie to leave the medical unit and rejoin everyone in the mess hall, which was where dinner was currently being served along with some important announcements.

Charlie did his best to feel better about his failure as he wheeled his way from the medical unit to the mess hall and though he was quite upset that he wasn't yet able to walk there for himself, he could now easily move himself around in his chair – small victories he guessed.

"Ah, Mr. Sinclair," Cesari's voice boomed as soon as Charlie entered the hall. It was a container-shaped building made from corrugated metal panels, though it was much, much larger than a standard forty-foot affair. The thing was at least one hundred foot long, fifty feet wide and tall and had two heavy metal doors at one end to mark the entrance. Charlie was actually pretty happy that he didn't have to open the doors himself, as even though he felt much stronger it would've been difficult to open them outwards and towards his chair without simply getting in his own way.

Charlie silently wheeled himself to the back end of the hall where five long metal tables with accompanying benches were laid out, big enough for probably fifty recruits on each side, though Charlie didn't have the time to count before the chief instructor spoke again.

"You are all officially from this moment Cadets of the Earth Space Corps and are no longer recruits," he announced. "Your ranks are to be determined by myself and myself only. The next available rank to you all is 'Ordinary Cadet', and then for those who progress with merit, 'Able Cadet.'"

Charlie wondered if Cesari included him in his 'all of you,' though the instructor hadn't taken the time to single him out, so he probably was included. Charlie did wonder though if it was actually of any use to have a cadet that failed almost every baseline test that they'd placed him in.

"The five tables you see before you are your class specialisations," Cesari continued. "These are Heavy Arms, Assault, Scout, Support and Special Ops and your specialisation has been selected for you based upon mostly your baseline assessment scores. Your specialisation cannot be changed, and it is what you will eat, sleep and breathe during your time here. Any Questions?"

Not a single cadet even made the slightest movement.

"Good," the chief continued speaking. "Once your specialisation is read aloud, you will then move yourself to the corresponding table, you will then collect your uniform from the end of the table and take it to your seat. Is that clear?"

"YES CHIEF INSTRUCTOR!" The chorus came back from the cadets and the synchronicity had already notably improved.

"Your uniform serves as an indicator of your given specification. Heavy Arms are blue, Assault red, Scout green, Support yellow and Special Ops are white. Stand by." Cesari waited for a moment to make sure his instructions were clear and then started reading names from a list on a data pad he brought up to eye-level.

"Singh, Bakara. Scout." This was evidently the first name on his list and a small dark-skinned boy with short black hair scurried over to the table with a pile of clothes that had some sort of green flashing showing on them and took a seat.

"Orlov, Sergei. Assault." Again a boy, though this time light skinned and fair-haired, moved himself to the table with red uniforms.

Charlie tuned out most of the other names until he heard Mauro Latori being placed into Heavy Arms, and Laura Giardini being placed in the Scouts. He also took little note of Matty Henderson being placed into Heavy Arms alongside Mauro and certainly spared his friend no envy about that.

"Last and by all accounts, least: Sinclair, Charlie," Cesari finally announced. Charlie's breath caught in his chest at the mention of his name. He had already thought sniper would be a good fit for him as shooting a rifle was the only thing he'd shown any aptitude for thus far, though the word that followed, along with the toothy grin from Cesari shocked him entirely.

"Special Ops. Secondary Specialisation. Alpha."

A few of the cadets turned to look at Charlie as he still sat in his wheelchair, either shocked that he had been made a cadet, shocked he was not placed in the sniper squad or shocked that he was the only person to be designated whatever a secondary specialisation was. All in all, nobody knew what to do.

Cesari spoke again when he could see his words were causing some discomfort amongst the cadets. "Each of you will be given a secondary specialisation as you train. For Heavy Arms these are berserker and artillery. For assault, blitz and cover. Scout, recon and sniper. Support, tech and medic. Special ops," the chief instructor looked directly at Charlie as he spoke these words, "alpha and communications."

It didn't tell anyone much about what the roles would entail, though the cadets did recognise the names of the specialisations, and their subcategories and essentially what would be expected of them in the long run. Nobody quite knew what this 'Alpha' role was going to be though, not being one traditionally used in earth militaries, movies or even the games that many of the cadets had played previously. Charlie knew though that because he had been told he was one, life wasn't going to be easy as an Alpha.

Now that the ceremony had concluded and each cadet had been given their specialisation and therefore table, it was time for the food to appear. Charlie had visions of the pizza that he'd had during his journey to the planet, though once each cadet had received a covered plate in front of them, he could already tell from the aroma that it wasn't to be. Dinner tonight was water, bread, porridge and a fat (though overdone) steak. The military on this occasion had apparently decided on hitting the macronutrient requirements for the cadets above anything else, especially taste.

Charlie didn't particularly care that the food was a disgusting mixture that tasted like crap; he enjoyed the fact that he could eat for himself, his arms having gained even more strength as the day had gone on.

"Did you see Matty lift those walls up like they were nothing?" Charlie overheard two of the boys near to him on his table talking about the events of the day.

"Yeah, and when he jumped on that wheelchair kid..." the other replied, though he stopped once he realised how close Charlie was to their conversation. "Uh... sorry," the boy said to Charlie, who was actually taken aback by the apology.

"Next time he'll have to deal with my walking stick if I keep getting stronger like I am," Charlie quipped with a smile. Something told him that if he wanted to make friends in all of this, he was going to need to learn how to laugh things off.

The boy looked shocked at the response for just a moment, then broke into a large grin. "I'm Joey Ashman," he introduced himself.

Charlie looked at the other boy who'd just filled his mouth with a slice of dry bread. He did his best to talk and Charlie deciphered his name through his mumbling to be Luca Strano.

Contrary to how he thought this was all going to go down, Charlie actually had already made a few friends. Laura and Mauro were at different tables so they weren't close enough to converse, but Charlie saw on a number of occasions both of them looking over to check to see that he was getting along OK, and that alone made him feel so much better.

Luca and Joey were actually pretty decent people too. They recounted Charlie's fight with Matty Henderson to him with a fair amount of detail, apparently impressed by the technical ability of the much stronger boy and not just his overbearing aggression. As the three of them spoke and discussed fighting in general, Charlie could tell that the Special Ops corps had taken in some pretty perceptive cadets with a good knowledge of technique and tactics – which still bore the question of what he was doing there.

"I did pretty well on the firing range," Charlie protested after the other two had teased him one too many times for not even lifting a hand to defend himself against Henderson.

"Ah yes, the cheater brings up how he cheated to win, of course!" Joey said with a wide grin. "You place your rifle on your perfectly stable wheelchair and the other end on a concrete wall and expect us to accept that? Try holding the thing up for yourself next time, eh?"

Charlie raised an eyebrow as the penny dropped to why he'd been thought of as a cheater in that particular test, though he didn't let it discourage him.

"Maybe next time I will," he replied and folded his arms across his chest. "Then you'll be even more disappointed to be beaten by the cripple and without him even having to use his chair for support. How terrible you would feel then; imagine all the people looking at you because you're different."

For a military encampment the evening was surprisingly relaxed and the officers in the camp didn't seem to take any issues with all of the cadets getting their downtime. Charlie presumed that mealtimes were just that – downtime - so it would be normal for everyone to simply unwind and forget the deeds of the day. However, the time did eventually come when Cesari announced loudly that the cadets would need to leave the mess hall for their dorms.

This turned out to be another surprise. The cadets weren't in long dorms full of bunk beds like Charlie had seen in the movies, rather the accommodation was more like a student-style living arrangement. Each dorm, which was again a large metallic arrangement seemingly made of three containers connected together, had five segregated bedrooms, a kitchen and a communal living area complete with a comfy sofa and a couple of armchairs. Each bedroom had a personal terminal, desk, bed and bathroom and the thing was, it was all just so *nice* inside. You could hardly tell you were inside a container as it was so tardis-like. It was huge, softly carpeted and the painted walls and light fittings just made everything feel so *warm* and homely.

Living arrangements were pre-determined though, which meant that in each dorm there would be one member of each of the specialisations. Charlie wondered if that was to prevent conferring and cheating if there was any studying to be done, or to give each cadet a wider range of shared experiences. All Charlie knew for sure though were his new roommates.

In Charlie's dorm, he was thankful to find that both his friends had been placed along with him. There was Mauro, Laura, a boy called Kori Nakamura assigned as an Assault and a girl named Stephanie Marsh who was a Support. Charlie hadn't been able to decipher who Kori and Stephanie were, though when he, Laura and Mauro entered their new dorm shortly after receiving their assignments, the three found both Kori and Stephanie sat in the common area of their new home.

Laura and Charlie didn't say anything when they all locked eyes, though Mauro couldn't help himself. "Hey roomies!" he said happily. "I'm Mauro. This is Laura and Charlie," he added and both Charlie and Laura raised a sheepish flat hand to say hello.

Kori Nakamura nodded slightly back at Mauro and replied. "Kori Nakamura. It is a pleasure to make your acquaintance Mauro Latori, Laura Giardini." It was obvious to everyone in the room that the boy had totally ignored Charlie in his greeting and Charlie was OK with leaving that be, though apparently Laura wasn't.

"You got a problem, Kori?" she asked curtly. "Don't like the wheelchair? Or do you just have a problem with kids with no hair?"

Charlie felt the top of his head at that statement, not having ever really thought about that issue before, though it had been mentioned twice in as many days. She was right though, he was bald as an egg – a by-product of the repeated brain surgeries he kept having.

"It's because he's a cheater," Stephanie interrupted the conversation, standing up off of the sofa in the middle of the room. "He cheated on the firing range and he couldn't pass any of the other tests. Also, you heard what Cesari said about everyone being only as good as the worst team member right? This is going to end up with us doing extra pushups or star jumps or something – we can all see it."

Laura took a step forward to the girl who was now evidently a couple of inches shorter than her. "Listen right now," Laura raised a finger threateningly and practically growled her words. "Everybody here is here for a reason. Everybody made it as a cadet so if you don't like it, I suggest you take it up with the chief instructor. Otherwise, if you don't like something I suggest you take it up with me. Got it?"

Charlie was so shocked at Laura's demeanour and absolute confidence in herself that he barely noticed when Stephanie sat back down on the sofa as though the pair were wolves vying for the position of alpha. If that were the case, then Laura had just won with aplomb.

The three friends decided then that it was best if they simply went straight to their rooms. There was no need to try to force some awkward small talk after everybody had made their feelings known and Charlie had

had enough of being awake for now anyway.

Inside Charlie's room was a long, full-length mirror on the door of a narrow wooden wardrobe and he stopped as he caught his own eye in it as he rolled past. He placed his hands on the handles of his chair and pushed himself up to stand before it, pulling his t-shirt up and over his head and dropping it onto the floor to get a good look at himself.

He looked at his head and face first. The bruises had started to heal but that just meant they appeared a disgusting shade of yellow around both of his eyes and across his nose. His brown eyes were sunken and gaunt. His hair had still made no effort to begin to regrow, leaving his head entirely bald, and again Charlie raised his hand to his head to feel it, not quite believing it. His shoulders, ribcage and collar bones protruded from his skeletal form. He tried to take everything in at once but all he could see standing before him in the mirror was a husk of what should've been: what looked like a malnourished boy who'd been sent to this camp by accident, especially when standing next to the other, healthy cadets. Charlie didn't even bother to remove the rest of his clothes before he made the effort to stumble and fall onto the small bed and wriggle himself under the covers. The last thing he thought before closing his eyes for sleep was that if he couldn't walk back to his wheelchair in the morning, he would be starting the day by crawling over to it. '*Thank God the floor is carpeted and warm*', he thought.

Chapter 9

The rude awakening of the next morning came in the form of a loud air-raid siren that was sure to have awoken everyone in the camp at once. Charlie had been awake before it had started though he wasn't sure if it was because he was having trouble sleeping properly in his new environment or if he'd simply had enough sleep. Either way he didn't feel groggy or exhausted, so he turned in the bed and placed his feet on the warm floor to yawn and stretch before the inevitable annoyance at the frailty of his body set in.

Today, though, was different. Today Charlie felt the muscles in his legs moving at a much more acceptable pace, responding well to his mental commands and shifting themselves quickly to the edge of the bed on their way to the floor. His stomach muscles too - they pulled him up to his seated position without the usual burning sensation as they struggled with his unfamiliar weight.

Charlie looked at his chair positioned about three short paces from his seat, then raised himself up to standing as he was getting used to doing. He didn't wobble though this time. This time he felt strong, sturdy and natural. He placed his left foot forward and felt strength again in the movement. Then he pulled up his right foot to take the first step he'd taken alone in so very, very long. He couldn't help but smile; He had finally done it. He had walked.

There was no indication that Charlie was going to fall down and he took pace after pace in his room, growing in confidence each time one of his feet struck the floor and the other left. He never thought anyone could be so grateful for the simple fact that they could walk but he was, and his smile practically touched his ears as he walked and walked, faster and faster. This was like magic to Charlie and he wasn't going to waste a single moment of it.

Eventually, he realised that he would be lagging behind if he didn't get a move on, as once he took note of his surroundings, his terminal was displaying a fifteen-minute countdown that'd already dropped by seven, gloriously walking minutes.

Thankfully, putting on his uniform didn't require more than a minute, then brushing his teeth and using the toilet flashed by in a moment because he now didn't have to manoeuvre his chair through doors or do everything sitting down with no strength in his body. He thought about everyone else just taking these mundane tasks for granted and, no matter what happened, how he would never ever take the abilities he'd regained as anything other than what they were – a miracle.

His uniform was a tight-fitting dark blue flight suit style affair with white streaks down the arms and legs. He presumed that all of the cadets' uniform were the same with just different colour flashings to denote their specialisations. Charlie took one last good look at himself *standing* and *walking away* before he left his room and re-entered the communal living space.

Laura and Mauro had apparently waited for Charlie, where Stephanie and Kori had decided it was better to get to the mess hall early than to wait for the entire group. Charlie didn't take offence to that, as it was probably the right call – if they were late because of him it could mean that they would all be punished and he didn't need that on his conscience nor his mental scorecard of why the other cadets might take issue with him.

Laura practically beamed and Mauro's eyes bulged as the pair watched Charlie *walk* out of his room super casually as though it was the most normal thing to do in the world.

"So I uh... I didn't need the chair, I was just faking it," Charlie said with a sheepish grin. He felt as though humour and sarcasm was definitely the way to go, otherwise he might simply have cried about how good this all actually felt.

Laura ran over to Charlie and immediately threw her arms around him in a giant hug, having read the situation perfectly, and Mauro simply gawked at him. Truth be told, Charlie was worried that she was going to knock him over although her embrace was light and careful, which he was eternally thankful for. The last thing he needed was to be knocked over and break one of his weak body parts, confining him to a wheelchair again.

That would not be a fun piece of irony.

"What... what happened?" Mauro asked eventually once Charlie and Laura had separated.

"I don't know," Charlie replied honestly. "I woke up and I just felt so much stronger. I took one step and that was it – I just kept going!" His smile was still so big that it seemed to infect the other two and the three all patted each other on the back and chatted merrily as they made their way to the mess hall.

"Cadets!" Cesari made his announcement once everyone was seated and awaiting their breakfast. Charlie was so hungry that he could practically hear his stomach rumbling constantly. The instructors all sat in front of the five specialisation tables as they had done the night before and Charlie wondered if any of the others actually ever had a turn to speak.

Not many of the cadets had noticed Charlie walking into the back of the mess hall with the other two, although some had and they stared silently at him trying to figure out what his game was.

"Last night I received word from up the line," Cesari continued. "In three weeks from now there is to be an inspection by our benefactors. You probably don't have to be told, but these inspectors will not be human."

Charlie knew that Dr. Kono certainly wasn't human, though he had never seen him outside the medical unit so he didn't know if that was common knowledge. Either way, Charlie wasn't surprised and he wondered how many of the other cadets were, given that they were on an alien world.

"This is our first opportunity to show these benefactors what the human race is capable of. You are expected to work hard until you can work no longer. The days ahead are going to be long and difficult but I can assure you they will get easier. Do not let your head drop and keep striving for better. This is how we all survive," Cesari concluded. It was one of the more positive speeches that Charlie had heard, almost optimistic in fact, and it made him remember what the doctor had told Charlie about Cesari – if anybody knew what it took to survive out there in the universe, it was him.

Breakfast was served after the announcement and this time large vats of what turned out to be porridge was brought to the five tables along with stacks of bowls for the cadets to help themselves with. Charlie waited his turn patiently and made the effort to note the names and faces on the table closest to him. In the seats next to him sat Elliot Kelly, Neville Young, Manuel Mancini, Luke Rook, Phillip Anderson and Anthony Johnson who had apparently decided to stick together as males with not a single girl amongst them. Beyond that he could see Jean Martin and Xi Ling chatting as a pair and Lucy Cooper and Emily Wood in a similar situation. Beyond that, though, the faces and names were still unknown to him.

Charlie didn't attempt to join in with the conversations happening around him. He couldn't be sure who actively disliked him and who just hadn't taken a moment to try to include him yet so he ate his porridge quickly and in silence. It was nice though , creamy with a jam core – it was surprising really, having been expecting some sort of gruel.

Cesari stood up again once everyone had more or less finished eating, though it was evident from his action that he'd expect everyone to be finished now, whether there was food left in front of them or not. "Cadets," he called. "Your combat gear is what you are expected to wear to all of your lessons and although it looks like a pretty basic pyjama-suit, I can assure you that it is a very advanced piece of equipment. Your gear has been designed to measure over a thousand metrics from your body and collate them wirelessly into your personal file, held in the medical unit by Dr. Kono. They include but are not limited to your cardiovascular health, your physical condition, loads, stresses, movement and composition. As you grow, we will know about it. If your heart rate increases by even a single beat, we will know. If you go somewhere you shouldn't be, we will know." He made it almost sound like a warning, though Charlie didn't see it that way. The way he saw it was a method by which to track the way his body was sure to improve during his time at the camp.

"These suits will also measure your PIP level. Now this stands for 'Perceived Intervention Percentage', and is the level at which the various modifications that have been made to your bodies have manifested in your system. Essentially, the higher your PIP level the better you are at becoming all you are meant to be. You can now all view your own PIP level at your personal terminals in your dorms, though I suggest that you keep this information to yourselves as the indicator is personal and not universal. I will also add that there is a lock on the maximum PIP level all of you can achieve, though it varies from cadet to cadet. My advice to you is to do the best you can and ignore these numbers if you can. Do not get bogged down in the nitty-gritty of growth and comparison and focus on being the best *you* can be, as it may not be comparable to the best another cadet can be."

Charlie's ears pricked up at the last statement and he wondered if the chief instructor was talking about him. Was he at a disadvantage because his starting point had been complete paralysis, or did Cesari know that

Charlie supposedly didn't have a lock on his PIP level as Dr. Kono had told him. What Charlie did want to do, though, was take a look at his stats and see what he could do to advance as quickly as possible.

Once breakfast was over, the cadets were told that their timetables would be sent to their personal terminals, and to go and have a look to see where they should all be going next. Charlie's timetable was displayed right there on the glass screen waiting for him when he arrived.

Day one: eight AM for two hours: CCS (Condensed Conventional Schooling); ten till twelve: Weapons Skills; one hour lunch; one till three: hand to hand combat; three till five: PT. This was the schedule for the full first week, with the same classes every single day up until Saturday, which was simply labelled 'War games.' Charlie thought that seemed pretty ominous, but the word 'games' at least was there to lighten the mood.

Checking the time on the terminal, he knew that his next stop was going to be whatever CCS was, though when he checked with Laura and Mauro, he discovered that they had entirely different schedules to himself and each other. It stood to reason that the schedules were keeping the same specialisation groups together so that they could be trained together in the same ways.

Before Charlie left to go to his first class, though, he searched his terminal for his own physical stats as after Cesari had announced that particular function of the flight suit he was wearing, he'd been interested in learning more about himself, and what he could be doing to grow more.

When he found the screen in question though, his mouth hung agape at the sheer volume of information there was about him right before his eyes. An outline of what he presumed was his own body was showing on the screen and there was a line of toggles to the right that when pressed each overlayed a new metric onto the body. From blood flow, blood pressure, muscle load and muscle fatigue, to stress levels, testosterone, sweat, body temperature, there was literally everything available to him right there at the push of a button. What was even more impressive, was that the data was in real-time. When Charlie raised a hand to press a toggle for muscle load, a very slight yellow glow came from the outline of his arm, and when he pressed the button and let his hand fall back down to his side, the loading subsided. He watched his pulse increase at the sheer wonder of the data too although he managed to bring that back down under control when he found what it was he was looking for: his PIP level.

Two measly percent. That was it. The whole ordeal of learning how to God damned walk again, from going from a total paraplegic to someone who could walk under their own power. To *be* a miracle. That, was worth just one single extra percentage point on his PIP level? Charlie was dumbfounded and annoyed.

Just as he was beginning to boil over, Mauro walked into the room with a piece of bread half in his hand and half in his mouth that he must've carried with him from the mess hall. He mumbled through his full mouth to Charlie when he saw how acutely annoyed he was. "What's up? Don't like your timetable?" Mauro asked.

"What's your PIP level? Did you look?" Charlie asked quickly, still annoyed.

"Yeah... I looked," Mauro replied still chewing. "Five percent."

"Mine is four," Laura said as she walked into the room to join them. "And we're going to be late if we don't leave right now. That's not something I want to do with the chief instructor looking for reasons to punish us."

The three walked and talked before splitting up to get to their respective class modules.

"What's your level anyway?" Mauro asked having finished his stolen food.

"Two percent," Charlie replied in a huff, though slightly reassured that the others hadn't steamed ahead too far with their own levels.

"That's not bad!" Laura replied. "Nothing to be annoyed about anyway – we're all at about the same level then. Plus you had to start on the back foot, what with the chair and stuff. Just think of it as you having more room to learn and grow."

Laura's words actually made Charlie feel a lot better about himself and it helped that she was right. There was *so much* room for him to grow, and actually thinking about it, if the difference between nought and two percent meant for him that he would be able to walk again after being entirely paralysed, he could only imagine what ten percent would mean, or even twenty. Charlie calmed himself down with that thought and left the pair to get to his condensed conventional schooling lesson, though he was still not entirely sure what that was going to entail.

The training centre that Charlie had to go to was actually a brick building, which was very surprising as he hadn't noticed any construction materials used other than the container-like corrugated metal that made up the mess hall and dorms. This building, though, had been tucked away and by being half-cut into the sheer valley face, it was clear that whoever built it was able to minimise the use of bricks but still make it seem as though it'd been constructed from such because the interior was actually a cave more than a building.

Inside was a large auditorium with long curved seats and benches stepping down toward a large stage with a huge white screen pulled tight across it. It seemed that once again Charlie was the last to enter the class as the rest of what he already knew were the Special Ops cadets were sat in their clump of around fifty, facing the screen on the stage.

Charlie quickly took a seat alone at the back of the auditorium and was surprised to see standing at the edge of the stage, Dr. Kono ready to give the class its first lesson of the day.

"Well it seems we are all here now," the doctor said as Charlie sat. Charlie jumped as Kono's voice came at a conversational volume from some speaker behind him. It made sense, as so much else had done, as well – this way the teacher wouldn't need to make any effort to be heard.

"Now, with a show of hands, are any of you familiar with photosensitive hypnotic induction?" Kono asked, though not a single hand raised into the air.

"Ah, so I guess we're going to have to take this one all the way from the beginning then aren't we," he said, though Charlie felt that it was partly to himself rather than just to the class.

Another thing that Charlie had to wonder about was the fact that none of the other cadets seemed fazed about the lizard-man taking the class. Had they met the doctor before or were they just that shocked to see an alien that they'd come out the other side of shock and landed on acceptance?

"Have any of you seen a movie where someone is hypnotised by flashing images on a screen?" Kono asked and this time a few nods returned. "Good. Now what we are going to do in this class is to show you concepts on the screen behind me, lessons if you will, that humans of your education level would be expected to learn. Observe."

Kono pressed a button on the top of a small cylinder in his hand and the screen flashed for a fraction of a second and if anyone had blinked, they'd have missed it happening.

"Did anyone see what that was?" Kono asked with a grin.

A boy a few rows in front of Charlie raised his hand and Kono nodded his head at him to allow him to speak.

"Sir, I think it said 'This is just a test. Don't put your hand up," the boy said slowly.

"Thank you Rook, you are the perfect example of a difficult subject," Kono said with a smile. "To everyone who didn't get the message, I assure you that you read it, though your brain took the subliminal command and processed it to the point where it was obeyed. Rook here, although he read the message and remembered it, did not have his brain process the information therein, and therefore didn't have the automatic response to follow the instruction. Moving forward from here, it is important that you do not try too hard to comprehend the subjects that you are going to learn. It will be better for you to open your minds and concentrate on learning as a concept rather than as an objective and everything will go a lot easier for you. "

A girl raised her hand to interrupt Kono with a question of her own and the doctor acknowledged her question.

"Sir? But if this really worked, then why doesn't everyone learn this way? Surely it would save so much time and money, wouldn't it?" she asked.

"Emily Wood, good schooling, intelligent and eager to learn though rigid in her approach in doing so," the doctor replied as though reading from the girl's personal file. "Emily, I have two answers to your question so I shall leave it up to you to select which you prefer. One: what do you think would happen if educating young minds became a task that could be carried out in weeks rather than years in this very manner. Did you know in your home country, the place you humans call America, there are almost four million teachers currently employed? These people devote their entire working lives to the goal of educating young minds year after year. And the combined estimated spend per year on the education infrastructure itself is over a trillion of your American dollars. That is around one twentieth of your gdp every year, spent on something that could be replaced overnight with a cheap, quick fix that has just made four million people unemployed all in one go. I am sad to say that if the education system were to be replaced in such a way, it would cause havoc on almost every continent of earth overnight, both economically and personally. Jobs lost, lives ruined and all for... well that leads me into option number two. The only human beings that are able to process the information shown via this very technique are the members of the GAP program, i.e those who have had their genetic code modified to allow them to do so. In short, you Ms. Wood. Only you have the ability to process the information you are about to be given in such a way that it is retained, your neural pathways being able to form at an accelerated rate in response to subconscious instruction and cues."

Nobody else interrupted the doctor or let them be a part of his devilish traps to name and shame them before he readied his next lesson on the projector screen. All of the cadets knew they were right not to do so after seeing Rook and Wood sink down into their respective seats in embarrassment, Rook even covering his brow with an open hand.

The lesson began on the large screen and Charlie adjusted his posture to a more alert stance. He was interested in how this was going to work and wanted to make sure he didn't miss anything and get left behind again. It was one thing being at the bottom of the class physically but to add to that by being left behind academically would've been just too much for his mind to handle.

On the screen flashed the single word 'mathematics,' and Charlie braced himself for a lesson in something that traditionally he'd been pretty good at, and was keen to see if that knowledge would trickle over to this new learning style and environment. He was disappointed though with what happened next.

After a moment of nothing happening after the initial introduction, Charlie watched as text, numbers, equations, symbols and diagrams flashed onto the screen before disappearing again. It was so quick that before he had the chance to process what it was he was seeing, it was gone and the next image had taken its place – again disappearing before Charlie could get to grips with whatever it was. After a moment, Charlie deflated and let his posture relax into his chair, and resigned himself to the fact that this wasn't going to be something he could control. He would simply have to watch and see if anything went in, as the doctor had said.

Some pictures and numbers did stick out though, and Charlie could remember them as though their form had been burnt into his mind's eye and the more the screen flashed the more things he seemed to remember, though their context was lost on him for the moment. None of the numbers or symbols seemed to be making any sense to him, he couldn't even think of any situation where he'd seen them portrayed like this before, so instead of trying to remember and to understand, Charlie's mind began to wander off as his eyes followed the images on the screen.

"OK, that's about enough of that," Dr Kono said as he pressed his button to stop the images flashing on the screen. The lights in the room also increased to a more sociable level. "Did you all learn something?"

Nobody answered the doctor again, though Charlie had no idea why the lesson had stopped so abruptly and after such a short period of time.

"That's a bit of a trick question I must admit. In the last two hours, you have been shown an entire term's worth of mathematical concepts and equations and though you are not expected to remember, well anything, your minds will now over the next hours and days decipher that information and organise it for later recollection. Does anyone have any questions?"

This time Charlie couldn't help himself and raised a hand into the air.

"Ah, Mr. Sinclair," Dr. Kono acknowledged the raised hand. "That arm is nice and straight, and it looks like you don't have any trouble holding it up there – that is very good to see. What can I answer for you, my young prodigy?"

Heads turned and eyes glared at Charlie, presence had just been politely introduced by the lizard-man. Charlie felt as though he shouldn't have put himself in this situation but he asked his question anyway.

"Did you say… two hours?" he asked. "It felt like just a few minutes."

Dr. Kono smiled. "Are you telling me that you fell asleep during my lesson Mr. Sinclair? Usually students try to hide that fact." Some of the cadets snickered at the statement and Charlie felt his face turning hot and red. "I'm just kidding you, of course," the doctor continued. "The fact that your conscious mind shut itself off was an indicator that your subconscious or unconscious mind had taken over. This is a good sign and in fact the very way in which this learning is designed to happen. You can liken it to a waking dream if you wish – and let me tell you, with some of the more boring subjects, this is going to come in very handy."

With that, the class was over. Charlie had made it through lesson number one, day number one and it'd been quite the experience. It was not something he'd been expecting to enjoy, but what Dr. Kono had told him and the rest of the class made him excited at the possibilities that the future held for him. The capacity to learn at such a rate combined with the growth his physical body could go through made him feel almost as if he could become a superman overnight, and he liked that thought very much. Nobody else would appreciate it to his degree though, having gone from not being able to move at all to possibly becoming stronger than he'd ever thought possible of mankind.

The class left the auditorium chatting quietly to each other and Charlie recognised most of the faces as they passed him, most walking quicker than him as they were much more used to that menial task. Charlie didn't mind though, he let them pass him as he contemplated what'd just happened. He tried his best to arrange the symbols and formulae that he could actively remember in his mind, though he could only remember one or two, which was disheartening but it didn't make him stop trying.

The class went straight from the auditorium to the firing range and was greeted by instructor Rosewood, the shorter blonde instructor who'd been present when Charlie had found something that he was actually pretty good at. The class formed up into five lines of ten before her as she stood to attention.

"So who thinks they're pretty good with the rifles then?" The first words coming from the instructor were a challenge rather than a welcome and some of the class turned to look at Charlie and smirked at the fact that he didn't have his handy wheelchair rest to work with now.

"Ah, Mr Sinclair, our resident sharpshooter. Why don't you come up here and take the first shots then," she said and Charlie positively went red.

Charlie slowly made his way past the other cadets, overhearing the hushed words of 'cheater,' and 'good luck without your chair,' though he tried to pay them no mind. He did however stumble a little when an elbow from the crowd knocked him off-stride as he passed the last few cadets and made it out to the front.

Rosewood picked up a familiar Lee-Enfield rifle from the stands that held a handful of the weapons and handed it to Charlie whose hands had begun to shake slightly. He was worried that maybe his good score in the baseline test had all been because of the chair, and if he failed miserably now it'd just mean that everybody was right about him – that he was a cheater.

Charlie turned with the rifle to look at the firing range. It was exactly the same as before – targets laid out at varying distances from the concrete oche designed to allow the shooter to rest their firing arm on.

"Listen to me Charlie," Rosewood whispered as the pair turned their backs on the rest of the cadets so that no one else could hear their conversation. "It takes skill to do what you did in the baseline testing. It was not luck nor coincidence so get that out of your mind. You have the ability to do this so block everything else out and go do what you did last time, OK?" Then she raised her voice for the benefit of everyone else. "Sinclair, you're up. Take aim and fire when ready."

Charlie stepped up to the concrete barrier with his rifle and knelt behind it. He held the wooden handguard in his left hand and his right took the grip, pulling the butt of the weapon tightly into his shoulder, and he rested his left elbow atop the concrete wall, aiming the rifle down-range.

Charlie looked through the sights of the weapon and aimed at what he thought was the middle of the first target. Then he pulled the trigger... and nothing happened.

"You have to load the weapon first, Sinclair," Rosewood called out from behind Charlie who closed his eyes in embarrassment, picked up a single .303 round from the ammo box to his side and pushed the bolt into place.

He re-readied the weapon and took a deep breath. The other cadets had been right, this was much more difficult to do when you didn't have a stable ground to foot the heavy weapon on. Charlie could tell that the rifle weighed at least four kilos and under normal gravitational conditions, that meant that the force exerted on his shoulder and elbow was somewhere around forty newtons – although how did he know that? His mind raced at the new knowledge and for a moment he forgot what he was doing until he heard a few muffled laughs coming from the cadets behind him. Charlie felt his pulse increase and the vein in his neck began to pulse.

Charlie looked down the iron sights of the rifle and aligned his shot at the first target again, he took a deep breath and squeezed the trigger.

Pop. The paper target had a new hole torn through it and Charlie could see it was in the 'eight' ring. Not a bad shot, he thought to himself, and the class fell silent behind him. If he needed to prove that he wasn't a cheater, this was going to be the way.

"Mr Sinclair will you please just use a pre-filled magazine this time?" Rosewood said from behind him, sounding very impatient. Charlie looked at the ammo box and sure enough right next to it was a magazine full of ten rounds ready for attachment to the base of the rifle. He picked it up and clicked it firmly into the base of the gun. It wasn't something he was trained to do, but like all twelve year old boys he knew what a magazine was for, and the fact that once you heard the click it meant it was in place.

Charlie reloaded the rifle with the bolt which expelled the spent cartridge onto the floor and readied a new one. Then he took aim down the range at the second target.

This time Charlie didn't waste time thinking about the pressure on his body though he was acutely aware of its presence. He breathed in, and squeezed the trigger again.

Pop. Another hit, though this time just on the ring between the three and the four so not a perfect shot by any means although again he *had* hit the target. Again the class behind him was silent and he reloaded the weapon without further instruction to align his third shot.

Charlie looked down the iron sights again and this time he felt his pulse quicken to the point where he could hear his own blood rushing in his ears. He blinked a couple of times and then it happened again – the target down range filled his vision and he could see it perfectly. It was so far away and had looked so tiny when he'd first aimed at it but now it was the size of a car. He could see the ink on the paper, the thin black lines between the scoring rings and he could see exactly where his shot was aimed. He took a deep breath, held it then squeezed the trigger.

Pop. Silence. Rosewood had her binoculars up to her eyes that she'd used before to call the scores of the more distant targets and the class awaited the latest result.

"Bullseye, Mr. Sinclair. Nice shot," she announced loudly enough for everyone to hear and the class of cadets remained silent.

Charlie smiled to himself but didn't respond before lining up shot number four. Again the target grew much bigger and clearer than it should've. He lined up the sights as best he could though he could already tell that his aim was off. The sights moved too fast to line up and whenever he adjusted his aim, the sighting simply whizzed past the target. He was simply not strong enough to line up this next shot, his arms were tired already and the effort of continually adjusting was just too much.

He didn't take the shot. Placing the rifle down on the concrete block he quietly announced to the instructor that he was unable to hit the next target.

Rosewood didn't say anything for a moment and just looked at the cadet. Then finally she spoke, apparently having come to an internal conclusion.

"Knowing your limits," she announced loudly, "is an important lesson to learn. If you are not absolutely sure that you are going to hit what you're aiming for, sometimes it is just better not to take the shot at all. Thank you Mr. Sinclair you may now retake your place in the class.

This time on his return to the back of the group, no one said a word and Charlie was satisfied that he'd proved his point well enough - that he wasn't a cheater – he was actually just pretty good at something, chair or no chair.

The class then spent a lot of time analysing what Charlie did right and wrong, his firing stance, breathing patterns, how long he took to line up his shot etc. all the way down to how hard he pulled the trigger. It was fascinating at just how much detail there was that went into shooting a bullet down a range, and by the end of the lesson all of the cadets felt that next time they would be doing a lot better. Charlie did have to wonder though, why they couldn't simply learn all of this in the auditorium with Dr. Kono, which he voiced to instructor Rosewood.

"Concepts can be learnt with the doctor of course. Typical classroom things like maths, English, science – even foreign languages. But when it comes to something more hands-on, you're going to have to actually put in the time to grow both muscle memory and the *feel* of the exercise. After all, you can learn about lifting weights in a classroom but when it actually comes to moving the iron, there's no substitute for the real thing,"

Rosewood explained and Charlie understood, after all it made frightfully good sense to him.

In addition to the lesson on firing, the cadets were taught how to maintain the old fashioned rifle; how to strip and clean it and then put it back together. It seemed like a bit of a misnomer to Charlie, and although he was positive that these old fashioned rifles weren't used anywhere in the world in any meaningful way anymore he carried out his orders without question, stripping and remaking the weapon over and over. He couldn't help thinking, though, that soon they'd bring out the shiny new guns for them all to have a go on.

Chapter 10

"I heard something about you a minute ago," Mauro said with a piece of bread in his mouth *again* as he fell onto the bench beside Charlie.

"Me too actually," Laura said as she plopped herself with her tray on Charlie's other side. Charlie felt blindsided at the interruption from his two friends who he hadn't seen all day, but he was still glad to see them now. Being quiet and trying to stay away from the attention of the others was both tiresome and annoying.

Lunch times seemed to be a universal for the cadets, which made sense as whoever it was making the food would only have to do it once and en masse. Cadets were scattered amongst the mess hall and spaces were being filled as more and more filed in from whatever class they'd just been to, and a low background hum of excited conversation was slowly filling the room as the cadets filled in their friends and peers about what they'd been up to in their first lessons. From what Charlie could overhear it was a lot of the same same.

"What?" Charlie asked surprised, "about me?" His heart beat slightly faster as he anticipated something bad.

Mauro leapt to the opportunity to tease Charlie and made an effort to look forlorn about what he had to say. Eventually, he put Charlie out of his misery.

"Some of the other cadets are saying that you did quite well on the firing range again, but this time you didn't have a wheelchair to help you." Mauro smiled proudly as he spoke and grasped Charlie's shoulder. "I knew you could do it!"

Laura smiled too and chirped in with a comment of her own. "Plus now people might stop calling you a cheater, right?"

Of course she was probably right. By proving that he could do it without that particular aid, at least Charlie had a counter argument. Plus, now that he could walk on his own two feet the only thing keeping him standing out from the others was his somewhat smaller physical stature.

"You're right!" Charlie exclaimed. "Now all I have to work on is my abysmal personality and nobody will ever bother me again!"

The three laughed together until the hulking form of Matty Henderson entered the mess hall and it was clear that he made a beeline for Charlie and his friends. Henderson wasn't hulking by adult standards, though for a twelve year old he was certainly in the upper percentiles of growth.

"Did he get bigger?" Charlie muttered out of the side of his mouth to Laura as Henderson didn't break eye contact with him.

"Well, now that you mention it..." came the whispered reply from his side, but before the pair could say any more, Henderson was too close and he came to a stop, standing over the three with a full tray in his hands.

"Going to tip that over me?" Charlie said before the larger boy could say a word - *and was that the beginnings of a moustache?*

Henderson smirked but didn't say anything at all. What he did do though, was slowly tip his tray onto Charlie's lap, covering his flight suit with lukewarm porridge.

The mess hall went quiet with everyone apparently seeing exactly what had happened, though before Laura could jump up from her seat to give Henderson what for, Charlie laughed.

"What a guy!" he proclaimed loudly for everyone to hear with a grin from ear to ear. "I finally get feeling back in my legs and you're nice enough to warm them up for me!"

Henderson smiled at Charlie's deflection, then tipped an entire beaker of cold water on top of the porridge on Charlie's lap.

"There, cooled it down for you, cheater," Henderson replied.

Charlie's cheeks reddened but he kept his smile firmly plastered across his face. "You won't have anything left to eat or drink now. Shame though – a growing boy like you must be hungry." And with that, Charlie picked up a slice of buttered bread and made a big show of how delicious it was. It wasn't his finest work, but Charlie knew how to pick his battles – and with whom. Matty Henderson, he knew right now, was way, way out of his league. But he would get there; he just needed time.

As if by some divine intervention, the next person to enter the mess hall was instructor Rosewood and seeing her enter, Henderson moved away from Charlie and his two friends who were free to talk properly once again, though Charlie's lap was decidedly mushier than previously. He tried to wipe himself down subtly but it wasn't his finest clean up.

"What were your first two lessons like?" Charlie eventually asked the pair as they ate.

"Nothing too strange really," Mauro answered first. "We did some weights, carried heavy bags around and stuff. My arms hurt now but I get the feeling we are going to need all the strength we can get. Does make me hungry though!" he added, forcing way too much bread into his mouth. At this rate, Charlie thought the boy was going to turn into a slice of bread.

"What about you Laura? You're a scout class, right?" Charlie didn't need the green flashes on Laura's arms to remember her class, though the constant reminder was handy.

"Oh, yeah…" she said slowly. "We did some shooting practise and then some kind of perception class… it's hard to explain but I guess it's to get us learning to use all of our senses and not just focussing on one target?" Laura didn't seem to be totally on board with the training, though Charlie smiled at the thought of the pair getting to grips with the CCS lesson with Dr. Kono.

The mess hall eventually filtered back down to empty as the cadets made their way to their next lesson, which for Charlie was something that he really, really wasn't looking forward to: hand to hand combat.

Hand to hand combat class looked like it was going to be exactly as it sounded. As Charlie approached the lesson's location, he noted the cool white sand that must've been collected and dispersed across a large arena specifically for the purposes of this class. He thought it looked like the whole ordeal was going to be barbaric. Alongside the sand were also dumbbells, barbells, weight benches, cable machines, weighted logs, barrels and resistance bands. Charlie laughed internally at the thought of trying to lift any of the weights laid out, as previously he'd barely been able to lift a slice of pizza – and before that his empty hand.

The hand to hand combat instructor was not the beast of a man that Charlie had been expecting, rather he was tall, not thin, but definitely not a muscular type. Over six feet tall and with a bald head, his eyes were slightly drawn which gave him the look of someone who was not to be messed with, and his straight expression told Charlie that he would need to concentrate throughout just to make sure this man didn't have any reason to resent him.

"Cadets, my name is instructor Lawrence Wilson and I am your hand to hand combat instructor."

The class as one stood to attention but didn't reply.

"Now traditionally in the forces where I'm from, a martial arts system called 'defendu' is used. Now this is a mixture of jiu jitsu and boxing. Does anyone have any experience with either of these techniques?"

One or two hands raised in the group of cadets.

"That's good, not too many bad habits to have to break," he said, which caused the hands to drop rather quickly.

"This system of hand to hand combat has been designed to finish any confrontation as quickly as possible with overwhelming force. I want you to know that whilst this is good in principle, there is one main downside to this method of conflict. 'Defendu' has no means of block or parry within its system, there is only offence or attack. I want you to know right now that defence is as, if not more, important than offence when used correctly. Defend yourself appropriately, and attack when necessary. Defend appropriately, attack on necessity. Repeat it."

Some of the class mumbled the words back to the instructor.

"Again!" he shouted.

The class replied with more vigour this time.

"Again!"

"Defend appropriately, attack on necessity!" The cadets chorused as one and Charlie felt chills run down his spine as he spoke. He was anxious to learn if this system was actually going to allow him to go toe to toe with *any* of the other cadets here.

The class progressed with the cadets being partnered up based upon their size. Charlie, being particularly small and weedy, was paired with Xi Ling who seemed unhappy with the pairing but not enough to raise the issue verbally. Instead, Charlie felt as though she was putting a little extra effort into her strikes to his padded hands.

One of the pair wore pads and the other light gloves for the first half the lesson, then they'd swap for the second half. The system was fair and although they all received instruction on throwing straight punches as well as hooks, Charlie could tell that the emphasis was placed on defending the strikes – taking the momentum from his opponent and keeping them off balance. Essentially, Charlie could see that the goal of this exercise was to let your opponent strike, strike and strike again while all the time you removed the power from those strikes and kept your balance. What he found amazing though, was the fact that not many of the other cadets had been learning that lesson – most of the kids holding pads thinking they were there simply to help the attacker in their training.

"One more thing cadets," the instructor called amongst the sounds of grunted punches and slapping pads. "I am the instructor for you *only*. The other classes will all receive their own specialist training so whatever you learn from my class may or may not be replicated throughout the other cadets. Bear this in mind when you come to bouts against other specialisations, as though you may not be able to anticipate all of your opponents' moves, neither will they know your intentions."

Charlie wondered immediately what he meant by bouts with other specialisations, though it seemed Xi Ling picked up on this too as her attacks doubled in speed and power. Although Charlie had been getting better at utilising his own body, he was pushed back and eventually he tripped and fell to the ground.

Xi Ling looked smug at her achievement, though Wilson immediately appeared in Charlie's line of sight having come over to see what had happened.

"Sinclair," he said quietly so that just Charlie and Xi Ling could hear. "I would usually say that sometimes you're going to face bigger and stronger opponents, but in your case you will face nothing but. You must use your opponent's own movements, overconfidence and balance against them if you stand to win a fight, do you understand?" The instructor looked a little forlorn at the small boy who'd been knocked down by an especially small girl, although it did look as though he believed in his own words.

Charlie nodded slowly without a word, raised himself to his feet and brushed himself down. Raising the pads again, he retook his ready position and nodded to Xi Ling who smiled sarcastically before throwing her first straight punch.

Charlie immediately saw it this time. The girl's right shoulder tensed and thanks to the tight-fitting flight suit Charlie saw her muscle pulled into action to draw back her arm. It was all in slow motion and so obvious to him now. He watched her arm as it drew back and in his mind's eye calculated its trajectory to make contact with the pad he held up in his left hand. At that moment he knew he had three options. One: he could let the punch hit the pad and do nothing; two: he could move the pad to meet the punch early and remove some of the force that would otherwise be accumulated; or three: he could move out of the way entirely.

Ultimately, Charlie chose option number two and slapped the pad into Ling's gloved fist. The noise that the contact made was deafening but Ling looked shocked when her own strike, caught early, challenged her balance and she took a single step backwards. To Charlie, this was in itself the greatest victory he could've hoped for.

Ling then balled her fist again and attempted the very same punch, again with the same result. She took a step back, but this time Charlie took a step forward to press his advantage.

Ling's face reddened with embarrassment and shame, and she began throwing a flurry of straights and hooks at Charlie's pads which he in turn met punch after hook after straight until he began to move out of the way of the punches entirely. He could see as he moved that Ling's eyes were almost entirely closed with effort and frustration and he parried and dodged over and over until he eventually saw it. Ling's body leant back in one final vow to knock her target down and before she knew it, as her fist flew through the air, Charlie took a large step to his left and the girl stumbled and fell to the ground. Charlie smiled to himself but held out a hand for Ling to take and bring herself back up to her feet. She didn't take it.

Some of the rest of the class had begun to take notice and Charlie didn't know if the attention was to his credit or if they were annoyed at him still. In any case the main issue at the front of his mind was that he'd done it. He'd taken down a stronger opponent without actually throwing a strike. Of course he knew doing it again might've been a bit of a stretch but that didn't really matter. With each passing hour and day he could feel his strength growing alongside this enhanced perception that he'd been experiencing. It was disorienting, but it was useful.

When it came to Charlie's turn to be on the offensive, he didn't aim to make Ling look bad as she had done with him. He didn't try to push her back or knock her over, he simply planted his feet firmly on the ground and concentrated on the form of his punches. The last thing he wanted to do – especially on his relatively new-standing legs – was fall flat on his face and make a fool of himself. He'd already seen what overplaying your hand did to your balance in this situation.

Ling had smiled to herself knowingly a few times during Charlie's offensive training and he could tell that it was because where he had not taken openings to press forward or try to off-balance his opponent, she felt she knew better. Charlie didn't care though, the girl could think what she wanted and he was content to simply get all his muscles moving together in the way he wished. By the end of the lesson, Charlie's arms and shoulders ached from having to hold his arms to the ready for the entire duration of the class – and what he didn't like about that was the fact that the PT lesson was next.

This one turned out to be less of an tutored class and more of a way for the cadets to gain some strength and endurance. The two hour class consisted of resistance training and an hour's jog around a standard four hundred metre running track circling the training sands. Of course Wilson was there to give instruction on form for lifting weights but apart from that it was pretty much a free for all. The good thing was that this meant there wasn't a requirement for sixty sets of weights for all of the cadets at the same time; rather most preferred to simply start their run and do whatever they could with the weights afterward. Charlie, swimming upstream as ever, decided that he would start with the resistance training as the area was quieter and a run seemed like it was going to be difficult.

Having already been shown by Wilson the basic compound exercises such as squats, bench press, bent over rows and deadlifts, Charlie decided that these were his best bet to start with. After testing some of the weights that were lined up in weight order he picked up the lightest set – a tiny pair of one kilo dumbbells that none of the other cadets had seemed interested in.

Holding the weights in his hands, Charlie embarked on a routine of what he thought were exercises although without proper instruction he knew that it wasn't going to be the best. Nevertheless, by watching some of the other cadets and with some light instruction from Wilson who didn't seem too interested in helping anyone with such light weights, within moments Charlie began to feel his muscles burning. It'd been so long since he'd used them so vigorously and his own perception, paired with Dr. Kono's atrophy assessment, led him to the conclusion that anything was better than nothing. He knew though that he really, really needed to get stronger, and quickly.

Charlie pumped the irons for what felt like forever, although the light weights felt as though they were probably made of plastic. He kept going until his arms shook and simply stopped responding to his commands and although he was used to that particular sensation, this time it felt so different. For the first time in a long while, he'd set out to tax his muscles to their limits and that is exactly what he'd achieved.

His arms and upper body in general ached as he made his way out to the compressed running track and Charlie cursed his past self for letting him get into this state before such a long jog, though he was determined to use his recovering body to its fullest capabilities.

Charlie walked for the first few paces before testing the waters with a light jog at just a little over a walking pace. Once he was sure he wasn't going to crumple into a heap on the ground, he burst into a full jog. He wasn't fast, of course, his muscles were not only weak from the resistance workout, they were still much weaker than they once had been and still way behind the other cadets. All in all, a lap of the four hundred metre track took him about four minutes and although it seemed so, so slow compared to the rest of the cadets who constantly lapped him on his journey, Charlie was happy. And what was more, by the end of the day he had run for an hour without stopping.

He'd counted about fifteen laps of the track in that time and Charlie simply couldn't believe it when he'd come to a final halt. Some of the other cadets looked at the former paraplegic with confusion, some with annoyance and some with hatred but none of them could take away what Charlie had just achieved – what he never truly believed that he'd be able to do ever again in his entire life.

The class was ultimately dismissed and in the time it took for Charlie et al to return to the mess hall for their dinner, he was amazed to note that his flight-suit had magically wicked away all of the sweat that'd been pouring off his body. He put it down to intelligent alien engineering, though he couldn't be sure if that's how workout clothes were designed to work anyway.

The mess hall was already abuzz by the time Charlie plopped himself down between Laura and Mauro forcing the pair apart. He wondered why the class tables seemed to be ignored, but looking about he didn't see Cesari anywhere in the room and assumed that the cadets had started taking certain liberties with their seating arrangements. He liked that fact though as it meant he could talk with his two friends again.

"Guess who just ran a marathon?" he beamed at the pair who seemed a little surprised to see him moving quite so fast.

"Well I know it wasn't you," Mauro stated flatly before Laura could open her mouth.

"Dammit Mauro let the boy say his piece before you jump down his throat like that," Laura replied before looking at Charlie. "What do you mean 'ran a marathon?' she asked in a completely placid tone.

"Well..." Charlie started though he'd been somewhat caught off guard by Laura's immediate change of mood. "When I say 'ran' it was more like a fast walk or a slow jog... and marathon..."

Laura still seemed interested though Mauro interrupted Charlie again before he could finish.

"Please tell me it was more than a lap of the track!' he seemed ready to burst into laughter and Laura shot him a stern look.

"Well yes... fifteen actually so what's that, like, six kilometres? I suppose that's only really three point seven miles per hour so not that impressive really," Charlie said.

Laura and Mauro both looked at Charlie with their mouths slightly open.

"What?" Charlie said when neither of them said a word.

"You ran six kilometres when yesterday you needed a wheelchair to get about?" Mauro asked not quite believing what he was hearing.

Laura was troubled by something else though. "Did you just do that sum in your head?" she asked.

"What sum?" Charlie asked before realising what she had meant. "Oh... not really, I guess I just kind of knew the answer. Weird."

Laura narrowed her eyes at Charlie who felt like he was now very much exposed and he didn't like it. Eventually he had to fill the gap with something to make sure Laura's gaze didn't burn a hole in his head.

"What's for dinner anyway?" he asked.

"Steak," Laura replied without letting her gaze drop.

"And chips?" Charlie asked hopefully.

"No." Laura replied.

"You know the steak isn't half bad this time," Mauro said whilst chewing. He'd definitely missed what was happening between his two friends and gone straight back to stuffing his face.

That was the moment that Charlie realised he was hungrier than possibly he had ever been in his entire life, and made his way to the serving trays at the far end of the mess hall. Happily armed with an overdone medium rare fillet and a charred jacket potato, he retook his seat next to Mauro and the more relaxed Laura, and stuffed his face.

Apparently only able to deal with one feeling at a time right now, once Charlie had eaten his fill, his body decided that it was essentially in tatters. His muscles ached and his shins throbbed from the running. His arms could barely hold themselves up and sitting on the hard bench hurt his lower back. He needed rest and as much of it as he could get.

The three spoke about their lessons without too much detail as the whole day had seemed to have passed in somewhat of a blur for all three of the cadets, and they made their way back eagerly to their dorm and inviting beds without causing any issues with any other cadets for once. Charlie was happy at that and tonight he knew he was going to sleep well.

Chapter 11

The offensive alarm sounded again the next morning and this time Charlie wasn't awake to pre-empt it. He'd slept hard and so completely that the sound ripped him from his peaceful sleep and confused him as to which reality he was in – was it his dream where he'd been eating a delicious lasagne with the Browns, or was this reality where if he didn't make it to the mess hall for breakfast in the coming minutes, he was sure to take a verbal beating from Cesari. After shaking his head and wiping his face with his hands a few times, Charlie realised that it was the latter, and he needed to get out of bed.

Charlie practically leapt out of the bed for the first time in what felt like forever and the action made him happy. His smile was so wide as he began to pull on his flight suit and he almost didn't catch his reflection in the mirror as he wrestled with getting his feet into the leg holes of the bottom half of the garment.

Had his body started filling itself in? There was just no way. Charlie held his arms out to his sides and examined himself closely in the full length of the mirror and he was sure that he wasn't imagining it – his atrophied and wasted body did look bigger and healthier. It wasn't up to the standards of any of the other cadets but he knew a different him when he saw it. His legs looked rounder at the top, his stomach was certainly straighter, his ribcage wasn't so pronounced and his shoulders were rounder and looked stronger to him. His arms, though, that was where the big difference was as both his triceps and biceps had definitely grown by at least half an inch in their respective circumferences.

Excitedly, Charlie pulled up his body stats on his personal glass terminal and looked at both the outline of his physical stature and the numbers that accompanied it. He couldn't remember everything that made up his being, but when he looked at his weight and muscle mass, he could tell that he'd put on a full kilo of muscle mass that had presumably been apportioned to his body as a whole. Sadly taking note of his PIP level, though, it remained unchanged at just two percent.

"Shit," he muttered to himself, though as he spoke Laura opened the door and entered the room.

"Well there's no need for that welcome," she replied to the swearword he'd spoken for his own benefit and Charlie couldn't tell if she looked annoyed or upset.

"No I didn't mean…" Charlie stammered in response. "I mean…" he said as he looked at himself in the mirror. "Do you see this? Do I look bigger to you?"

"You know bigger isn't always better," Laura scowled as she replied but Charlie didn't seem to notice as his eyes were firmly fixed on his new stature. "In fact…"

"Looking good boss man," Mauro said loudly as he entered Charlie's room and Charlie instinctively felt as though his timing had just saved him from something unpleasant. "Flex those arms!"

"Is everything a joke to you?" Laura asked as she turned on her heels and exited the room before either of the two very confused boys could answer.

"What's her problem?" Mauro asked and Charlie just shrugged.

"Try eating something!" Mauro called after her though there was no response.

"Do I look bigger to you?" Charlie asked Mauro as his only peer left in the room.

"Hell yeah," Mauro replied. "You've put on size everywhere. I mean you're still small in comparison to basically everyone else but you're definitely growing man. Speaking of which… breakfast?"

Charlie smiled. If there was one thing for which Mauro could be counted on it was his hunger. Nine times out of ten when Charlie saw Mauro he had his mouth full of something and it kind of made Charlie feel happy. The boy was clearly enjoying life so why not?

Breakfast was a little more imaginative this time though and Charlie could tell that Mauro couldn't have been happier about it as the pair took their seats on a bench next to each other, although Laura was still nowhere to be seen.

"Eggs! Can you believe it? I love eggs so much!" Mauro exclaimed. "On brown toast too, like we're kings!"

Charlie did share the sentiment to a degree, though he lacked the full emotional range to fawn over fried egg on toast as Mauro had. Instead he stuffed a forkful of the delicious breakfast into his mouth and simply smiled.

"Mauro?" Charlie said before he fully swallowed his mouthful. "Why did you come here?"

His friend swallowed his own mouthful of breakfast before he replied. "I told you, they said I could be like superman!"

"No, I mean really, how did it happen?" Charlie pressed.

Mauro looked a little deflated and took a moment to exhale before he answered the now serious line of questioning. "Well... I guess you'd find out eventually, as we're supposed to be friends and all," Mauro replied slowly. "My older brother, Marco, he's in prison. Been there for a long time now and my parents do everything they can to go and see him. They work so hard, then have to make sure I'm looked after and I get to school on time and stuff you know? It's hard on them. But this army guy told my parents they'd look after me like it was some glorified boarding school and I knew it would lessen their burden. At first they weren't having none of it. Eventually I spoke to Marco about it without mum and dad knowing and he told me that he'd been asked by who I assumed was the same army general to see if I wanted to go, and if I did they could make his sentence more lenient. So here I am. My parents hated it but it was a win win for everyone – less burden for mum and dad and out of prison sooner for Marco, right? Plus, you know... I might get to be a superman at the end of it."

Charlie smiled at Mauro but inside his heart ached for what must've been a terrible situation that he could empathise with so well. Charlie knew exactly how much it hurt to feel like a burden and that feeling was still somewhat evident every time he looked around at the other, larger cadets of the GAP program.

Laura then took a heavy seat on the bench beside Charlie and placed her tray on the table delicately. He could see in her face that she wasn't in the best of spirits, though he wanted her to feel as included as Mauro in their conversation. Charlie liked Laura, she was already a good friend and he didn't like seeing her upset and certainly didn't want her to feel excluded.

"What about you, Laura?" Charlie asked the girl. "What brings you onto the GAP program?"

Laura didn't look up from her tray for a long moment and Charlie watched her face contort through a series of emotions that were almost certainly all negative.

"I...I..." Laura stammered before taking a deep breath and starting over, composing herself. "I had a great home," she said. "Loving parents, I did well in everything in school. I was both academic and active, I did all the sports I could and still got straight A's... then something happened. My dad... he lost his job at the factory he worked at and he started drinking. It wasn't really an issue but it became one more and more and at first I didn't see it but then it got worse. It went from a drink every now and then to him getting drunk every single night. He fell asleep early most evenings but as he gave up hope in finding new work he started opening his bottles at lunch times, and when I returned home from school he seemed so down all the time. Then he got angry." Laura stopped talking but both Charlie and Mauro knew better than to interrupt her as she poured her heart onto the table before her, not raising her gaze for a second. Mauro moved from his place on the bench to her other side so the pair encircled her.

"One evening, dad woke up after passing out for a while and mum made a comment about his drinking and he just lost it, you know?" Laura continued. "I tried to push him back down onto the sofa but he was so heavy I just couldn't do anything about it. He hit mum and shouted at me to go to my room. I called the police..." Tears had started rolling down Laura's face at this point and Charlie had put his arm around Laura to comfort her whilst Mauro handed her a crumpled tissue. Laura didn't seem to care that Mauro had most probably already used it to mop up whatever crumbs he'd had around his mouth.

"The police didn't do anything," she said after sniffing back some tears. "But dad knew what I'd done and he didn't talk to me for a few days afterwards. I don't know if he was embarrassed or if he just hated me from then on but then an army general visited me at school and took me out of class to have a chat. The general told me that once people started doing the things that I said dad had done, that they didn't really ever change and I'd have to deal with that for the rest of my life... He gave me an alternative though."

"Let me guess," Charlie finally interrupted seeing Laura come back to herself. "He said he would sort everything out for you if you just joined the GAP program. The military would look after your mum and your dad would get all the help he needed?"

Laura looked shocked at the question and nodded slowly. "Almost...

they said they'd give dad a job too which would get him back to who he was and also keep mum safe... how did you know?"

"It's a bit of a common theme around here," Charlie replied eyeing some of the other cadets. "They give you a sort of win-win situation – an offer you can't refuse - and here we are. I just wonder if it was the same for everybody or if we're just the lucky ones."

"It can't just be a coincidence though, can it?" Mauro asked through a mouthful of grapes that he seemed to be able to materialise from nowhere. "I mean if it was just the three of us then we'd be pretty damn lucky to find each other and become friends."

"So both of you too?" Laura asked before Charlie could answer and both he and Mauro nodded.

"Miracle cure for me, obviously," Charlie said raising a single arm into the air and wriggling his fingers.

"My uh... my brother's in prison," Mauro said. "Shortened sentence for my volunteering."

"Huh," Laura said thoughtfully. "Definitely too much of a coincidence but I don't know about any of the others. Maybe we should start asking people?"

"Does it matter?" Charlie said. "We're all here together now so who cares how and why, really?"

"Don't you want to know if the other cadets chose to be here or were forced into it? Maybe it'll give us some insight as to why some of them act the way they do. I mean, think about Henderson, don't you want to know if he's acting out because of some issues back home that forced him here, or if he just really is a colossal dick?" Laura asked and Charlie smiled. Matty Henderson was a colossal dick and he couldn't have put it better himself.

In a lighter mood, the three then discussed what they thought the day's lessons were going to entail for each of them though they knew ultimately it was going to be more of the same. No matter how much they dreamt of alien technologies, weapons and futuristic fighter jets, there was no evidence of such and the dreams were just that, dreams.

A creature of habit, Charlie went through the rest of his day in very much the same way as the previous – classes followed by lunch and total physical exertion, a crawl into bed at an early hour. He barely even took a moment to look at himself in the mirror or check his daily stats on his terminal; he was simply too exhausted as he knew that by pushing himself he gained results and he really, really needed to catch up with everyone else.

As usual, the other cadets had gone out of their ways to ignore him but the low-key insults had all but disappeared as Charlie made actual progress in using his own body to carry out his day. Truth be told, as soon as he'd been able to ditch the wheelchair, the other cadets had stopped looking at him as though he was different and simply accepted that he was just another one of them, albeit smaller and weaker by some factor.

CCS Class with Dr. Kono hadn't borne any new results, though the subject had changed to a mixture of Earth Geography and History, which Charlie saw as a huge waste of time given the fact that Camp Rebirth, as it was called, was on an alien planet so the flashing images of earth and its statistics seemed entirely moot at this moment. He did figure though that when he and the other cadets eventually went home, these were probably lessons that they were expected to have learnt – at least that's what Kono had told them all when one cadet had asked that very question.

Sleep was all that occupied Charlie's mind when he re-entered his dorm and he could tell that all of his roommates had had the same idea as the communal living area was empty and none of the lights were on. Well, he was either the first one back or they'd all gone to bed – either way that was his own intended destination anyway. His bed felt so comforting to his entire body as he flopped down onto the mattress after slinking out of his flight suit, that the moment he closed his eyes a second later, he was asleep and his body had begun to repair itself ready for the next day of hard work.

The next morning arrived shortly after Charlie had closed his eyes, though this time: no alarm. Charlie felt as though he wasn't very well rested at all as he rubbed his eyes and he looked around the room for what had awoken him from his much needed restorative sleep. Eventually his eyes fell on the glass terminal on the desk at the foot of the bed, which was flashing bright red every five seconds. Charlie counted the time between flashes and confirmed that it was indeed repetitive so he got up and walked over to it, slightly annoyed with it. Internally he thought that if it was giving him a low battery warning or something, he was going to break it.

The terminal sprung into life as Charlie approached it which shocked him out of his drowsiness somewhat and he became much more alert.

"Charlie! It's good to see you," the smiling lizard-like face of Dr. Kono appeared on the screen as he spoke in a hushed tone. "Sorry it's so late – or early, whichever you prefer - but the important thing is that I apologised, OK?"

Charlie blinked twice but his expression didn't change, nor did he reply to the doctor.

"Anyway," the doctor continued without encouragement, "I wanted to let you know that I've been monitoring your statistics over the last couple of days. You've made some good progress with the loading your body has sustained."

Charlie nodded slowly, now more interested in the conversation. "Yeah... I feel stronger," he whispered back to the doctor not wanting to wake the whole dorm. "B...but my PIP level hasn't moved."

"Well technically it's moved a little," Kono replied. "Three percent as of right now, though I wouldn't scoff at that!" he said with a wide smile. "Just look at the changes you've made thus far."

Charlie knew the doctor was right and he'd already thought the same thing – total paralysis to lifting weights in a matter of days was a Jesus-tier level of miracle. He nodded for the doctor to continue.

"Now this all brings me onto the reason for my contacting you at this unfriendly hour. I want to talk to you about your PIP level and what we are going to do to accelerate your growth."

Charlie was now completely on board with the conversation and alert. When it came to his physical improvement he was interested in whatever it was the doctor had to say.

"I feel as though a by product of the removal of your level cap – which as I said before should very much be kept to yourself –your growth may present as logarithmic rather than linear, that is to say you will achieve faster growth at the beginning of your training that will level off over time. What we have seen in this short period would seem to support that fact."

Charlie felt his pulse quicken as the doctor spoke and realised that what he was hearing was exciting.

"What I am suggesting, Charlie, is an additional training regime for you and you alone with the sole purpose of maximising your growth in this early period."

The doctor waited for Charlie to respond. Charlie thought about what he was saying then the penny dropped – the doctor wanted him to do *extra lessons*.

"I'll do whatever is needed to catch up... but there are only so many hours in the day," Charlie replied after turning Kono's words over in his mind.

Again the doctor offered a lizardy smile as he spoke. "I was thinking something like an hour before your usual alarm call. Then you can return back your bed afterwards and no one will know what you've been up to. It can remain our little secret."

Charlie immediately wanted to accept but was still hesitant about the secrecy of his involvement in the GAP program and needed answers to some of the more global questions he had.

"Doctor… why don't I have a cap on my PIP level? And why can't I tell anyone? And lastly… why me?" Charlie spoke without over-emoting in a calm and calculated manner. These were things that he wanted to know but inside he knew the reasons behind them didn't make a difference to his immediate situation.

The doctor looked thoughtful for a long moment before he replied to Charlie, seemingly having an internal conversation about the detail the boy should learn at this juncture.

Charlie spoke again before the doctor, having noticed the struggle. "I know I may seem young but I'll understand. I just want to know more," he urged. "So I can be better."

"OK Charlie, I will tell you some of the things you deserve to know," Kono replied on his internal conclusion. "To answer your questions in reverse: You were chosen by your government because of a number of factors. You were in the foster system for a long time and with a range of different families and institutions, it was therefore determined that in the very first instance, your familial bonds would be easier to break due to the shortness of their creation."

Charlie blinked, unable to reply. He remembered how he cared for the Browns and everything they'd done for him and how they loved him back, but he could see though how the government would come to this conclusion given his personal record of hopping between families and the like.

"Second," Kono continued. "Why you can't tell anyone about your unlocked PIP level? Well that question is rather loaded so I will condense the answer as such: The Intergalactic Council – let's call them 'sponsors' of the GAP program - insisted upon a hard cap across all of the human cadets so that you could be controlled. It would do no good to create an army of 'supermen'," he smiled knowingly at the word, "then have them dominate you as they grow to an unknown strength. It is true that the GAP program is experimental and the first trial of its type using the human adolescents of earth."

Charlie picked up on some of the subtext, the things that the doctor wasn't saying but didn't press the issue. He'd distinctly heard that Kono had specified 'the humans adolescents of Earth', and the 'human cadets', which made Charlie think that there could be similar programs being run on other races and possibly there were humans out there that weren't from earth. Questions for another time he thought.

"Thirdly, why don't you have a cap on your PIP level? I will give you three answers and you may choose the one you prefer," Kono repeated the technique he'd used in Charlie's very first CCS class. "Your physical stature started out at a disadvantage. Therefore, by shifting your ultimate level cap upwards would allow you to catch up with the rest quickly. Two: Because you were entirely paralysed, I wanted to see what would happen if your body had the chance to rewrite all of the bad habits that other cadets may have had engrained in their very beings. That is to say, because you were a blank page, the genetic enhancements would be able to do things that they wouldn't have otherwise. It is just a theory though one I would like to test. Thirdly, I just like you, Charlie." The doctor smiled as he finished his answer and Charlie immediately came to the conclusion that out of the three answers, two were probably true – whether or not Kono liked him was neither here nor there – although if he was going to help Charlie grow faster he was all for playing the game a little bit. He guessed though, that the doctor's scientific curiosity was probably the reasoning behind all of this rather than some innate sense of caring for the boy.

"With all this being said, I would like you to report to the location shown on your terminal immediately," Kono concluded. "Your next training session awaits."

Charlie made his way to the location that had been blinking away on his terminal. From the top-down view of the canyon which showed all of the buildings and training areas in a sort of 2D arrangement, he could tell that it was a little deeper into the valley and away from anywhere that was overlooked or that would be seen by others. The doctor must've been serious when he'd said this was to remain a secret.

Pulling on his flight suit and fully awake, Charlie made his way silently out of his dorm, careful not to wake any of the other cadets, and slipped out of the main door and into the cool, dark night.

When he arrived at his personal training grounds, he was greeted by the sight of a huge military-style assault course on bright sand complete with nets, bars, balance beams, climbing walls, hanging rings and everything else he'd ever imagined assault course contained. At the beginning of the course stood someone familiar to him, and she smiled at his arrival.

"Charlie," the instructor greeted him as he approached her. "It's good to see you again, though I think I prefer to see you walking," she added.

"Instructor Shepherd?" Charlie sounded shocked at her presence, and he was.

He wouldn't have mistaken her anywhere as all he could think about was that over-dramatic fear she tried to force into her eyes when faking the alien boarding of their transportation to the planet. He wasn't annoyed at the scene or the lie, rather it made him smile as to how easy the whole ordeal was to decipher.

"I will be your instructor for the next hour, so I expect you to do as I say. If I hand you a gun and tell you to shoot something, I expect you to do it, not analyse the situation and poke holes in the plan, is that understood?" Shepherd asked, though she did so with a smile and it made Charlie feel at ease, the instructor seeming to be very caring and not at all like some of the others he'd had the misfortune to be taught by. Charlie nodded happily in acceptance of her terms and Shepherd clapped her hands together.

"How's that upper body strength coming along?" she asked, appearing to appraise his shoulders and arms.

"Um... good I think?" Charlie responded though not entirely sure how he should've.

"Good. Now get up on those rings and let's see how far you can swing!" she replied pointing to a line of hanging rings on the course.

The pair then walked to the start of the ring section and Charlie gaped at just how long it was. There must've been fifty rings hanging from the overhead beams before him and at a height of about three metres he knew there was no helping himself along.

Charlie gripped the first ring in his right hand and held it as tightly as he could, his knuckles turning white in the anticipation of the challenge ahead. Letting his feet slip off of the platform behind him and simultaneously reaching for the second hanging ring, Charlie felt his grip shift and fought against letting go of the wooden apparatus. He managed to grip the second ring and grasp onto it for dear life before coming to a complete stop, hanging for a couple of seconds then falling to the ground, landing hard on his feet.

"OK," Shepherd said with a short exhale attached. "First things first. When you land, bend your knees. That looked painful. Second, this is all about your grip strength which I had a suspicion would be lacking for you as you haven't had to use it for a while. Third, there is also a technique component. You must time your movements to keep your momentum which will speed up the task and make it easier at the same time. Try again."

Charlie climbed back onto the raised starting platform and retook his ready position. This time, he was determined not to make such a fool of himself and he closed his eyes before taking a hold of the first ring. Then he let himself slide off of the platform once more and although he did manage to take the second ring and actually let go of the first, his grip failed him. This time though, when his feet hit the floor he made sure to bend his knees and he did note that it made for a much softer landing. If he wasn't going to improve on the actual task of swinging from ring to ring, he was damn sure that he was going to improve on something else.

The act of attempting to swing and then failing went on for almost an entire hour before Shepherd informed him that it was time for him to return back to his dorm before the others were awake, though she did give him plenty of positive reinforcement before he left.

Charlie couldn't help it, he felt like a failure - he'd made it to the third ring but simply didn't have the strength in his grip or forearms to make it any further. To his dismay though, instructor Shepherd had said that this task was going to be repeated until he could make it all the way along the line of rings –a task that sounded like it was going to take forever.

Although he was absolutely disheartened by the lesson as he had hoped for something a little more specialised and effective than simply swinging from ring to ring, Charlie was still grateful that Dr. Kono was trying to help him grow and that instructor Shepherd was taking the time to try to help. Even if right now it felt like a waste of time, Charlie had the distinct feeling that if he kept trying and never gave up, he would be improving in no time.

Chapter 12

Three days had passed since the first time Charlie had laid eyes on the damned ring-swing and for three straight days he'd arrived an hour before the rest of the cadets had awoken, sneaking from his dorm so as not to give away the game. Instructor Shepherd had been there each time though Charlie hadn't yet heard anything else from Dr. Kono.

"This is the day, Charlie, I can feel it!" the instructor said happily as Charlie approached groggily. He'd found the compounding fatigue was absolutely draining as with each passing early morning combined with total physical exhaustion, it meant that he never had the chance to entirely recover and repair. He was surprised though that actually he was managing to still get on with it even through the pain and tiredness.

"What was it yesterday? Twelve?" the instructor asked.

"Thirteen, I fell on the fourteenth after I lost my grip," Charlie replied having recalled the incident perfectly. "I think if I could just hold on a little tighter for a little longer I'd get it."

Shepherd nodded, then added "let's get to it then," and ushered Charlie onto the starting platform. There was something about her reply though that made him think and his mind whirred into overdrive.

As with every single attempt he'd made, Charlie walked onto the platform and took a hold of the wooden ring closest to him. The apparatus felt comfortable in his hand, almost as if his palm was expecting the cool smooth edge of the wood. Against the wood he could feel the hardening callouses of his hand and he enjoyed the sensation – it was like scratching an itch now.

This time though Charlie had a new tactic to deal with the course and as he took the ring in his hand he did not close his grip tightly around it, rather he locked the ring in the crook of his finger joints and forced them into place in a somewhat open grip. Letting go of the platform, Charlie swung from the first ring, then to the second and third until before he knew it he was half way down the course. His grip strength no longer a factor and his forearms no longer aching from overuse, Charlie found that his new technique allowed him to hold on for longer and the momentum that carried him forward just seemed to grow and grow until he was there – he had made it to the far end of the course.

"YES!" Charlie announced happily as he leapt from the platform and he could see that Shepherd too was delighted.

"What did you learn?" she said as she smiled to the young cadet.

"That you don't tell me everything I need to know," he blurted out before he could stop himself and the instructor narrowed her eyes.

"I mean, sorry instructor," he quickly followed up. "You never told me to change my grip on the things, so I was always overtaxing my muscles trying to just hang on as hard as I could."

"So what did you learn?" Shepherd repeated but slightly slower this time.

Charlie thought long and hard before he answered, then finally he spoke. "I learnt that you don't need to be the strongest to accomplish a given task. Technique is sometimes better than force and also, it is important to ask more questions about a task before attempting it in case there is a better way."

Shepherd nodded, "Correct!" Then added with a smile, "AND that I didn't tell you everything you needed to know – sometimes it's better to learn things for yourself - that way people tend to remember the lesson a little better."

Charlie smiled back at the instructor, knowing that she was mainly just teasing him though she was right, he would certainly remember this lesson.

"Charlie, there's something coming today that you need to be prepared for. Your first week of training has come to an end and I am sure that you have seen that 'Wargames' is planned for today?" Instructor Shepherd asked.

"Yes I saw," Charlie replied. "I guessed it was something that would use what we'd learnt in training to make sure it was all going in?"

Shepherd shook her head slightly at Charlie, "In a way you are right, it's there for your training to be used, though the wargames are not to be taken lightly. There are real dangers within them and you will need to remain calm with your wits about you if you wish to do well in them. The most important thing though, is that as an Alpha you will need to be able to rely on your teammates and they on you. You won't be able to get through this alone..."

Charlie caught her meaning as he knew more than anyone how good a job he had been doing at remaining unnoticed by the others as much as possible. As he'd grown and started catching up to the others over the week – albeit slowly – he seemed to stand out less and less and that suited him right down to the ground. If there was a way he could blend into a larger group whilst a lesson was being carried out then he did it. He hadn't pushed himself on the firing range nor had he attempted to knock down any of his opponents in hand to hand combat, and for the most part nobody had really taken any notice of his existence. The one thing he did have going for him though, was his two best friends, Mauro and Laura, and the thought of having them on his team made him smile.

Shepherd seemed to read his mind and shook her head once again, "Giardini and Latori aren't always going to be enough. You need a full squad working together as a team Charlie, and the quicker you make that happen the easier all this is going to be. You need to look a little *closer to home*," she urged.

Charlie nodded slowly in response, already thinking about just how he was going to win over his two roommates, Nakamura and Marsh – if he had to start somewhere that was going to be the simplest way.

After Charlie returned to his dorm, he sat alone in the communal area on the fabric sofa for what he thought was the first time, waiting for the rest of the dorm to awaken and discover him there. He was going to go back to his room and see if the bastard alarm would let him have a lie in given that it was technically a Saturday, though he couldn't be sure and didn't want to miss his opportunity to catch the others before they left for breakfast.

Just about wondering if the alarm was going to sound or not, Charlie heard the all too familiar siren and blinked in anticipation. Three or four minutes passed before he heard the first footsteps and a door opening and he realised that the first one out of their room was Kori Nakamura.

"Kori," Charlie said to his roommate as he made a short awkward eye contact with the boy, who didn't answer.

"Kori, listen," Charlie tried again. "There's supposed to be something called Wargames today and we are going to have to work as a team. I know you don't like me and all but I have reason to believe that things are going to be so much easier if we just all work together."

Kori stopped mid-step as though Charlie had said something that he was interested in.

"What do you mean, you have reason to believe?" he asked with a scowl and Charlie knew he'd just messed up.

"I... uh," Charlie stammered trying to come up with a suitable lie quickly.

"Have you been cheating again, cheater?" Kori asked as he took a step toward Charlie who now felt very much on the back foot.

As the week had progressed there had been slight differences appearing between the class specialisations. Most notably this came in the way of the heavy arms cadets who had been growing larger and more muscular. Being an assault, Nakamura hadn't presented in such a large way, although he did appear strong, menacing and quick and Charlie could tell that the boy was readying himself for a fight as he spoke.

"No!" Charlie protested and raised his palms in a calming gesture, "I just asked an instructor and they said we'll be working as a team."

"Then why didn't they tell anyone else? What else do you know, Charlie?" Nakamura was practically growling at this point and Charlie could tell that there would be no talking him down from this ledge.

Another door creaked open and Charlie immediately caught Laura's eye from behind Kori as she stepped into the sitting room. Kori, however, didn't seem to either notice or care, the result was the same either way.

"What's happening here?" Laura said as she read the situation and took note of the aggressive and defensive postures before her. Kori still didn't speak although both Charlie and Laura noticed that his knuckles were balled and his fists white.

"I was just saying that we all need to work together in this wargames today. I asked an instructor about them and they said..." Charlie attempted to answer though was interrupted by Kori.

"He's fucking cheating again," the boy spat out, practically foaming at the mouth. "The fucking cheater is cheating again!" Then Nakamura took a menacing pace toward Charlie and Laura moved quicker than Charlie ever thought possible, arriving behind the boy in an instant. She placed an arm around Nakamura's neck and the other under his armpit and pulled him into a solid rear-naked choke before the pair fell to the ground and Laura wrapped her legs around his waist from behind. Within just a few seconds Charlie could see that all of the anger had left Kori's body and Laura loosened her grip so as to not completely choke him out.

At that moment, both Mauro and Stephanie Marsh exited their rooms and were greeted with the sight of Charlie sat on a sofa and Laura holding a submissive Kori Nakamura on the ground.

Stephanie didn't say anything immediately but Mauro seemed to be buoyed by the situation, smiling widely and moving closer to see what was happening, apparently coming to the conclusion that this was a lesson in hand to hand combat and not an actual altercation.

"You OK now?" Laura asked Nakamura who blinked and nodded slightly. The pair both stood up and the tension in the room abated somewhat.

"Charlie, what did you do?" Laura asked of her friend who made an effort to look shocked at her accusation. "I know you did something, Kori wouldn't just flip out like that if you didn't say anything," she argued.

Charlie exhaled. "Look, can we all sit down?" he asked. "It's just about the wargames. We need to work as a team. Instructor Shepherd said…"

Shit, Charlie knew he'd made a mistake as soon as the name came out of his mouth. Laura looked confused and Kori went bright red again – the perfect colour to match his assault specialisation. Mauro didn't seem to understand what was happening yet and Stephanie sat down to listen to what was going to happen next.

"Charlie?" Laura said before he could say any more. "Who the fuck is instructor Shepherd?"

It was now Charlie's turn to go bright red and he knew it was time to tell the actual truth as the group would probably have seen right through anything but.

"She uh… she's like a bit of a… private tutor," he said, though the words 'private tutor' came out in a very small voice and the resulting shouting from the group was enough for Charlie to sink into the sofa and made him want to disappear.

"Are you FUCKING KIDDING ME?" Laura was the first to respond to Charlie's statement.

"This is brilliant," Kori chimed in with a sarcastic smile on his face. "The cheater strikes again!"

"Come on man, that's not cool," Mauro added and took a seat next to Charlie which made him admittedly feel protected by the larger boy but also incredibly embarrassed.

"Can we all get private tutors?" Stephanie asked with her first words that'd ever been said directly to Charlie and it was an opportunity for him to speak again.

"I can ask," he replied tentatively. "But honestly it's only been a few days and it was because I started off so far behind. I still am, as you can tell. I just needed to catch up – or at least try to. I'll ask if we can all have lessons if it helps us all but right now we have to make sure we are all going to work as a team to get through this next thing."

The next minutes passed with Charlie making promises to include the rest of the dorm in his private lessons as well as talking through how they'd gone, what he'd done and the progress he'd made. The only thing he stopped short of though was telling anyone at all about the unlocked status of his PIP level or his conversations with Dr. Kono. They didn't need to know about any of that just yet. He knew he couldn't trust them all completely.

Eventually the group seemed a little more positive about the prospects of working together and all of them actually chatted with a degree of happy optimism which shocked Charlie. It seemed that by actually taking the time to talk together, the two outsiders to his group of three were far more amenable to accept him as a human being rather as something to be either avoided or insulted. Charlie liked this new dynamic and wanted to make sure he didn't do anything to jeopardise it.

The group was still talking as they made their way to the mess hall for breakfast and sat together discussing how each of them could use their specialisation to work together towards a common goal. As it turned out, Stephanie was a tech specialist and not a medic, which sounded far more useful whilst they'd be playing the wargames, though none of them could prepare for something they didn't know was coming.

Breakfast was porridge again and Mauro pined for his eggs, complaining that without a varied diet his muscles were going to waste away. Charlie joined in with that statement saying that if he didn't get eggs again he'd probably just fall back into using his wheelchair. Surprisingly, both Stephanie and Kori laughed at Charlie's joke and he beamed at both of them.

"You know you said you needed to catch up to everyone," Laura said as Charlie filled his mouth with lukewarm porridge. He replied with a mmm mmm as though to say 'yes, go on'.

"Have you looked in a mirror lately?" she asked rather slowly and cautiously, though when he thought about it, Charlie realised that he hadn't had the time – he had simply carried out his classes, trained until he was exhausted and fallen into his bed – there was no time for self appraisals.

"No…" he said slowly after swallowing. "Am I still bald?"

Mauro spat out a small bit of porridge before he caught himself from laughing again but Charlie ignored him.

"Actually, yes," she replied. "You've got short black hairs sprouting up all over the place... but I was talking about your body. You must be twice the size you were when you arrived. We've all grown hugely actually but you seem to have caught up very quickly. I'd say in a few days at your rate you'll be right on par with most of the cadets here – with the exception of Henderson... and Mauro here. But I think he just eats too much." Mauro could tell it was a joke though because although he did nothing but eat, the Heavy Arms Specialist was not fat by a long stretch – he was just bigger overall.

"CADETS!" the very loud shout interrupted everyone in the room and they instinctively snapped to attention at Cesari's booming voice. "Today is the day of your first ever Wargames. This scenario is called 'The Gauntlet' and I expect you to treat the entire exercise as a live fire event. That is to say if you are injured – or killed – within the games, it will count against both you and your squad. The Gauntlet is an objective based scenario in which your squad must reach the top of a hill which is defended by enemy forces. Your squads are made up of your dormitory allocations and you will be ranked according to your score which will be made up of a range of factors, not least of which, as you will imagine, is speed and casualties taken." The entire room was silent as they listened to the chief instructor describe their day's activities. "You will await your turn on the course in the mess hall and be taken squad by squad to The Gauntlet, then you will report back to your dorms and await the completion of the day so that the detail remains secret until all squads have completed the course. Do you understand?"

"Yes chief instructor!" The cadets chorused back and the instructor gave a devious smile.

"Your scores will appear on this terminal above my head," He pointed upwards to a large flat terminal that could be read from even the back of the room and listed were all of the Special Ops Cadets. "These are your squad leaders and it will be in your interest to obey their commands when they are given."

Charlie scanned the list of names for his own and saw it about half way down the list between Neville Young and Manuel Mancini. They weren't in alphabetical order, though when Cesari called for the first squad – Joey Ashman's – he could tell they weren't in the order to be taking the Gauntlet either.

The squad left the mess hall with Cesari and the room burst into the sound of the cadets trying to guess what was going to happen, what tactics they might employ and hopes that they were going to top the leaderboard by the end of the day. That all fell into silence though when the leaderboard was replaced by 'Squad: Ashman' and a timer that started counting the seconds from zero. This was how the cadets were going to follow the progress of the other squads and not a single pair of eyes in the room was on anything other than the scoring terminal.

Fifteen seconds passed with nothing interesting happening, then the timer abruptly stopped and the scoreboard reappeared. Now though, next to Ashman's name was a time of fifteen seconds and the horrifying words: 'Squad Deceased'.

The room fell silent and nobody looked away from the scoreboard. The silence was interrupted by Cesari opening the door a few moments later to the mess hall and shouting for the next squad which looked utterly terrified at the prospect of facing the Gauntlet. Luca Strano's squad trouped out of the mess hall and every single cadet in the room felt for them.

The next score followed baited breaths once the timer had started and the second squad was clearly more cautious in their approach, making it to a full three minutes before the 'Squad Deceased' message accompanied their time on the scoreboard. Some of the cadets practically whimpered when the note appeared on the screen but others looked away in an effort to double down on their determination.

Then it was time for Jean Martin's squad to go, of which Matty Henderson was the heavy arms member. Charlie watched them leave following Cesari and noted with surprise that the large muscular cadet was smiling as he walked – apparently his overconfidence had no limits.

This time the timer simply kept going. Five minutes passed, then ten, then fifteen. When it was just shy of twenty minutes the scoreboard reappeared with the time next to Martin's name along with two notes: 'Gauntlet Complete' and 'Four Deceased'. Charlie could take a good guess at who had survived the Gauntlet, though with his whole being he wanted to believe that passing this test was not simply a matter of physical stature.

His squad was up next and the five of them walked to the start of the Gauntlet with a deep sense of dread and foreboding amongst them.

As they followed Cesari deeper into the valley for a good few minutes it became apparent to all of them that it was actually getting darker as the sun above them was being obscured by the high and narrowing walls of the valley to either side of them, Eventually they came to a stop before three other instructors who stood to attention awaiting their arrival. There was a metal control room at the start of the Gauntlet – and the actual thing was a marvel to behold. Carved into the valley wall was a course running at a moderate incline complete with winding paths, camo netting, sheer rock faces and obstacles that could be both used for cover and would need to be traversed. From their starting position, though, the squad could see nothing of what was awaiting them past the first turn into the maze and the rest of the scenario rising off into the distance.

"This is to be treated as a live fire scenario," Cesari repeated to the squad. "Your weapons, the enemy weapons and the turret at the base of the Gauntlet will fire electroshock rounds. These are non-fatal ammunition but will render body parts unusable if hit, or will knock you unconscious if you are hit in a vital area such as the head or torso. Also, as you are probably about to find out, these rounds are extremely painful. Your turret will also fire these non-lethal rounds, so I suggest you watch out for friendly fire." The squad continued to listen intently without replying. "Your objective is to make it to the top of the Gauntlet and raise the flag that you will find there. Your time will be recorded along with any fatalities. If you do not complete the objective your time will be recorded but the course will be considered a failure. Do you understand?"

"Yes chief instructor," all five of the cadets replied and all of the instructors made their way without a word into the control centre to watch the cadets as they ran the Gauntlet.

"You may begin when ready. The clock will start the moment you enter the Gauntlet," Cesari's voice now came from a speaker atop the control centre.

The cadets were in shock and they all looked at each other silently. Laura took it upon herself to eventually speak first.

"What should we do? We can't just stand here," she said.

"I can't see anything from here though, so we need to get in there, right?" Mauro asked hesitantly and Charlie couldn't agree more. There was no assessment of the situation to be made until they actually entered into the Gauntlet itself.

"I think we just go for it then?" Kori offered and the rest nodded their agreement before all walking slowly in a straight line towards the entrance to their test and crossed the threshold to start their timer. None of the squad said it, but they'd been expecting to be given weapons, or equipment though none had arrived. Charlie for one thought that then perhaps they were expected to collect things as they went from inside the Gauntlet itself.

On entering the Gauntlet, before them was a solid stone wall with a wooden ladder attached to it and two paths, one leading left and one right but no sign as to which way was the correct path.

"There are five of us, how do we decide which way to go?" Stephanie said quietly and without any confidence in her voice at all.

"We stay together for now," Charlie replied. "This is going to all be about teamwork so we stick together unless it's necessary for us all to separate."

Mauro then took a hold of the short ladder and took two steps upwards before looking down at the others to relay what he could see.

"There's a turret up there – some kind of fixed heavy machine gun looking straight up the hill – I think I can use it to give us all cover," he reported.

"That would make sense – you are a heavy arms specialist," Charlie said. "But wait..." his mind had started to function at that all too familiar higher level and his perception was telling him that something was off.

"Cesari told us about that turret, though he knew that we'd see it straight away," he said. "He told us about the turret and its ammunition twice - it was almost like he was telling us to make a move for it... you don't think that..." He trailed off as he spoke and searched around for a large stone to throw in the air and when he found one he tossed it up high toward the platform and turret. Immediately the stone was hit with heavy machine gun fire that decimated it and the echoes of the gunfire all but deafened the squad before fading away to nothing.

"Shit, thanks," Mauro said jumping down from the ladder a little too quickly. "I guess we need to be a little more careful, huh?"

"So... left then?" Laura said picking the direction at random, "and leave the turret behind?"

"I think so," Charlie agreed, I don't see how we can get a hold of it without one of us getting hit in the process." Nobody mentioned the clear deception of the chief instructor that had attempted to have one or more of the cadets killed. Now wasn't the time to feel hard done by.

Cautiously the squad took the path to the left and stopped at the first corner before Charlie threw another stone out to see if it would get shot at like the first. At this turning and the next, nothing terrible happened and the stones simply fell to the ground unharmed. When they breached a third corner though, the squad came face to face with a long, straight stone staircase that was very clearly not under any sort of cover, with sheer cut walls on either side of it. A path carried on past the staircase though it didn't seem to offer anything out of the ordinary.

"Another trap?" Mauro asked as he peered side-eyed at the staircase.

"Maybe," Charlie replied, "though I don't see the point. We don't have to go up it so why would we risk it?"

"Because we have to get to the top of this Gauntlet," Kori said smugly, "and what's a better way to get up there than on a staircase?"

It did make sense to Charlie but he didn't see what the purpose of the obstacle was. After a long moment though, he decided to take the chance as Kori had said – they needed to go up.

After a few tentative steps, the squad could tell that they were making good progress in an upwards direction. Then Charlie saw it, the machine gun that had fired at their own turret was perched on a cutaway platform just above the staircase to their right, sat on a stabilising tripod. It was within reach of the staircase so Mauro took a jump and pulled himself up to where it sat and picked it up although with some effort – the thing must've been very heavy. Attached to the trigger was a small black box with a laser coming from it, and testing a theory, Mauro put his hand in front of the beam. Immediately the weapon fired a volley of rounds which almost caused the cadet to drop the thing, though thankfully he held onto it.

"It's got a sensor on it to get it to fire automatically," he said down to the squad, though slightly louder than necessary as the gun firing had caused his ears to ring. Of course the rest of the squad had already figured that out, though they nodded along with his assessment anyway.

"Bring it with you," Charlie said to Mauro, though he was sure that was his plan anyway.

At the top of the steps things really started to change for the worse. As soon as Charlie placed a foot on solid ground, a single gunshot rang out from the distance. It was like the sound carried in slow motion, and on complete instinct, Charlie could tell that the shot had been fired from a few hundred metres away and directly at his head. It was all very much like it was in slow motion and Charlie fell immediately to the ground before the bullet made its way from its barrel to his person. It ricocheted off the wall behind where his head had just been and he exhaled deeply. Luckily for the squad, Charlie had been the first up the stairs.

"Shit Charlie, that was some quick thinking," Kori said from his own prone position on the stairs. "How did you do that?"

Charlie shrugged, "Just lucky I guess."

"Bullshit," Mauro called from the back of the squad. "Bet he's got a private tutor for his reactions!" Charlie could tell he was joking and it made him smile.

"What do we do now?" Stephanie asked.

Charlie thought and tried to analyse his situation again, though it was difficult when it was forced and not instinctual.

"How fast can you run?" Charlie eventually asked Laura. "When you choked out Kori... I've never seen anyone move that fast."

"It's... part of the recon training, we do sprints a lot," Laura replied and it clicked into Charlie's mind as she spoke. Mauro as a heavy arms specialist was slow and strong, and Laura as a recon was quick and agile. This was the whole point of working as a team and he wondered how the others were going to fit into this system.

"I'm going to make it fire again, then I want you to run into that cover, OK?" Charlie instructed and Laura nodded confidently.

He slowly rose to his feet and immediately a single shot rang out again causing him to fall to the ground to avoid it. He felt the wind pass him as Laura sped off almost in a flash and slid to the ground herself behind a large cut stone. Smiling back at Charlie she gave him the thumbs up.

"You see anything?" he spoke loudly so Laura could hear him clearly and she called back.

"Yeah, once you get past that gunfire there's cover here. There's something else too..."

Laura disappeared from view for a short moment then she threw something heavy that landed an inch from Charlie. Examining the object without raising himself to his feet he saw that it was similar to a car door - black metal and very solid. Before he could announce it to the squad, Kori spoke loudly from the rear.

"It's a riot shield!" he cooed. "We've been training with them... hold on."

Kori crawled up a couple of the steps and came to a stop beside Charlie. Carefully he picked up the shield and crouched down behind it then nervously took a few shuffled steps forward.

Bang! Ting. The shot rang out and ricocheted off of the riot shield this time and Kori was thankfully unharmed.

"Quick, go!" He ushered the rest of the squad and they didn't need to be told twice. As one they ran behind the protective cover of the riot shield and across to where Laura had found safety.

The squad took a short moment to catch their collective breath and let adrenaline levels drop before they moved onwards from their cover.

They rounded another blind corner, but this time with no stones to test the waters with, Charlie peered around it carefully. Thankfully no gunshot rang out and there was nothing that caused him any immediate danger. There was however a series of hanging rings crossing a gap in the carved hillscape that would lead them on to their next destination. He stood with his mouth agape at the familiar obstacle and the only thing he could think of was how glad he was that instructor Shepherd had trained him specifically for this very obstacle.

"I... uh... I..." Stephanie spoke quietly. "I don't know if I can do that."

Charlie refrained from saying that it was easy, as he knew it was anything but, having actually trained in this very task extremely hard.

He turned slowly to face Stephanie before speaking as he wanted her to understand that he actually believed in what he was saying.

"Stephanie, I know it seems difficult and I know you think you can't do it. I've had that very same thought so many times in my life and so many times it caused me not to even try. There is no shame in failing something if you give it your all but that doesn't mean you shouldn't try." He made his speech then turned his attention to the task at hand. "Besides, this is all about technique and momentum. It's not that far to swing, you just have to keep moving - watch."

Then he curled his hand around the first ring as he had done so many times before and narrated his actions as he began to swing.

"Don't close your grip all the way it'll just tire you out. Put the rings in the crook of your knuckles and swing in an unforced and natural pace."

Charlie swung and gripped, let go swung and gripped fifteen times before his feet touched down on terra firma on the far side of the apparatus and the group clapped and cheered as he touched down. Laura then followed suit, then Kori – who left his riot shield behind as it was too heavy to bring along. Both made it with ease though it left the group split, with Stephanie unsure of herself and Mauro not wanting to leave his heavy machine gun behind – though he knew he was going to have to do so if he wanted to make it across.

"Mauro, you have to drop that thing," Charlie called across the chasm. "You won't be able to hold on with it."

Mauro knew Charlie was right but it didn't stop him from pouting as he left the weapon behind. Then when he swung across the rings, Charlie noted that he didn't swing rhythmically like the rest had done so far, rather he relied on his brute force and strength to cling onto the rings and force himself across. It looked difficult and exhausting although he did make it, panting when he landed.

"Come on Stephanie, you can do it!" Laura called back across to the lone cadet who looked worried. She was almost at the stage of giving up, her arms tightly folded across her chest when Charlie called out to her.

"If I can get up and walk out of a God damned wheelchair you can do this! Stop thinking about it and just go!"

These seemed to be the exact words that Stephanie needed to hear and she shook herself off and leapt at the hanging rings. Her momentum took her flying along the course in no time at all, so fast in fact that when she reached the other end, Mauro had to practically catch her to prevent her from falling onto her back. However it'd happened though, the group had made it across.

The last obstacle then presented itself to the group. They knew it was the last because at the top of a wide and long path uphill, stood an empty flagpole, but on the way was a turret placed on either side of the path pointing a laser across its line of sight. It would not be possible to run past these guns and Charlie couldn't see any way to get through them without taking some heavy damage.

"They're M382's!" Stephanie cheered happily as she peered up the hill at the turrets. "We've learned something about these ones..." She brought a hand up to her chin to think then eventually snapped her fingers as she remembered what it was.

"The thing about these turrets is..." she spoke as she moved cautiously onto the hill and into the turrets' domain. "They're run by an artificial intelligence that's designed to identify threats. It's a bit of a dumb one though, so if we move slowly... and remain unarmed... make no threatening moves..."

Then all of a sudden, she had done it, she was past the firing arcs of the turrets and standing safely on the far side of the hill just metres away from the flag and their final destination.

The group looked at each other questioningly then one by one they followed Stephanie's lead, moving slowly, cautiously and unthreateningly to where Stephanie crouched down behind a piece of handy rock cover. Amazingly, they all made it past the turrets and collectively let out a breath as they looked happily up at the flagpole.

One thought dawned on Charlie as he contemplated the group's final move. Cesari had spoken about their own weapons as though it was expected that they'd have something to fire back at, though up until now there hadn't actually been any reason to use any weapons. In fact if Mauro had carried the heavy machine gun through to this last task, the turrets would probably have painted them as hostile. Again Charlie added that fact to the mental list of things Cesari had done to try to get him or his team killed within the Gauntlet and filed it away and out of his mind.

"You think there's any more surprises up there?" Mauro asked as the squad looked at the flagpole with a mixture of anticipation and happiness.

"No idea," Charlie replied. "But we're about to find out I guess," and with nothing else to do, Charlie walked slowly toward the flagpole and began pulling on the rope that would lift the solid yellow flag up the pole. Almost immediately he was joined by the rest of his squad, each offering a pair of hands to help in the task. Although it wasn't a difficult one, he was happy for the camaraderie.

"Gauntlet Complete!" Cesari's voice carried up the hill from the loudspeaker attached to the control centre and the group all but fell to the ground. It was over – they had done it and if there was anything more exhausting than actually running the gauntlet for the first time, it was the feeling of their collective adrenaline draining from their bodies.

Chapter 13

The scoreboard had updated as soon as the 'Sinclair' group had completed the Gauntlet with no fatalities and a time of forty eight minutes, twelve seconds. It wasn't anything to write home about but their squad was the first to complete the challenge without any casualties, although they were still slower than Henderson's group.

Charlie and the squad returned to their dorm immediately as instructed and all fell onto the sofas in the communal living area. A moment passed before anyone said anything, then all five of the cadets burst into a cacophony of celebration, laughter and exclamation.

"Did you see that?" Charlie had shouted and responses came in the way of "yeah, I was there," and "how did we manage that?"

"I can't wait to see Henderson's face when he sees we kept our whole squad alive - he's going to be so pissed!" Mauro said with a huge grin on his face.

In truth the whole squad knew that it was a whole lot of luck that had got them through but there was a good portion of teamwork too - if they hadn't been matched so well and had worked so well together as a team, they were sure to have all perished.

The large glass terminal in the communal area hadn't yet been touched, but acting on instinct, Charlie tapped it to turn it on and it filled with the same information that the terminal in the mess hall had been showing. The Gauntlet rankings and the communal area turned into something akin to a football match with the cadets all eagerly anticipating the scores. Charlie's squad sat in first place, despite their time being slower than Henderson's group, their score apparently having been calculated higher due to their lack of casualties. Another fact that was sure to get Henderson's blood boiling.

Each time a new squad's timer started, the cadets cheered them on as though they could hear them and each time one was wiped out they would all boo and spare a moment. On about half of the occasions, though, a squad would complete the course although always with at least one casualty. By the time the entire list had completed their runs through the Gauntlet, not a single group other than Charlie's had completed the task without casualties, and not a single group had completed it faster than Henderson's. That meant that Charlie's squad had won the day.

"Shit," Charlie muttered once the commotion had died down after the last squad on the list had completed the Gauntlet. "We won?" He almost couldn't believe it.

"HELL YEAH!" Mauro shouted loudly though Laura could see something was troubling Charlie and she realised what it was.

"This paints a target on all of us, doesn't it?" she said aloud for everyone to hear. "They're all going to want to beat us next time, which is going to mean a harder time in training and possibly some of the others (basically Henderson) going out of their way to bring us down."

Stephanie looked worried but didn't say a word, although Kori decided to announce his allegiance with "who cares, we're better than all of them and this just proves it!" He was cocky and admittedly it was somewhat warranted, but Charlie knew this was just going to be the beginning of something bigger.

Eventually the group found themselves tired from the day's activities and as there were sixty squads participating in the gauntlet it had actually taken all day for the entire scoreboard to be filled, even continuing into the evening with a cursory dinner being delivered to their door from the mess hall – jacket potatoes, cheese and beans. Charlie did promise, before he retired alone to his room, that the rest of the cadets could join him in the morning for his additional training session if the instructor would allow it. He wasn't sure if the training was on though with the week being all but over, but decided that if it wasn't, a little extra session between the five couldn't hurt either.

When Charlie was alone again he took the time, as he wasn't entirely exhausted to the point of collapse for once, to appraise himself for the first time in days and he started with the mirror.

Taking his flight suit off completely and stripping to his underwear, Charlie could see huge differences immediately. His legs were beefier and the gap that had once sat between his thighs was now completely gone. His hip bones were no longer awkwardly protruding from his skin and his ab muscles were clear and defined. His chest had taken a sharp, muscular shape and although nothing was large or out of proportion, his entire body had started to change in ways he'd never thought possible. His shoulders and arms were more defined than he'd ever seen them too and as he raised his arms up he could tense them into peaks that made him smile. The boy smiling back at him was almost as much of a stranger as his body was.

His jawbone had become more pronounced than he'd remembered and his face had thinned to a more adult shape, but the real change was the top of his head. Where it was once a shiny bald deal with not a hair in sight, he had grown a not insubstantial amount of thick, black hair. He had been told by the others that he had been sprouting hair already but this... this was something else entirely and lifting a hand to touch the new hair, tears welled in Charlie's eyes as he felt his own head.

After a few more appraisals and poses to see what his new body looked like from all angles, Charlie moved his attention to his personal terminal and the stats that would shed some more light onto his progress. The first thing he noticed was that his muscle mass had increased by a full three kilograms, and he'd apparently grown a few inches taller too. He wondered what that translated to in terms of his apparent age, though as the cadets only had one another to compare with it was difficult to decide. Charlie figured he definitely looked at least a year or two older than he should have and his accelerated growth was another reason to make him smile.

His PIP level though – that was what he was truly interested in. This was the one thing that no kid back on earth would be able to compare themselves to and the one thing that was doing all of the leg work in the background (pun very much intended) to affect all of the changes he was going through. His emotion toward his new level though was once again mixed. Six percent. Was that good? He wasn't sure but he was simultaneously annoyed that it wasn't much higher and happy that it seemed to be growing at an actual tangible rate. Again Charlie wondered what was going to happen when he reached the higher percentages of PIP level and what the limits of the human body were actually going to be.

Eventually there was nothing left for Charlie to do other than get into bed and go to sleep as it had already become late. He wasn't as totally exhausted as usual, so it took him a few minutes to actually fall asleep, the actions of the day and the choices he'd made in the Gauntlet spinning around his mind. His last thoughts before falling completely asleep were of Henderson, and how he was going to be so annoyed that he'd been placed second to Charlie's own squad.

The next morning Charlie's alarm that he'd set woke him up at his usual training time and he could tell from the sounds of unsteady footsteps and groans coming from the other rooms that all four of his roommates and friends had also awoken to join him for his private training session. He smiled at the memory of his own fatigue during the week and knew exactly how they felt at having to get up at such an hour, though he knew that it was worth it – without those lessons he would surely have not made it through the Gauntlet alive – or even as a part of a team.

"Morning!" Charlie said as he exited his room and saw Laura stumble out of her own doorway. Her hair was messier than he'd ever seen before and her eyes were barely open. She looked like a mole. Laura wore her flight suit almost correctly, though one of her arms hadn't quite made it all the way through a sleeve yet and she glared back at Charlie without saying a word. She walked toward, then past him and out the dorm's door into the dark morning air and Charlie knew that she would be woken up properly in the cool outside atmosphere, as he had been every morning. He smiled to himself at his friend's reaction to being woken so early.

Mauro was much chirpier about the situation, replying to Charlie's greeting with a 'good morning' of his own, accompanied by a stretch and a yawn.

The three waited outside the dorm for Stephanie and Kori to join them, Charlie partly not wanting to catch Kori's bad side, but when they were joined by the pair, Kori seemed the most awake of the group and Stephanie remained as quiet as ever, her arms folded across her chest.

"You ready for this?" Kori asked in an excited tone before anyone else could speak. "I'm about to teach you all a lesson in... uh... learning lessons." Kori winced as he spoke the last sentence, clearly not having thought through what it was that he wanted to say before he said it and Charlie snorted.

The five cadets walked happily to where Charlie knew the assault course was – and that he hoped was where instructor Shepherd was awaiting him. To his relief, she was standing exactly where she always had been for their lessons. As the group approached, the instructor addressed Charlie.

"Charlie? You didn't say you were going to bring along extra students; you know that costs extra, right?" she said with a stern look on her face.

"I... uh..." he started, then pulled himself together. "They kind of dragged it out of me and after the Gauntlet. I kind of thought I owed it to them."

"Right, then I guess we'd better make a start, more students means less time, so chop chop." She clapped her hands and ushered the group towards the start of the assault course and not just the hanging rings portion. Charlie figured it was about time he got to have a go at the whole thing and smiled as he followed the rest of the group.

"Charlie," Shepherd said quietly as he was the only cadet in earshot as they passed. "You haven't said anything about... you know, have you?"

He thought for a moment then realised she was talking about his unlocked PIP level and assured her quietly that still nobody knew anything about that particular fact.

For the next hour, the instructor did what Charlie had seen her do best – give lessons that weren't quite lessons in what they seemed. She taught initiative, lateral thinking and self awareness whilst covering it as an assault course and the whole time Charlie could see exactly what she was doing, after all he'd fallen for it the first time too. If a task needed to be repeated it might not have been because you weren't strong enough, maybe the lesson was that you needed to ask for help – or if your technique was off then maybe her encouragement and reassurance was there specifically for you to question your own abilities – later to find that you were simply doing it wrong from the beginning. Instructor Shepherd's teaching techniques were certainly odd to Charlie, though from his own experience they were frightfully effective.

"That's enough today then!" she called an end to the class and all five of the cadets looked unhappy at the fact it was over, it was clear to everyone that they wanted more. "I am happy to continue training you all in this manner for the time being. I feel that the benefits to you outweigh my own fatigue and effort," she winked to let them know she was being somewhat sarcastic. Though *If I ever feel like you aren't putting in one* hundred percent effort... I will not hesitate to go right back to bed. I like sleep, you know."

The group left the assault course for the morning and headed back to their dorm and Charlie was looking forward to not having to sneak in so as to not telegraph his presence to his unknowing roommates. Fate however decided upon a different path and as they say, there's no rest for the wicked. Standing by the door to their dorm was the hulking figure of Matty Henderson.

There was no hiding their approach as it'd taken too long for the group to notice the larger cadet and they'd been speaking merrily. Charlie's hands automatically balled into fists and he felt both Laura and Mauro's hands on his shoulders comfortingly.

"I knew it," snarled Henderson. "I knew there would be some reason that *you* would complete the Gauntlet and here you are, sneaking off getting some... what is this ... private lessons? I bet it's Cesari isn't it? Acts all tough in public then whilst everyone else is asleep it's all 'oh here are the answers to your next test, Charlie. You make me sick." His face was contorted with rage and Charlie was half surprised the boy hadn't lost it already from looking at him.

"What are you doing here?" Laura snarled at Henderson, choosing to ignore his little rant.

"I just came to give Sinclair a little pre-breakfast beating," Henderson said with a smirk. "You know, let him know he's not the big dog around here, no matter what some stupid fucking scoreboard says."

"Sorry Henderson, do you mean you care that much that we were top that you needed to come see us? Aww that's so sweet of you," Charlie replied falling back on his sarcasm to escalate the situation once again. Really he knew he should learn to keep his big mouth shut but Henderson really pushed his buttons and he kind of couldn't help himself.

"I'm going to teach you to shut your fucking mouth," Henderson practically spat out, apparently not caring that this was now a five on one situation.

Stephanie took a slight step backwards somewhat threatened by the bigger boy, although Kori and Laura took ready stances and Mauro stood protectively between them all. Looking at his friend, Charlie could see that Mauro had grown into a bit of a hulking beast but Henderson was bigger still.

"Come on Matty," Mauro said in a placating tone, "There's no need for it to all come down to this now, is there?"

Henderson didn't respond though and did something Charlie didn't expect. He punched Mauro, hard in the stomach and the boy fell to his knees apparently very winded.

In the speed of the moment, Matty Henderson then took his opportunity to lunge for Charlie, who could see the blood red anger in the larger cadet's eyes. He could see everything in fact - the way Henderson's muscles tensed, coiled and exploded to move his body toward Charlie, the way his fists balled, tensed and cocked and the way that if Charlie didn't do anything to get out of the way, how he was going to be knocked clean out. It was all in such slow motion and all so clear… but still Charlie couldn't do much about it.

Charlie moved his head to the side as quickly as he could to avoid the leading fist of his attacker but it did nothing to stop Henderson crashing into him in a kind of rugby tackle. The sheer weight and momentum of the attack saw them both fall to the ground with Henderson on top of Charlie. The cadet then balled his fists again and began raining blows into Charlie's arms, chest and face over and over. Charlie tried to block and defend but after just a few blows he found that his technique was lacking and the punches made it through.

Laura and Kori who'd been knocked back by the initial lunge made it back onto their feet and within an instant of seeing what was happening they both wrapped their arms around Henderson's and dragged him off of Charlie and to the ground. Henderson then shrugged them both off of him with somewhat ease, took a look at Charlie, smirked, dusted himself off and turned and walked away as though he didn't have a care in the world.

Charlie though didn't see any of that though. He was unconscious and hurt.

"Sorry Charlie," Mauro wheezed as he attempted to deal with the blow he'd been surprised with, "I'll get him ne…" Mauro stopped when his eyes fell upon Charlie.

The young cadet was on the floor unconscious, face covered in blood, cuts, swelling and bruises. He was in a bad way and all four of his squad mates knew it, although they hadn't realised that such damage could be dealt in such a flash.

"Go get help, now!" Laura said commandingly to Stephanie who immediately ran off to where the instructors would be at this hour while Laura made sure Charlie's airways were clear and that he was breathing. She wasn't a medic in any sense of the word but she knew that trying to move him was probably going to be a bad idea. She comforted him as best she could with words of encouragement intermixed with threats of revenge whilst the group awaited Stephanie's return with help. Kori was shaking where he stood though it was from anger and not fear, and Mauro looked embarrassed that he had been taken out of the fight so easily.

"Don't worry Charlie, it's going to be OK," Laura whispered to her friend. "And the revenge we're going to have on that fucking asshole is going to be sweet."

"Just wait until I get my hands on him, I'm going to rip his God damned head clean off his shoulders," Kori agreed, though Mauro kept silent at his internal struggle between failure, worry and anger.

It took a couple of minutes, which to the squad felt like a lifetime, for Stephanie to reappear jogging towards the dorm accompanied by none other than the large chief instructor. If Charlie had been conscious he would've preferred literally anyone else but him, but the chief immediately scooped the broken cadet up carefully in his arms and carried him away toward the medical unit. Before he left he muttered a low "Stay here," to the group, to which there came no reply, though there was silent obedience from the group of four.

Chapter 14

"Why must you continue to wake up from some life-threatening ordeal in my medical unit?" Dr. Kono's voice was all Charlie could hear when his consciousness returned to him and though he hadn't even opened his eyes yet, the doctor somehow knew that he was back in the land of the living.

"I... just love it here... so bad," Charlie replied slowly then opened his eyes to be greeted with an offensively bright light coming from all around him in the room. "Instructor Shepherd?" he asked surprised as his gaze fell upon his private tutor. She waved in response but didn't say a word.

"Follow my finger," the doctor instructed while holding up a single scaly digit before Charlie's eyes. It moved from right to left and back again and Charlie followed it with his eyes. "Do you feel this?" he said and then pinched Charlie's nose.

"Yes," he replied almost comically nasally but also casually, "but it doesn't hurt?" It was more of a question than a statement as Charlie was almost positive that one of the first blows that Henderson had landed had broken his nose. Then it dawned on him as to what that meant.

"How long have I been here for?" he asked slightly panicked.

"Well, in terms of earth years..." Kono looked forlorn and winced slightly before speaking again.

"YEARS?" Charlie practically shouted before Kono could complete his sentence.

"Oh come on Kono, that isn't nice," Shepherd piped up from the corner of Charlie's field of vision. "It's not even been a day Charlie, just a few hours."

"...as I was saying, in terms of earth years... it would be zero," Kono finished. Then he broke into a wide toothy lizard grin which made Charlie feel both slightly scared and slightly more at ease.

Charlie then looked at Shepherd. "You aren't a normal instructor, are you?" he asked flatly. He wasn't sure if he'd come to this conclusion before or if it was just that right now it was the first thing he'd concluded, but it didn't matter, he was positive that something was different about her.

Dawn Shepherd looked slightly surprised at Charlie's statement, but after a moment of feigned shock she spoke. "So what am I? Some sort of alien?" she asked, challenging Charlie's assessment.

He thought for a moment then spoke clearly. "No, you're human, but not military," he started. "Your acting skills are not up to par but you do like to try. Your training methods are different to anyone else's, focussing more on the thought process than actually completing the task. You care for cadets in a way that other instructors don't and you seem to be closely linked to Dr. Kono here."

"So what does that all add up to then, Sherlock?" Shepherd teased.

"You're a... counsellor? Or therapist? Something like that. I've been to a few myself actually but you don't fit the bill exactly," Charlie summarised.

Shepherd practically beamed at Charlie's words. "You have a way of deducing things don't you?" she asked, but didn't wait for a reply. "You're right of course - I'm not really either a counsellor or a therapist, rather I am here specifically to ensure the mental wellbeing of the cadets, where Kono here is much more attuned to the physical side of things, as you might have been able to tell from his humour. Actually, thinking about it, what do you make of Dr. Kono?"

Charlie looked at the doctor for a very long moment and squinted his eyes a few times. Eventually he spoke of his in depth deductions. "He's a lizard," he stated flatly.

Shepherd blinked, then burst into laughter at Charlie's joke. Even the doctor chuckled to himself though it was hard to hear over the instructor. Eventually she calmed herself and managed to pull a sentence together. "Anything else? Maybe next you'll tell us you think he's a doctor!" She laughed again and it made Charlie chuckle too. Sometimes everything around here was just so serious.

"OK," Charlie said eventually being more serious now. "He's here as a medical doctor and clearly has the ability to tend to our physical needs. He's versed in both human genetics and our physical bodies so I would assume that he is also a very good scientist – by our standards anyway. The fact that we don't have a human doctor here also reinforces that fact, so I'd say he's doing more research on us than we think. Now, combined with some other factors..." Charlie was reluctant to talk about his unlocked PIP level when the walls could very possibly have ears, "... I believe that he also sees himself as a bit of an authority unto himself, and will skirt the limits of what's allowed to get the results he's looking for."

This time both Shepherd and the doctor were amazed because Charlie had once again been right on the money.

"Almost," the doctor replied once he'd managed to close his mouth from the excitement. "I won't just skirt the limits of what's allowed – I'll fragrantly ignore them!" He paused with a toothy grin. "With that being said, I have a bit of an experiment I'd like to try out with you."

Charlie didn't like the sound of that and Shepherd's posture went practically rigid at the statement.

"Your nose has entirely repaired itself Charlie. It was definitely broken when you arrived here earlier, and in fact your bruises have all but faded," the doctor said with an air of curiosity in his voice.

"You don't want to..." Charlie started having caught the doctor's meaning almost immediately. He looked at Shepherd with wide eyes until she caught on.

"You can't!" she protested, "I won't allow... that."

"I assure you it will be entirely safe, instructor," the doctor said. "And as painless as possible. Of course I wouldn't be so brash as to say that it will be completely painless..."

"No," Shepherd said with authority and Charlie immediately saw that she had some pull over what Kono could and couldn't do.

"Charlie, I want you to know that this really is necessary for my research," the doctor spoke to the cadet without addressing Shepherd's objection and Charlie could tell that his own decision would be enough to sway the instructor's.

"What do you want to do, exactly?" Charlie asked slowly.

"Well, I'd like to break some of your bones," Kono said seriously and Charlie let out a snort.

"Then, I'd like to see if your body repairs itself as quickly as it has done with your nose and bruises here. Of course I can break your bones through medical procedures and under anaesthetic so you wouldn't feel a thing, but afterwards, while you're healing, it could get a little sore."

"You think I'm going to stand here and allow you to torture the boy?" Shepherd asked loudly.

"It's not *torture*, the doctor practically hissed. "This is scientific experimentation to help all of us and not least Charlie here. Imagine knowing that your body will repair itself in a given amount of time, and also knowing how long that could take and what factors could speed it up? How do you think we learn all of this information instructor?"

"I... um... I think I'd like to give it a go," Charlie interrupted their argument. "But slowly. Like break my nose again first and time it. I know how much that one hurts and I can take it. Then next week do an arm – just, I don't want to miss out on any training OK?"

Shepherd's mouth hung agape at Charlie's words and the doctor grinned hungrily. Charlie could tell that he thrived on learning new information and this was one of those times where their goals would align. He really did want to know if and how fast his body could heal itself. He also wanted to know if any of the other cadets had that ability too – something he could test out on one cadet in particular.

Charlie spent the night in the medical unit because Shepherd wouldn't let him out of her sight, or even alone with the doctor. She'd reassured him and let him know on no less than ten occasions that he could change his mind at any time, then it would all stop but Charlie was not ready to quit just yet.

The doctor had quickly injected four places around his nose with the local anaesthetic and after just a few moments to allow the solution to work its way in, the lizard-man quickly punched Charlie hard in the face. Shepherd had initially objected to the barbaric method, though the doctor said that it was the quickest and easiest way to get the result he needed from the experiment and after all, it was too late anyway.

The strike didn't hurt in the slightest although it did knock Charlie unconscious. As his vision faded to black the last thing he could think about was how exactly the doctor was planning on breaking his arms, legs or, heaven forbid, his spine.

Kono and Shepherd kept Charlie under observation all night until they were sure he wasn't going to awaken in horrific pain. To the contrary, what they did witness was the bruising around his nose and eyes all but disappear over just a few short hours, his nose slowly but surely righting itself. By the time morning had come around, you wouldn't have even been able to tell that Charlie had been injured.

"Charlie?" Shepherd's voice woke the cadet from his dreams of breaking Henderson's nose in the name of science.

"No... not ready to get up yet... break something else," Charlie joked dryly as he opened his eyes and the instructor smiled down at him.

"Maybe next week," she said. "It's time for you to go get ready for breakfast."

The first thing Charlie did before making a move to get up and out of bed was to bring his hands up to his face to assess the damage. To his surprise, though, he felt nothing out of place and, much more importantly, no pain.

"You did… quite well," Kono said as he entered the room. "Six hours to mend the break and then a short time for the bruising to disappear. Extraordinary, really Charlie."

The statement made Charlie smile to himself almost to the point of blushing. It seemed that every time he interacted with the doctor he had something positive to take away, and this was a biggie; no longer would he have to worry about hurting himself, safe in the knowledge that his own body was now very much on his side.

Instructor shepherd passed him his clothes for the day, saving him from having to get back to his dorm dressed in just a medical gown – which had been a mild worry but something he had been prepared to do. Upon inspection there was something slightly off about this new uniform though and when he unfurled it he could see what it was. Along the arms and legs were a single golden pinstripe running their length and on the left shoulder sat a single, hollow outline of a golden chevron.

"This… isn't mine," Charlie said as he came to the conclusion that this was either not really for him, or the much less likely scenario that he had just been promoted.

"Oh, it is though Charlie. I'm happy to announce that you have been promoted to the rank of 'Ordinary Cadet'," she burst into a wide smile and added "congratulations, you earned it."

Charlie's expression didn't convey a sense of pride and accomplishment though, rather the opposite. The first thing that he could think of was that this was just another thing to single him out from the rest of the class. He was tired of everyone thinking he was different and the last thing he wanted was a bright golden badge to remind everyone of that fact.

Un-ecstatic as he was though, Charlie donned his new uniform – which fitted as though it was made to measure – and made his way out of the medical unit and across the way into the mess hall where he knew everyone was already. He had a few visions of entering the room and everyone becoming silent at his entry because of his new uniform, but when he actually entered not a soul noticed. The cadets were bunched around one of the tables not taking any notice of anything that was happening around them. As he drew nearer, he recognised the four faces at the centre of the mass: Laura Giardini, Mauro Latori, Kori Nakamura and Stephanie Marsh.

Charlie slunk his way through the crowd, which was by no means an easy feat, and when he arrived at the table he saw what everyone had been so concerned with – the rest of his squad wore the uniforms of Ordinary Cadets too - gold pinstripe and a hollow golden chevron included. What Charlie then realised was that the rest of the cadets didn't seem to be berating them for their promotions, rather they were offering congratulations, asking advice on how to get there and also presenting their shock that the squad had remained intact during the Gauntlet, when no one else had. Matty Henderson, though, was nowhere to be seen.

"ATTENTION!" The loud voice filled the mess hall as Charlie made it to the epicentre of the gathering and took a place on the bench beside Laura, who smiled at him with a question mark, though didn't make a sound so as not to invite Cesari's wrath.

"As you may all be aware, and I take it from your current positioning in the mess hall, the Sinclair squad as a whole has been promoted to the rank of Ordinary Cadets. This is a reward for achieving first place on the leaderboard from this week's Gauntlet." Cesari said. He was smiling which Charlie immediately took to mean that he wasn't unhappy with the development, rather quite the opposite, and that made him feel tense. The chief instructor continued. "You all now have a squad to aspire to and to look up to. These cadets are now your betters and it would be wise for all of you to try your utmost to emulate them." With each word he spoke, his grin grew wider and Charlie's own expression grew grimmer and grimmer.

The faces of the cadets that Charlie could see also contorted mostly in unhappiness, though a few looked absolutely disgusted at the statement and Charlie knew that things were about to get a whole lot worse for him and his friends.

"There are of course perks of promotion," Cesari began his closing statement and Charlie's ears pricked up at that. "The specialised training centres are available only to Ordinary and Able cadets. These are designed to further your abilities in your given specialisations and I expect you to all take advantage of these centres when you are able to." He looked directly at Charlie when he spoke his last few words. "Your very lives may depend on the skills you will hone during your time here, so do not waste a moment."

Charlie couldn't tell if the chief instructor was giving him a warning for his own good or a threat, but either way the result was the same – he needed to train as hard as he had ever done to ensure he grew properly in both stature and skill. Added to his internal to-do list was to survive whatever Henderson had in store for him whenever the boy returned from where he was hiding.

Eventually the mess hall returned to the cadets eating their breakfast and now giving the 'Sinclair Squad' a wide berth, understandable, given the fact that everyone had effectively been told the squad was better than them. Mauro practically didn't notice the change though, stuffing a toasted muffin topped with sweet strawberry jam into his face-hole.

"The thing is..." Mauro spoke with his mouth overflowing, "If we just keep training at that specialised thing... we're just going... to get better than everyone else, right?" He swallowed his mouthful at the end of his sentence as though it punctuated his statement.

"Yes... but I doubt that it's going to last very long, I mean everyone will have to get promoted eventually won't they?" Laura asked and Charlie could tell she was anxious about the situation.

Charlie nodded along with the group's pondering until he reached out with the question he'd forgotten to ask.

"What did you do for your R&R?" he asked.

"Oh man, you aren't going to believe it..." Mauro replied half excitedly and half conspiratorially. We had... PIZZA!"

Charlie snorted out a laugh at Mauro's excitement, and when the larger heavy arms cadet didn't offer anything past the food they'd eaten, Kori Nakamura interjected. "There's a whole bunch of sports fields just through the valley there," he nodded in the general direction of 'outside'. "Football, basketball, ultimate frisbee, tennis – you could go on the assault course..." he smiled at that fond memory.

"So basically things that are fun and involve some kind of fitness?" Charlie asked, having come to the conclusion that this 'R&R' was more like cardio in disguise; still, the others made it sound fun so he didn't want to rain on their parade too much.

"Honestly it was quite fun," Laura replied. "Plus I got to take down a few people playing frisbee," she smashed a fist into her hand as she spoke and smiled menacingly, though Charlie could see that it was harmless fun.

"We didn't get our promotions until this morning so people weren't as annoyed with us as I think they are now," Stephanie offered. "It was fun though – I played some tennis."

Charlie didn't envy the squad their relaxation time, but he also didn't want to tell them about the secret and somewhat unethical experimentations that he'd been subjected to. Thankfully for him, either none of the squad had realised that he had healed extraordinarily quickly, or they simply didn't want to ask. It did stand to reason though, that perhaps they just thought that the alien doctor had some advanced tech that could get them back to normal, no questions asked.

"What about... you know who?" Charlie asked eventually after looking around to find the large, aggressive Henderson still absent.

Stephanie went bright red at the mention of Henderson's absence and Charlie immediately recognised that something had happened after he was taken away.

To save her the embarrassment of telling the story, Kori spoke before she became too uncomfortable.

"This one played a masterclass," he said pointing a thumb at Stephanie who reddened still. She found Henderson after you went off to get your healing done, then told him that she wanted to tell him all about our squad's secret deal with Cesari to make everyone look bad. She worked him up to such a frenzy that he was practically calling for Cesari's head by the end of it... but the best part about it? She'd done it all while broadcasting a comms signal to the officer's mess! The chief basically flipped out and threw Matty in solitary for a few days to 'cool off', I've never seen anything like it and Cesari was *so so* mad."

Charlie looked at Stephanie, who despite looking proud of herself, he could tell that she was quite ashamed of her deception and he looked to comfort her.

"Thank you, Stephanie," Charlie said earnestly. "Honestly I've never had anyone fight my corner before like you guys all do." The girl rose a little in her seated position, buoyed by his words.

"Hang on," Charlie said coming to a realisation. "How the hell did you send a comms signal?"

"Oh you haven't realised?" Mauro said as though he was the cock of the walk. "There's a smaller portable terminal in the drawers under your personal terminal in your room. I can't believe you didn't know about it!"

"Oh shut up Mauro," Laura berated him. "You wouldn't have known about if it Stephanie hadn't told you, none of us would."

Charlie smiled at Mauro's attempted deception and was excited to have a go on the personal terminal that they were talking about. He wondered how many of the cadets knew about it, though he feared the secret was probably already out by now. It didn't matter anyway – he couldn't take the thing out whilst training so at best it was just another way to check his stats at the start or the end of the day.

"So tell me more about this pizza? Is it better than the one I had on the way here?" Charlie asked Mauro, who immediately returned to his annoyance that Charlie may have had pizza before him. Wanting not to be outdone though, he proceeded to tell Charlie all about how this particular pizza, was the best pizza ever made.

Chapter 15

Charlie had decided not to bring up the subject of his miraculous recovery to the rest of the group and, to his relief, none of the others brought it up either. He wasn't sure if that was because they didn't realise what'd happened, or if it just didn't factor as an interesting thing in their daily lives. Either way, he didn't want to outright lie to his friends, but he knew that telling them the entire truth was a dangerous game to play, especially after the warnings he'd already received about precisely that.

The next week had begun with lessons as normal, though it was apparent that an unexpected by-product of wearing the next-level Ordinary Cadet's uniform was that Charlie was called on first for every single question, example or practical demonstration, being the only Special Ops specialisation to have achieved that rank. It wasn't particularly difficult as he generally was able to carry out the given tasks anyway, though it did ruin his plans to stay well hidden within the pack. If anything, the uniform was akin to wearing a sash and badge that both said 'happy birthday!' – at best it got you some attention, at worst it made people want to push you over. True to statistical form, Charlie experienced both ends of the spectrum.

For the second week of training, there were two new lessons introduced to Charlie's group of sixty Spec Ops cadets, namely 'Combat Manoeuvres' and 'Special Units', although if Charlie thought that this meant that a lesson was going to be replaced, he was sorely mistaken. The other lessons were shortened slightly, but the addition of these two new classes added an extra hour to the length of the cadets' days. This not only meant that there was more to learn and absorb, but also the levels of fatigue that began to be displayed throughout the entire group were palpable.

Tacked on to the end of the working day, the two classes were to be taken back to back and first up was the Combat Manoeuvres class. Cesari, who was the instructor for the Special Ops cadets in this class, collected the cadets from their PT session where Charlie had swapped his tact of weights first, and run afterwards so that he wasn't totally exhausted for whatever this new class would bring.

The group followed silently deeper into the valley and eventually out the other side completely. It was odd to think that this was the first time Charlie had actually left the safety of the high rock walls of the camp, though in truth the new environment relieved some unknown claustrophobia he had been harbouring and when he was greeted with the sight of open dirt and sands, his shoulders dropped, relaxing slightly.

Before the cadets was a mixture of rolling sand dunes that rose and dipped away into the distance, patches of hard packed orange mud and the occasional thin and unhealthy looking tree or bush. Charlie couldn't fathom exactly what they were expected to do out here, but had the feeling that with Cesari at the helm, it wasn't going to be pleasant.

"Cadets!" he shouted snapping Charlie and everyone else to attention. "Welcome to Combat Manoeuvres, you're going to love this." He grinned menacingly. "Your goal in this class is to learn that you will not always have equal or stable footing with your enemy. Sometimes the very terrain beneath your feet will cause you almost as many problems as those who seek to kill you. Sometimes your enemy will have stable firing positions where you may not." Charlie remembered the Gauntlet and how that sounded very much like what Cesari was talking about here.

"You will be expected to traverse terrain under fire. You will be expected to move while firing. No matter how skilled you may or may not be at the firing range," Charlie was sure that Cesari was looking him dead in the eye as he spoke these words, "when there is no stable base to fire from, that does not mean you will simply lay down your weapons and accept your fate. Do you understand?"

"Yes Chief Instructor," The chorus replied as one in perfect synchronicity.

"Now we need a volunteer to demonstrate to the class the importance of the techniques you are going to learn from here on out." He scanned the class a little over dramatically for Charlie's liking then stopped squarely on him. "Sinclair, you're up as our resident 'best efforts' at creating a Special Ops cadet." 'Shocker', Charlie thought.

Charlie took two steps forward but before he could take any more the rumbling sound of an engine roared behind the cadets and they all turned as one to see what was making it. Rolling up towards them was a large four by four sand buggy type vehicle laden with camo rucksacks, high-tech looking weapons and other assorted equipment. The buggy then proceeded to drive around to the front of the group and tip its contents onto the ground before the class.

"Oh, and one last thing. In a combat situation you will be expected to be carrying your gear, so…" Cesari stated menacingly.

Charlie was the first to pick up a backpack, which must've been filled with bricks because it was extremely heavy. In addition he clipped a water canteen on a belt around his waist along with two ammunition magazines before turning his attention to the weapons on the floor. He didn't recognise them, but they seemed like they were much more up to date than what they'd been using at the firing range.

"The weapons you see before you are the Mark Four Standard Tactical Assault Rifle, or STAR. These weapons are the standard issue for new marines of the earth military because of their reliability and effectiveness. Eighty five round mag, seven hundred rounds per minute and if you hold the trigger you'll be spent in round about seven seconds, and that, boys and girls is a position you do not want to be in. You will be expected to learn everything about these weapons during your time at Camp Rebirth though today these weapons are not to be fired." Cesari narrated the efforts of the cadets gearing up and eventually there was nothing left on the ground before them save for disturbed dust and sand.

Charlie took another step forward once the class had come to a halt and stood to attention before Cesari. The chief instructor was huge and stoic though Charlie did feel that he himself was actually beginning to grow taller against the larger man's frame, and wondered if the accelerated growth of the GAP program cadets would eventually allow them to outstrip their instructor's impressive stature.

"Sinclair," Cesari said officially. "You are to move in that direction," he pointed off into the distance, "retrieve the flag that stands there and return it to me."

Charlie squinted but no matter how hard he tried he couldn't see any flag and assuming that it was obscured by sand dunes, hills or other features of the landscape, he decided to simply start moving at a walking pace.

"You have ten minutes," Cesari said loudly to which Charlie responded by moving quicker though he was impaired by his backpack, weapon and equipment.

The first difficulty that Charlie found on his journey towards the mysterious flag, was that trying to move up a slight incline in the sand whilst weighed down substantially, was nigh on impossible. The sand kept falling away beneath his feet and no matter how hard he willed his legs to move, he simply kept sliding back down, scoring deep cuts into the hills.

"You're dead, Sinclair!" Called Cesari, who was apparently aiming a rifle at him. "Move faster!"

Charlie changed tact at that and decided to start moving at an angle along the first sand-hill. It made things easier though his movements were still taxing and strained.

"Dead again Sinclair! If you don't start moving then I'm going to come up there and run *you* up the flag pole!"

Try as he might though, Charlie simply couldn't get up the hill quickly enough without Cesari calling out about his failure and eventually the chief instructor called time on Charlie's endeavours.

"What you are looking at here," Cesari gestured towards Charlie who was both sweating and panting, "is an example of how trying to do something by yourself can be a futile endeavour."

Charlie's jaw dropped at the instructor's words and he immediately felt as though he was being made a fool of by Cesari once more.

"Teamwork will be essential for you in many situations that you may find yourselves in. There will not always be perfect concrete roads for you to drive down in APC's, there will not always be jets, carriers or even spaceships to give you support out there in the universe and this is a lesson that you will need to learn now if you are going to make it as soldiers," Cesari concluded.

The session then moved onto ways in which the cadets needed to work together to make it up and over the inclines and dips with their equipment in tow, sometimes the group holding each other in daisy-chain like lines, other times they simply passed the equipment between them as they moved. One time the group even lay flat on the floor so that others could crawl up and over them but the one thing that was for definite was that together the task was manageable where alone, Charlie had failed.

The lesson finished after the group had all made it to the flag and back and Cesari had them moving along the compacted flatter ground in waves to complete the lesson. The front line would move forward and kneel, pointing their weapons to cover the advance of the second line who would filter through and past them to take a knee of their own and so on and so on. This way of movement ensured that the cadets covered each other at all times and also maintained a constant stream of advance in a forward direction, all of which seemed so simple to Charlie, though actually getting the movements synchronised as a group did take some practise.

Eventually Cesari called a halt and the cadets moved out in search of their next lesson: Special Units. Charlie was expecting the group to be collected by a new instructor and taken away to the location of the next lesson, but Cesari told them to wait in place for the rest of the class. This would be the first time that different specialisations would be mixed, and Charlie dreaded the thought of being paired up with the heavy assault cadets – and Henderson, who he was still yet to see after their fight. Well more accurately, Charlie's beating.

The cadets that arrived though were thankfully support class – which meant that Charlie got to see his friend Stephanie again, and although they weren't as close as he Laura and Mauro, he was glad to see a friendly and smiling face – not to mention another Ordinary Cadet to take some of the focus off of him.

The class that ensued was completely different to anything Charlie had experienced before and he could start to see how the different roles would interact within a squad. Each Special Ops cadet was given a partner from the support class – Charlie had mercifully been paired up with Stephanie – who was then given a drone equipped with a camera to fly up into the air over the dunes. The Spec Ops cadet then was blindfolded, spun around a few times and through an earpiece needed to make it to the flag again, only this time with just the Support cadet as their eyes and ears. For this first class that was pretty much the extent of the lesson and it was tricky though not impossible. However, Cesari said that as the lessons went on there would be the introduction of obstacles and other hidden dangers for the cadets to deal with, each lesson therefore becoming more difficult and more complex than the last.

"I'm just glad I got you to the flag and back without you disappearing off down a hole," Stephanie said with a shrug. "It's a good thing we've been practising with those drones every day otherwise I'd have had no idea how to get you there."

"You did great, Stephanie," Charlie reassured the girl though her expression was still a little forlorn. "Next time I guess we'll have more to deal with then, huh?"

The pair were the first to make it back to the mess hall out of the squad of five that they usually preferred and were talking about the lesson they'd shared. Charlie found Stephanie to be a quiet girl, though once he got her talking she did seem to come out of her shell somewhat.

"Guess who just got the high score in the Assault training?" Kori's voice practically oozed with cockiness as he slumped down at the table alongside Charlie and Stephanie, shortly followed by Mauro, though the group still lacked Laura.

"You only got the high score because I was on your team watching your back," Mauro replied with a smile. "If I hadn't been there to take out that drone behind you, you'd have gone down for sure!"

The pair picked at each other for a few moments before filling in the rest of the squad as to what their training had entailed. It seemed that the assault cadets had to make it across an obstacle-laden battlefield defended by drones that shot tasers at them when they presented themselves as targets. Working together with a fixed-in-place heavy weapons cadet on a turret, it seemed that once again the lesson had been focussed on both movement and teamwork, though Charlie did wonder what the recon cadets were getting up to whilst all of this was happening, not having another specialisation to partner up with.

The week seemed to pass by in the blink of an eye for Charlie, who barely had anything else to do other than train, learn, eat and sleep. In the morning he was up so early with his squad to join instructor Shepherd on the assault course, and the additional lessons in the afternoon meant that if he thought exhaustion was a thing before, he had no idea what real tiredness was because this was simply on another level. He did have one thing to look forward to though, and that was R&R.

With the choice to do whatever the cadets liked within the confines of Camp Rebirth during their downtime, Charlie chose to ignore his alarm call in lieu of getting a few more hours of well deserved rest. He was motivated generally of course, but sometimes you just had to pay back that sleep debt if you wanted to survive the next week, and that is exactly what he did as a matter of urgency in his first ever R&R day.

When Charlie eventually awoke and rolled out of bed he did the usual – check to make sure his body had healed from any injuries he'd incurred, then turned to the full length mirror in his room to see what changes his body had been through so far. Another week having passed, the changes were clear and stark.

Charlie's hair had grown back to about an inch in length, which was still quite short for his liking but was displaying growth that he'd never expected. He was certainly taller and very evidently more muscular as the training he had been participating in was sculpting his both young and genetically enhanced body. His face though, that was something he had to lean in closer to fully appreciate. His jawline was positively defined and he could start to see the beginnings of tiny black hairs upon his chin and if he really had to put an age on how he looked as a whole, he would have said sixteen.

Shocked, he turned to his terminal to bring up his body stats and the first thing he confirmed was that both his height and muscle mass had increased again. His PIP level too had reached eight percent and he filled with warmth at the continued growth on paper that he was experiencing. He made a mental note to find out what levels his friends were and although he wanted to know what everyone's level was in the camp, he knew that was probably a bit of a wish too far.

Charlie decided that with his newfound and greatly rested body, the first thing he wanted to do with his R&R time was to complete the baseline testing again to actually get a good idea of what improvements he'd made on a tangible level. Pulling on his flight suit, he left his room behind and entered the communal living room where Laura was also entering from her room at the same time.

"Good morning Sinclair," she said in a mocking tone that was clearly meant to be an impression of Cesari. "Why aren't you out on the training fields turning that useless body of yours into something better?"

Charlie smiled at the attempt but didn't bite her bait. It was a good try at an impression but she just couldn't get her voice to go as deep as the Chief Instructor's.

"Well I was just on my way actually," Charlie mimicked her deeper attempt. "I just wanted to make sure that we could practise some teamwork first. Teamwork is everything here, and you are only as strong as your weakest link."

The pair laughed and Laura told Charlie that the others had already left for breakfast and most probably had already finished that, so it was just the two of them to have their breakfast together. Charlie enjoyed Laura's company and took no issue with the others leaving early – she always had such a matter of fact way of saying things that was refreshing to hear, it was what he liked about her the most.

Breakfast for the day was a choice – which was something Charlie had never expected to see, though Laura told him it was like this last week when he'd been out of action for their first ever R&R day. It was a huge buffet of all kinds of cooked foods, bacon, sausages, three kinds of eggs, toast, cereals, fruits and everything Charlie had ever imagined that a posh hotel would provide for its guests in the morning. Not having had the opportunity before, Charlie piled his plate high with everything he could fit on it, regardless of if it went together or not. If the apple had a bit of bean sauce on there, so be it. Laura had porridge and a yoghurt which practically disgusted Charlie and he let her know it.

"I think I want to try the baseline tests again this morning," Charlie said once he was sure he couldn't physically fit any more food into his body. One thing he was grateful for at this very moment, was the fact that his gene-edited body seemed to be able to quickly use the food that he provided it with, meaning he was only sickeningly full for a few moments before he felt he could move around properly again.

"Really?" Laura started, then she caught herself as she realised why he might've wanted to carry out such a task. "You know it doesn't really count going from a zero to a one, right?" she joked at his expense. "Besides, I still don't think you'll beat me on anything now you don't have your wheelchair to cheat with."

Charlie made a mock effort at being offended, though in truth he knew that the joke was said in jest without any malice. It did remind him of some of the shade he'd received from some of the other cadets though, and the still notable absence of Matty Henderson, who presumably was still in some kind of confinement. Cesari must've been really pissed by whatever he'd said.

The pair joked for a little longer and Charlie couldn't help but notice that, like him, Laura had grown what must've translated into a number of years in the short time the cadets had been in Camp Rebirth. Her long black hair braided down her back looked as though it had grown noticeably and her figure was decidedly both more muscular and toned. Like him also, she'd definitely grown a couple of inches too.

Charlie led Laura to the first task that he'd attempted upon arriving at the camp, the strength test and happily it was entirely deserted, the other cadets apparently enjoying their free time. Charlie moved to the first wall though Laura stopped him with an outstretched arm and indicated silently that she wanted to try first. Charlie stepped back to let her pass.

Laura practically skipped through the first four weighted walls without so much as a strain in her expression and Charlie felt an immense amount of pride as he watched his friend carry out the task. He knew the fifth wall was heavy though and wondered at what point she would start to falter. To his amazement though, she made it through with a little effort. Then she passed wall six and Charlie felt his palms turn sweaty.

At wall seven, Charlie found himself almost screaming her words of encouragement and his own muscles straining in support as she dragged the weighted wall up and over her head, then stepped under it, quickly letting it fall back to the ground with a loud thud. Both cadets at this point looked amazed as the progress she'd made in such a short period of time was amazing, and had allowed her to lift the forty kilogram wall where before not a single other recruit had managed it – that was until Charlie stepped up to the first wall. Charlie had made it to wall number eight, a full fifty kilograms.

The tone was set right then and there for the rest of the day with the pair exceeding every single record that'd been set just two weeks ago and in most cases smashing right through them. Charlie and Laura both completed the speed and agility course in record times with both grabbing a hold of two of the extra point rings available on the course, then both hitting every target on the firing range with the archaic Lee Enfield rifles. It was the hand to hand combat test that Charlie was unsure of, having still not actually been on the winning side of any of the real fights he'd had at the camp.

"Don't go easy on me," Charlie said happily as the pair faced off against each other on the hot sands. He raised his hands in a boxing-style approach to signify the fact that he was ready and Laura took her previous open handed grappling-style stature in response.

Laura didn't take any chances though, knowing that Charlie was now stronger than her, though she had the speed advantage as well as the technique. She lunged for Charlie looking for the double leg takedown but Charlie had seen it coming, analysing both her posture and previous fight in the blink of an eye. He didn't move out of the way though, he simply threw his legs back and wrapped his arms around her neck so that she was facing the ground and he was on top of her. For Laura this was her worst nightmare – the stronger opponent had got a hold of her and it was going to be murder to get him off.

She threw her body to the side and spun underneath Charlie who was pretty unsure of what was happening beneath him, until Laura took a hold of his collar in a baseball bat choke and within a moment that he couldn't help but struggle in, he was forced to tap out to her superior technique.

"You need to show me how you did that," Charlie coughed and Laura simply smiled back at him.

"Again," she said.

The pair fought over and over and whenever the bouts came to grapples, Laura won without reply – though Charlie never stopped learning. Whenever the fight was left standing and striking, Charlie couldn't be matched as he was able to read the throws of punches and kicks without too much effort, dodging and parrying with seemingly little effort. It was in these matches that Laura asked Charlie for his instruction and though his end of the fight was probably around ninety percent instinct, he tried to help her where he could and narrated what he was actually doing to keep her off balance.

As much as it didn't sound very much like rest and relaxation, both of the cadets never stopped smiling between rounds and before they knew it the day was over. They'd been training for the entire day and were drenched with sweat and sand, a few patches of blood and a bruise or two but nothing that would last more than a couple of hours, Charlie knew, and if Laura didn't already, she was going to find out the next morning.

Eventually as the day drew itself out they had to retire to the mess hall for dinner, followed by a debriefing both to and from Mauro, Kori and Stephanie who'd spent the day playing football. Although they weren't as battered and bruised as Charlie and Laura, they were just as sweaty and possibly even dirtier. As far as the group was concerned as a whole, sleep couldn't come soon enough.

Chapter 16

When Charlie reached the weights area for the first time after a weekend of R&R (though truthfully it couldn't be called either rest or relaxation), he wasn't sure what to expect. Having beasted through the baseline tests to somewhat of a shock, a part of him knew that pushing weights and running track should've been easy.

Lying flat on his back beneath the long barbell, Charlie had loaded forty kilos onto it as he already knew he could lift that weight over his head without too much difficulty. He breathed out once and hefted the bar into a bench press. Not feeling as though the effort was too taxing, he then pushed it again, and again, and again and to his surprise before he knew it he'd managed fifteen reps of the thing.

It wasn't a full and bending bar of course, but compared to just a couple of weeks prior, the feat was absolutely nothing short of miraculous. Testing himself with heavier and heavier weights on the bar, Charlie found that he maxed out at around seventy five kilos, which was more than his own body weight and, not that he would know it right now, but for his age and weight category, this would've actually constituted a world record.

Laura, who had arrived at the training location having apparently been allowed to leave her previous lesson early for whatever reason the instructor had allowed, joined him. She did not manage the same feat and couldn't help but both encourage Charlie and face bewilderment at his miraculous development.

"How the fuck did you lift that, Charlie?" were the exact words she used, though Charlie couldn't think of an answer quickly or assuredly enough and said "I'm not really sure." Laura narrowed her eyes.

"Is there something you need to tell me?" She asked in an accusatory tone which Charlie didn't like, though upon reflection he knew that he was hiding something from her, and as they spent more time together he felt that he could trust her with his secret – the one thing that he'd been warned not to do for fear of harsh repercussions. Charlie internalised the whole situation and concluded that if he didn't come clean now, it would mean an outright lie – then possibly an end to their friendship in the future, a price that he was not willing to pay.

"I...," Charlie started to speak but his voice caught in his throat. Clearing it, he tried again. "I don't have a lock on my PIP level," he said quietly in an exhale and immediately he felt a weight he hadn't known was there melt away from his back. His shoulders relaxed and fell and he looked into Laura's eyes to search for the disapproval he knew she would feel.

"And...?" She asked.

"And... nothing," Charlie replied, not exactly sure he knew what she was getting at.

"So that's it, you don't have a lock on your PIP level?" She asked with narrower eyes still. "What does that even mean?"

Charlie didn't realise what she'd missed in the statement, though thinking about it he could see that the statement alone didn't really hold much weight without the explanation that the doctor had given when he'd explained it to Charlie himself. So he then spilled the beans about everything and anything, from the moment he woke up on the space ship to the first time Kono had broken his nose in his experimentations.

"He broke your nose again?" Laura asked at the end of Charlie's speech. Apparently it was the thing she cared about the most – not that he was a miracle of nature, not that he was strong as an ox and not even that he could heal broken bones in a matter of hours – it was the fact that a doctor would intentionally cause him pain and harm.

"Don't they have to say an oath or something to do no harm?" She asked in a bit of a frenzy.

"I think so," Charlie replied. "But I don't know if that counts for lizard doctors or not. In any case I said he could do it."

"I don't care if you let him do it, it's not right Charlie, don't you see? You have to see that?" Her anger was somewhat overtaken by the concern for his wellbeing and Charlie could do nothing but feel utter care and concern from his best friend. He could see now that she didn't care what he was, how strong or advanced he was becoming; all that she cared about and all that she had ever cared about was the fact that he was cared for and happy.

"I... I don't know how to deal with this Charlie," she said slowly and he could see a tear welling in the corner of her eye. In the end though, rather than saying anything more, she hugged him and held him tightly against her body.

The two cadets hugged for a long while and Charlie could feel Laura's shoulders rise and fall which betrayed her hidden tears of concern and he imagined her anger toward the people who had caused him harm. Eventually though she pushed him away to arm's length, wiped her face and announced, "so you think you're strong do you?" with a bit of a forced smile attached.

If Charlie had any inclination that Laura had been going easy on him before, those thoughts were well behind him as the two spent a good hour training their hand to hand combat skills next to the weights and benches with a group of cadets watching their bouts. It was strange though as Charlie felt as if they were the only two cadets in the world locked in some private dance that nobody else could see; he didn't even hear the cheering and jeering as Laura pressed her will unto Charlie, taking him down at almost every turn.

In the end, both of the cadets were battered and broken and retired happily and quietly to their respective rooms for the night to rest and recover.

The next morning, Charlie was awoken early by the alarm sound coming from the terminal on the desk and groggily made his way over to answer it. He wasn't happy about it and knew that he hadn't managed to get in a full night's rest, but when doctor Kono appeared and ordered him to make his way immediately to the medical bay, he snapped to attention and put on his clothes. He did note too, that his body had completely healed and was ready for the next day's training.

Charlie thought about sneaking off to the doctor, but a niggle kept him from doing so right away and before he left, he knocked on Laura's door, told her to get dressed and to come with him to see the doctor. Laura didn't object even once.

"You didn't show up this week Charlie, I thought we had a deal?" The doctor said without looking up from his desk, though if he had he would've seen two cadets enter and not just Charlie.

"I don't care about your deal," Laura practically spat before Charlie could say a word in reply. "What you're doing is disgusting. Don't you have any sense of humanity?"

The lizard-man raised an eye to take in the two cadets and sighed before he spoke. "Funnily enough I am not a human, so at what point do you think I'd learn about a sense of humanity?" Kono replied. "And if you think what I am doing is disgusting then you might like to have a look into the history of your own race and you might see that large advances in many fields are made specifically because of hardships and pain, such as war for example."

"I don't care about history, I care about right now. History is there to teach us not to repeat our mistakes, not to encourage us to copy them," Laura countered and as much as Charlie knew that his friend was fighting his corner, he could see that neither Laura nor the doctor were going to change their thought process.

"Listen," Charlie said. "You're both right. It's a terrible thing to carry out experiments on people – when they don't agree to it – and it's also important to learn from history, but I really don't see any other way to learn the things I need to about myself, other than the way that we're going about it here."

"The doctor looked pleased at Charlie's words but Laura's expression didn't change. She didn't agree with any of this and she wanted everyone to know about it.

Charlie wondered if the doctor had called him in so that the two of them would be alone without the annoying presence of instructor Shepherd, though that plan had been well and truly foiled by the presence of Laura, who was as against the situation as the instructor was, if not more.

"If you really want to do this Charlie, I'll be here with you, but if you do anything that Charlie doesn't want," she pointed a finger at the doctor, "I'll break your nose and see how you like it."

Kono raised a scaly hand to his nose-slits and shrugged to himself and Charlie could tell that he was wondering how exactly Laura planned on carrying out her threat – even Charlie could see that the doctor didn't have a nose, per se, to break.

"Don't worry, this time the break will be under a general anaesthetic and will be carried out surgically," Kono said to Charlie as though that was going to make things better. "You aren't going to feel a thing."

The doctor was right of course. Charlie didn't feel a thing after he was rendered completely unconscious after the anaesthetic was administered and actually enjoyed the flying dream again that he didn't really know he'd been missing. Unbeknownst to him also, Laura stayed by his side until he awoke some hours later, the pair both missing the majority of their classes for the day - repercussions be damned.

When Charlie eventually woke up, Laura was sitting on the floor in a corner of the room and Kono was absorbed with something displayed on his terminal. He could see that twelve hours had passed on the digital clock on the wall and when he shyly moved his arms to his head to see how much they hurt, he was astounded to note that there was neither any pain nor a lack of range of movement.

"Huh?" he announced to the room. "Why didn't you do it?"He looked to Laura as if to ask if she had stopped the doctor in his experimentation but she simply looked back at him bewildered.

"Uh, Charlie," Kono said. "We did carry out the experiment. Your arm was broken completely and has fully healed in the time you have been under."

Charlie blinked at Laura who raised her eyebrows back at him and he could see the emotions that battled inside her – happiness that he was OK and sadness that he'd had to undergo such an ordeal. She couldn't really know though that in fact Charlie hadn't had to deal with any sort of ordeal, he had simply had to have a nice nap and wake up well rested and, all things considered, pretty happy.

Charlie stayed with the doctor for the remainder of the day to make sure that there was no residual damage and other than a few mobility and strength tests in the medical bay, which were nothing to write home about, it was a pretty boring ordeal. What he did find strange though, was the fact that none of his friends had come to see how he was and in his segregated existence he began to wonder if Laura had told the rest of the group about his deep dark secret, and that they'd decided that they didn't want to be friends with him anymore.

What he did learn later though, was that in reality they didn't have a moment to spare to talk about Charlie and how he was doing because Matty Henderson had finally made it out of confinement, and he was as pissed as pissed could be. The large cadet – although it was noted that because of his confinement, lack of training and proper nutrition, he was now not that much of a larger boy – had taken to making sure classes and training were as difficult as possible for Mauro, who was now larger than Henderson. Henderson was very careful though not to let his temper get the better of him, but he kept the group on edge during meal times by sitting within earshot, apparently trying to figure out exactly how they'd been promoted so quickly, still sure that Cesari had something to do with it. It was almost paranoia at this point and whenever the group of four Ordinary Cadets tried to ignore his presence, he'd make himself known again by speaking to them from his seat as though he was a part of their conversations. The group had decided not to interact with Henderson at all, though on occasion Laura had to pull Kori back from the edge of breaking that pledge as his temper got the better of him. Stephanie was the best at it though, as she was used to remaining mostly silent.

When Charlie rejoined the group it was breakfast time and he was happy to see all of his friends still grouped together comfortably. He was also happy to note that there still wasn't another Ordinary Cadet amongst all of Camp Rebirth, which made him feel pride for his squad above anything else. What he didn't like to see though was Matty Henderson sitting not five feet away from his friends with a murderous stare in his eyes.

"I know you can hear me Sinclair so I'm only going to say this once," Henderson said at a little over a whisper, though Charlie could definitely hear him clearly. "I'm going to get you for what you did. It might not be today, it might not be tomorrow, but I will get you."

Charlie chose to ignore the promise and barely even looked at Henderson before taking his seat amidst his friends and plopping his tray of porridge down on the table. Regardless of Henderson's words, he was happy to be back and there was nothing that was going to sour that mood today.

The group's conversation turned to the fact that Charlie had had a day's absence and there was little he could do to prevent it now. He'd already told Laura his secret and he knew that lying to his friends was simply not an option as it would only serve to make things worse for him in the long run. What he did do though, was get the group to wait until Henderson had finished his food and had moved away before he spilled the beans to the rest of his friends in a whisper. Laura looked pleased at his decision though the other reactions were mixed.

"You mean you can get stronger than me?" Mauro offered the first answer when Charlie had finished speaking, and after leaving a long pregnant pause.

"Afraid so, big man," Charlie smiled.

"Shit, and here I was thinking I'd be the one always looking after you," Mauro replied with a smile of his own.

"Don't worry Charlie, you'll never be better than me. And if you are stronger or faster then you'll never do it with as much style as I do," Kori offered with a smile of his own.

"I very much doubt that," Charlie replied. He was happy that his friends had taken the news so well and were so understanding as he had once imagined them all hating him forever for keeping this secret. It was in this moment that he realised what true friends were.

"I knew there was something different about you," Stephanie added her two cents, "I never imagined it was going to be something as big as this though Charlie. Do you know what this means?"

To Charlie's surprise, the timid girl had been the only one of the group to *really* understand what all of this meant, and he smiled at her in return.

"It means that my powers are going to be limitless," he said matter of factly, then threw in a wink to Mauro as he replied. "I'm going to be like superman."

The week passed with not much of anything different happening other than the new daily ritual of training before classes started. It was difficult but the group knew that whatever they could do to advance themselves as quickly as possible was going to help them out immensely in the long run. The cadets had also been told that their first inspection – and by aliens no less – was still on schedule to happen at the end of this week, so they needed to impress, or at least try to.

The early morning sessions had mostly turned into hand to hand combat drills, with two pairs of cadets going at each other until one tapped out, then the odd one out jumped right in. It made for difficult rounds but it meant that the training was intense and varied, placing members of the squad at advantages and disadvantages with varying amounts of rest in between. One cadet could be waiting for five minutes for one of the fighters to break through a defence, or they could tap out then almost immediately move into the next fight. All in all, the method was effective and all of the squad members felt more confident in fighting with each day that passed.

All of this was of course coupled with the fact that all of the cadets in the GAP program had grown in their physical stature, most presenting as late teens already in size and strength. The thing that Charlie noticed the most though was that the conventional schooling classes with Dr. Kono had been taking a strong hold in his – and presumably everyone else's - minds.

Concepts, ideas, histories and general knowledge had been embedded in Charlie's brain and the things he knew would sometimes shock him. For instance in one of his shooting classes he was tasked with firing on a distant moving target and he actually managed to calculate in an instant the time it would take for his round to meet the target, taking into account initial velocity, friction due to wind resistance and the almost indeterminate parabola of the travelling projectile. It wasn't a sit down and work it out kind of deal – his mind had just done it all for him. There was no way these alien inspectors were not going to be impressed with advances like those, they were just simply too impressive already.

Eventually the sixth day of the week arrived and along with it the transport ship that housed the inspection team. The cadets had all amassed outside the high metal gates of Camp Rebirth and stood to attention in five ranks of sixty whilst the small metal spaceship landed slowly before them. It seemed like a small ship to Charlie perhaps because he'd been expecting a huge battleship of some description, though in reality the vessel was a long cylindrical shape of about fifteen metres culminating into a point, and at its rear was a large cross with an engine pod at each point.

The cadets had learned nothing of spaceships, their design or the methods by which they functioned and this arrival had left most of them holding their breaths.

A door slid open at the centre of the ship and a ramp slid the short distance down to the ground. The cadets waited for their first glimpse of an alien being – and of course that was a lizard man.

The first alien life form to exit the transport, to the exhalation of the cadets, was a Kanaan, just like Kono. The similarities of race were very obvious, though this alien lizard creature wore a long black robe covered diagonally with a golden sash. He was also absent the doctor's almost human expressions that Charlie had grown to actually enjoy. This lizard looked both serious and annoyed.

Next came a large muscular creature with yellowish skin and four arms that it held together before itself in a regal like stance. It looked as though it was bald though Charlie couldn't tell if this was a hairstyle choice or if the race didn't actually grow hair. Judging by the stature of this alien though, he felt as though asking him would be a bad idea.

A third alien being then came into view as the first two started moving down the ramp to allow her space. This one was very different to the others though mostly because everyone could see that she didn't walk on just two legs. She had a long black tunic covering her entire body and most of her lower half, and Charlie could see that she walked on eight thin and sharp looking legs. She also wore a veil covering her head and face and Charlie theorised internally that this being didn't enjoy the bright sunlight of the planet.

When the aliens had made it down the ramp and had come to a halt, Cesari spoke to his cadets.

"Cadets, ATTENTION!" He yelled. "I present to you your sponsors from the Intergalactic Council. Jorell of the Ascara," The four armed alien nodded slightly. "Korvin of the Kanaan," The lizard-alien copied the gesture, "and Callantra, of the Scriven." The veiled octopod didn't have to gesture to let everyone know who she was, and that lack of greeting seemed to Charlie to telegraph the feeling that she felt like she was better than everyone else and it made him feel immediately uncomfortable.

When Cesari had finished speaking his words of introduction, the three aliens spoke quietly to him, making a few gestures to the cadets in general and then they came to some sort of group conclusion and Cesari pronounced to the cadets again.

"You may all leave for your R&R now, all except Giardini, Latori, Marsh, Nakamura and Sinclair. Dismissed."

Chapter 17

Charlie felt as though there was a foreboding wind building around his squad as the five cadets moved to stand together to attention before their chief instructor and the alien visitors. He desperately wanted to ask why they'd been singled out, or at least to speak to his friends to make himself feel better, but he knew that moving now and bringing more attention to himself would be the worst thing he could have done.

Eventually, the three aliens and Cesari walked up to the five cadets and stood before them, looking them up and down.

Jorell was the first to speak. "You are the only five humans that have achieved a promotion to the second rank of advancement." His words formed a statement and not a question so none of the cadets moved or spoke. "I expected you to be bigger," he said.

"These are all effectively children, Jorell," Cesari spoke in a soft tone that Charlie had never heard before, "Though they are large for their age because of the program, and they will continue to grow."

Jorell nodded and walked the line of five cadets in an appraising manner without saying another word. This was then followed by the lizard-man, who stopped before Charlie and sniffed the air animatedly.

"There is something different about this one," the alien said suddenly whilst looking Charlie dead in the eye. "I don't know what it is but his scent is not the same. I can't say if that is odd for humans though so far you have all smelt similar. Why is this?"

Charlie didn't answer, not knowing if the question was directed at him or Cesari. Thankfully the chief instructor answered on his behalf.

"Sinclair did not have the use of his legs or body when he arrived. The doctor said that he has made remarkable progress, so maybe that's what you are detecting?" Cesari offered.

"I am not sure, though I cannot say for certain either way. I will need to speak with Kono before I make any judgment of this case." Korvin replied and moved past the line to join Jorell in hushed whispers.

Callantra, the last of the inspectors, did not take her time appraising each of the group and instead practically glided on her eight legs to stand before Charlie.

With the female alien standing before him, even through her veil he could see that her skin was dark, almost black and that she had six black eyes and two protruding fangs. Truth be told, he was pleased the veil was there.

"Hello, Charlie," the alien spoke melodically though her words felt to Charlie as though they were dipped in venom. This was then accompanied by a voice in Charlie's head that was identical in sound and feeling, though he knew that instinctively it was for him alone. *"What are you trying to hide from me?"*

Panic. Charlie couldn't help but feel his heart rate quicken and his palms grow sweaty though he tried his best not to telegraph any further discomfort.

"It must've been difficult in the beginning, to not have the full use of your body," *"I can feel your fear and I will find what I am looking for."* The voices both spoke at once and Charlie had a hard time separating the statements. His breath quickened and he suddenly became acutely aware that the world had turned dark as though black clouds had filled his head.

'Have I gone blind?' his mind asked though to his surprise and horror, an answer returned from the darkness.

"You have not gone blind, I am searching," it said.

"Tell me, why is it that you five have been promoted over the other humans here?" *"Why are you able to grow at an accelerated rate over and above that of your peers?"*

Charlie shut his eyes tightly and began to put up a mental defence. He wasn't sure what the capabilities of this alien were, though he felt as though the fact that she was asking these questions of him meant that he had some say in what she was learning. Then it hit him – he didn't *have to* answer the questions; hell he didn't even have to submit to her will.

'I... don't... know...' Charlie replied in his mind, hoping that lying wasn't too big of an issue over the mental link. *'We just... keep... training, everyday... non-stop...'* he could feel the weight of what felt like ten

gravities pulling him down to the ground as the spider-woman tested and searched for any information that Charlie was hiding but he held his ground. It felt as though his knees were going to buckle and he could feel the warm trickle of blood coming from his nose, and then it stopped. The world around him returned to normal and he watched as the alien moved away from him to join the others that'd arrived with her.

Charlie was shaken, though he knew he'd won here. He'd kept his secret to himself and had stood up to the scrutiny of the creature that'd been so deafeningly terrible.

The inspection party then decided that they would like to speak to the doctor, and the five Ordinary Cadets were told to accompany the party so that they could be used as the demonstration subjects for the data that the flight suits collected. Charlie felt like he'd rather be anywhere else than in the vicinity of the alien spider-creature, but he knew that obeying orders would always come first, so that is exactly what he did.

As they walked in silence, Charlie and the others traded glances as though they all felt that something was a little off, though none of them were silly enough to voice their concerns.

Dr Kono was in the medical bay and seemed surprised to see the three aliens, Cesari and the five cadets, and instructor Shepherd, who looked concerned at their appearance but was managing to hold herself together. Charlie wondered if she was used to being around aliens other than the lizard-like Kanaan.

"What is wrong with this human?" The Kanaan named Korvin asked the doctor and Charlie became acutely aware that both their names and the name of their race started with a 'k' and his mind wandered off into thoughts of the rest of their race.

"There's nothing wrong with Charlie," Kono replied without looking up from his screen, tapping away at something the rest of the group couldn't see.

"He has a different scent. I know he is different," the lizard pressed.

Kono stopped typing and looked up to meet his kin's gaze. Grasping his hands together in the very human gesture he thought for a moment before speaking. "Charlie here was entirely paralysed when he arrived here. His bones have been broken and mended, his nervous system has been all but entirely remapped and his muscles have been torn and rebuilt stronger. What did you expect to see from such a cadet?" Kono asked matter of factly.

"The rest of the humans have the same genetic recoding, so what you say could be true about almost any of the others. This one is different still."

Korvin pressed.

Charlie could tell that the lizard had picked up on something about him and he simply wasn't going to let it go, and he hoped that the doctor had a better explanation up his sleeve than simply saying that this was normal.

"Do you think..." Charlie spoke before the doctor would have to lie on his behalf again - if anyone was going to lie, he was going to make sure it was him. The room turned and looked at him as one. "Do you think that it's because I had a brain tumour and had to have some kind of specialist therapy?" he asked, tapping his head.

Shepherd then spoke up quickly before anyone else. "He's right," she said. "He would have had to have gone through a regimen of radiation and chemotherapy wouldn't he? No other cadets have had that sort of treatment..."

"ENOUGH!" The lizard inspector interrupted her. "Kono, I know you and I know exactly what you are like. Tell me now, have you done something to this human that you should not have?"

The room now turned to face Kono who to his credit seemed utterly unfazed by his kin's outburst.

Kono stared daggers at Korvin, before simply responding with "no."

"I believe that this matter is settled then," Jorell spoke to reduce the tension and move the conversation onto more important matters. "Show us the progress that these cadets have been making with their enhanced genetics."

Charlie and the squad managed to talk quietly with instructor Shepherd whilst they waited for the inspectors to be brought up to speed with the cadets' training and improvements over the weeks. She apologised for being absent of late and said that it was because she'd been working with Matty Henderson of all people, making sure he was looked after during his confinement. Charlie really didn't care though, the last meeting between them, like many others, had left a sour taste in his mouth.

"How tangible is the difference between the cadets? What are their growth rates like?" Charlie overheard the larger Jorell asking Kono as they scoured the data on his terminal.

"The cadets have made impressive progress by human standards," Cesari said in a tone that Charlie had never heard from the chief instructor before. "Compared to regular human cadets, these kids really are something to behold."

Charlie felt entirely buoyed by Cesari's words as pride washed over him, though he couldn't help but feel that the conversation was being led down a path that was ultimately going to be bad for him.

"I do not wish to compare these humans to regular ones," Korvin said with a sneer. "I wish to compare them to each other as obviously this gene editing program will make them superior to their kin in almost every way."

"A proposal," the melodic voice of Callantra filled the room to everyone's surprise and Korvin was still grinning as though this had been the plan all along. "Why don't we arrange a competition in which these humans are to face each other so that we may see the differences in their advancement?" she asked.

Cesari replied first. "We have the baseline testing that we can..." though Callantra interrupted him before he could finish his statement.

"I am not interested in the testing that you have carried out and the numbers that scroll across a screen. I wish to see these humans in battle against one another so that they may be showcased for all that they are." *'There will be no hiding from me in the heat of battle'* the inner voice said in Charlie's mind.

"They aren't animals!" Objected Shepherd, though it seemed that she was alone in this statement. "You can't just make them fight and see who's the best, like some game of marbles."

"You are right of course instructor," Callantra spoke to the room and again Charlie could see that Korvin was smiling as though all of this was supposed to happen. "So instead of a test I propose that we make this a competition, and one with a prize that the humans would be interested in winning. It will be voluntary of course, though I expect we can come up with something that they would willingly fight for."

"Yes, let's say that the winning squad will get a vacation to the D forty-six station?" Korvin said though it seemed far too rehearsed and far too quick for Charlie's liking. All of this was so obviously manufactured, but he could do nothing to prevent it from unravelling right there before him and he held his tongue.

Of course none of the cadets knew what this 'D forty-six station' was, though by the sounds of it, it was a prize to be coveted. Once it was agreed that the cadets were going to compete for such a prize, the inspection team, along with Cesari, Kono and Shepherd, devised amongst themselves a contest for the prize.

The contest was to be a standard hand-to-hand squad based tournament, sixty squads of five, which they had already been placed into, to go head to head one at a time, squad against squad. This would mean that in order to win outright, a squad would have to win five matches in a row unless they caught a lucky bye in one of the rounds with an odd number of teams. Charlie's own squad, upon hearing the idea became immediately thankful that they'd been training their hand-to-hand combat skills as a squad for hours on end, so each felt that they might have had the advantage and couldn't help but smile at each other, though things were never as easy as that, were they?

The inspection team had left Charlie and his squad alone with Kono and Shepherd once the pre-determined contest had been 'planned' to start the very next day, Cesari saying that he would announce it at breakfast the next morning. Once they had been left alone, though, Kono beckoned the cadets over to his station where he could whisper to them conspiratorially without fear of being overheard.

"Charlie, you know this is all about you, right?" he said. "They think they know something, but really they don't know anything. I implore you to keep your mouth – and your mind - shut at all times from now on unless you are explicitly told exactly what they know about you." He spared a glance at Charlie's four friends and squad mates. "Whatever is known right now must be kept to yourselves at all costs, and I do not just mean verbally. I say again, you must keep your mouths and your minds closed for all our sakes." He stared into Charlie's eyes for a few moments before Shepherd spoke to ease the tension in the room and Charlie was very thankful for that.

"Besides, you're going to be fine, I've seen you all fight. Plus you really will enjoy the station – though I've heard it called Omnis station by the humans that have been there – the Intergalactic Council really is terrible at naming things." Shepherd assured them.

"Have you been?" Laura asked the instructor and the question sounded genuine although Charlie felt that she was doing anything to change the subject.

"No, I haven't. Actually only a few humans have been to my knowledge so the information is a little anecdotal at best, but from what I've heard it really is something to behold, with relaxation, games, shopping, even food and on offer are all the best things from around the universe. If I didn't know any better, I'd say that offering it up as a prize really is a little too much."

Mauro's eyes practically bulged. "They have FOOD from around the universe? The – best - food?" His mouth was practically watering at this point. "Charlie, we have to go, we have to win! I *need this*," He proclaimed and it made Charlie smile widely, somewhat forgetting about all of the ulterior motives that the inspectors might have had.

"I really think this is a good opportunity for all of us," Stephanie agreed and Charlie was surprised that she'd spoken up. "I bet they have some really advanced tech up there."

"What about you Laura?" Charlie asked. "Is it the food or the tech you want?"

Laura didn't say anything for a short moment while she thought. "I want to see the other aliens and how they interact with each other," she said. "We haven't really had the chance to learn anything about the universe so that's what I'd really like to see."

"It's clothes for me, before you ask," Kori interjected quickly. "And sunglasses. That's what I want."

The group spoke about the things that they wanted to see on the station, should they win the chance to go up there, but Charlie remained quiet about his own ambitions. Truthfully he didn't care too much about the station beyond the fact that he wanted his friends to get everything they wanted from it, but what he really wanted was simply to win the tournament. By doing so he would show everybody – and himself – that he was worthy of his new uniform and would shut down all of the cadets who had accused him of cheating in the past. That was what he wanted more than anything. Acceptance.

The squad decided that the best course of action for the rest of the evening was to talk amongst themselves and decide upon how to work as a group of five in a fight. It was going to be difficult for sure, but they felt that they had a distinct advantage over their competition, and this was going to be a battle that was theirs to lose. They decided upon using their cadet-like specialisations and how they liked to fight in their training matches to their advantage as it seemed like the most logical course of action. Mauro would take on the biggest opponent, Kori and Laura would move in to fight as quickly as possible, closing down two enemy fighters, Charlie would defend, block and counter as he'd become used to doing and Stephanie would take whoever was left of the opposing team. It was a good plan though they were acutely aware that this was never going to be a one size fits all situation, and they were probably going to have to roll with the punches, literally speaking.

"I just don't know how useful I'm going to be," Stephanie voiced quietly as the group continued their conversation into their own communal living space.

"Are you kidding me??" Laura asked incredulously. She was the real fighter of the group with the experience of actual training in grappling from her time growing up, and if anyone was able to analyse the fighting styles of the group and their worth, it was her. "You fight so technically,

I've never seen anything like it," she protested. "Even when I'm sure I have you in a choke hold that would normally mean my victory, you're able to find a pressure point in the weirdest place and all of a sudden I'm on the floor. You really have a knack for the technical side of fighting and it is so effective you don't even know. And you Charlie, you're stronger now than you were but your ability to dodge and counter strikes… there are just no words for it, it's like trying to fight a mongoose!" Charlie smiled at her words but she continued. "Mauro is nigh on impossible to take down to the ground because he's so damn big and strong and Kori fights like if he loses then someone is going to steal his brand new pet puppy. You are all really good fighters and I'm not just saying that," she concluded.

"Thanks Laura," Mauro replied before anyone else had the chance to. "But I'm not just big and strong I'll have you know, I also have a sensitive side," he joked.

"Yeah, sensitive to hunger pains," Kori jabbed at him and the group laughed together. Silently they all thought that it didn't really matter what the result of the tournament was going to be, as long as they all got to fight together and have a bit of fun.

Chapter 18

The brackets for the tournament went up the following morning, similar to how the Gauntlet rankings had been displayed, and Charlie saw that his group was to compete in the very first match of the tournament against Phillip Anderson's team of him, Torolev, Hardman, Kahn and Wu. None of the cadets had stood out in any meaningful way and as Charlie's squad took to the sands for the opening fight of the tournament, the crowd of spectators, being all of the other cadets, the instructors and the inspectors, were obviously expecting an absolute walkover from the side of the Ordinary Cadets. Buzzing about their heads was also a small orb about the size of a cricket ball that Charlie couldn't identify, but assumed it was perhaps a recording device owned by one of the inspectors.

Wooden stands had been erected in a large semi circle around half of the hand-to-hand combat training area so that all of the cadets and spectators could see the fights as they happened, totally unlike the Gauntlet where the actual task had remained a secret up until the moment a squad was due to take the test. This was good news though, Charlie thought, because this way he'd be able to see how the other cadets fought and perhaps devise strategies to beat them if they were drawn against them. Being a part of the first match of the day though meant that this first fight was going to be a blind one, and his team was going to have to rely on their skills to make it through it.

One of the worries that Charlie had had during the morning of the tournament, was trying to decide how much breakfast he was supposed to eat before a fight. He didn't want to eat so much that he couldn't move properly, that was for sure, but he also didn't want his body to fight itself with an empty stomach, searching for an energy source that wasn't there. In the end, he'd thought to eat a little, but stopped himself when he felt what he judged to be half full. The last thing he wanted was to be punched in the stomach and throw up on the floor. He wondered if he was overthinking it, but decided that even if he was, what was the worst that could happen?

Mauro hadn't had any such worries and Charlie had watched with wide eyes as the larger cadet ate no less than five eggs, three rashers of bacon, two sausages, a small bowl of beans, mushrooms and six or possibly seven slices of buttered toast – Charlie couldn't tell because one of the slices was so thick, he wanted to count it as two. Mauro didn't speak during breakfast but his determination to eat as much as possible was a little more pronounced than usual, so Charlie chalked it up to anxiety before the big day. All of these memories chased Charlie's mind's eye as he stared down his opponents who stood his equals across the hot sands. It was a sunny day with little wind, perfect conditions for a fair fight.

The five Ordinary Cadets of Charlie's squad lined up before Cesari who stood in the centre of the makeshift arena, facing their opponents without giving away any emotion on their faces. The crowd turned silent so that Cesari could be heard by all.

"This is to be the first match of the tournament," he proclaimed. "Sinclair's squad versus Anderson's squad. As you will note, Sinclair's squad is the only team here to consist of Ordinary Cadets and as such it is expected that they will perform well and defend their rank. This squad should be an example to all of you as to what you should be striving for and in this match we expect great things from them. The rules are simple, you must fight until all members of a team have been either rendered unconscious or have otherwise tapped out. Each team member who taps out is to remove themselves from the field of battle immediately after their surrender if they are able. There are no weapons and no specific rules within the fighting, though consider this: your tactics are being watched and counted by everyone here, so don't be surprised if one fight your team has is very different to the next. Does anybody have any questions?"

Not a single sound came from the crowd at the question the chief instructor posed, and with that he held his hand in the air and proclaimed "FIGHT!" before moving back and out of the way. There was no real need for him to referee the match, especially as the list of rules was so limited.

Charlie didn't think that the fight was going to start so immediately and stepped his right foot backwards to steady himself. He wasn't sure exactly what he'd been expecting but a 'ready, steady, go at least would've been nice.

For a long moment no one made a move on the sands until Torolev, who was notably the largest cadet of the opposing group, started walking towards Charlie's team and to Charlie's horror he was making a beeline straight for him. Mauro realised what was happening and took his place in front of Charlie and a moment passed before the large pair engaged in their segregated bout.

While Mauro and Torolev moved away to take each other on, Kori jumped in toward Hardman as his assault counterpart, Laura grabbed a hold of Kahn by his collar and Wu and Stephanie raised their hands tentatively, both cautious and unwilling to give up the opening move. That left Charlie to enter into a contest of his own with Anderson, who he'd seen training on a daily basis for a while and wasn't too concerned that he would offer any more of a threat than the rest of his own squad had in their training rounds.

Anderson, who was cheered by the crowds as he raised his fists at Charlie, smirked cockily but restrained himself from throwing any insults at the Ordinary Cadet. Charlie silently raised his own guard and moved into striking range with a straight face; he didn't want his expression to betray any emotion for the coming fight.

The first few strikes came toward Charlie who simply moved out of the way to allow their momentum to pull Anderson toward him. The punches failed to land all but thin air and Charlie did his best to block out the sounds of the crowd and the 'ooh's' and 'aah's' that were apparently focussed primarily on his own bout. He could see that each time a strike missed, Anderson's face grew redder and angrier at his inability to make contact and the fact that Charlie was yet to actually offer any effective offence of his own. Charlie just hoped that the rest of his team weren't having too much trouble in their own fights, though he could not even see what was happening around him let alone help anyone even if he so wished.

Eventually, Charlie saw an opening as Anderson swung with too much of his strength and he stumbled forward showing the back of his right shoulder to Charlie. Charlie in turn, not wanting to miss any opportunity, snapped at the cadet's shoulder with a left hook and Anderson yelped in pain as his arm went limp. Charlie moved away and Anderson regrouped, his right arm shaking, and he was visibly uncomfortable.

This all seemed so easy for Charlie, who effectively had to simply concentrate on move and counter as the other Special Ops cadet simply punched himself out, still growing more and more frustrated by the minute and making mistakes that Charlie knew he could jump on.

Anderson moved in again but Charlie could see that from his gait, he was protecting his right shoulder by keeping his body turned ever so slightly further than he had done before. Charlie decided that a fun way to carry out the rest of this fight was going to be to see how far the other cadet would go to protect this new injury so he jumped to his left and watched as Anderson spun on the spot to keep his posture between Charlie and his own injured shoulder. Charlie smiled.

Knowing the weaknesses of your opponent was always a good thing during a fight, though this was just simply on another level and Charlie lunged forward at Anderson's flank, causing him to turn in surprise in order to keep his guard. As he did though he presented his side to Charlie who threw a straight-jab combination that caused Anderson to yelp as his un-injured arm and ribs took the full brunt of the blows. The cadet didn't even offer any kind of retaliation for the strikes and Charlie almost felt bad about it.

It was then that Charlie decided that finishing his opponent quickly in case the others needed help was probably going to be a good idea, so he swept Anderson's leading leg with a fair amount of force causing him to fall to his back on the ground. Charlie didn't waste a moment and mounted Anderson before he had a chance to do anything to right himself. From there it took just a moment to pull Anderson into an arm-bar, causing him to call out his surrender loudly, saving his arm from being broken. Anderson rolled to his front and crawled to the edge of the sands where Charlie could now see Torolev, Hardman and Kahn awaiting him. All that was left was for Stephanie to finish off Wu, but as they both realised that all of Charlie's squad was now bearing down upon her, Wu indicated her surrender and left the sands of her own accord. It was a total walkover and although Wu's surrender had come without an actual finish to the fight, it was still a good and decisive victory for the Sinclair squad.

"That was easier than I expected," Kori said as the group took their position in the stands as the next groups took to the field.

"They just didn't know how to fight," Laura replied without taking her eyes off of the match that had already started – there was evidently going to be little waiting around. "I don't think many of the cadets here are actually trained to fight properly, let alone as a team."

Charlie watched the fight on the sands as Laura spoke and he could see what she meant. Two of the cadets were trying to pull each other down to the ground with no technique at all, the largest in the group was walking a smaller opponent around the sands in a kind of headlock though it was evident he had no idea what to actually do next, and the rest had seemed to have jumped into a kind of free-for-all bundle type deal in the middle. There was no way these groups were going to pose a challenge for whoever actually won this competition and Charlie began to daydream about visiting the crowning jewel of the alien lifestyle.

Charlie and his team took the time before their next round to talk amongst themselves and what they thought the alien space station was going to be like, though one important thing that did crop up, was what they were going to call themselves.

"We can't just be 'the Sinclair Squad'," Kori had said looking disgusted. "It's just not fair!" He was smiling as he spoke so Charlie knew that he was simply teasing. "It doesn't say anything about the rest of us."

"What about 'Charlie's Angels?'" Laura said with a chuckle and a secret wink to Charlie, which made him laugh too.

"Knockout Nakamura and the Fearsome Four?" Kori offered though his suggestion was met with silence.

"Mighty Mauro and the Four Musketeers," Mauro suggested now fully invested in the conversation.

"Listen… I didn't come up with the name, but I kind of like it," Charlie smiled. "It lets everyone know what's what, right? I'm the main guy and you four are just there to help me."

The rest of the squad stared blankly at him for a moment in silence, though the penny dropped pretty quickly that he was joking.

"Oooh … what about the A-Team?" Laura offered to break the silence and Charlie snorted.

"Just be thankful that my surname isn't Simpson," he said. "Or we'd all be known as the Simpsons."

"Killer Kori, plus four?" Kori said totally ignoring Charlie's observations, and his suggestions just seemed to keep coming. It was obvious to all of the cadets though that Cesari wasn't going to entertain a squad name change like this but it filled the time.

It took two hours for the first round of fights to end and when they did just thirty squads remained in the contest. It had been obvious to Charlie and his squad that just a few of the other squads were comfortable in the situation, though some really did look as though they were going to be hard to beat. Henderson's squad, for example, looked like it was going to be a force to be reckoned with, as they'd steamrolled their opponents with overwhelming force in under a minute.

Charlie's squad was then informed by some stroke of luck or divine intervention – he was not used to being on the fortunate end of either – that the first bye had been awarded to them, allowing his squad to skip the second round, gaining entry into the third without even taking to the sands

The Sinclair Squad in the next round, then took to the sands to fight against a team that had already fought and won in two matches, meaning that they definitely knew what they were doing.

Their opponents, the Darefski squad, consisted of a larger girl as lead accompanied by four boys named Sebastian, Cooper, Zirkov and Chance and they all looked confident walking across the sands toward Charlie's team as though they were completely assured of themselves. Charlie made sure he kept eye contact with Darefski the entire time so as to not betray any fear or anxiety about the upcoming match. This time, though, his squad had concocted a new plan – it was risky but he felt as though it was going to work.

As soon as Cesari gave the motion to begin the fight, Charlie and his team immediately sprung as one straight at Darefski and before she could do anything to move out of the way, they took her down to the ground as one. Laura then mounted the larger girl and took her in a choke hold without a moment's pause. While this was happening, the rest of the opposing team took an unsure step back and it was all that Charlie's squad needed to remove Darefski from the fight entirely.

"Hey that's cheating!" one of the opponents called out, though nothing came in reply from Cesari who was watching the bout in relative nonchalance.

"Haven't you heard?" Kori called back across the sands. "It's what we do!" He smiled as he spoke then leapt towards the opposing cadet who'd dared to speak, the ferocity of his attack causing the boy to stumble. Charlie didn't need to watch that fight to see who was going to come out on top. What he did notice though, was that a second cadet – he was sure it was the boy named Cooper – was moving toward Kori and his own opponent in a bid to help him out. This wasn't going to be good for Kori, so Charlie dropped his shoulder and ran as fast as he could on an intercept course.

Charlie's charge hit with ferocious force and bundled Cooper to the ground knocking the wind out of him. From there it was easy to force a submission by simply applying a little force to his throat with a well placed forearm. Charlie then returned to his feet to see just two opponents left and his entire team still standing.

There was nothing the remainder of the opposing team could do to fight in a five on two situation, although they did try and try hard. All they could do was huddle up close together and defend from the strikes that reigned down upon them, but in the end it was simply too much and both cadets took the knee and conceded the bout. Charlie liked it when fights ended like this – nobody had to get too hurt and everyone was shown to try their best. Charlie's team was through again to the next round and as it was the fourth of five, it was the semi-final with just four teams left in the competition. Jean Martin's squad containing Henderson, Manuel Mancini's, Charlie's squad and Xi Ling's were all that was left to fight for a prize that they all coveted, though Charlie wasn't sure if he wanted one of the other squads to knock out Henderson's group so he didn't have to fight his mortal enemy, or whether he wanted the chance at some revenge for himself. He just didn't think that was going to be an easy feat based on the way that their team had been decimating their opponents so far.

Charlie held his breath as he held his portable terminal in his hands awaiting the announcement of the next bracket, still unsure of what he was hopeful for. Then the words finally popped into existence. Mancini's group was to fight against Henderson's and Charlie was to fight Xi Ling. That was probably for the best anyway as he'd trained with the quick to anger girl before and knew exactly what he needed to do to push her buttons. A plan set firmly in his mind, he was sure that his team was going to win the day.

Charlie wiped the dust and sand from his hands once the bout was over and Xi Ling pulled herself up and away from Charlie. In truth the battle was a foregone conclusion before it had even begun and was simply a formality that had played out to plan. There wasn't a need for complex planning or a Hail Mary as in the fight before, just a simple move, block and counter like he'd done on a few occasions before when sparring with Ling. A few insults thrown regarding her inability to hit him did help to speed things up a little too.

The sun had faded in the sky with the last semi-final being played out and not a soul in the place was surprised to see that Jean Martin's squad, featuring Matty Henderson was going to be the opposing team to Charlie's in the illustrious final. Charlie had just started walking off towards the mess hall when a hand grabbed his wrist from amongst the other cadets and pulled him aside. He wanted to resist, although he didn't really feel any danger in such a crowded place.

Chapter 19

Charlie was pulled away from the other cadets and it took him a moment to realise who exactly it was that had accosted him. To his surprise it wasn't another cadet ready to take him down a peg, nor was it Henderson there to cripple him before the big fight. The person who'd pulled him away and was leading him off towards the medical bay, was Instructor Shepherd.

"Instructor? What are you doi..." Charlie managed to say as the pair entered the medical bay to a waiting Dr. Kono. Shepherd crossed her arms across her chest and wore a stern look on her face.

"Doctor?" Charlie amended his question to once the door closed behind him.

"Charlie," Kono stated.

"Is there something I can help you with?" Charlie asked after no-one said a word for a long minute.

"Charlie," Kono said again though paused and Instructor Shepherd cut in.

"There's something going on here with the inspectors," she said. "They know something and they want to get you up to that station so they can see if they're right. I know you really don't want to hear me say this Charlie, but you're going to have to lose your next match."

Charlie blinked twice, not entirely sure if he understood what she was saying. "You want me to throw the fight?" he asked eventually. "You know who it's against right? And you saw what he did to me the last time?" Charlie could barely believe what he was hearing.

"I know Charlie, but..." Shepherd started though this time Kono interrupted her.

"If you win, Charlie, their assumptions about you are going to be confirmed. They know how fast you've been growing and they're more than suspicious already. If you go up against Henderson and win, not only will they be proven right that you are further along your evolutionary path than you should be, but also they'll have you to themselves up there and we won't be able to protect you. You need to think about this Charlie because it isn't just your life that's on the line here."

"You've said all this before but you haven't really told me *anything* about what that actually means," Charlie replied. "You keep saying that I need to keep my PIP level a secret and the fact that my bones can repair themselves overnight, but why is that such an issue?" Charlie's face had turned red and both the doctor and Shepherd exchanged worried glances.

"The thing is," Shepherd spoke in a soothing tone now. "As a part of the agreement to set up this facility with the long term view to use humans as soldiers out there in the wider universe, the PIP level lock was kind of a deal breaker. Without the lock it was feared that the humans could run out of control and, you know, go after their makers."

"I get that," Charlie said with a nod, "but it's just me – even if they did find out couldn't they just take me out of the program or put me in jail or something?"

Dr. Kono took the lead again and Charlie wondered if this was their version of a good cop bad cop thing. "The Council is very black and white – which is kind of the reason why I disagree with them on a lot of issues but that's beside the point. The agreement was for humanity to go through this test in lieu of being destroyed entirely – a breach of the agreement would mean that the only course of action left to the Council would be destruction. Do you see, Charlie, either the GAP program works as planned, or human beings will be removed from existence."

Charlie's mouth hung agape at the doctor's words as the sentences fell into place and their meaning set in.

"And you thought that it would be a good idea to go *against the agreement* then?" Charlie air quoted the words as he spoke. "You thought that you'd just have a go and see what I could do, risking billions of lives because of what? Morbid curiosity? Scientific experimentation? Or did you just want to see if you could get away with it?" He had to make an effort to keep his voice low as he spoke to ensure that unwanted ears didn't overhear, but he thought he was pretty safe.

"Take a seat, Charlie," Shepherd soothed again. "It's a lot, I know, but there are good reasons for everything."

Charlie didn't want to sit down though. His whole body was shaking and he felt the weight of burden bearing down on his shoulders.

"You've ruined everything, you know that?" he said quietly. "I could have been *normal*."

"You're so much more than that, Charlie," Shepherd stated flatly. "You need to trust that this was the only way. You alone had the means to unlock your full potential and you prove that day in and day out. All we are asking is that right now you keep your head down and don't show yourself as above the rest."

"Fuck," Charlie said quietly, coming immediately to the conclusion that there was nothing he could do about it. He was angry for sure, but he knew that showing that anger and acting upon it would mean the end of the world – literally.

"Throw the fight, make a good show of it if you want and it'll be all back to normal by the day after tomorrow," Kono gave a half hearted lizard smile as he spoke, but Charlie heard the apprehension in his voice. The doctor was scared and Charlie had the feeling that if the GAP program went down, the doctor was going right along with it.

"The day after tomorrow?" Charlie asked honing in on the doctor's statement.

"Yes because it is late now, the final is going to be held first thing tomorrow, then the inspection team will depart the very next day with the winning squad," Kono explained. "You just have to make it through the next two days then you won't have to worry about anything else, I promise."

Charlie narrowed his eyes as he saw an opportunity. "Fine, but you'll owe me for this," he stated flatly. "When I need something from you, I expect you to help me out. *Both* of you." He looked pointedly at Shepherd and both she and the doctor nodded slightly, releasing him from their custody. Charlie would like having a favour in the wood from those two, they always seemed to know what was going on and some information might just be enough to save his skin one day.

Upon returning to his dorm and finding the entirety of his squad in the communal living space, Charlie knew that he needed to tell them about his instruction to throw the fight, though he knew that the conversation was going to be a difficult one. He knew that if he didn't pass off the information in exactly the right way, his friends wouldn't be happy about the situation at all. In the end, he decided to tell them all the truth immediately without hesitation or editing. He spoke in one long sentence and told them exactly what he'd been told and as he relayed the information, the squad punctuated his words with gasps, mutters, growls, putting their hands over their mouths and looks of concern. The emotions that took a hold in all of them warred for dominance, though by the time Charlie had finished speaking, the room was full of nothing but care and support.

"It's a shame we won't get to see the station," Laura said eventually in a sombre tone, "but some things are more important, right?"

"Yeah like what's for breakfast tomorrow?" Mauro said with a smile and it made Charlie feel immediately at ease. He should never have thought that his friends would be anything other than caring. What they did need to do though was to decide how they were going to go about losing the fight without getting actually hurt by Henderson and his squad. They all agreed that the previously larger cadet was going to be the one doing all the work again with the others not too much to worry about; they'd all seen the previous fights.

It took a while, but they eventually concocted a plan that made the most sense. Charlie would take Henderson one on one and simply defend himself – effectively keeping him away from the rest of the fights, then Stephanie would pair against Singh who would offer more of a fair fight so it wouldn't really seem suspicious if the bout went either way. The next part was a little more devious and all five of the cadets knew that it would take some pretty skilful acting to pull off.

Charlie and his squad took to the sands the next morning and were greeted by the smiling faces of their opponents, though Matty Henderson seemed to be the one getting the most enjoyment out of the situation, grinning widely and punching a fist into his other open hand.

The crowd gave a sharp intake of breath as one before Cesari took no time in announcing the beginning of the fight, and the two teams jumped into action without a single missed beat. As planned, Henderson and Charlie engaged first because that's where the real fight was going to happen, then Stephanie and Singh disappeared from view trading blows although it was apparent that neither was going to take the early advantage. That was when it was time for Mauro, Laura and Kori to enact their master plan and the squad would see if the luck of the gods was going to favour them today.

The three ran at Felix Target, whose eyes widened at the surprise attack, and as they grew closer, Mauro and Laura barged into each other jostling for position and the first blow. Tiring with the back and forth though, Mauro shoved Laura away from him and to the ground, right at the feet of Sergei Orlov, who didn't waste his opportunity in mounting the girl and choking her to submission.

Mauro then turned his attention to Orlov with an apology to Laura, but with his back turned, Target leapt onto Mauro's back and wrapped his arms around the larger cadet who in turn could do nothing to shake off his attacker.

Kori was left to fight Jean Martin who was confused with all the commotion that was unfolding before her. If anyone was looking, they would've noticed the suspicion that grew there at the Sinclair squad's sudden lack of teamwork and ability. Kori leapt towards the girl and attempted to baseball slide between her legs although through the telegraphed and poorly executed attempt, Martin placed a well aimed boot right onto Kori's nose, rendering him immediately unconscious.

Charlie blocked a tenth straight blow from Henderson as he continued to step back and away from his mortal enemy. He was surprised at the strength of the attacks and wondered if he would actually even be able to stand against the cadet as it was, even without having to throw the match. Charlie's forearms ached and his shoulders screamed in agony from holding himself up against the barrage, but he knew this show needed to be a good one so lying down and submitting was simply not an option.

Henderson feinted a left jab and Charlie watched it in almost slow motion as it travelled half the distance towards him before being retracted to give way to a strong right hook. He saw every minuscule movement of the one-two attack and would've had no trouble dealing with the clumsy sequence in reality, though he saw it as an opportunity to let the strike connect. He gritted his teeth and moved out of the way of the false jab only to be struck by the hook. It felt like he'd been hit by a train and he stumbled backwards but made the effort to stay on his feet. Then Henderson predictably charged in for his trademark double-leg takedown and Charlie didn't even have to feign being forced to the ground, the weight of the attack doing everything it needed to in order to lift Charlie off of his feet and slam him onto his back.

Charlie felt the sand hit his back, winding him slightly as he was dropped completely by Henderson's strike and a small part of him was happy that it seemed like everything was going to plan. He let out the tiniest of smiles before the shadow of his opponent fell over his face. Once again he felt the first blow break his nose, then after three more hits darkness fell upon him and his fight was over.

Charlie would later discover that although his squad did manage to put up quite the fight regardless of their plan, Henderson's squad had won with their superior numbers. The failure of the rest of his squad would be what hurt him the most though, after all they'd all been put in this position because of him.

"Charlie?" The all too familiar voice of Dr. Kono filled Charlie's world as he awoke once again in the medical bay after having suffered a defeat in a fight and also another break. This time though the first thing he did was bring a hand up to his nose to see how it felt and to his surprise, it was absolutely fine. Charlie opened his eyes.

"Ah here we are," Kono said in a polite manner, though what Charlie noticed first was the fact that Cesari and the inspection team were all in the room too with him and the doctor.

Jorell looked as though he was pretty mad at whatever was happening, his four arms crossed across his chest as though he didn't want to be there in any way shape or form. Korvin was difficult to read, his lizard features not telegraphing what was running through his mind though Charlie could see that Callantra was smiling beneath her veil – as much as a spider-being could smile that was, of course.

'Hello again, Charlie,' the voice inside his head rasped as he made eye contact with the telepathic being. 'Do you have something you'd like to tell me?'

It was clear that nobody else in the room could hear what Charlie could hear, or they were otherwise ignoring them because Dr. Kono spoke next.

"You can ask any questions you'd like of Charlie now that he is awake," he said, "though humans do tend to get a little belligerent after they've just lost a fight."

Cesari smirked at that knowing all too well what the doctor meant – most humans did hate losing and would go out of their way to prevent that from happening in most situations. "Now don't you worry about all that now son," he said in a very level tone that Charlie didn't know if it was because he was being particularly sympathetic, or if he just wanted to team up with the only other human in the room. Either way it didn't matter, Charlie was happy to see this side of the chief instructor.

"There was a moment," Callantra said aloud so that everyone could hear her rasping voice, "where a choice had to be made during the fight. It would determine the outcome at a pivotal moment and at that moment, Cadet Charlie here made the wrong choice. This is why his squad lost the fight," she assessed. Of course she was right but Charlie had the feeling that this wasn't a good thing for her to have noticed – especially if she was looking for such a sign the entire time.

There was a knock at the door and as Cesari called for whoever it was to enter, Charlie's heart both raised and then flipped as the rest of his squad entered the room. This could not be good in any way.

"Do any of you have anything you'd like to tell us?" Callantra spoke as soon as they entered and acknowledged Charlie with a silent look. All of the cadets stood to attention and didn't say a word.

"You, Latori, you pushed your friend and comrade Giardini to the ground in frustration. This is a trait that you do not have documented in your personal file nor one that you have shown in any other fight. Nakamura, as cocky as you are I have yet to see a human being more willing to put himself in a position where he can get so easily knocked unconscious as you did in that round. Tell me and I ask this of all of you, we're you trying to lose that fight?"

Charlie watched as nobody made either a sound or move and he was proud. Out of the corner of his vision though he saw Kono make the slightest move of his eyes to meet Charlie's. He could tell with that gaze that he was being told to do absolutely nothing.

There was silence for a long minute and Charlie could tell that his squad mates were being mentally questioned by the telepathic octopod, something he was eternally unhappy about though knew there was nothing he could do to stop it.

All of a sudden, Callantra took two steps toward Stephanie and Charlie could see her beginning to grimace and shake – she was on the verge of giving everything away.

"Alright!" Laura spoke up loudly when Callantra's face was just inches from the visibly uncomfortable Stephanie's. "We threw the fight, OK?"

Every head in the room snapped to look at Laura as she spoke those fateful words, and if looks could kill, Dr. Kono was doing everything he could to shoot laser beams at the girl who was about to bring his world crumbling down.

"What in God's name are you talking about?" Cesari started to question but Callantra shushed him before Laura could answer.

"We... threw the fight," Laura repeated.

"Didn't I tell you?" Callantra hissed in the direction of the other two members of the inspection team. "Something to hide, I knew it! Humans can never be trusted..."

"Now hold on a minute," Cesari spoke with authority and it silenced Callantra in her spiralling monologue. "Now these cadets might just have a reason for throwing that fight and my God I hope it's a good one."

"You are well respected amongst the Council members, Marcus Cesari, but if these cadets are hiding something from an official inspection team then that is an offence against all coaligned space," Callantra spoke menacingly.

"That's enough for now, Callantra," Jorell spoke unfolding his arms. "These cadets have a right to explain themselves, just as anyone else would have. We must not repeat the same mistakes that have been made in the past."

Cesari rounded on Laura. "Tell me everything, now."

"Ok..." Laura replied. "We got ahead of the other cadets by training right? And I mean we trained really, really hard. We got up early and worked later to work as a team - that's why we're the only cadets who've earned a promotion right? Well, if we go off on some leisure cruise then it'll give everyone else the chance to catch up. We don't want anyone else to catch up."

She'd made a very convincing statement and Charlie could see the corners of Cesari's mouth curve ever so slightly upwards in pride.

"That," Cesari said, "...isn't that bad of an explanation, actually."

"I want to see his stats, right now," Jorell said to Kono who was making himself very small behind a glass desk as though he wanted the room to forget that he was there. The four armed alien had gestured with his head toward Charlie.

"Why?" The lizard doctor replied, though Charlie could tell that this wasn't an argument that Kono was going to win.

"I do not need to give a reason," Jorell said. "Now."

Kono tapped a few times on his glass terminal and spun it on the spot so that the entire room could see. Charlie could see that the stats showing were his own – he knew them like the back of his hand by now.

"This student has shown excellent progress during his time as a cadet at Camp Rebirth. The GAP program has served his physical body well and his PIP level has been increasing steadily, now sitting at eleven percent for a few days. There is nothing out of the ordinary here and his progress is well within the limits as theorised at the beginning of the program," Kono narrated as Charlie's stats flicked from screen to screen. It was difficult to hear actually, that he was 'normal' though this could be one of those occasions that he'd been warned about – where being 'normal' could save your life.

The three aliens listened to Kono's speech and scrutinised the data that was presented to them, though Charlie could tell that one of Callantra's many eyes was focussed in on him, not letting him relax for an instant.

'I know that there is something different about you and you can trust me when I say I am not to be made a fool of,' the voice sang in his head. 'You have played *your part in this well, but do not think that I am such an easy opponent to best.'*

Charlie, in turn, did nothing to betray the fact that he'd heard the voice in his head, staring continuously at the terminal that the room was looking at his stats on.

"Uh, can we go?" Mauro asked whilst the room was both silent and evidently more interested in Charlie than of the entire squad. Cesari was about to agree but was interrupted by Korvin, the other lizard-man who was yet to make his opinion on the matter clear.

"This squad forfeited the match on purpose to manipulate their own path. This is not acceptable behaviour from a race of soldiers," he said though it didn't sound insulting, rather just an exacting reality. "There must be a punishment for this behaviour. Their orders were to fight and they did not follow those orders to the best of their ability. I... have a proposal."

Charlie saw Kono close his eyes as though he knew something bad was coming.

"This squad leader, Sinclair, should stand alone as the one to take the punishment on behalf of his team," Charlie's pulse quickened at that and his palms became instantly sweaty. "I propose that the final fight be repeated although this time, as I have said, Sinclair should stand alone. The contest carries until either Sinclair is rendered unconscious or the opposing team is."

"That's barbaric!" Laura shouted though when the entire room snapped their attention to her, she retreated into herself somewhat.

"What you are proposing is barbaric," Cesari spoke before anyone could berate Laura. "It's just not the way things are done here."

Charlie was surprised that Cesari had come to his defence, knowing full well that the chief instructor had a very barbaric streak within himself. After all, Charlie had been on the receiving end of that weapon before.

"These kids... these cadets may look as though they're adults," Cesari continued, "but they're still only twelve, thirteen years old.

At that, Charlie looked at his friends and he saw exactly what the man was saying. His squadmates didn't look like your average pre-teens. They weren't small, weedy and soft skinned – they looked as though they were in their late teens or perhaps even touching their twenties, with Mauro growing a slight stubble that shadowed his chin. It seemed that without the comparative nature of other age ranges about them all, it had become difficult to realise that their ageing had accelerated far quicker than anyone had actually realised.

"Technically speaking," Kono replied now a part of the conversation as it pertained to his expertise, "these cadets can be thought of as about nineteen when compared to their Terran counterparts in both physicality and general education levels. I can't particularly speak to their emotional maturity, though Shepherd has assured me that their growth is level across all aspects. For all intents and purposes, the GAP program has aged these cadets at an accelerated and level pace."

Charlie blinked.

"And you think that makes it OK to send a cadet in one on five to be beaten to within an inch of his life?" Cesari asked sarcastically.

Charlie was unsure why Cesari was suddenly so protective, but if he thought about it the man had been pretty fair – although he took the opportunity to single Charlie out on any occasion that presented itself to him, he never expected any more or any less from any of the cadets.

"I think that it is both a test and a show of that happens if you don't follow instructions," Korvin replied levelly. "These cadets must know that above all else obedience is required if the human race is to prosper within our space.

"It wasn't obedience you wanted from me when I was sent to the far reaches of Council space to fight alongside the Baccus as equals. And I didn't hear you complaining when I brought you the scalps of your enemies after years of my own volunteer service," Cesari practically growled and started to remove his outer layers of clothing.

When Cesari's skin was bare, Charlie winced at what the chief instructor showed to the room. From the top of his shoulders, diagonally to his hips, sat two long, wide scars that crossed over in the middle. It was evident that the wounds had been stapled together at some point because alongside the scars were the telltale dots of the technique used to pinch the skin together to aid its healing. Charlie didn't miss either, the smirk that showed on Callantra's face as Cesari made his revelation.

"How much blood and pain do you need before you realise that human beings are helpful to the greater good, and not beasts to be controlled?" Cesari asked.

"The answer is irrelevant," Korvin replied simply. "You are one amongst many, and those many must be taught. You are a military man; do you not understand this principle?"

"I understand it alright," Cesari replied. "But I also believe in a fair fight, not a bloodbath for entertainment and punishment – we aren't in the dark ages anymore."

"May I make a proposal?" Callantra chimed in sensing that neither of the headstrong individuals were going to forego their posturing. She continued without anyone answering and Cesari began to put his undershirt back on. "Why not replay the fight, though this time with Sinclair here pitted against the one that rendered him unconscious. It would be a fair fight and I am sure that both cadets have something to gain from the scenario?"

"No way!" Laura shouted but before anyone else objected, Charlie spoke.

"I'll do it."

Chapter 20

It seemed that the mood in the room turned instantly sour, with the negative thoughts coming from the humans plus Dr. Kono, who all turned to look at him astonished.

"What the hell do you mean you'll do it?" Laura practically shouted and threw her arms into the air. "What aren't you getting about this Charlie? They're trying to punish you and you're sitting there smiling as though they'd just given you a bowl of sweets!" She was so animated that it almost made Charlie laugh.

Charlie hadn't realised that his smile was so evident, but he knew something deep down that the others didn't, the one thing that nobody had really taken into account in all of this. Charlie knew that he could beat Henderson in a fair fight.

"Listen... I've only been here for a short while, but in that time I've been teased, screamed at, accused of cheating and attacked on more than one occasion. If standing out there before that bastard lets everyone know that I'm here for the right reasons, then that's a price I'm willing to pay. Besides, what's the worst that could happen? He breaks my nose again?"

Kono shot a look at Charlie as if to remind him not to say anything too incriminating but he didn't need reminding – he wasn't going to spill the beans about anything to the inspection team.

"Ah then it is settled!" Korvin clasped his lizardy hands together as though the conversation had reached its conclusion. "Though I wonder what the stakes shall be – after all we don't want you throwing the fight again, do we?"

"I have a suggestion," Callantra rasped and Charlie could hear the smile in her tone. "After all, this *is* to be a punishment. For the opponent, we can offer promotion on his victory, he has done nothing wrong in this and by all merits he has proven himself to be an able fighter so I assume promotion isn't too far away anyway?"

Cesari winced and Charlie could tell that he didn't like it when anyone other than himself decided the fate of his charges, though he did nod ever so slightly at the assessment.

Callantra continued. "For Sinclair – if his reasoning was truly due to advancement - then let's say if he wins the fight, he will accompany us as planned to the station along with his squad... and if he loses, the entire team is to be placed in segregation for, oh I don't know, a week?"

"But that...!" Laura began to object though Cesari held up his hand to stop her in her tracks.

The chief instructor didn't say anything for a while as though he was turning the proposal over and over in his mind, hand still raised. Eventually he spoke a single word: "Fine." Then he added, "But if he wins, I'm coming to the station with him."

All of the cadets looked at Cesari, stunned. There was just something about him that Charlie couldn't place. Something that he showed every now and then - a spark of humanity? No, it was more specific than that, it was almost as though he cared about his cadets.

"Oh and I will have to come as well," Kono added to which nobody responded. "I have to... well it seems nobody is listening anyway so let's say I have a master plan to kill Charlie and eat his rotten corpse."

Charlie snorted out a laugh though nobody else in the room seemed to be in any state to laugh along with him. To them, something big had just happened and there was a mixture of worry, concern, delight and foreboding filling the room. It was strange. It kind of made the air feel thick.

Charlie wondered errantly why Kono had announced that he would be coming along, though suspected it was to keep an eye on him to make sure he didn't spill the beans about anything he shouldn't, though he needn't have worried, Charlie knew how high the stakes were.

Once Charlie was cleared to leave the medical bay, he was given one hour's notice of the beginning of his upcoming fight and he'd been told by Mauro that Henderson had accepted the idea with glee. Apparently the boy was looking forward to 'putting down the cheater' again, though Charlie knew that Henderson just still wanted to get his revenge.

Taking to the sands with the crowds around them once again pulsing with anticipation, Charlie watched as Henderson balled his fist with a crack of his knuckles loud enough for him to hear even at the distance he was currently standing at.

Before he knew it, the fight was begun by Cesari with a single shout, and Charlie was right back into the frying pan.

"Don't you ever learn?" Henderson sneered as he rounded on Charlie, the large cadet surprisingly light on his feet.

"I will when you start giving lessons worth learning," Charlie replied, though he winced at the poor rebuttal.

Then Henderson *ran* directly at Charlie who barely had time to raise his fists and plant his feet in readiness.

Henderson's body and momentum hit Charlie like a freight train, though to his surprise and evidently that of everyone in the crowds around them, Charlie stood his ground and took a hold of Henderson around the neck.

Henderson writhed trying to escape. Charlie moved with him keeping a flowing grip that wasn't going to be easily broken. Henderson swung his arms at Charlie who kept his lower half just out of reach and eventually the crowds began to snicker and laugh at the way the fight was panning out.

Henderson growled and put an almighty effort into righting himself, and as he did, Charlie let go. Henderson flew upwards and as he did, Charlie followed his momentum with a vicious uppercut to his opponent's face. The force wasn't what it should've been because of his momentum, but it still lifted the larger boy off of his feet and deposited him onto the ground with an *oof.*

Charlie didn't press his advantage and waited for Henderson to spring back up to his feet, which he did momentarily. Checking his nose though, there was a single trickle of blood circling Henderson's mouth.

Henderson raised his fists and smiled. "Not this time cheater," he sneered.

Charlie didn't respond with words this time, repeating the act of planting his feet and raising his fists in readiness.

Henderson moved in and swung a heavy right hook which Charlie dodged effortlessly, then followed with a jab that was blocked but not countered. Charlie knew that he didn't have to rush to end this fight, it was like the whole thing was choreographed and he could see every action that was being taken, every punch, swing and...

A boot hit Charlie in his ribs with the force of a cannonball and he felt them crunch and break. There was nothing he could do to stop his body falling to the ground. As his body landed, Charlie rolled and he righted himself just in time to see Henderson's boot aimed directly at his face. He got out of the way of this one though. Henderson swinging for a 'lights out' kind of punt, Charlie grabbed the boot and twisted it with all of his might. He felt Henderson's knee pop out and could actually hear the ligaments straining and snapping beneath the larger cadet's skin. Henderson yowled in agony.

Separating again, the cadets panted as they righted themselves, Charlie holding his ribcage that burned like almighty hellfire and Henderson half-limping in place, not able to put any weight on his ruined leg. Charlie could see now that his opponent wasn't going to be surrendering easily any time soon.

Charlie hit the offensive and feinted a jab before swinging in with a straight that Henderson blocked with his forearm – which hurt Charlie – followed by a countered knee into Charlie's gut that caused his ribs to burn even harder and winded him. It was clear that both cadets were skilled fighters and whenever either tried to press their advantage, it ended badly for them. Both stood again facing each other, though now a little more hesitant to make the first move.

Charlie shook his arms to try to force his body to forget the pain it was in.

"Is that all you got?" He channelled his inner movie insult as he taunted Henderson, trying to get under his skin.

"Oh, we haven't even started yet," came the reply, accompanied with a slow limped walk toward Charlie with his fists raised.

Henderson then unleashed a torrent of blows against Charlie's guard who did his best to block and evade the strikes, though with each one he felt his body bruising, straining and becoming less effective. He knew that if he didn't do something quickly, the larger cadet was going to overpower him completely.

And then he knew what he had to do. The world around him had turned to slow motion and Charlie watched the punches coming at him as though he had a lifetime to analyse them. He knew their speed, force, trajectory – he knew it all. He also knew that there was only one way he was going to win this fight and with that in mind, he purposely mistimed one of his blocks to a left jab, letting Henderson's fist collide with his jaw. He timed his movement to roll with the blow, turned his face to the ground and threw his leg at Henderson's leading – and good – knee. He heard it snap more than he heard Henderson scream.

The fight was all but over and Charlie knew that all he needed to do was tap out his opponent, which sounded like it would be an easy task given that he couldn't actually stand any more, but Henderson evidently wasn't going to give up that easily. Charlie rounded on him and as he came close Henderson made the monumental effort to raise himself to a seated position, placing his broken legs between himself and Charlie. It was quite the task to pass the legs, useless as they were because every time Charlie made the move to step past them, Henderson spun on the spot with his hands outstretched. This was unfamiliar territory for Charlie and he wanted to make sure he didn't make any silly mistakes.

Feinting left then right, Charlie threw his body atop Henderson, flattening him down to the ground. He grabbed a hold of Henderson's arm and forced it with his body weight into an Americana submission but Henderson fought back with pure strength alone. Inevitably though, technique won out and Henderson could hold on no longer. Charlie snapped Henderson's arm back and dislocated his opponent's shoulder. This time though, Henderson didn't scream out in pain. He was straight faced and accepting of the loss of his arm. Still he did not submit.

"Why won't you quit?" Charlie breathed so that only Henderson could hear him, though his response was simply a smile. Charlie knew he would have to take this one all the way.

Charlie switched his body around atop Henderson and wrapped an arm around the back of the cadet's neck. Henderson didn't even try to stop him. Charlie placed his forearm against the front of Henderson's neck. Again his opponent made no effort to prevent the choke that was obviously coming. Charlie watched as consciousness faded from Henderson's reddening eyes until he felt his entire body slacken. Charlie rolled off and away, and stood as the victor. Something felt sour in the victory though and Charlie wondered if that was Henderson's last laugh.

The crowd was positively stunned into silence for a long moment before an instructor ran onto the sands and raised Henderson's legs in the air, shaking them to bring him back to consciousness . Then everyone erupted into cheers, whistles and claps. Charlie could hear above the rest, the noise of the crowd and the loud voices, his friends chanting his name with glee.

"You did it Charlie, you actually did it!" Laura cooed with glee once the squad had been reunited following the excitement and the conclusion of the tournament.

"Yeah, well done man, seriously," Mauro added with a slap on Charlie's back that hurt a little more than it really should've done – maybe he needed to get back to do a little more healing before hugging anyone.

"When you took that punch to the chin, damn I thought you were out for the count, we all know how hard that ogre hits!" Kori said with a shake of his head.

"Oh please, he did that on purpose," Laura said, "so that he could counter, right?"

"Nah, no-one lets themselves get hit like that," Kori objected.

The cadets all gave their opinions about the fight and what Charlie did and didn't mean to do while he remained silent. He liked to hear what they thought about the situation, and he liked even more that he knew the whole truth and it was frustrating them nearly to the point of argument.

"Sinclair. Now!" Cesari's voice boomed above everything else as the squad walked and Charlie instinctively stood to attention and moved toward where the sound had come from. He knew better than to keep the chief instructor waiting.

Wordlessly, Cesari led Charlie to his office in the camp and sat down behind a very old fashioned looking wooden desk. It was surprising to Charlie that it all looked so old-fashioned, though really Cesari did seem like the kind of person that enjoyed his staple creature comforts.

"You won," Cesari said without looking up from his desk. It was strange to Charlie, who had become used to the man's eye contact and accusatory gaze. Now though, he couldn't seem to bring himself to meet Charlie's eye line and it made him uncomfortable.

"I did, sir," Charlie replied officially and that seemed to straighten Cesari's gait in his chair.

"I mean... well done. It was... unexpected," Cesari said slowly. "Honestly, I never thought you would be able to turn yourself around the way you have. I'm... I'm proud of you Charlie."

Charlie blinked. There was something really not right. Something he could sense but didn't know exactly what it was and it made him anxious.

"Th... thank you," Charlie replied. "I have... we have all been training really hard."

"Some things take talent as well as training Charlie."

"Right."

Cesari was visibly as uncomfortable as Charlie with the awkward conversation and both of them clearly wanted to leave, though because the chief instructor had called this little meeting, there was nothing for Charlie to do other than grin and bear it.

"Well..." Cesari said. "We'll all be leaving in the morning for the station, that's... why I called you in here." It seemed like Cesari had made his mind up about something and Charlie could tell that there was a level of anxiety that had left the instructor with that decision. "At first light the transport will take your squad, the doctor and myself along with the inspection team and I just... I guess I wanted to give you a bit of a warning I suppose."

"Have you been on the station before?" Charlie blurted out.

"Not this one, but others. I guess they're all the same." There was no sense of pleasant reminiscing about the station in his tone. "Listen, when you're up there, keep to yourselves. Don't be drawn into anything that you don't know the full situation about – some of the aliens that you'll meet have ways of getting into your head, of making you do things you wouldn't otherwise do. Keep your heads down and your wits about you, and tell the others the same too."

Charlie furrowed his brow though he nodded. Why would the chief instructor impart such a warning when by all accounts this trip should've been a reward for hard work well done? The entire situation made Charlie worry about what exactly was happening out there in the big bad universe, and the information he was given was the first thing he relayed to his squad mates and friends as soon as he returned to his dorm after leaving Cesari to worry alone.

"Have you seen Shepherd in all of this?" Laura asked immediately once Charlie had finished speaking.

"Actually, no," he replied. "I don't know where she's got to, but it would've been nice to get her perspective, right?"

The team had come to trust instructor Shepherd since their private tuition; they all knew the role that she played for the cadets as a whole and that level of care just wasn't something that could be faked.

"Do you think she's going to come with us?" Laura asked though Charlie shook his head.

"I think they would've said so if she was."

"Who cares?" Kori eventually broke the silence that followed. "We're going on an *alien space station*! Isn't that just so cool!?"

Of course he was right and everyone knew it; getting to go aboard the station was the real prize, regardless if it meant that Charlie and, by extension, the others would need to remain vigilant. After all, who wouldn't?

Chapter 21

The transport ship from the planet to the station was thankfully just big enough for the squad of cadets to remain segregated from the alien complement, as well as the doctor and Cesari, who presumably weren't sharing either – not that it would matter but Charlie guessed that with seniority would come the ability to dictate living arrangements whenever the situations arose. He was also thankful that he didn't have to spend any actual time with the aliens other than the doctor; every time he thought about Callantra and the sound of her voice inside his mind it made his skin crawl.

"Did you ever find out just how quickly you could heal?" Mauro asked, making idle conversation to pass the time. There was a terminal in their small room, though with the trip taking a total of two days to make, there was only so much TV one could watch.

"Yeah mostly," Charlie replied nonchalantly. "It's a few hours for broken bones by the looks of it. Bruises much faster and I don't know about you guys, but I don't think I've actually coughed in weeks."

"Shit, hours?" Mauro replied his mouth hanging open. "Is it the same for everyone?"

That was a very good question actually and it wasn't something that Charlie was able to answer. Stephanie, though, did know something about it.

"I don't think so," she said. "I mean not that anyone has actually been hurt to the extent that you have, but I overheard them saying that Henderson was going to be out of action for a good week. I don't know if that meant fully healed or just back to walking but either way it sounds like you have the ability to heal a lot quicker than anyone else."

"That's so cool," Kori said. "You're like superman!" The statement made Mauro frown.

"Don't worry big man, you'll always be superman to me," Charlie said, remembering Mauro's biggest wish.

"So should we leave you two alone or...?" Laura made a disgusted looking face before the cadets shared a laugh. It was nice to know that they weren't on the clock, waiting for the next training session or otherwise preparing for a lesson in God only knows what. In truth, a little R&R was exactly what they all needed.

The journey actually passed remarkably quickly as the cadets discussed what they liked most about life as cadets, the station that they were headed to, the alien races that might've existed, and the future of the human race within the Council governed space. Not one of them fully trusted the aliens, that much was evident, although as they had no real reason not to so they made the effort to not pre-judge anyone or anything they might encounter.

When the transport ship docked with the station, Charlie and his squad were collected by Cesari, the rest of the crew having departed before them, and he offered one more piece of advice before the door slid open.

"Remember what I said Charlie. Keep your head down."

Charlie nodded in silence, accepting that the chief instructor knew what was best for him.

The transport ship had docked in what seemed like a private bay that overlooked a much larger docking area, although in truth it could've been a cargo area because below them was an open dockyard full of spaceships of all shapes, sizes and colours bustling with the activity of automated cargo drones filling and emptying, alien beings traipsing back and forward as though it was the most normal thing in the world. From his vantage point, Charlie could see that there were aliens of all kinds, Baccus, Ascara, Kanaan to name the few that Charlie and his squad immediately recognised, then insectoids, humanoids, hairless, hairy, yellow skinned, blue skinned, tentacled, multi-eyed – the place was so diverse that Charlie couldn't believe what he was actually seeing. The two races he noticed were not present, though, were humans and Callantra's kin, the Scriven.

"Excuse me," a small gnome-like alien said as the group neared the exit of their docking bay. "Are you humans?" His voice was high pitched, nasally and whiny, exactly like how Charlie expected a gnome to sound.

Charlie went to answer politely, but Cesari, hearing the beginning of the conversation, moved to stand between them.

"We are. Now please leave us alone," he stated flatly.

The alien looked defeated but made no motion to move away. It was strange, the thing really did look like a short, fat human although his skin was tinged pink and he had ridges on his forehead.

"I'm sorry, and please forgive me," the gnome thing sounded anxious at his own words, "but I've been sent to collect you... you've been invited for an audience with the station Overseer."

"You have to keep your wits about you here Charlie. You never know who means you harm in this world." Cesari spoke down to Charlie with no regard for the feelings of the alien.

"Please, just follow me," the gnome repeated.

"I think we should follow him Sir," Charlie said, noticing that the chief instructor was not carrying any weapons. That would've been strange in itself, given all the warnings of hostilities, but Charlie internally decided that there must've been some kind of system of punishment or law on the station.

"Can we go shopping here?" Laura asked from the rear of the group as she noticed the shops and businesses that lined the walls of the station below them. She too had apparently chosen to ignore the presence of the gnome alien, following Cesari's lead.

Cesari thought about it for a moment and inevitably concluded that if the cadets were in open, public spaces then they were probably safer anyway.

"Yes... but remember you don't have anything to trade with here, so you'll be strictly window shopping is that clear?" he replied.

Laura and Stephanie positively beamed at each other.

"Please, I don't want to have to force you to..." the gnome said, though his statement was interrupted by a loud voice that sounded far more authoritative coming from all around them.

"Humans aboard this station, you are required to report to the station Overseer immediately. Failure to do so will result in your expulsion from the station."

"Well I think we should probably go and see the Overseer first," Cesari said with a smile and started walking towards the gnome-thing.

"That's what I was saying all along!" The gnome protested. "You may call me Voris..." though his speech was apparently falling on deaf ears as Cesari moved as though he was being accosted by an Istanbul salesman.

"I think we're supposed to follow this... Voris was it?" Stephanie said from behind Charlie, and Voris practically puffed out his chest at the acknowledgement of his presence.

"Oh look what you've done now, you've gone and made it feel important. We're never going to hear the end of this…" Cesari huffed.

Stephanie ignored the chief instructor and spoke directly to Voris, who was practically grinning from ear to ear. "Please lead the way," then she added, "manners don't cost anything."

Voris then led the group to a small elevator that felt like it went straight upwards and required a keycard to get to where it needed to go. When it came to a halt, the doors opened to a large open, carpeted room that to Charlie just felt so opulent. There were sofas and chairs scattered around and it looked as though it was a slightly lower budget version of a Caesar's Palace penthouse. Sat on a red velvety sofa, was a thin grey skinned alien with slits for nostrils and a tuft of dark grey hair atop his head. When it saw them enter the room from the lift, it stood up to its full height of a long seven feet. Charlie heard Stephanie gasp.

"Welcome. Please come and take a seat," the creature gestured with a long open hand to the sofas in the room, it's voice was smooth and official which was kind of what was to be expected from the look of the thing. "I am The Overseer and I am pleased to welcome you… humans… to my station, as well as the famed Marcus Cesari no less."

Cesari didn't seem to care, or he didn't acknowledge it if he did.

"Hi," Mauro said. "Do you have any food up here?"

Laura turned to stare daggers at the larger cadet, though before she could decide whether or not to hit him for his stupidity, The Overseer spoke again.

"Ah yes, please help yourself to whatever you like. I'm sure you'll find things to your liking within these quarters. I would like to speak to this one alone though," he pointed a long, thin finger at Charlie whose mouth fell agape.

"Me?" It was all he could manage to muster.

"You can speak with me first," Cesari cut in with authority.

"I am afraid I know all about you, Marcus Cesari and whilst I would like to speak with you in the fullness of time, right now I would like to speak with this one."

Charlie didn't quite know what to do, but had the feeling that doing exactly what this 'Overseer' said was probably the way to go – after all, for all he knew if the creature decided he didn't like him, perhaps he would just throw him out of an airlock or something. However, a quick scan of The Overseer revealed no obvious weapons or even a threatening demeanour – past the presumed importance of the creature anyway.

Charlie followed The Overseer into another much smaller room where two small sofas faced each other. The Overseer immediately sat on one and gestured for Charlie to sit at the other. It was weird and the proximity made him feel uncomfortable.

"Ah Charlie, it is good to meet you in person," The Overseer said.

Charlie didn't respond although his expression changed subtly to one of slight confusion.

"I watched your last test in the competition you know," the alien said and picked up a small baseball-sized sphere, turning it over in his hands, appraising it. Charlie recognised it as the thing that was buzzing about as he fought Henderson and concluded that it must've been some kind of drone or camera that The Overseer had watched his fight on.

"These things are very useful for gaining information on the people that are looking to visit my station. I must admit I was impressed by your skill when fighting with the larger human during your contest."

Charlie nodded slightly, still unwilling to vocalise his thoughts.

"Charlie Sinclair, conversations are so much more enjoyable when they are conducted between two beings. Would you like to have a conversation with me?"

Charlie frowned at that somewhat, wondering exactly what it was the alien thought they were doing already, though realised it was The Overseer's way of saying that he wanted Charlie to actually speak instead of simply making vague gestures.

"I... uh. I'm sorry," Charlie replied. "I'm not used to really... speaking with..." he resisted the urge to simply say aliens – though that wasn't strictly true as he'd spoken with Kono on many occasions and had no problems with it. What he meant was that he wasn't used to speaking with aliens that could probably do or mean him some harm.

"With figures of grand authority?" The Overseer finished Charlie's sentence for him. Charlie nodded.

"How about we do it this way, I ask you a question then you answer, and ask me a question of your own?" The Overseer offered. Again Charlie nodded.

"Hmm. OK." The Overseer paused though Charlie felt that it was for effect rather than the fact he had to actually think about anything, He had the distinct feeling that this being already knew exactly what questions it was he wanted to ask.

"How old are you?" The Overseer asked.

"Thirteen... but I seem older." Charlie replied.

The Overseer nodded. "That was an easy one, wasn't it? Now you go."

"How many humans have been to this station?" Charlie asked the first thing that came into his mind.

"Twelve. Why do you say you seem older?"

"Because of the GAP program. My body grows faster than the other humans."

The Overseer nodded.

"Am I in any danger on this station?" Charlie asked his next question.

"Whilst you fall under the remit of my care, no. Why did you throw the fight before your last?"

"We didn't want to come to the station," Charlie repeated Laura's lie. "We didn't want to fall behind in our training."

The Overseer's forehead twitched almost imperceptibly though Charlie noticed it as though it had been punctuated with a loud scream. The Overseer either knew more than he was letting on, or had some ability that let him know when Charlie was lying. He needed to test the theory to be sure.

"Do you know the Chief Instructor?" Charlie asked.

"I know *of* him, though I don't think that there are many that don't. What is life like on Earth?"

Charlie froze for a moment. Did these aliens know about the planet and how many humans were there? Was this a way for them to glean information from him?

"It's... quiet," Charlie said and again he noticed the twitch. "The people there are sparsely populated and life is pretty boring." *Twitch*.

The Overseer looked at him blankly for a moment and then Charlie realised that The Overseer knew that he knew. "So now you know that you cannot lie to me Charlie, why don't you tell me what is different about yourself."

Now was the time for full panic mode. There was something that this creature was doing that allowed him to see when Charlie told a lie, and that meant that he couldn't say he wasn't special and he couldn't deny his altered PIP lock. What he needed to do was hope that the alien didn't have any suspicions that were close to the truth, and to only tell truths that would get him out of this situation.

"I... uh..." Charlie stumbled over his words and The Overseer listened intently. "I... when I came into the GAP program – you know about that, right?"

The Overseer nodded.

"Well when I came into the program, I was in a wheelchair. I was paralysed totally from the neck down. I couldn't even eat or drink for myself."

The Overseer listed his head to the side slightly and Charlie didn't see any sign of the twitch – he was on the right course.

"Then after the start of the program, and as my PIP level began to grow slowly and steadily, I got the use of my body back. I got stronger and have been continuing to grow stronger ever since."

"And why do you think that you have grown quicker than your cadet kin?" The Overseer asked. It was the one question that Charlie knew he had no way to back out away from. He couldn't lie but also, he couldn't tell the truth. His pulse quickened and his palms started to sweat. Charlie could begin to feel the weight of humanity bearing down on his shoulders, and then…

Charlie's vision started to blur. The timing was impeccable, if there was one time where he actually wanted to pass out for no good reason, it was right now – to avoid having to answer that question – to not have to be the reason that humanity as a whole was condemned to erasure…

He felt the warm carpet on his cheek and his vision disappeared, but not before he noticed the bare, long grey feet of the alien and the movement of its shins as The Overseer stood from his seated position. The last thing Charlie thought - hoped for - was that the thing wasn't about to kill him.

Chapter 22

"Good morning, Charlie." Dr. Kono's voice said happily and Charlie couldn't help but feel like he'd been awoken by the lizard doctor far too many times.

"Where am I," Charlie asked.

"You're on board the station still. Don't worry; I had a feeling that this was going to happen – and here I am. Ta-da!" Charlie opened his eyes just in time to see Kono break out the jazz hands and he smiled slightly. His head was pounding though.

"I thought we'd gotten through all of this," Charlie said. "My brain stuff…the tumours… what happened?"

"Well…" Kono replied slowly, obviously unsure of how to continue.

"Hang on, you knew this was going to happen?" Charlie opened his eyes fully and noticed that the medical bay was frightfully similar to that of Kono's domain back on EP1.

"Well… suspected might be the better word for it," he replied. "But I'm happy to report, and I'm sure you'll be happy to hear, that this time we did not have to carry out any surgery – rather the treatment was not invasive and therefore… you still have all of your hair!"

Charlie didn't smile.

"What did you do?" He asked through gritted teeth.

"I suppose it's about time you knew the truth, Charlie. The reason you suffer these growths on a somewhat regular basis is not a simple coincidence. Well, oh where do I start? Your first tumour/blackout/surgery occurred as you were just about to hit puberty, right? Well the reason for this was because of – amongst other reasons that I won't go into right now – a heightened emotional situation where your new hormones were essentially flooding your body."

Something about that clicked for Charlie. Each time he'd suffered one of these growths, it had come on the back end of an emotional response - this last one being the thought of being pushed into a corner from which his only way out would cause the human race as a whole to be wiped from existence.

"Your muscles grow because of the GAP program. Your new genetic coding takes the stresses and strains that you place upon them and helps to repair and grow them as a result of that loading. The beauty of the program," Kono spoke as though he was very proud of his baby, "is that it works in exactly the same way as a regular human body would react, only on an accelerated path. A normal person will go to a gym and lift weights, his muscles will grow and that's just how it works. A member of the GAP program will lift a weight once, then the next time will perhaps be able to lift another just a few hundredths of a percentage point heavier than that. As you tax your body, it will grow, and it will grow quickly."

Charlie had guessed most of this and it wasn't particularly new or useful information, and then it hit him. His jaw dropped.

"The GAP program is making my tumours grow in the same way, isn't it? I get extremely emotional and they latch on to whatever coding you've carried out to the point that they need to be cut from my brain?"

Kono held up a small syringe with a long needle. It contained a bright pink liquid. "Well, not cut out any more, shrunk actually," he said with a lizardy smile.

"Whatever," Charlie said waving the syringe away.

But there was one piece of the puzzle that wasn't making sense. "My first tumour though, I got that one before I even knew about the GAP program, so either that one was real or I'd been... I was on the GAP program before I even knew it?" He closed his eyes tightly as though to wish away that train of thought and thankfully Kono had an alternative explanation for him to deal with.

"No, you weren't a part of the GAP program before you knew it. Actually. Your father was." The lizard said softly.

"My father?" Charlie said. "He died with my mother in a car crash when I was three."

"Or..." Kono said invitingly. Charlie didn't want to say the words though. "Your father was a member of the GAP program before you were born, and some of his advanced and edited genetics had passed on to you at your conception."

"But... you said only adolescents could join the GAP program. And why didn't I heal quickly after my first surgery?" Charlie asked both questions immediately as his mind processed the information.

"First, I said it was *better* for adolescents as adults are generally mostly fully formed so their editing is limited. Actually, the first trials were on the humans that volunteered to fight with the Council members in the far reaches of occupied space, and they were all human adults – as much as we're all aliens here we don't go around experimenting on children... unless it's *very* necessary. Secondly, you didn't heal because your coding was not activated. Essentially it lay dormant inside your system until it was activated at your own actual GAP implementation. The tumour in the first place was sort of a *blip*, and I'm sure you'll forgive me when I tell you that you are the *only* human that has ever received a natural GAP inheritance from their parent. Mostly because, well, there was only ever one human that survived those trials out in the far reaches of space."

'OH. SHIT. NO.' Charlie's mind screamed. "You mean..."

Dr Kono nodded with a huge grin on his face, like the cat who'd got the cream.

~ Thirteen years prior ~

Dr. Kono had followed Cesari back to Earth aboard the same vessel that the Intergalactic Council had provided for their transport. It was the least they could do for the man who was the sole survivor of the war against the Scriven and the failed incursion onto their planet. They would now have to decide if it was worth still trying to take the planet by force, taking charge of the resources it provided, or whether it was simply best to remove it from existence altogether. The Council had had to make this very decision on many occasions, but it was becoming more and more difficult to recruit soldiers to fight on the ground. On the occasions they did destroy entire planets from orbit though, they lost out on cultures, technologies and resources that they could possibly otherwise have assimilated.

The GAP program had been somewhat of a failure for the doctor. It was his hope that through gene editing of existing military personnel from Earth, he would be creating a race of obedient and well trained super soldiers; however of this first trial of twelve, just one had returned. Marcus Cesari, had proven one thing though: that human beings can be resourceful and very, very hard to kill. The way they approached war and fighting was just something that he had never seen before, and if there was any way he could perfect his therapy, there would be no stopping an army made up of these beings.

When the transport arrived back on Earth – of course hidden from the general populations of the planet – Kono took up a research base in a continent that the humans called America, in a facility known as Area 51, whilst Marcus Cesari remained a serving member of the United States Marine Corps, although due to his ordeal he had been afforded a healthy amount of 'off-duty' time to debrief, unwind and relax.

Dr. Kono had requested that Cesari was tailed as a part of his ongoing experimentation with the GAP Program, and was pleased to note that the man carried out his next three months by indulging in what humans called 'life'. He would eat fatty foods, drink coffee in coffee shops and even took a lover though when his three months was up, Cesari was recalled to his station and Kono had turned his attention elsewhere.

It took a long time for the doctor to realise what the issue was with the GAP Program. The aged human body simply didn't take well to being manipulated into differing growth patterns from what it already knew – and the answer to this quandary was simple. Like shaping a bonsai tree, the GAP program needed to focus on humans that were still growing, so that they could be formed into exactly what the program required. Human pre-adolescents were going to be the answer to this question, and it took Dr. Kono twelve long years of research and petition to come to this conclusion.

Of course, the powers that be on Earth did not wish for what was essentially children to be used in this manner – experimentation on lives that had so many years yet to live – but Kono had put forward many arguments to the benefit of the program, least of all the avoidance of the destruction of the planet. If the humans had something to offer the Council, they would be safe, or at least until they were no longer useful that was.

~ Present Day ~

"Cesari. That absolute lunatic… is my real father?" Charlie articulated slowly.

Kono nodded, still grinning widely.

"So all of this was just some elaborate plan to get me and him back together then? I mean, seriously, what the fuck is wrong with you?" Charlie said.

"Oh… actually no, it's not all that elaborate really," Kono replied.

"You're in the program, he's in the program, it wasn't all that much of a coincidence really."

"Then why didn't you tell me?"

"Does it make any difference at all?" Kono asked.

It was a fair question actually and once Charlie thought about it for a moment, he internalised that no, actually it didn't make any difference.

"Yes it does make a big fucking difference." His words and emotions didn't agree with his mind. "He's my *dad*. How could that not make a difference? Everything I went through…" he looked down at his hands as though searching for answers there.

A knock at the door interrupted the pair and Charlie scowled at it as the Doctor told whoever it was to 'enter'. It seemed that Charlie's feeling of betrayal hadn't quite made any difference to his demeanour. Either he didn't care or he simply didn't understand the feeling.

When the door opened, the rest of Charlie's squad was peering into the medical bay with looks of concern on their faces, although they really should've become used to this scene by all accounts. Behind them though, stood The Overseer, much taller than the cadets, with a straight but unconcerned look on his face.

"Charlie is not yet well enough to field questions, Overseer," Kono said clearly for everyone to hear. "He will need a good night's rest and tomorrow he will be feeling much better."

The Overseer nodded slightly then turned and disappeared into the corridor. Charlie actually liked that the doctor had done him this favour, though still felt disheartened at his betrayal.

"Fancy a game of frisbee?" Mauro was the first one to speak as the squad entered the room and closed the door behind them. Charlie was in no mood for fun and games though and immediately relayed to them all his Earth-shattering revelation.

"You have got to be shitting me," Mauro was once again the first to speak, though it appeared he didn't have much competition. All of the cadets' mouths hung open with their eyes wide. Eventually they managed to gather themselves.

"You knew?" Laura accused the doctor and Charlie felt a sense of relief at the fact that she'd also taken offence at that revelation too.

Kono simply nodded.

"You're a fucking lunatic!" She accused, pointing a finger at the lizard-man.

"Well it's not the first time I've been called that, actually," he said though he didn't look upset by it.

The rest of the squad also voiced their concern for the doctor's mental health before surrounding Charlie on the bed, who told them about what his inherited GAP genes meant for him and the reasons behind his repeated brain surgeries. Not a single one amongst them said a word until he'd finished, then as one they hugged him.

"He really is going to be a Superman," Kori said as the group separated, Mauro snorted.

"Don't worry, we'll find you some sunglasses too Charlie so you can look better than Kori while you do it." Stephanie said quietly.

"You'll still never be able to beat me," Laura added quickly.

"I'm glad you're OK," Mauro said quietly and it seemed that the room agreed wholeheartedly with that statement.

After a few more minutes of catching up and a few more insults directed at the doctor, the gnome-like creature Voris appeared and announced that he'd been sent by The Overseer to accompany the squad to their respective quarters.

All along one side of a long corridor and all next door to each other, the rooms that the cadets had been given were opulent. Carpeted in a soft red weave and containing a large silken bed, with separate bathroom facilities just like there was back on Earth – Charlie wondered exactly how this would cater for all species, although for all he knew these rooms could've been arranged specifically for their arrival. Or perhaps these were just the 'human rooms'. He didn't know and he didn't particularly care.

Charlie undressed down to his underwear and stood in front of the long mirror that constituted the back of the door into his room. It'd been a few days again since he'd actually taken the time to appraise himself and by his account there had been some big changes.

He looked at the almost stranger in the mirror as he stared back at himself. He must've been six feet tall and he knew that his friends were around that stature too. A defined muscular chest protruded above abdominals that were well on their way to being chiselled into his midsection. Arms that he could've only dreamed of a year ago bulged with new muscle. He wasn't huge by bodybuilder standards, he simply looked as though he was in great shape, as if he went to the gym a few days a week. Nobody would've been able to guess his age - they wouldn't have even been close - he looked as though he was in his early twenties. The shocking thing now, though, was that in the mirror he could see some of his father, Marcus Cesari, staring back at him.

Charlie went to bed with a smile on his face at the sight of his new body. There was never any way in a million years that he would've expected to look anything like the way he did; just a few short months ago he was entirely confined to his chair with round the clock help. That thought made him remember the Browns. They wouldn't recognise him like this and he wondered if they'd even believe his story, that was of course if he ever got to see them again, they were so far away after all. He hated the fact that the pair who had truly become his family had been left out of the loop. He wanted to call them or just let them know he was OK, but that was a thought for the morning. For now he would think about all of the times they'd helped him and loved him. It was the reason that he'd become the man he was, after all.

The next morning arrived with a frantic knocking at his door. It sounded like it was going to be something to worry about, but Charlie was pleased to see the smiling face of Mauro once he opened his door to the boy, and behind him the rest of his friends.

"It's... BREAKFAST!" Mauro exclaimed with a look of delight on his face and Charlie couldn't help but join him in his excitement.

"And we need to get some clothes too," Kori added, pinching at his tight flight suit. "These things are nice to train in and all, but they aren't exactly the height of style, are they?"

"Alright alright," Charlie replied. Just let me wake up for a minute first."

The group waited impatiently for the two minutes that Charlie took to do his morning business, constantly calling him to ask if he was ready yet, and when he did reappear they practically pulled him out of the room as one. Back down the corridors they'd used to get to their rooms and back down into a lift that they all knew led to the station proper, the group practically held their breath as one as the doors slid open with a hiss to reveal everything they'd ever imagined the station would offer.

"Oh... my... God..." Stephanie muttered before anyone else could articulate. "Do you see *that?*" She pointed upwards at the huge pulsing blue neon cylinder running through the centre of the station. "It's... so big!"

"Uh, Steph..." you're looking at the wrong thing," Mauro said, teasing her head back down to eye level; "Look."

A few steps led down from the lift into the station proper and Mauro had been right, it was a sight to behold. Like a large convention arena, there were stalls of all kinds, shops and traders peddling their wares: food, clothes, trinkets and anything and everything that the universe had to offer from all of its civilised planets. The smells, sights, sounds and general business was overpowering and as though that wasn't enough, the entire place was filled with every kind of alien being that the squad had never seen before. To the back and sides of the market bullpen were corridors that led off and away to other establishments such as restaurants, higher class shops and recreational areas. It was easy to tell this because above each arched corridor an illuminated sign flicked through a set of languages including English telling everyone what was beyond them.

"...we don't have any money," Laura whispered to Charlie before any of them could muster a move.

"What kind of money do you think they take?" he replied quietly out of the corner of his mouth, to which Laura simply shrugged.

Without a way to discover the answer where they stood, the group decided to simply move into the crowd and ask the first vendor that they could see. It looked a lot like Jorell of the Ascara that had been on the inspection team, so Charlie at least felt comfortable asking questions of the being.

The squad had come to within just a few metres of the vendor and his stall, but before they could reach it, they each felt a hand on their shoulders and when they turned, they were greeted with three alien beings that did not look as though they enjoyed being messed with. The things looked like humans, though they had three eyes in a triangular pattern and their skin was a royal blue; they also didn't make any eye-contact with the cadets, simply looking above their heads and off into the distance. It was also clear from their uniform that these were whatever the station called security.

"Get your filthy hands off me!" Kori exclaimed as he brushed the security guard's hand off.

"Good morning humans," a small voice came from much lower down and from behind the creatures, suddenly, Voris appeared.

"Apologies for the rudeness of my greeting!" he smiled wickedly. "I have been sent to give you these:" he handed each of the cadets a small glass card that fitted comfortably into the palm of their hands. "As you haven't visited our station before, you won't know how things work around here. These cards hold your currency – station credits – that can be used to purchase anything on the station. One can normally earn these credits by carrying out jobs or tasks on the station, but because of the nature of your limited visit, your cards have been pre-loaded with a small amount of funds so that you can sample some of the delights of the station. This has been ordered by The Overseer who expects to see you all again once you are ready."

Charlie took the card and turned it over in his hand. It was a strange device and he couldn't see any markings on it whatsoever, so there was no way to know exactly how much money he had to play with, or even if he was simply being pranked by the small alien creature.

"One more thing," Voris grinned. "This station has a security complement," he raised his eyebrows as though to acknowledge the three blue aliens who still hadn't made any moves to acknowledge anything around them. "Follow the rules and you won't run into any *trouble*."

"What are the rules?" Laura asked before Charlie was about to say the exact same thing.

Voris held up three fingers in turn as he spoke the rules. "One: No fighting in the open. If you want to fight then you can do it in one of the arenas set up for that. Two: No stealing. If you steal from any of the vendors here then you will likely find that all of them will turn against you very quickly, and three: The Overseer's word is final. If you are told to do something by The Overseer, you do it and you do it immediately."

Charlie frowned. "Seems simple enough. What if someone starts a fight with you and you defend yourself?" he asked.

"There is no tolerance or interpretation of the rules," Voris replied grandiosely. "If there is a fight, then all parties are to be punished equally."

He didn't like the sound of that, and it left the system open to gross manipulation, although he parked his thoughts in lieu of the most important thing on his mind at that very moment – breakfast.

Mauro took the lead in finding somewhere suitable to eat and the group dutifully trusted his nose on the matter. After all, if anyone knew food it was going to be him.

Arriving at a non-threatening, quiet looking kiosk with tables and chairs around it, the group took a seat and watched as a glass terminal lifted from the centre of the table and flashed a few times before landing on English as its displayed language.

"This stuff is just all... so amazing," Stephanie cooed with wide eyes, though before she had a real chance to appraise anything, Mauro had begun tapping on pictures of food that none of the group recognised, with names and ingredients that were entirely alien to them.

After a frank discussion about what they all thought might have been dangerous to eat, the group as a whole decided to order five separate dishes that were all entirely plant based; they had no business eating the creatures that lived on other planets, much to the dismay of Mauro, who reluctantly caved.

Charlie's food was both delicious and filling. When it arrived he was worried that it was going to be bland as it looked much like a hollowed out sweet potato filled with boiled spinach, but to his delight the flavour was beautiful. Unlike anything he'd ever tasted, what he could most closely associate his dish with, was a mixture of fried eggs, bacon and beans, although he did wonder how much of that was actually manufactured in his own mind. The food had been brought to the table by another alien race who Charlie'd never seen before either, essentially a humanoid cyclops.

The group all seemed to enjoy their food with not a scrap left once they'd finished and after discussing their meals it was evident that they could all compare what they ate to human dishes that they enjoyed. It made Charlie wonder if there was a telepathic component to the food or even the menu to give them exactly what they wanted – after all, it wouldn't be beyond the realms of possibility for the station.

Once they'd paid for the food that they ate by holding their small station credit cards up to the terminal, which beeped happily, the squad had planned to go in search of Kori's fabled clothes, though when Charlie looked towards the lift they'd arrived on, he could see Voris and his three guards watching the group intently from afar.

Charlie nodded towards the aliens. "I think he wants us to go see The Overseer right now."

Laura looked over at the observant beings. "So? Then he should say so shouldn't he?"

"You want to risk breaking any of those three rules?" Charlie held up three fingers, mimicking Voris sarcastically. Laura chuckled.

"You're right, better not keep him waiting, he might throw us out of an airlock or something," Kori said and the group put a pin in their shopping with a definite 'to be continued.'

On the way back to The Overseer's room, Charlie worried about how exactly he was going to deal with the line of questioning that'd been conveniently interrupted the last time the pair had spoken. Moreover, he was worried that he would manage to navigate the situation without spilling the beans, but one of his friends didn't. He turned the scenario over and over in his mind until he concluded that the only way he could get them all out of trouble, was to waste as much time as possible and hope that Cesari or Kono came to his rescue. Statistically speaking, the longer time passed without his secret coming to light, the less likely it was to happen during their visit. Of course, conversely, the longer the secret remained hidden in general, the higher the probability that it would come out in the grand scheme of things, but Charlie chose his statistics on the current situation, rather than on the universal constants.

"Ah, hello again Charlie," The Overseer said once the pair were alone once again. It was as though their conversation had never missed a beat.

"Tell me about this station," Charlie said before The Overseer could get another word in. He knew it was a rude way to start the conversation, but he also knew that this being liked to partake in conversations that took turns, like a game of chess. Right now though, Charlie was playing for time.

The Overseer was silent for a long moment before he spoke, but when he did, he seemed almost happy about it.

"My father was actually on the team that built this station you know. I always wondered where his work would take us and look at where we have arrived." He looked around the room with an air of fondness in his eyes. "It was of course built initially as a listening outpost on the far reaches of the controlled space, but as the Council grew to more and more distant planets and galaxies, it became an important part of life that, well, everyone needed to not only resupply, but also to relax. My station is well known for its recreational facilities as well as our shipyard and marketplace. By all accounts, this station is the place to be for anyone who's anyone."

Charlie nodded along as The Overseer spoke and didn't really have to feign any amazement; what he was being told was fascinating.

"Now tell me about you, Charlie. Where do you come from?" The Overseer asked.

"Now that's a loaded question," Charlie replied pushing his back into the soft sofa. It was actually very comfortable so although he was still filibustering in a way, he was pretty happy about it. Then he chose his words very carefully. "When I was three the people who were raising me died in a car crash. As you could imagine, a three year old with no parents would... actually could you imagine? What do you know about raising children? Anyway as I was saying..."

The Overseer raised his hand. "That is not what I meant. And personally, I think you know that."

"You're right," Charlie conceded. "I come from a country called England if you must know. London to be exact which is a city situated in the south east of the country, though in terms of continents..."

The Overseer raised his hand again. "It is very rude to purposely mis-answer questions during a conversation, Charlie."

The door slammed open and Cesari barrelled his way into the room.

"Don't say another word, Charlie," he said and with that, Charlie dutifully shut his mouth. Cesari had arrived just in time.

"He's working with the inspectors and he's trying to get you to talk,"

Cesari said. "Keep your mouth shut. Do you hear me?"

Chapter 23

"Sorin, there have been some changes to the situation regarding the humans and the GAP program and we will be making our assessment clear with the Council in the coming days." Jorell of the Ascara spoke to his old friend through his glass terminal. "Our recommendation will be the destruction of the race and their home world, though I know that this does not fit your plans well as we had discussed."

"My friend, of course you must make your recommendations as you see them, I would never think to try to sway your decisions," Sorin practically sneered. He knew the game well and precisely how to play it. "My only fear is that we may waste an opportunity here that does not often present itself. By all means if it is your view that the human race and their planet is useless to the Council, then the threat they pose should be removed, as you say, though those that have been indicted into this program of advancement may be a key to our survival in the long run. The stories of Marcus Cesari – who by all means is just one human and on an early and unrefined version of the program, killing hundreds, possibly thousands of the Scriven's finest warriors - are not easy to forget or ignore."

Jorell sat back in his chair and thought for a moment about what Sorin was saying. "Indeed the feats of Cesari are marvelled, though as you know the Scriven are now allied and are as members of the Council. There are some that do not wish to see this race of beings, and even less so Marcus Cesari himself being inducted to our fold."

"And as the Scriven were once enemies and are now allies, do you not see a possible similar path in the future for humanity if this course of action is not taken?" Sorin asked and Jorell could tell that his friend had thought of answers for everything he might say. Regardless, Sorin was right – there was more than one race and on more than one occasion a previous enemy had been inducted into the Council. Granted it wasn't always as quickly as the Scriven had been, and seldom did the race harbour so much thinly veiled animosity to another race.

"What would you have me do, my friend?" Jorell finally asked, knowing that the quickest way to discover Sorin's agenda would be to ask for it outright.

"As I have said before, friend." Sorin replied. "My goal has always been to offer the Council an alternative to outright war and destruction where alternative paths may lie. Let me take the humans from the GAP program from all five of the sites around the planet and use them to further the aims of the Council. I am sure there are conflicts that require a timely conclusion as we speak, no?"

"You know there are," Jorell spoke quickly. "Though letting these humans live and trusting them for their compliance would not be an easy task – especially if their home world is to be destroyed."

Sorin cut in. "Their compliance is not of particular importance," he said. "The humans of the GAP program, will either fight, or die."

Chapter 24

The room had come to a silent Mexican standoff with Charlie, Cesari and The Overseer not exactly sure how they were going to resolve the issue, though Cesari looked positively mad. In contrast, The Overseer looked both assured of his own stature, and unconcerned.

Behind Cesari though and through the open door, Charlie could see his friends and squad mates trying to glance into the room, but behind them he could see Voris and the three alien security guards walking along the corridor towards them menacingly. The net was closing in and he didn't know what to.

Thankfully, the guards walked straight past his friends and in that instant Charlie decided that they weren't in any danger here. These aliens didn't know about his secret, the doctor's meddling, none of it at all. The most likely scenario that fell into place in his head was that the inspection team and The Overseer suspected him of some individual crime – finding or taking something that allowed him to cheat the system off his own back, rather than the truth – a large conspiracy in which Kono was the ringleader in advancing the human race past the means of the GAP program. That meant that if Charlie could escape from this place and keep his secret as a fugitive, the rest of his friends, the camp and humanity would almost certainly be spared.

Cesari, sensing the danger approaching, glanced at Charlie, who in turn shifted his eyes to the approaching guards who were almost at the doorway now. To Charlie's surprise, Cesari turned and leapt at the three overpowering brutes and shouted for Charlie to run, hide or find a hanger

– just do whatever he could to get out of there. Charlie, being a good soldier, ran.

The Overseer barely moved as Charlie pushed all of the strength he could muster through his heels and sprang away, past his friends in the previous room, through the open doors and down the narrow corridors. He could hear footsteps both behind and in front of him though he spared that no mind. That was until, of course, a security guard appeared in the corridor before him, again a huge being with royal blue skin and three piercing eyes.

His course had already been set though and Charlie dropped his leading shoulder and continued his charge. The security guard, apparently not threatened by the charge, stood his ground.

That was a mistake.

The force that Charlie had managed to muster in his charge, carried by his momentum and subtly shifted centre of gravity, meant that as the pair collided, Charlie came out the other side and simply carried on running. The security guard, however, hit the ceiling before landing flat on the floor. Charlie didn't even spare a moment to look back.

He entered the lift that would take him back down to the busy bullpen below and he pleaded with whatever being these things called God that it wouldn't require a keycard to do so. Today was Charlie's lucky day and the lift quickly slid right back down to the ground floor and opened to the familiar sight of crowds of aliens, shops, stalls and everything else that had existed before, going about their usual business and clearly unaware of the mortal peril Charlie had found himself within. What he did notice immediately though, was that a distress signal must've been sent out to the station's security as all around him and through the crowds, he could see more of the large security guards filtering towards him.

Without delay, Charlie ran into the crowd.

Initially he worried that it would be difficult to move through the density of the station, though as he moved quicker and quicker past the activity of the day he found that his advanced perception was helping him along his way. Things had slowed down for Charlie and he dodged, ducked, dipped and dived past alien shopper and shop alike, never even clipping a single errant shoulder. He could see the guards still following in his mind's eye, though he knew all he had to do was lose them in the crowds and then make it back out to where the ships were. He didn't care if he needed to stow away or learn how to fly a ship of his own accord but he knew that the station had nothing left for him now.

Then he saw it. His mind's eye mapped out the path to the arched exit of the bullpen and out into the cargo shipyard that they'd seen upon their arrival. That was where he needed to go.

A zigzagging path through the shops and shoppers would create the most confusion for any of his pursuers and he followed it perfectly, his body complying with every single request no matter how acrobatic it seemed. He spun, dove and juked between everything and everyone until eventually, he was clear and mere feet away from the archway and salvation.

Then his luck abruptly ran out.

Three of the large aliens moved from hidden cutaways either side of the archway, and skidding on his heels to look behind himself he saw another five filter slowly from the floor where he'd just arrived from. This was it, there would be no escape now.

Charlie's hands were zip tied behind his back once he'd surrendered and fallen to his knees. He was amazed at the feats that his body had allowed him to accomplish in the chase but couldn't help but feel as if he should've done better. What buoyed him the most though, was the fact that he wasn't even panting. His heart rate had already returned to resting and he felt as though he could do it all over again without so much as a word.

Then he was dragged to his feet roughly and pulled back towards the lift he'd arrived on and no one in the entire station seemed to bat an eyelid. He thought about shouting out for help but really, did he want to get anyone else into trouble? Would anyone else even help him?

The lift then took the three guards and Charlie downward for a few moments and opened into a new hallway though this one led around a right angled corner and to a wide open room that was bisected by black metal bars like an old fashioned jail cell. Inside the cell sat Cesari in the far corner, and the rest of Charlie's squad. Perhaps his assessment of what the aliens thought of the humans had been wrong.

Charlie didn't say a word as he was ushered into the cell and it was closed tightly behind him with a clang. He took a seat on the ground next to Cesari, who didn't look up.

Nobody felt like talking, all of the cadets realising the gravity of their situation.

"I'm sorry Charlie, I should never have let you come here," Cesari said quietly, the first to break the silence in the room. "The rest of you too."

Laura shifted to sit closer to Charlie and Cesari, though no one else moved.

"It's not your fault, Sir," she placated. "We knew what the risks were and it's not like we did anything wrong anyway. They have to see that, don't they?"

Cesari exhaled but didn't reply. He knew how these aliens worked but he didn't want to quash any hope that the girl might've harboured.

Charlie knew though. Well more accurately, he read through Cesari's body language the fact that it wasn't going to be as simple as that.

"Tell us about how you got those scars," Charlie asked eventually.

Cesari looked up and met Charlie's eyes. In those eyes and not for the first time, he saw a part of himself and knew that he owed the truth to his son - a stranger or not.

"The war was brutal. I mean you have no idea what it's like to have to fight alongside aliens you never knew existed, against other aliens that just want to kill you. Every day you don't know if you're doing the right thing – if you're on the right side. I fought until I didn't have to think any more." Cesari paused and Charlie could see the disparity in his face. "I just had to keep going, you know? Just to keep myself together. Fight and fight and fight. Keep killing, never stopping because the moment you stop, you'd die. Ramirez, Johnstone, Carter, Asimov, King, McCulloch, Hernandez, Wilson, Hunter and Foley all found out the hard way. We were surrounded by these creatures we'd been sent to clear out. We didn't know it then but they were a subspecies of the Scriven – you know the race that Callantra is from."

Charlie nodded solemnly without altering his expression.

"They'd sharpened their legs to razor edges so that if one even touched you it would cut through you in an instant. These bastards were big too – the size of a car – anyway we stood together and the Baccus had already retreated to their transports. They weren't made for war, but we were. Don't get me wrong, they fought as well as they knew how, but they just couldn't cope with the realities of the pain of fighting. The Scriven, though, they knew exactly what to do. They'd maim, removing limbs so that you wouldn't die, just feel the pain they caused and it seemed to feed them, to spur them on. Ramirez fell first. His weapon jammed just at the wrong moment and he took his eyes away from the enemy for one second to try to clear it." Cesari closed his eyes. "Johnstone, Carter and Asimov fell together completely overwhelmed by a swarm of the enemy. They fought bitterly to the end but eventually their ammo ran short and once one link in the chain weakened, that was it. Foley and I were eventually the last two. He… he couldn't handle it. Foley took his own life to leave me to fend for myself, one human alone between two alien warring races. I nearly followed Foley."

"What did you do?" Charlie asked quietly, absorbed by the story.

"I held on. I said to myself that there was no way I was going to be killed on a planet I had no business in being on so I found a defensible position, collected up all the ammo from the rest of the guys and sat with my back to a wall for three days. The Scriven attacking me piled up and up until eventually it was hard for them to even get to me over the bodies of their dead. If the Baccus didn't come back for me, I would've probably been done within another day."

"So the scars?" Charlie gestured to Cesari's back and the place where he knew the two scars crossed over.

Cesari smiled, "There's nothing heroic about those. When I saw the transport land near to my position I dropped everything I could and ran. It was only ten or fifteen seconds away at top speed but let me tell you, those eight legged bastards can move. One caught up to me as I reached the transport and even though it was cut down by the Baccus, it managed to leave its mark on my back before it took its last breath. If I hadn't been a part of the first GAP program I don't know if I would've made it through all of that."

"And then you had me?" Charlie asked, skipping over some of the gorier details.

"Well... as you might imagine..." Cesari spoke slowly as though unsure of the words to use. "When I got back to Earth, there were a few things that I craved. I wanted a burger. A smoke. The company of a good woman..."

Charlie didn't need to hear the end of that sentence. "But why didn't you stay with my mother and raise me? Do you have any idea what I've been through?" He didn't mean it to, but his voice sounded pleading almost to the point of desperation.

"I didn't know..." Cesari replied quietly and he looked very ashamed. "I was posted back to the military and that's where I stayed for the next few years. I just... didn't know, Charlie." He raised his gaze to meet Charlie's again and Charlie could see the wetness of tears filling them and he could empathise through his own feelings. He could see that Cesari was telling the truth. His dad was telling him the truth and if he'd have known, then perhaps things would've been different for the both of them.

"When did you find out?" Charlie asked quietly once he was able to talk again.

Cesari lowered his head. "Just before the final fight between you and Henderson. Kono told me everything."

"Ok," Laura said quietly once the room was sure that no one else was going to offer any mind-blowing revelations. "So tell me, if this Council or whatever it is, is so all powerful that they can wipe out the human race all in one go, why do they need God damned soldiers anyway?"

Cesari looked up to meet her gaze and Laura saw in his eyes the change from father to instructor in that very moment.

"Giardini, do I need to explain everything as if you're five?" he asked and Charlie was sure that Laura had just cemented herself as the new butt of all of Cesari's nastiness. "Think about this – the world has nuclear weapons, so why do humans need an army to fight each other? Total annihilation, as much as it may sound like it is the aim of many conflicts, is almost never the goal of war. Why destroy something when you can take it, or use it to your advantage? In most conflicts throughout history and by extension the universe, total destruction has almost never been used."

Laura didn't respond and Charlie could tell that she'd understood the concept, as had he.

"So who was my mum? My real mum I mean?" Charlie asked quietly.

Cesari took a deep breath and exhaled animatedly. "I don't know how to say this Charlie, but I'm afraid I never took her surname. Like I said, I was home on leave after the GAP program trial run and I'd just had spider-creatures try to kill me over and over. Your mother's name was Maria. She was beautiful, and to me she reminded me what humanity was all about. That's all I can tell you. You remind me of her actually, and myself."

Charlie could almost feel the hurt oozing from his father as he spoke the words and decided that it was probably a good idea not to press him any further. After all, it did sound as though there was nothing more he had to say on the matter anyway.

As though by some divine intervention, on the far side of the cell that the group shared, the alien inspection team appeared and Jorell didn't spare a moment before he made his announcement, reading from a glass terminal without emotion.

"The human beings of the GAP program have demonstrated that they cannot be trusted to carry out the instructions given to them by The Intergalactic Council. It is with regret that following our visit our subsequent recommendation regarding Camp Rebirth and all of the other locations around the planet designated 'EP1' is to be termination of the program. We understand as a group what this will mean for the human race as a whole, though fail to see any alternative."

None of the cadets nor Cesari could believe what they were hearing and were totally dumbfounded. Not a single one of them could make a noise in answer. Charlie did notice though, that underneath her dark veil, Callantra was smirking.

Cesari was the first to raise himself to his feet once he was sure the alien had stopped speaking.

"Are you fucking KIDDING ME?" He practically screamed as his knuckles turned white around the metal bars.

"Wait... do you mean that you're recommending that the entire human race is to be destroyed?" Laura blurted out before Cesari had the chance to explode and the rest of the cadets began to mutter amongst themselves worriedly. Jorell though, chose to respond to Laura over the larger Chief Instructor.

"The GAP program was enacted as an alternative to total annihilation of the human race. It was a testing ground for the malleability and usability of a cross section of the human race. With the failure of the program, the only alternative is to act upon our initial assessment of destruction."

"Why?" Stephanie's voice came from the rear of the cell quietly and she moved forward toward the bars. "Why does it have to be serve or die? Who are you to decide what races deserve to live or die?"

"What Stephanie's trying to say, Kori joined her, and then Mauro, "is who the fuck do you think you are?"

Jorell chose to ignore the outburst though Korvin spoke on his behalf, the lizard man practically hissing. "You humans do nothing but fight. You fight over land, over resources, over religion, over words. The smallest perceived sleight can set you off on a course to total war. This has been your way for centuries. It is what fuels you, what advances you."

"So what?" Cesari spoke now as though he was protecting the cadets from the words. "That's exactly what you wanted for your Council, isn't it?"

The Kanaan continued speaking as though he hadn't heard Cesari at all. "But the countries and military powers around the planet Earth have reached a turning point. What you call nuclear weapons are a weapon of mass destruction and not precision tools. Usually when a civilisation reaches the technological level that the human race has, that technology is turned towards good - the advancement of the race, a search for the stars. Human beings, however, are hell bent on war and destruction. It is all you know, and all you care to know."

"And?" Mauro said from beside Stephanie. "We have to make sure we have the means to defend ourselves, especially..." he paused for a moment, "especially when this 'Council' can decide who lives and who dies at the drop of a hat."

"Do you see?" Callantra hissed. "These humans are just like the others. They will do nothing but fight, betray and live in the belief that they are better. There is no training them to do our bidding. There is no compliance. There must be destruction."

'You should never have crossed the Scriven,' Callantra's voice rasped in Cesari's mind, though it was somehow internally loud enough for Charlie to hear.

'The Scriven will always have their revenge.'

Chapter 25

The only way that Charlie could track the days that were passing during his incarceration, was because of the two meals each day that were brought to their cell by the large three-eyed security guards. Of course he didn't know if this translated to twenty-four hour periods or not, but his levels of fatigue told him the timing wasn't too dissimilar. Putting a number on it, they'd been in the cell for about three weeks in total – although they'd been allowed to leave to use the toilet and to shower periodically – though Charlie assumed there was something in the food keeping their bodily functions suppressed as he barely needed to use the very human-like, flushable toilet.

The group had wondered how long their existence in captivity was going to last and none of them could come up with a definitive reason as to why the inspection team had both told them their plans for the human race and that they had allowed them to live, given those plans. The group had theorised that the aliens either didn't have the authority to make the decision alone – Charlie recounted that they'd used the word 'recommendation' – or they had something else in mind for these rule breakers. Maybe they wanted to parade them around in front of The Council members or the human race in general as the reason for their decision.

Not one of the inspection team nor The Overseer had come to visit the group in the entire time they'd remained in their cell and it gave the group the chance to talk amongst themselves at first, although soon a collective silence had washed over them, each inwardly dismayed at the potential loss of their families and friends back on Earth.

They had learned, though, that Kori Nakamura was an orphan much like Charlie. Originating from Japan, his parents had fallen ill with an unknown pathogen at the same time. His grandparents already having passed and with no other family to speak of, he had brought himself up living on the streets until he was offered the chance to join the GAP program to become a better version of himself. Handily, it also offered a warm place to sleep and all the food he would need. Charlie didn't miss the fact that Kori was the only one amongst the group who had been told what the GAP program was before he joined up.

Stephanie was the youngest of seven sisters, and by all accounts her family was struggling. She'd had it in her mind to leave the family home as soon as she could. Being the smallest voice in a cacophony of louder ones she wanted to disappear and never be thought of again as soon as she could. Her options had been somewhat limited though and without money there was little she could do. Stephanie had begun to write a blog. It wasn't well followed or even liked to a huge degree but she kept up with it, and sure enough some readers enjoyed the trials of her daily life, the way she thought about things and deconstructed information. It was when she'd started talking about how things worked in greater detail that the military had made contact. Stephanie, according to their analysts, was brilliant – and they did that they could help her become so much more.

Day twenty-three was the day for change in the prison cell that the group called home. This day, their first meal was not brought in by the usual hulking three eyed security guard. Today, the being carrying their large tray of food was very thin and had very little muscle tone. Underneath his blue sash with golden trim, his skin was a translucent blue and if Charlie looked closely, he could see almost the entire network of veins just beneath its skin.

Charlie jumped when Mauro spoke loudly to break the silence at the alien's entrance.

"Is that... PIZZA?" The larger boy exclaimed as he sniffed the air. Charlie was surprised at the announcement though after he took a deep inhale, he too could smell the sweet aroma of tomato sauce on a deep pan, oven baked breaded base.

"How do you do that?" Charlie asked sideways with a frown.

"Greetings, humans!" The alien proclaimed as he placed the food tray on the serving hatch. "I trust you are being well looked after here?"

Cesari exhaled through his nose but took the food that was on offer. Mauro was not far behind him, waiting as though he was a dog ready to have his lead put on for his daily walk. Nobody replied.

"My name is Sorin," Sorin announced with a smile. "And I am here to rescue you!" he raised his arms to his side as though he was Jesus.

That earned him a few looks of confusion from the cadets.

"Rescue us?" Laura said before taking a large slice of the pizza from the tray. She couldn't help herself, what the group had been eating so far whilst in captivity had been... bland. "It's you lot that put us in here!"

Sorin had a look of visible confusion on his face for a long moment before it returned to its previous assured smile.

"Ah..." he said. "You think all aliens to you are equal don't you. If one race does something you don't like then all aliens are bad?"

Laura blushed, she hadn't meant for her statement to sound so sweeping and she could see that Sorin was actually right. "N... no," she replied. "I meant that... well... if you're here to rescue us then why wait until now? Where were you three weeks ago?"

"It took my ship three weeks to get here," Sorin replied simply. "I don't just wait in stations to rescue humans and, well, the universe is a very big place..."

Laura stopped talking for fear of making any more of a fool of herself.

"Don't be fooled, Giardini," Cesari said. "He's not here to rescue us." The Chief Instructor also took a pizza and shuffled out of the way for Kori and Stephanie to slide a slice off the tray.

"Plus..." Mauro announced through chewing. "Maybe we don't want to be rescued... You ever... think about that?"

Sorin looked confused again. "You don't want to be rescued? You know what they have planned for you right? For all of you?"

"Don't worry about him," Laura replied on Mauro's behalf. "Yes, we would like to get out of here, but what exactly is it that you are offering?"

"I'm glad you asked," Sorin replied grandiosely. "I am offering you the chance to see the universe. To be a part of something much bigger than anything you have imagined before. To see the stars and work together with a race of beings that always have the best things at the forefront of their minds..."

"He wants us to be his army," Cesari said flatly, interrupting the statement. "Just like The Council, just like everyone else. We're soldiers and that's all we'll ever be to any of these races." He didn't speak with malice or discomfort, it was more of a matter of fact statement, as if he didn't care at all.

Sorin opened his mouth to object.

"Oh don't get me wrong, I don't mean it as a bad thing," Cesari continued before Sorin could speak. "I'm just saying how it is. To me it doesn't really matter. Soldier here, soldier there... it's all pretty much the same. If what you're saying gets me out of this cage though, I'm all for it." He punctuated his statement by taking a bite of pizza and walked away to the back of the cell to sit down.

Sorin looked decidedly taken aback. He was shocked that Cesari had concluded his intentions correctly, but even more shocked that the man didn't even seem to care.

"Is that it?" Laura asked. "Do you want to use us as soldiers?"

"Well, uh..." Sorin replied. "Yes actually. You see I am what is known as a Talchiar..."

"Don't care. Already said we'll do it," Cesari spoke up nonchalantly, interrupting the blue alien. Charlie liked this side of Cesari, it made him seem so much more human than his persona as Chief Instructor had.

"Well be that as it may..." Sorin replied. "I am in need, in the long term, of an army of soldiers that will fall under my command and perhaps even pilot ships of their own."

"You want to give us a ship?" Stephanie cocked her head and stood up. Charlie had noticed that when the conversations had turned to technology, she was all ears.

"Uh well... not... uh right away?" Sorin replied. This was possibly the first time that the alien had ever been a part of a conversation that he didn't fully control himself. He was totally astounded by the lacklustre way in which the humans conducted themselves and, frankly, it put him on the back foot. Stephanie sat down again hearing the 'no' in his statement.

"So you'd all like to come willingly?" Sorin asked, still unsure if the conversation was going to plan or not.

"Duh," Laura replied.

Nobody else said anything.

"Is that a yes?" He asked again.

Laura rolled her eyes and huffed. "Yes, please spring us from jail and take us back to exactly what we were doing before we were put in here. Thank you very much."

"Oh," Sorin replied. "Well now I almost feel bad for the pizza..."

Mauro's head snapped about. "You don't have any more, do you?"

"Well no," Sorin said. "Sleeping drugs are quite expensive and..."

Charlie's vision went fuzzy. He knew this feeling all too well.

"Good morning, Charlie," the voice came from the darkness and Charlie could only assume that he was either dreaming right now, or had dreamt the entire space station ordeal, because the voice that he heard, belonged to Dr. Kono.

"Are you KIDDING ME?" He announced loudly, bringing a hand up to his forehead in his instinctual way to check if anything on his face was broken after the lizard doctor had got his hands on him. Opening his eyes he recognised the layout of yet *another* medical bay that'd been set up specifically for Kono, though not one he'd been in before.

"Oh don't be like that, Charlie," The doctor smiled. "I haven't done anything to you... well not yet anyway."

Charlie could tell he was joking, though that feat alone was more of an art than a skill.

"You've been away for a while now Charlie, haven't you?" Kono announced. "Sorry I couldn't be there to help you out but I just didn't fancy joining you in there – I didn't want to blow my cover as you humans say. Anyway. Had a chance to check your PIP level recently?"

Charlie shook his head.

"Nineteen percent," the doctor announced with a grin. "Very, very impressive. No doubt you have discovered some new things your body is capable of? Superhuman strength? Invisibility maybe?"

"I'm a bit stronger, and I can run and recover really quickly. Also my perception is, well..."

Before Charlie could finish his sentence, the doctor threw the pen that he was holding in his hand directly at Charlie, who caught it without so much as a thought.

"Holy shit!" Charlie said.

The doctor made a note on his terminal but didn't respond to the outburst.

"It's good to see that your new accessory doesn't impair your physical functions," Kono said.

"New... accessory?" Charlie stated slowly but the doctor was already pointing towards his neck.

"Don't panic about it," Kono said as Charlie brought his hand to his neck and felt the metallic collar that encircled it. It wasn't overly tight but it was enough that it wouldn't move around and he certainly wouldn't be removing it over his head. He could feel a hinge at the back though so assumed that was the way he could get it on and off.

"Our sponsor has insisted that all of the cadets they have on board wear these devices. Essentially they're shock collars, so I wouldn't go around breaking any rules. Other than that though, you're right as rain." Kono explained.

"So now we're slaves... and you're not," Charlie summarised. "Amazing."

"No, not slaves, soldiers." Kono announced. "Just like before."

"Just like before, but with shock collars." Charlie stated.

"Exactly."

"Where are the others? And where are we?" Charlie asked.

"Well, we are aboard a spaceship on its way back to Camp Rebirth. You're the first one to wake up after the pizza – probably because of your ever enhancing body and its advanced metabolism. I need to make a note to keep an eye on that; the last thing we need is for anaesthetic to not work on you without us knowing – or even worse that it would wear off right when it shouldn't... Your squad and the Chief Instructor are in the next rooms down the corridor, you can go and see them if you like. I must warn you though, better to not go anywhere else at the moment – the crew might get a little... trigger happy," he gestured to his neck and grimaced. Charlie did not want to test that theory.

The rest of the squad, including Cesari, were indeed in the adjoining rooms and each of them wore the same collar as Charlie, as he pointed out to them as he gathered them up one by one until they all stood together in Cesari's room. Mauro was pulling at the collar but it wasn't moving and Stephanie was peering into a mirror as she tried to spin it around her neck with a very inquisitive look on her face.

"What do you think they have planned for us?" Stephanie said absently as she was absorbed by the collar. "And what about the other cadets? Do you think we're all just going back to train again?" Her question was directed to the room, but it was obvious that Cesari was the one who was supposed to answer – he was still the one in charge after all.

"I don't think that things are going to be 'normal' in any way, actually," he replied. "This Sorin character seems to be keeping something from us and I don't like it. Personally I much prefer when people actually say what they mean, you know."

"He's right," Charlie agreed. "He had to knock us out to get us to come with him. That tells me that he didn't have permission to do what he did, or at least official permission. I wouldn't put it past one of the inspection team having a hand in our escape. If he had permission then why wouldn't he just get ten security guards to force the collars on us and walk us out the front door?"

"Oh, you think ten security guards would be enough to take me down?" Kori snorted out.

"Oh shut up Kori, I think I can still see that boot print on your forehead" Laura said.

"We were throwing that... that doesn't count!" He turned red. Laura smiled wickedly.

"Anyway..." Charlie continued. "I doubt that everything is as clear cut as it seems. And do you know what a 'Talchiar is?" he asked Cesari.

"Not a clue," The Chief Instructor replied. "Probably some grand idea to make this one feel better about himself. They're all a bit like that."

"And Callantra?" Charlie asked.

"Yep, that's a Scriven. Not as big or as sharp as the ones that gave me my scars, but still dangerous," Cesari answered.

"But you're OK with her being on the inspection team? Isn't that like a conflict of interest or something?" Charlie asked.

"It wasn't something I was happy with, don't get me wrong. She clearly has an agenda but there's nothing I could've done about it. Anyway, Marsh, have you figured out how to spring us from these God damned collars yet?"

Stephanie practically jumped at the mention of her name and squeaked out a response, "N... not yet. Was I supposed to?"

"Then what in God's name have you been doing this whole time looking at that thing in the mirror?" Cesari said flatly.

"Oh... I uh... I suppose," she looked back in the mirror at the collar around her neck. "It's got an electronic locking system. I'd guess that it takes a specific signal to unlock and another to shock but I wouldn't like to try to run through frequencies just in case we got the wrong one."

"If the crew can all activate the collars, then wouldn't they have to have, like, a remote control or something?" Charlie asked.

"That's likely," Stephanie replied thoughtfully and clearly more comfortable about discussing technology than anything else. "Though each collar must be individually controlled, right? Or everyone would be shocked if one prisoner decided to run off?"

Cesari winced but didn't answer. Charlie saw it though and wondered if that was exactly what the collars were designed to do.

"I'd say we need a portable terminal – like the ones we had back in the camp – those glass things seemed pretty universal." Stephanie said. "The aliens on the ship probably all have one each.

"Well, I know one way to test that theory," Cesari said, and opened the door to the corridor. He then inhaled loudly and yelled at the top of his voice for help.

Within a few short moments, three of the translucent blue aliens that looked remarkably similar to Sorin arrived at the medical bay and walked in, causing the cadets and Cesari to all back away from them to make room.

"Oh look, it's a smurf!" Cesari said animatedly, though the others didn't say anything. He muttered to himself about his humour being wasted on this generation, but was interrupted by one of the aliens. Charlie was surprised that they didn't seem to be carrying any weapons, though that just further reinforced the notion that they had control over the shock collars.

"Can I just distract you for a second?" Cesari said as he ushered the three aliens toward him. They didn't seem worried and dutifully took another step further into the room.

Charlie saw Laura bring her hand up to her forehead in utter despair at the deception, but she kept her mouth shut.

Then Cesari punched the middle alien in its face. Hard.

It collapsed to the ground in a flash and Charlie had moved before it even hit the metal floor with a bang. In that moment he'd moved behind the alien on the right, taking a hold of its head with his back to its own. He knelt to the ground and backflipped the being over himself and to the ground. Then he took the lead and punched it in its face, rendering it unconscious. The third and last standing alien then took a large step back and retrieved a glass terminal from inside its uniform. Before Charlie or Cesari even moved, the thing had tapped it with a long thin finger and a huge grin on its face.

Cesari jerked his back straight, his head angled towards the ceiling and Charlie could see the veins in his neck straining against the current. It looked like more pain than the man could endure and eventually he fell to the ground, convulsing.

What Charlie did notice though, was that the alien didn't seem to be able to activate all of the collars at once so there must've been some kind of menu system to navigate on the terminal. Not wanting to waste his moment of opportunity, he leapt at the alien.

Stephanie held the terminal in her hands turning it over and over, examining it as Cesari brushed himself off, bringing himself back up to his full height.

"Well that was… unpleasant," he announced sounding very much out of breath. "Seriously it was like getting wrapped up in an electric fence, but the fence was made of razor wire."

Just as he finished speaking, his collar clicked open and he moved his hands to remove it immediately. "No thanks," he announced. "I prefer my uniforms without unnecessary bling."

"Wait," Charlie said. "We can use this to our advantage, can't we?" he looked at Stephanie, "Can you deactivate the shock part with that?"

Stephanie looked at the terminal for a short while before answering with "I think so?"

"Great," Charlie said. I have an idea.

Chapter 26

Sorin sat and watched The Council members deliberating on their latest findings and the recommendations of the inspection team that'd arrived. It was strange that the team was yet to make it back for the meeting although it wouldn't take anything away from the severity of the situation that they all found themselves within – least of all because of the video link that'd been established. Once again, The Council members were to decide on the fate of the human race, and once again there were arguments for both pro's and con's.

"Our recommendation can be summarised as the following." Callantra was the one speaking and Sorin could tell she was trying her hardest to use her least threatening and most emotionally unavailable tone. He knew the trick well too, remove feeling from the equation and focus simply on facts – it made difficult tasks easier to swallow for others.

Callantra continued: "The human race is not to be trusted and we feel that there is no alternative at this moment. We must shut down our program of artificial advancement and remove the threat that they pose to all of us from the universe. It is what should've been done in the beginning and now that we have experimented with an alternative path, we can see that it has been fruitless."

"It seems a little dramatic, don't you think?" The Intari member spoke in his high pitched, small voice though Callantra did not respond to him directly.

"The humans have displayed a willingness to deceive us, and have committed crimes aboard the well known and well populated Omnis station that alone caused many innocent bystanders to fear for their lives. On top of this, all we continue to do as a Council to make them stronger and smarter to the point that they may rival our own acuity. You must all see now that this must not be allowed to continue."

The Council members muttered dully amongst themselves for they knew that it wasn't so long ago that Callantra's own race had been their mortal enemy. They knew that by the rules of the Council and its membership they needed to be fair and concise, but some simply couldn't see past the black eyes and long fangs of the Scriven. It was simply too soon.

"But they don't have any ships! And no way to leave either their home world or the planet that we are conducting our experimentations on!" the Intari replied loudly once the muttering had abated. "Where is the harm in leaving them to grow to see which path they lead?'

Callantra almost hissed in the smaller being's outright disobedience but held herself back; she knew that this was not the time.

"Human beings are like a virus, a plague," she explained calmly. "If we let them grow and expand, they will multiply. Once this happens they will look to make more space for themselves in the universe and that means they will come for your planets, your home worlds. Before you know it they will integrate across the universe and there will be no stopping them. Are you willing to put the lives of your families and loved ones at risk simply to see 'where this is going?" she asked sarcastically.

"N... no," the Intari responded wavering slightly, "But still... they don't have any ships... so where is the threat?"

Callantra smiled because she had an answer to this question. "Tell me, when you are dealing with a plague like this, what happens when one single minute cell of that disease escapes the quarantine?" She paused dramatically. "If one single human is allowed to live then we are all at risk. If even one of them makes it off of the planet and escapes our watchful eyes then it will be too late. We must stop this madness right now."

Sorin, who'd remained silent through all of this, heard the meaning in the statement and sat ever so slightly more upright in his chair. Truthfully he hadn't been listening intently to the spider-creature because the sight of it made him feel quite sick. He wasn't from a particularly warring race and the thought of the way these Scriven creatures conducted themselves in battle was frankly frightening to him. He knew though that his friend Jorell had made him a promise, and this was as good a time as any to remind him of what that was.

Sorin spoke loudly and clearly for everyone in the meeting to hear. "But with plagues, pathogens and viruses, with the right containment we keep and study those don't we? Because one day they may provide the solution to a problem that was not thought of before. It sounds to me as though this is a question that can be answered by proper containment and supervision rather than total destruction, honoured Council member."

The link fell silent and Sorin sat back to allow his words to percolate the members. He was proud of his counter-argument but was happier once Jorell of the Ascara spoke in response.

"That is a very fair point Council member Sorin. We must not be hasty in our decision making and of course our recommendations are just that – they are not binding and we three cannot and will not decide the fate of an entire race by ourselves.

"Perhaps there is an alternative path that can be taken?" Sorin replied in a very leading tone.

Jorell spoke again. "There are three paths that I can think of in this scenario. The first is that we allow the humans to continue as they are – though I feel that this is not preferred by any of the members here now. The second is that the human race is to be destroyed as a whole and we remove them from our thoughts. Third," he gave a slight sigh before he spoke, "we can destroy the human home world and allow the cadets of the GAP program to carry out their duties as intended."

"I can offer my ship and those of my kin," Sorin replied quickly. He'd been waiting for just this moment.

"I… have no issue with Sorin taking the GAP humans away to do the bidding of the Council," Jorell stated and with that, his promise to his friend had been fulfilled.

"NO," Callantra stated loudly, almost losing her cool. "The humans must be destroyed. If just one of your own family members, and I speak to everyone here, is killed by a human because you made the wrong decision then their blood is on your hands. These beings cannot be trusted and must pay for what they have done. There is no alternative, only total annihilation."

The room was silent for a long moment before Sorin spoke again. "I admit that your argument is clear and may well be in the best interests of everyone here," he said slowly. "In any case I will offer my ship as transport to take the humans back from the station to the planet's surface until your final deliberations have been made."

"Fine," Jorell said before Callantra could interrupt again. "But do not let even a single one of them evade you, Sorin. The Council will not accept failure in this case."

Chapter 27

With all of their collars on, although deactivated, Charlie had brought all of the cadets up to speed with what he had in mind. First, they needed to pay a visit to the doctor and then they would sit in wait until they reached the planet where the rest of the cadets were. Assuming that Sorin would either stick around on the planet for a short time, or immediately usher the rest of the cadets onto his ship, collaring the cadets for their compliance seemed like it was a thing that was going to happen. What they couldn't afford though, was for the three aliens that they'd tricked to tell the captain that one of their terminals was missing.

"Can I just distract you for a second? That's what you went with?" Laura said to Cesari as the group dragged the three unconscious aliens down the hallway. They were pretty light actually so none of them had any issues with the task.

"Hey, they don't watch TV, why do I care what I say as long as it works." Cesari replied. Laura just shrugged, still a little outraged.

When the group entered Kono's office, the lizard man reacted as if the three aliens being dragged in behind them was the most natural thing in the world.

"Hi!" Charlie announced to the doctor, who gave a curt 'hello' in reply.

"You know that favour you owe me?" Charlie started. "Well it's time to pay up."

"I don't recall..." Kono started but was cut off when the cadets and Cesari hoisted the aliens onto one of the tables, lengthways.

"We need these ones to stay out of action for a while. With a plausible excuse as to why," Charlie stated flatly.

"Hmm," Kono replied. "I suppose I can say something about there being a chemical leak on the ship – something that was fixed but I'd need to keep them under. Actually yes, I don't see why that would be a problem."

Cesari gave the lizard doctor the side eye as if he was trying to remember all the times the doctor could've deceived him in order to pay back some debt. In the grand scheme of things though, it didn't really matter.

"So what do you have planned then? Mutiny? The old take over the ship routine and sail off into the sunset?" Kono asked.

"Something like that," Cesari replied, apparently still wary of the doctor.

"A piece of advice though," Kono said as the group made to leave the room. "I'd refrain from playing with your collars, especially if you've opened them up already. Kind of gives the game away, doesn't it?" He was looking at Mauro who was apparently opening and closing his shock collar absent mindedly. Laura gave him a gentle kick in the shins and he whipped his arms away from the device.

The squad had the outline of a plan, though the finer details were somewhat lacking. Charlie had suggested that they wait until they landed back on the planet's surface to spring whatever they were going to do, though both Kori and Laura wanted to try to take the ship beforehand. It did make sense - once again statistically speaking the longer they tried to keep the charade up, the higher the chance they'd get caught. Plus the doctor needed to keep the other three aliens plausibly unconscious, and nobody knew for how long that was going to wash.

Cesari was the last to give his opinion on the matter.

"Listen up kids," he said. It was a bit of a misnomer now though, with each of the cadets presenting as though they were in their early twenties. "I don't know how to fly a big ass spaceship and I don't think any of you do either. That's why we gotta wait this one out. When we land, I'd bet that this Sorin character plans to take the rest of the cadets on the planet by force, so we have to be ready for that. There will be a moment when there are more of us than there are of them and we need to take that moment by the balls. You've all been trained and you know what you need to do. This is going to be a one shot deal, so we need to get it right."

Clichéd or not his speech was appropriate. The thing that worried Charlie the most in all of this, was that in no scenario could he see everyone making it out alive.

The Chief Instructor, noticing Charlie's concern, continued. "Listen up everyone. There's a reason that The Council wanted to use humans as soldiers and it's the same reason Sorin wants the same thing. The races in The Council don't like to fight. Yeah, I know they can talk a big game and can wipe out planets from orbit and all that – but fighting in close quarters, one on one? It's barbaric. They've evolved past all of that, and that is our advantage. We can beat them if we make them face the fight head on."

This actually made very good sense to Charlie, who immediately thought back to how easy it'd been to take down the three guards prior to the collar removals. These things just weren't cut out for fighting, for subterfuge and the like.

"So we wait then?" Mauro asked once Cesari had finished his statement. "Then pound them when we hit the planet like last week's mashed potatoes."

Laura rolled her eyes. "Does everything have to be about food with you?"

"Listen, if it's worth saying, then it's worth making it about food," Mauro replied. Charlie chuckled quietly at his friends.

If Sorin had been suspicious about his crew mates being knocked unconscious, or by Dr. Kono's explanation of that fact, he didn't show it. Or at least the group didn't get to hear about it. As far as they were concerned it was business as usual. They'd been told to stay in their section of the ship – which although was boring – wasn't confining in any way. They had food and water brought to them. The only thing lacking was any sort of recreational activity. They couldn't really tell if that's just how it was on spaceships or if it was a special case for them as prisoners. Either way, the journey back to the planet and Camp Rebirth was mostly uneventful and passed quite quickly, which Charlie and the group were all thankful for.

The ship landed with a small bump as it hit the ground but the group weren't collected from their section of the vessel. Presumably, Sorin didn't want to alarm any of the cadets still on the surface with the collars that the group was wearing – If he was going to try to talk them into coming along willingly, the last thing he wanted was for the others to look as though they were prisoners.

"This is it," Cesari announced to the cadets and as one they left the room and walked out of their section of the ship in search of the natural daylight the planet would afford them.

The first door they'd come to that led from their section was unsurprisingly locked and Stephanie took out the terminal that she'd used to unlock the shock collars and searched through the menus for a moment. When nothing happened, Charlie and Mauro each placed a hand on either side of the door and tried to prise it open. Beginning to give, the rest of the group offered their aid and within a moment the doors parted and revealed a long, wide cargo bay leading to the bright outside world. It made sense actually, if they needed to get everyone on board quickly, this would certainly help to accomplish that fact.

Between them and the planet though, stood two alien guards facing away from the cadets, both holding some kind of rifle.

Charlie and Cesari shared a glance before both simultaneously taking the aliens in a choke hold, covering their mouths and dragging them back into their segregated section of the ship. A muffled thud came from each of the cadets and both Charlie and Cesari returned a moment later holding the weapons.

On the edge of the cargo bay, Charlie could see that Sorin was standing before the massed cadets and he wondered how they'd managed to congregate so quickly, although thinking about it, it wasn't every day an alien spaceship landed on your doorstep.

He could see the gates and walls of the camp behind them, and noticed that the rows and rows of cadets were almost strangers to him. The three weeks or so they'd been away had turned the adolescents into tall, strong militaristic men and women, each one of them wearing a flight suit that betrayed their rank of Ordinary Cadet. At their front stood Matty Henderson, unmistakably, who'd grown a full head taller than the rest, apparently the time he'd been set back by in solitary already a distant memory.

Sorin was standing with his back to Charlie and his squad, alone, though Charlie could hear the speech he was giving to the cadets of the camp.

"...You can now all see that The Council does not think that you are fit as a race to stand as their puppets. I am offering you all the chance to come with me into the stars and become the things you were born to be..."

It was pretty much the same speech that he'd tried out on Charlie's own squad and he could see that although ruffled, the cadets weren't particularly falling for it. What they needed was instruction and without the Chief Instructor in their midst, Charlie wondered exactly who'd taken charge in all of this.

Charlie, Cesari, Stephanie, Kori, Laura and Mauro walked slowly forwards and out into view behind the blue alien. The cadets on the ground held their collective breath.

Sensing the disturbance, Sorin turned around to Charlie, who stood not a foot away from his face with his rifle in his hands. He didn't point it threateningly, though Sorin could tell that he had every intention of using it if he needed to.

"A... ahh, and here are our first recruits," Sorin announced loudly attempting to make light of his new situation. "We rescued your friends and instructor from the hands of The Council and here they are. Do not take my word for any of this, just ask them!"

"What do you think you are doing?" Sorin said quietly to Charlie, who didn't respond.

Sorin retrieved his small glass terminal from inside his sash and prodded at it almost in a panic. Charlie didn't make a move to stop him, safe in the knowledge that Stephanie had already deactivated the collars, so Sorin's actions would amount to nothing.

Sorin tapped the terminal a few more times in frustration before Charlie raised a single hand to his collar and unclipped it from his neck, dropping it to the metallic floor of the ship with a loud clang that echoed off into the valley.

Then Charlie picked up the alien by his neck and raised him off the ground by just a few inches. Once he was sure he'd made his point, Charlie then dropped Sorin to the ground, who did not make any attempts to stand back up.

"What some of Sorin has said is true," Charlie announced loudly so that all the cadets mustered could hear him. "The Council that had a part in starting the GAP program which we are all a part of has decided that the program is untenable, and to be terminated. We are all to be terminated." He waited a moment to allow what he was saying to permeate the crowd. "In addition, we have reason to believe that The Council will have determined that the human race as a whole is not one that they can tolerate. They plan to destroy Earth and eradicate humanity from the universe. This is not conjecture. This is the truth."

The crowd of cadets started muttering amongst themselves at that statement but Charlie knew he needed to continue.

"Sorin here," he nudged the alien with his foot, "Planned to enslave us all, to be used as his own personal army for whatever reasons he had in mind. He took us from the station, drugged us and placed collars on us like dogs to be controlled and that is what he had planned for all of you too. I have a plan of my own though if you'll listen."

The cadets remained standing to attention, indicating that they were willing to hear Charlie out. Surprisingly, even Matty Henderson remained silent at Charlie's speech.

"We need to rescue any other humans on this planet first. From what I understand there are other camps holding cadets within the GAP program. Then we must go to Earth to warn everyone what is coming and help however we can. Our friends, families and all of humanity will be relying on us to carry out this task and we owe it to each and every one of them to try as hard as we can to take these aliens down. We will show them that we are not out in the universe looking for war, but if a fight is brought to our doorstep, we will defend ourselves – and it will be the biggest mistake they'll ever make."

There were no cheers of agreement from the cadets, but there was a tiny movement right from the back and filtering through the ranks of cadets came Instructor Dawn Shepherd. She didn't speak up nor did she stop walking until she reached Charlie, coming face to face with him. Placing a single hand on Charlie's shoulder, Shepherd nodded once, then moved past him and into the ship. That was all the convincing that the cadets of Camp Rebirth needed to join Charlie and his crew and within moments they were all making their way towards and onto the ship.

Charlie and Cesari had passed their weapons to Laura and Mauro who were tasked with guarding Sorin whilst the rest of the cadets ferried equipment and weaponry into the ship. With three hundred well trained and genetically modified soldiers to work with, rounding up the alien crew of twenty was an easy task to carry out. Apparently Sorin had thought that the shock collars were going to be enough of a deterrent for mutiny so hadn't come mob-handed or even particularly well equipped. Now though, the ship was practically ready for war with a full complement of armed soldiers. The only thing they needed to do was make sure that the actual crew of the ship would either help them out, or do their work under duress. It didn't really matter which.

It was a kind of weird situation that Charlie had found himself and the rest of his squad in. There was a definite feeling of disparity between them and the rest of the cadets, which was outlined by the immediate separation of the cadets as a whole and Charlie's squad, who stood with the instructors. The ship itself had enough space for everyone on board, although it did mean that some had to share, and inevitably that meant that squads were going to be grouped up again wherever possible – it was the easiest way to sort everyone out quickly. What Charlie didn't like though, was just how easy it was for them to take the ship the way they had. In his mind, surely Sorin had something up his sleeve to get them all into the collars.

"I think we should leave behind all the food and supplies that the ship already had on board," Charlie said aloud after a long moment of pondering. He hadn't been expecting to voice any concerns but his thought process had led him to a single conclusion: Sorin was going to drug them *all* and put them in the collars.

Cesari, being the closest to Charlie replied. "It seems like a waste though, doesn't it? Besides why can't we use that against them? I mean the crew that are left might be a bit more willing to do as we say if they're wearing the collars, no?"

He'd thought about that already, but Charlie had concluded that the aliens left on board probably weren't going to be a threat to them. They had no weapons – all having been commandeered by the new human complement – no leadership as Sorin had been placed in a holding room to be interrogated at a later date, and no real desire to fight one on one. Plus they were seriously outnumbered by a race of genetically enhanced soldiers. They'd have to be stupid to try anything.

"Nah, they won't do anything," Laura replied confidently. "I've spoken to a couple of them and they were actually really against this whole thing. They said they'd show us how to fly the ship if we promised to take them back to the station."

It sounded like a good trade-off though Charlie worried about going back there. He had no idea what kind of firepower the station had, whether they were looking for him and his crew, or even if the ship that he was currently on had any weapons or defences of its own. He needed so much more information before he could commit to a plan, and the only way to get any of that, unfortunately, was to go and talk to Sorin.

Charlie told his squad mates to find out how the ship functioned and how it would all work under their command. He told Stephanie to ensure that teams from her own specialisation were versed on piloting the ship or effecting repairs as a matter of urgency – they needed to be able to fly and fix the thing if the shit really did hit the fan. He then told Kori to sort out living arrangements and to make sure everyone was as happy as they were going to be in their cramped arrangements. Laura would be in charge of security and making sure their captives were looked after and didn't cause any issues and Mauro - Mauro was going to be in charge of the kitchen.

It did occur to Charlie that the Camp had had instructors and staff for all of these aspects, but he didn't know much about these people and if he used the cadets to carry out these tasks, he was probably going to be able to keep a closer eye on them anyway. He didn't want to get into an 'I outrank you' situation with a dishwasher after all. Nobody seemed like they were going to argue about it either.

Taking Cesari along with him to his planned interrogation with Sorin, Charlie reflected on just what'd happened in what seemed like the flash of an eye over the last hours and days. He'd been so sure and assertive that nobody, not even Henderson, had said anything to contradict him or even glance at him with a sideways look. Remembering what Kono had said about his PIP level, he could only assume that things had been getting easier and would continue to do so because of the growth of that particular stat.

Chapter 28

"Hello," Sorin said happily as Charlie and Cesari entered into the small room that'd been repurposed to serve as the alien's cell. Similar to how Charlie and his group had been told to stay within one section of the ship, there wasn't an actual prison on board for Sorin to be held within, though they'd made do.

"Have you come to put a collar on me?" he asked, still smiling.

"Do we need to?" Cesari asked shortly, but Sorin shook his head.

"I think that if you wanted to kill me you would have done so already, so I'm not worried about that. I am of no use as a member of the crew as I imagine you have taken the others into custody. There are after all a lot less of us than there are of you. I do not intend to try to escape as there is nowhere to go and I assume that you do not wish to 'look after' me for a long period of time. I therefore assume that you are going to drop me off somewhere convenient for you once you have decided that there is nothing more that you can learn from me."

The speech was clearly frustrating for Cesari to hear, but it was logical as far as Charlie could see.

"Actually the others also want to be dropped back off at the station," Charlie said. "I assume that would work for you, too?"

Charlie noticed a very slight wince flicker on Sorin's face just before the alien nodded. He didn't mention it but stored the information for later.

"The thing is, we need to know more about this ship, what it can do and the circumstances surrounding our untimely departure from the station in the first place. You seem to know a lot about this Council and their procedures so we all think you should fill us in with the finer details," Cesari said authoritatively.

"Ah The Council," Sorin replied. "What a grand idea that was. You know when the Council was formed it was to ensure the safety of all of its members through both numbers and collective decision making. Now though, we can see clearly that, as you humans say, too many cooks can spoil the broth."

"What does that mean?" Cesari asked flatly.

"Well, think about it this way; they wouldn't collectively agree to include human beings in the Council itself because you are unpredictable and have the possibility to become much stronger as a warring race than many of the parts that make up the Council. You are a threat to some and a tool for others. You were placed in this program and then it was decided that you were a risk and their recommendation was to terminate you all. Why go through all of that extra work just to circle back to where they began in the first place? What the Council needs, I think, is leadership."

Cesari snorted. "And I suppose you think that's you is it?"

Sorin looked pensive but didn't answer.

"OK, so tell us more about this decision-making process. How long do we have until humanity is destroyed?" Charlie asked.

Sorin tapped his chin apparently deep in thought. "Well, their recommendation would need to be approved in the first instance so that could take a while. Then of course they'd close the program as it poses the biggest threat. Take that and then the preparations and travel time to Earth? I'd say one of your earth months, maybe two before the end of the line."

Charlie did notice something in the statement though. "And what if they don't take the recommendation and decide that the human race is OK to be left alone?"

The alien smiled broadly. "They never decide to leave a race alone. You are either a member or you are a threat. That is how it works and as you have crossed some of the more powerful races in the membership already, my assumption is that your fate is already sealed."

Then it hit Charlie - the reason that Sorin was so unfazed by his situation and the reason he'd turned up on the planet with such an unreliable and frantically reckless plan. "You didn't have permission to take us all, did you?" he asked.

"Nope," Sorin Replied.

"You thought you'd be able to take us all and get away with it before anyone noticed. The Council will probably have something to say now though, won't they?"

"Not really," Sorin replied. "Now you've taken the ship, you can drop us all at the station as we have discussed and I'll tell them that you overpowered us. It's not untrue anyway so technically we've done nothing wrong. I may have to include a little embellishment though - what great story isn't without a little flare?"

It really didn't matter anyway, both Cesari and Charlie knew. What they did need to know though was what the ship could actually do, and what dangers they might have to face in their planned defence of Earth.

"How does this ship compare to others of the Council in terms of firepower, and what kind of ships will be sent to destroy Earth?" Cesari asked.

"Hmm..." Sorin thought aloud. "In terms of ship's firepower? You aren't really in any luck. When I learned that I was going to spring you from your jail on the station, I didn't have much time to plan so this is simply a science and transport vessel. It is well equipped for scanning and living quarters – it even has some point defence cannons, but past that even a small scout ship would probably be enough to sink her."

Charlie was a little bewildered at the terminology that Sorin was using but it gave away Sorin's insight into the history of Earth and the human race, though Charlie kept that to himself.

"And food, supplies and the like?" Cesari asked.

"Ah, we did stock up on that front as we were planning to keep all of the cadets on board from the first Camp," Sorin replied.

"First camp?" Charlie replied before Cesari could speak again.

Cesari glanced at him side eyed. "Surely you know there are other camps in the program?" Cesari asked. "There are five in total, with three hundred cadets in each."

Charlie's enhanced perception seemed to be screaming at him now, and he felt that it wasn't right to speak in front of Sorin any longer. When the pair were alone again outside the room, Charlie spoke in a hushed tone. "This ship can't support that many cadets," he summarised. "There must be other ships coming, or one really big one to pick up the rest."

Cesari agreed with Charlie, although he wasn't sure what he could do about it. If their ship couldn't support the rest of the cadets and there were other ships on the way – and probably ones that would destroy theirs – they were stuck between a rock and a hard place. Either they stayed to defend EP1 and the cadets on the surface, or they left and let the aliens take the remaining cadets for their own. Both Charlie and Cesari knew that there was only one true choice here and although it meant the capture of the rest of the humans on the planet, it would mean that the cadets now on board could carry out their plan to try to save humanity from extinction. That, apparently, would be the price to pay for the attempt.

The pair dutifully relayed everything they'd learnt to the rest of the ship's complement via the internal comms system, the alien crew apparently living up to their word on teaching the humans how to use the ship.

When they'd finished their announcement, Stephanie appeared on the doorway to the bridge where Charlie, Cesari and a few of the other cadets were standing. Contrary to popular belief about starship bridges, this one was not the opulent, high tech neon-blue futuristic room with a view. This bridge was much more like an older fashioned tactical room with terminals showing outlines of the ship highlighted in different colours and layers. Apparently in space you didn't actually need to see where you were going – as long as the ship sensors were working correctly of course.

"I have an idea," Stephanie announced flatly.

As it turned out, Stephanie's idea was a bit of a Hail Mary, though if it worked it could save the lives of all of the other cadets on the planet. If it didn't work it was likely to get them all killed. That's just how it was sometimes.

The plan was simple: before their ship departed with the cadets of Camp Rebirth, they would visit each of the other camps and equip them with the knowledge of what was to come, along with the collar transmitter. It would be likely that these ships would be better equipped to place the humans in captivity as they would have had more time to prepare, so without the transmitter they might not have been able to escape. These cadets and their instructors would then have a fighting chance at a real mutiny aboard the ships that collected them, though in reality this might be something that Charlie and the rest of Camp Rebirth would never be able to discover.

The plan went as well as could be expected once the ship was off of the ground and speeding around the planet. It seemed that the rest of the camps had remained in the dark regarding the Council's investigation and subsequent decision, and the instructors and cadets of each of them seemed grateful for the knowledge and of the slight advantage that the transmitter would afford them. Of course there were so many factors that could go wrong – the aliens may have a different frequency for each ship, they may not even use the shock collars, or perhaps they'd simply just bombard the humans from space once they found out that Sorin and his ship weren't there to greet them. In any case, this was the best that

Charlie's crew could come up with, so it is what they did.

Phase one of the plan for the ship, was to take the alien crew back to the station unharmed. It seemed the right thing to do as good behaviour points were always a good thing to have. Plus they'd made the crew promises if they taught the cadets how to fly the ship and by all accounts they'd been extremely helpful, with the cadets almost fully up to speed in a matter of hours and certainly by the time they reached the station they'd have all the knowledge they'd need to resemble a proper crew. The ship had a lifeboat that would take all of the alien crew to the station which meant they'd kill two birds with one stone – the crew wouldn't be a burden or a worry, and they'd seem like the good guys for once.

Phase two thereafter was to head for Earth; it was the only thing left to do with the decision presumably made by the Council to wipe it out. After some more interrogation of the crew and Sorin, it became clear that their method of planetary destruction wasn't exactly orthodox. The sense that the Council did not particularly enjoy face-to-face combat extended to large scale interstellar body destruction evidently – they would send an automated weapons platform into orbit where it would essentially overheat the planet's core until it exploded. The science wasn't really important but what was interesting was the fact that as humans hadn't really reached the stars in any meaningful way yet, the Council would both take their time, and send a single unmanned platform to do the dirty work. It was the human's one golden nugget of information that could quite possibly be the very reason humanity and planet Earth might have the opportunity to be saved.

Charlie left the room and was greeted by the large, straight-faced stature of Matty Henderson blocking his path. He sighed internally. There were just so many things to be done when working on board a starship and dealing with this knucklehead definitely wasn't high up on his internal to do list.

"Listen here," Henderson practically growled. "I know you and I don't particularly see eye to eye, but I wanted you to know... there isn't going to be any trouble between us...OK?" He looked as though the words pained him as he spoke, though Charlie let him continue. "What I mean is... we have to work together in all of this, right, if we want to shoot our best shot at saving everyone. So whatever this is we have going on between us, let's say it's on hold until all this is over, OK?"

If someone would've said to Charlie that this was the conversation he'd be having with Henderson at that very moment, and those were the words that were going to come out of his mouth, he'd have called that person a dirty rotten liar. No amount of advanced perception would ever allow him to believe that he was going to be a part of a ceasefire with his mortal enemy. Apparently the shock of seeing new aliens, moving aboard a starship and hearing about the impending doom of the human race was enough to shake the cadet a little. Who knew? Perhaps if they were the last two human beings in the universe then they'd be friends.

~ Two weeks later ~

Life aboard the ship had been pretty uneventful and somewhat boring. There's only so much blackness of space that one can endure, and without the traditional gyms and recreational activities one would usually be able to make use of in a big open space, the cadets had to improvise. They'd sent the aliens along to the station on their lifeboat after they were sure that they could teach the cadets nothing more and their absence certainly took a little of the suspenseful edge away from the journey. It was almost as though every human aboard was able to let out a sigh of relief.

Thankfully, the instructors kept their lessons going as best they could, some classes easier to maintain than others, and Dr. Kono had managed to carry all of his CCS lessons over to the ship even without an auditorium. Truthfully, with all the concessions they'd made it wasn't so different from being on the planet, other than not being able to go outside, food being porridge three times a day and the air and water being recirculated as many times as didn't bear thinking about.

The cadets had named the ship – at first just anecdotally though later it stuck – the 'ES Revenge'. ES for 'Earth Ship' – it was just so fitting, plus it was a name that most thought would be appropriate given their task.

The last thing that'd happened, was that Cesari had announced that every single cadet aboard the ship was getting a field promotion, though not to Able cadet, but straight through to Ensign. It seemed a bit like it was a gestured promotion to Charlie, though the feeling of accomplishment and advancement that spread through the crew of the Revenge was palpable. It seemed to him that a little gratitude and acknowledgement went a long way with his friends and peers.

Kono and Shepherd had retaken their mantles as the ship's overseers of physical and mental wellbeing respectively and whilst Kono managed to fill most of his time with delivering classes to the crew as best he could, Shepherd had her work cut out with the low-level of background foreboding evident all around. If an Ensign wasn't worried about themselves, their friends or the human race as a whole, they were worried about their families or their pets back on Earth. In those respects there was a lot to worry about.

Charlie and his squad had managed to keep busy with routine. They carried out their lessons similar to the schedule they'd been a part of on the planet, but also took it upon themselves to oversee the running of the ship. It was strange that they'd fallen so well into a leadership role although nobody seemed to question it and they'd even begun picking up a few salutes as they'd passed others in the corridors or on the bridge. In addition, Charlie had reached a new high for his PIP level at twenty eight percent.

He suspected that his diet was holding him back somewhat, though he had nothing to compare it to as all of the Ensigns on board the Revenge had grown larger and stronger than any human being really had the right to do. Charlie though was positively ripped. His chest and arms bulged against his continuously tightening uniform and his jawline had grown so sharp that you could spread butter with it. Atop his head, sat thick jet black hair that he had to sweep out of the way whenever it became too unruly. What people had started to notice though, was the fact that Charlie was now the spitting image of their Chief Instructor Cesari.

The ship had become a kind of poor facsimile for the planet. The cadets mostly stuck to their squads, ate in routines and the instructors kept themselves segregated too. It was becoming clearer by the moment, and when Charlie actually thought back to how the lessons were conducted, that the instructors weren't hardened marines like the Chief Instructor, they were more likely mostly civilian instructors enrolled to train them all in their one specific task. After all, why would they get a soldier who spent most of his time fighting on frontlines or carrying out missions, to teach how to fight in hand to hand combat? Thinking about it, all of the 'real-life' combat situations that'd been proposed in their training had come from Cesari himself, a man that truly knew what real combat was like.

In a somewhat strange turn of events too, the Ensigns had all to a man and woman grown larger, stronger and faster than all of the instructors, save for Marcus Cesari who, although was now slightly shorter than most of the Ensigns, could probably still compare to them strength-wise. In any case, what this all meant was that other than very specific training and lessons, the instructors mainly stayed out of the way.

Both Shepherd and Kono had spoken to Charlie briefly to see how he was getting on, though at his current PIP level he had almost no reason to ever see the doctor. If he injured himself in training it was generally nothing that would last past the twenty minute-mark or so. If he was cut or received a nose bleed from an errant hit – although he generally had to allow that to happen on purpose – the bleeding would usually stop within five seconds and his skin would be back to normal and entirely healed within five minutes. By all accounts, Charlie was invincible.

Chapter 29

When the Revenge arrived in Earth's solar system, it wasn't the grandiose blue marble that'd been described by astronauts of the past that awaited the ship. This was mainly due to the fact that, once again, the Revenge didn't actually have a window on the bridge looking out into space. Of course the crew could go to another room to see what was happening out there - and some did – but the bridge was where Charlie, his squad and Cesari needed to be, just to make sure that there weren't any surprises lurking around the corner. Thankfully, as the ship was designed for scientific research, it's sensors would warn them of anything out of the ordinary in the system long before they'd be able to see anything with their bare eyes anyway.

In the system though, moving towards Earth, was a single object that the Revenge flagged as 'not supposed to be there' and the crew knew instantly what that meant.

The object was moving at about one tenth the speed of the Revenge, which was perhaps why they'd managed to catch up with it, and with what seemed like no time to spare and changing to an intercept course, the crew aboard the Revenge prepared to save their entire planet.

Once the scans of the object were completed by the ship and its sensors, the terminals happily displayed it in a three-dimensional rotating facsimile on the bridge. It was an orb about the size of a four story house, heavily armoured although it seemed that its one single weapon was the beam that would overheat the planet's core once it had acquired its target. It had entry points, presumably for maintenance crews to board it, though it was clear from the scans and what they'd been told about the weapon that it was currently unmanned.

It was a nervy encounter, but the crew of the Revenge essentially pulled their ship up alongside the weapon as it moved through space, matching its velocity and trajectory so that they could both get a proper look visually and start working on their plan to stop it from completing its mission.

The terminal, once Stephanie had played around with it for a few moments, then showed a countdown timer of how long the weapon would take to reach geosynchronous orbit with Earth. With that number sitting at around thirty hours, it meant that there was no real need to rush – and rushing usually caused mistakes.

"Can we shoot at it with the point defence cannons?" Charlie asked Stephanie who was trawling through lines of data that he didn't care to get involved in. Of course, with his enhanced cognition and learning speed, he could've taken the time to digest the data himself, but he didn't feel the need to do so with the technologically minded Stephanie on his team. You didn't usually have a dog and bark yourself.

"I don't think so," she replied. "It looks like the force that the PDC's would place upon its hull wouldn't be sufficient to punch through. They'd most likely dent it and if it wasn't an automated machine I'd say they'd probably piss it off too. It's kind of like banging on a reinforced steel door with a stick."

"So plan B then?" Mauro replied. He was holding an apple though for the life of Charlie he couldn't remember ever seeing fruit being loaded into the Revenge. Mauro winked at him conspiratorially.

"What's plan B?" Instructor Shepherd asked. She was always present when there were big plans to be considered – it was nice to have someone that was both level-headed and able to think outside the box in these situations.

"We go over there and blow it up from the inside," Mauro replied placing the apple in his mouth and punching his fist into his own open palm. Stephanie placed her hand on her forehead and sighed.

"First off, we don't know what would happen if we actually blew it up – it could be like a nuclear bomb going off for all we know and take out half the solar system. If it really is capable of destroying planets, then the power it must be able to amass should be unimaginable. Secondly, we don't even know if we can get inside it - what if they locked the door? Do you have a key? And thirdly, how do you damn well expect to get your ass over there to do any of this?" Her voice was becoming more and more high pitched as she spoke almost to the point that it was shrill by the time she'd said her last word.

"Uh… there are spacesuits in storage actually," Laura said quietly after a moment of silence that nobody wanted to fill. "I think we could get in them, we're not that much bigger than those blue aliens."

"And there are plasma cutters designed for carving through rock formations too – I saw them in one of the research labs," Kori added with a smile.

Charlie smiled. So now they could get over to it and maybe get inside.

"Stephanie," he said. "I think I have a plan."

Stephanie looked up at him with wide eyes as she started to comprehend his meaning. "Don't make me do it," she practically begged. "I *hate* space and I hate the thought of suffocating even more.

"Don't be like that, Steph," Mauro said. "Think of it this way, there might be pizza over there."

"Why would there be…" Laura started but just trailed off at the absolute absurdity of the statement.

"So, what is the plan exactly?" Shepherd asked looking very confused at the conversation that seemed to be happening almost entirely within subtext.

"Well the way I see it," Charlie explained, "Is that if we can get a team over there and cut our way inside, an expert in weird alien technology might be able to turn the thing around and send it back to where it came from – along with a little destructive power, just to let them know how it feels."

"I… I won't do it," Stephanie interrupted quietly. "I mean, I don't mind powering it down or whatever, but I won't send it off to be used against some unsuspecting world that may be filled with innocent bystanders, women and children. No single person should ever be able to push that kind of button."

Charlie, thinking about it, actually agreed. He certainly wouldn't want to be responsible for wiping out a planet of potentially billions of innocent lives just because someone else was going to do it to him first. As much as that was the picture of the human race that the Council wanted to paint, they just weren't like that. It was far, far too cold hearted. He also couldn't ask anyone else to do it on his behalf either.

"No, you're right Stephanie. Best case is that we disable it and send it off somewhere to self destruct where it can't do anyone any harm, and worst case, we deactivate it and leave it right where it is, right?"

Stephanie nodded slowly though everyone could tell that she still wasn't totally on board with the plan. Nobody could blame her really –

space just offered far too many unknowns and even the cadets of the GAP program – physically and mentally enhanced as they may be – could do nothing to prevent their own demise if they got caught without oxygen.

"So now that's settled then, who should go? I mean do we just draw straws?" Kori asked rather solemnly.

"Nope," Charlie replied with a wide smile. "I say if there was ever a time for Charlie's Angels to prove themselves, this is it."

Laura face palmed. "I thought we agreed we wouldn't use that one?" She asked without removing her hand from her face.

"Yeah but… you know, why not?" Charlie asked with a wide grin.

It didn't take long for the group to ready themselves for the spacewalk between the ship and the weapons platform. It was moving alongside the revenge pretty well perfectly, although they didn't want to get too close just in case they needed to manoeuvre and accidentally hit it as they still weren't sure how much damage it could do as an explosion rather than a weapon. A happy medium was to stay at a distance of two hundred feet and correct course if anything unexpected happened. This distance though was partly attributed to the crew having found, collected and joined all the rope they could find in storage, and that's how much they had. Not one of them fancied trying to make it across to the platform without a tether.

As the squad were forcing themselves into the spacesuits that the aliens had left behind – they were all black and rather tight fitting ordeals with golden visors that obscured the wearer's face – Charlie felt a large hand flatten on his shoulder. Turning, he saw the straight face of Matty Henderson staring down at him.

"Listen," the large Ensign said. "I want to come with you. I think I can be of some use over there."

He spoke loudly enough for the rest of Charlie's squad to overhear too, who all stood with their mouths agape.

Charlie's first thought was to ask why, though before he spoke, his mind told him to just accept the gesture and shut up about it, so he did. Charlie simply nodded and offered Henderson a helmet in his outstretched hand.

The rope didn't have a grappling hook on it or anything like that, so the best thing the group of six Ensigns could come up with, was to throw it out in a straight line with a knot at one end and clip themselves on to it. It wasn't fancy, but it would prevent anyone from being thrown off course. Besides, with the way the ships were travelling alongside each other and without any wind or air resistance, all they needed to do was push off and wait.

Charlie went first, followed by Henderson, Laura, Kori, Stephanie and finally Mauro, who had the large rock laser attached to his back as he slid along the makeshift zip line.

Charlie admired as he moved - just before he hit the side of the weapons platform with a slight oof – at just how easy it was to move around in their spacesuits. Quite unlike the oversized white ordeals he was used to seeing on the astronauts of Earth, these tighter fitting suits were much more suited to fine motor control where repairs on the outside of a ship might've been necessary and somewhat more frequent.

His feet found the small platform that'd been placed by one of the entries onto the orb and a few moments later the rest of the team had joined him. He wrapped the rope around a protrusion loosely so that they had their way back, but he didn't want to tie it just in case anything... bad ... happened.

Mauro unstrapped the mining laser from his back and placed it on the ground before the doorway, taking the time to make sure the door wouldn't actually open before he started to do anything else. As Stephanie had predicted, the door wouldn't budge.

The group then braced themselves for the impact that the laser was going to cause and daisy chained themselves around Mauro to ensure that any kickback from it wouldn't send him flying off into space. Happily, the laser provided no such force and as soon as he started cutting it was clear that within a few minutes they'd have made a perfectly human-sized hole in the doorway.

They knew that the interior of the weapon wasn't about to depressurise, mainly because with their scans they hadn't detected any atmosphere inside it – and why would it? If it wasn't going to have anyone inside as it moved, why would it waste power on making it habitable?

Only a few minutes passed before Charlie and Laura pulled open the broken and burnt piece of hull that allowed them entry into the weapon and before them they were greeted with a cylindrical column that spanned the internal diameter of the weapon with a single terminal visibly mounted in its centre at the end of a long walkway. It certainly made things easier not having to search for the terminal that Stephanie would have to hack into to get access to carry out her task.

What was even easier for the group, was the fact that they could just push off their entranceway and float right over to the terminal. Without atmosphere there was no gravity – sometimes things just seemed to work out for the best.

"Alright Steph, do your thing," Charlie said over their suit's internal communications system. The rest of the team had nothing to do but wait.

"Don't worry, we still have twenty-nine hours to go or something, so take your time!" Mauro said and Charlie could hear the smile in his voice. He also heard Laura audibly sigh over the comms network.

Stephanie tapped at the terminal for a long time before she said anything. She'd grunted, exclaimed, held her hands up in a 'what the hell' kind of pose and hit the screen with an open palm on more than one occasion before settling down into a very hacker looking pose of shutting down the world around her.

"OK, so I think I know how this thing works," she announced finally without looking around. "So there's good news and bad news."

"OK, hit me with it," Charlie said.

"So the way it works is a bit like – well, you know the large Hadron Collider?" she asked.

Charlie nodded. It'd been in his lessons although the intricacies of particle physics wasn't especially high on his 'to learn' list.

"Well it's a bit like that, but instead of sending particles around a giant loop to collide with each other, this works on an additional third dimension. That's why it's a big sphere."

"So what does that mean?" Charlie asked.

"Well basically the inside of this thing is going to get really, really dangerous when it's getting ready to fire. Then it will release that energy on its target and it won't matter what's in the way. Whatever it points at, it's going to destroy," she explained.

"Sounds like a pretty decent weapon to me," Mauro replied.

"Well, yes..." Stephanie said without taking her eyes from the terminal. "So the bad news."

"Wait that was the good news?" Kori asked in a higher pitch than he would've liked.

"Well yeah, I figured out how it works..." Stephanie replied, not quite sure what he was missing. "Anyway, the bad news. It uses its own propulsion engines to start building its internal energy, so once it stops moving then the engines turn to the internals and then there will be no stopping it. Once it starts, it can't be stopped – I mean it *really* can't be stopped."

Charlie heard something in her statement. "So if we just keep the thing moving, then it'll never be able to fire?" he asked.

"Well, yes," Stephanie replied. "But the moment it detects a geosync orbit, those engines will start the process and that'll be it."

"So never let it stop then," Mauro replied flatly. "Simple."

Then Henderson spoke, which made the rest of the team jump all at once. "You can't just send it away because then it might land in the orbit of an unsuspecting world and destroy it. You can't stop it right here because who knows what direction it'll fire in. You can't just take a torch to it and destroy it because that would take way too long. Short fact is we have less than thirty hours to figure out what to do with this thing and right now we don't have any ideas."

Everyone was silent for a long moment.

"That's exactly it," Stephanie said, and it was clear that the team wasn't expecting such comprehension from Henderson of all people. "We don't really have too many options here – but for now I need a little more time to figure out how to get into this thing. It seems like the navigation is locked out – or it's being controlled remotely. Either way right now I can't do anything other than view the readouts from it."

"Just do your best Stephanie," Charlie stated assuredly. "I know you can do this."

"Yeah, we're all counting on you," Mauro added rather unhelpfully. Laura kicked his shin and Stephanie got right back to it.

After a short while of silence, Henderson looked straight at Charlie and spoke over the comms link. "I need to know. What is it with you and Cesari?"

Charlie might've thought that the question was a trap, but analysing the speech pattern and tone that the Ensign had used he could detect nothing underhanded.

"It's... uh..." he spoke slowly trying to choose the right words, but again he decided that the best way to go about things was to say exactly how it was, leaving nothing out. He told Henderson about Cesari being his father, only finding out recently, and made the point that he'd never received any special treatment for the fact. To his credit, Henderson didn't seem surprised, but more importantly he didn't seem angry either.

"Well shit," were the words he chose when he did eventually speak. "That fucking sucks."

Charlie furrowed his brow at the response as it really wasn't what he was expecting. Then he continued to tell Henderson about his upbringing, the death of his parents, the system that he'd been a part of and the induction into the GAP program. He did stop short of telling him all about his interactions with Dr Kono and his unlocked PIP status though - there were just some things that didn't need to be brought up or rubbed into other people's faces.

Eventually after a lot of waiting around and a few segments of small talk, Stephanie spoke again. "OK, I think I have someth... oh, oh no."

"What is it?" Laura asked slightly panicked.

"Its, uh... well..." she looked embarrassed and took a deep breath before she spoke again. "When I made it past the firewall into the system, it sent out a distress signal. Whoever sent this thing, well they know we're here."

"The Council?" Charlie asked quickly, to which Stephanie nodded without turning her gaze away from the terminal. "Well shit. That fucking sucks." He looked at Henderson when he used his own phrase but Henderson simply shrugged.

"That means we have a new thing to deal with, doesn't it?" Laura asked though it seemed she wasn't looking for an answer. "We need to get this thing done and quickly."

Stephanie didn't answer but continued tapping on the terminal although somewhat more frantically now. Eventually her demeanour changed and Charlie recognised the fact that she was onto something.

"That's so stupid. Why didn't I think of that already?" she said to herself. Turning around to face the rest of the team she made her announcement.

"Well I have something, but you aren't going to like it."

"You know where the signal went?" Mauro asked.

"What? No. I mean yes I know where the signal went but that isn't the point. What I figured out is how to get this thing away for good."

"That's good, no?" Mauro asked.

"Well, yes." Stephanie replied. "This thing is loaded with fuel to both get it to where it needs to go and also start the firing process. So what we need to do is just..."

"Make it keep going until it runs out of fuel?" Charlie finished her sentence.

"Right! It's not so technical but it *would* work." Stephanie replied.

"Then let's do that," Kori said enthusiastically.

"It isn't... it's not that easy," Stephanie started, then Henderson interrupted her.

"Someone needs to remain onboard until it runs out of fuel," he announced. "They need to keep the thing moving until it doesn't move anymore."

The team remained quiet for a long moment before Henderson continued, moving toward Stephanie. "Well, you better show me what I have to do then."

"Wait, can't we just figure something else out?" Charlie started. "What about cutting the fuel lines, or breaking the navigation system – anything, we have the time and the equipment with us, right?"

Stephanie answered Charlie's questions solemnly. "We can't risk cutting anything anywhere near the fuel lines – one wrong cut and we destroy everything in a massive area. The computers too, I can't fool them into going against their very nature in such a small amount of time – the risk is way too high. I'm sorry Charlie, I can't think of any other alternative than…" she stopped talking as her eyes fell upon Henderson.

Henderson though, had already made up his mind. "We just don't have the time. Besides, if I get to kill myself saving your ass, it'll be worth it, trust me," He said.

Charlie could hear that his mortal enemy wouldn't be convinced otherwise, and just a short while ago he might not have been so upset at this turn of events. As it was, he didn't see any alternative to the plan. The team didn't even try to talk Henderson out of it though, not because of some deep engrained hatred for the man, rather it was because they couldn't come up with an alternative that didn't involve them all staying on board, or putting the Earth and the entire human race in dire peril.

The thing that none of the team mentioned though, was that even if their plan worked and they managed to nullify the planet-killer, there could very well be a fleet of alien warships on their way to carry out the task that the weapons platforms had failed in. *'One problem at a time though'*, Charlie thought.

Chapter 30

"Make sure you tell everyone I had to fight you to let me go. And tell them I won," Henderson said as he stood at the entrance hole the team had cut waiting for them all to leave. Truth be told, he was actually looking forward to a little alone time with just his thoughts, It'd been so, so long.

Charlie nodded. "I'll tell everyone you broke my nose for a fourth time. Or was it fifth? I could never remember. Matty Henderson, you have done humanity proud," Charlie smiled behind his visor and each of the Ensigns took a hold of Henderson's forearm in complete and total admiration. This was what the human race was all about – sacrifice for the benefit of others.

As the Ensigns pushed off away from the weapon, unhooking the rope behind them, they saw Matty Henderson one last time before he turned and disappeared inside the orb. Within just moments, the engines on the thing changed their angle and the weapon turned, and started moving away from the Revenge at speed. They all knew that this would be the last time they would ever see Ensign Matty Henderson.

Stephanie held up her small glass portable terminal once the group had made it back onto the ship to ensure that it hadn't been damaged in their travels.

"All good?" Charlie asked, desperate to think about anything other than the life they'd all condemned to end.

The girl nodded assuredly but couldn't bring herself to talk. The lump of guilt in her throat was simply too much to swallow.

"This is some real horse shit," Mauro announced once they'd all undressed from the spacesuits. "There was really nothing else we could do?"

"Don't you think we would've done it?" Laura hissed back at him. "If there was any way at all..." she couldn't bring herself to finish her sentence and just cupped her face in her hands. "Fucking hell," she moaned quietly.

The team let their heads hang in a mixture of shame and remembrance for a long moment before they all realised that they needed to get back to work. They needed to tell everyone what had happened, and about the distress signal but they knew it wasn't going to be an easy conversation to have. Besides, what could they do really? They were probably going to be outnumbered and outgunned soon, and they had nothing to use to their advantage – save for possibly the element of surprise – but with nothing surprising to hand, they all felt as though they were up the creek without a paddle.

"There's nothing we could've done differently and nothing we can change now," Cesari said once the Ensigns had brought him up to speed on the situation. "If you ask me, we need to defend Earth from whatever it is that's coming. Nobody else is going to do it and letting them know would just cause panic. I think we're alone here and as they say, it's going to be a long night."

The group separated for a long time after Henderson's departure and it was partly because when they each looked at one another, they could see the pain in their collective eyes. It was hard. It was the first time any of them had experienced real loss of someone so close to them.

To keep his mind off the loss of Henderson, Charlie spent a lot of time trying to devise a plan that would allow them to defend Earth, given the variables that he was aware of, though whatever way he looked at the situation he just couldn't see a way out. He needed more time and more information. He was aware of the tactics used by smaller forces within Earth's histories, guerilla warfare and the like, though none of it seemed relevant when dealing with the additional dimension that space seemed to offer. If he was going to come up with something, he knew it was going to have to be good.

Life on board the Revenge had become quiet again with a somber undertone and it made everyone feel on edge. The Ensigns tried their best to continue with their lessons where they could though attendance was starting to lessen and it was obvious that the instructors all had something else on their minds. It was, of course, not going to last.

"We've got company!" came the shout over the ship's internal communications system as the Ensign who was manning the station sent out the alert.

This was the alert that Charlie had been simultaneously waiting for and dreading and he sprinted the length of the ship from his quarters to the bridge. When he arrived, Cesari and Laura had already made it there and behind him after a few moments Mauro and Kori appeared.

"What's happened?" Charlie asked not even slightly out of breath.

"Looks like just one ship at the moment – the fastest one they had probably sent to scout the weapon," Cesari said. "It's to be expected really."

It did make sense. The Council wouldn't send an entire fleet out to answer a distress call from the weapon when they knew that the humans of Earth didn't have space-faring capabilities. The worst they'd probably think would be either a malfunction or space pirates trying their arm – assuming there were space pirates out there of course.

"So what do we do?" Charlie asked the room in general.

"It looks like they don't have any weapons at all," the Ensign manning the sensor station announced. Charlie could see that it was Felix Target, of Jean Martin's squad. It reminded him of Henderson.

"You want to try to blow it out of the sky?" Cesari said with a smirk.

"Hell yeah!" Mauro fist pumped. "I've been waiting for a real target to practise on forever!"

"Don't worry Latori, you'll get your chance; they're coming right for us." Cesari said. "Though I don't know why, unless they're planning to ram us there's really nothing else they can do."

"I'm receiving a communication from the scout ship," Target announced loudly. It reads: 'You are under arrest by order of The Intergalactic Council. Stand down now or you will be destroyed.'

"Don't say it," Laura said quietly.

"Yeah?" Mauro said. "You and what army?"

"You just had to say it didn't you," she sighed.

Then on the long range sensors, a much larger ship blipped into existence as though in answer to Mauro's question.. Apparently the scout ship, being smaller and purposely designed that way, hadn't shown up until they were practically on top of it but this new one, it must've been a beast.

The new ship was calculated at under an hour away at its current speed and the advanced readout from the sensor systems estimated its length to be over one kilometre with a veritable shit ton of armaments, and well, they were too long to list. Needless to say, the ship was going to swat the Revenge like a fly and probably not even think twice about it. The crew of the Revenge now had two simple choices: give in or fight. Either way, though, the fate of the human race seemed all but assured.

Charlie opened his mouth to speak but Cesari beat him to it.

"Mauro, please could you make that little scout ship go away?" he ordered.

The scout ship had come to a full halt just a few hundred metres off the port of the Revenge. It sat there totally still as though it was a scenting dog letting everyone know what it'd found and Charlie, having moved to a window that overlooked the vessel, watched and waited.

After a few moments, there was a very distant and dull hum from the hull of the revenge and then a shudder. Charlie watched as five balls of orange light scored through the blackness of space and impacted the small scout ship perfectly just a few moments later. The ship didn't even try to move. Then it exploded with a small shockwave that the Revenge felt, although it was nothing that caused any sort of panic. It had all just been so easy and Mauro had not missed a single shot with the point defence cannons.

"Well that's one down, who knows how many more to go," Laura announced as she walked away from the window.

Charlie followed her back to the bridge where Cesari waited and Mauro appeared soon after with a huge grin on his face. It was strange that he was so happy about taking the life of another, though Charlie could tell that it was partly because he'd actually got to do something helpful. God knew that if Charlie could take out some revenge like that for Henderson's loss it'd probably make him feel better too.

Stephanie then entered the bridge. It looked as though she hadn't slept in a week, her usually perfect skin drawing slightly grey and her eyes deep and dark.

"Guys, I need to tell you something," she said and continued speaking before anyone could interrupt her. "I know you said that we shouldn't contact Earth, but I couldn't just sit there and let everyone die without knowing why, or give them the opportunity to say goodbye to their loved ones." A tear rolled down her cheek as she spoke. "Everyone deserves that right, you know?"

"Jesus Marsh," Cesari said quietly. "That's one hell of a statement to give someone."

"I know," Stephanie sniffed. "I just thought it was the right thing to do."

"What did they say?" Charlie asked with wide eyes. "Are they putting everyone in bunkers or what?"

"Not exactly," Stephanie replied practically shaking. "They said they *knew* already and told us to wait for the justice of The Council."

There was a pregnant pause in the room.

"Shit," Charlie exclaimed. "They knew? And they aren't doing anything about it?"

"What can they do?" Laura asked. "The Council probably promised them mercy for our capture. It's what they do isn't it? Tell you what you want to hear so they get their own way, then do whatever they want anyway."

"We need to tell them the truth," Charlie announced forcefully.

"I tried. They won't listen," Stephanie replied almost sobbing. "They just think The Council will leave them be if we get taken in."

"Well it can't be changed now," Cesari announced matter of factly. "The only thing this changes is the fact that they know we tried to reach out and received a harsh no in response. We need a plan to stand and fight."

"What if we just gave ourselves up?" Stephanie sniffed in a tiny voice.

"You know that won't work," Laura said as she placed a hand on Stephanie's shoulder. "The Council has decided the fate of humanity already and whatever small promises they make in the meantime are all fake. There is no way out of this – it's now or never."

"Right," Charlie agreed forming a plan in his head. "Stephanie, go and send another message to Earth. Tell them everything we know about the Council, the weapon and the fate of planet Earth. Don't pull any punches - you're right, they need to know. This time though, if you can make sure your message is sent to as many locations around the planet as possible so that everyone gets to know – this can't be hidden anymore."

Stephanie immediately left the room to carry out her new task. It was obvious to Charlie that whenever Stephanie had something to do, it stopped her ruminating what she'd done, right or wrong.

"Now the rest of us, we're going to have to gear up. And I mean everything we can, and when I say the rest of us – I mean every single member of this ship," Charlie ordered.

It didn't take long to tell everyone about his plan, as he knew the simple ones were often the best. His thought process had begun with the very reason as to why humans had been chosen to play the role they had been for the Council, and although it was a rather long train of thought, it all happened in a split second.

The Council didn't like to fight. A fact that was made exponentially more evident by the fact they had even sent an automated weapons platform to destroy a planet. They just didn't seem to enjoy getting up close and personal. This fact was further bolstered by the huge battleship that was coming their way; they acted like a classic big bully – reliance on their size and the perception of their might to bend others to their will. This was going to be the one fact that Charlie's plan would exploit, coupled with the fact that during his Earth history lessons, he'd picked up a trick or two from the ancient Greeks.

Thirty-four railguns, eight plasma cannons, twenty-one point defence systems, a cargo bay full of plasma torpedoes, sixteen microcannons (whatever they were), eighty-two fifty millimetre tracers and one fully charged, one hundred percent powered force shield covering the entire vessel. That was what the readout of the enemy vessel had shown once it had come into a close enough range for their more complete scans to divulge. There were no two ways about it – it was a floating fortress.

The communications system lit up as soon as the Revenge had made her scans and text began to scroll across all of the terminals on the bridge.

'You have violated the laws of The Intergalactic Council and are under arrest. You are to power down your ship and any weapons systems and submit to Council law.'

There would be no misinterpretation here and certainly nothing to do other than comply. Charlie was sure a single disobedience would lead to their immediate destruction.

"Do it," he ordered flatly.

The Revenge went dark. The internal lights switched over to the emergency backup systems, no longer being powered by the ship's engines as they wound down to silence and not a single person on board made a sound. It wasn't necessary of course, but the foreboding shadow of the hulking battleship struck fear and awe into most things that encountered it.

The Revenge was bathed in shadow as the battleship moved closer and a pair of unimaginably huge doors began to part as though they were some terrible maw ready to swallow up the smaller ship as krill to a whale. There was darkness and silence, and it was deafening.

The doors closed behind them with a loud clang and Charlie watched through a window as the artificial gravity inside the ship kicked in and they hit the ground with a light thud.

'You are to stay inside your vessel. Do not make any movements to power your ship or exit from it,' the readout updated itself.

Charlie had wondered if they'd be escorted to their prison cell once aboard, but this was much easier for the aliens – out of sight, out of mind.

They had their prison, and they were sitting right in it.

The entire plan, though, relied on the fact that the aliens wouldn't simply start shooting at the planet – though if that was efficient, the theory was that if it was an option, they simply would've done it anyway. The more likely scenario was that once they had a plan, the Council would stick to it. The method of execution was a part of what they'd decided, so changing that now wouldn't have been so easy. After an hour of nothing happening, Charlie could tell that he was right.

The crew of the Revenge knew that timing was going to be important for their plan to work, and as they all stood in the corridors and behind the ship's exit doors, not a single one of them showed their anxiety of the situation. Holding rifles and wearing full body armour from the Camp's stores, they were ready to fight for what they believed was right.

They waited for their moment.

Eventually, the doors on the far side of the cargo bay in which their ship was housed opened, and a complement of armed alien soldiers filtered in, surrounding two taller beings that resembled the Overseer's race. Presumably these were important to the ship, though Charlie didn't recognise them. Their presence though, meant that if and when his crew exited the Revenge, the larger ship would not be able to vent the atmosphere into space, killing them all instantly. That was the enemy's first mistake and one that Charlie had been hoping for.

Nearly all of the aliens on board were the blue skinned Baccus, save for the few that joined them such as the more important looking figures. Charlie wondered if the Council had discovered Sorin's gambit and had decided to punish his race in general by sending one of their ships to bring them back into custody. It seemed a little archaic, though not beyond the realms of possibility.

The precession grew nearer and Charlie's grip on the handle of his rifle grew tighter. Adrenaline coursed through his body in anticipation of the fight that was coming, victory the only thing his mind would accept. Then… a dull thud, and a shudder…

Chapter 31

"What in God's name was that?" Cesari called out from his position closest to the door.

Charlie could see that the alien escorts and the important looking aliens were looking around quite obviously thinking the same thing, and they looked very worried.

Laura brought out her portable terminal and held it up. "I'm getting a message!" Then the screen changed to the face of a very human looking man, who by the look of him was very clearly a member of the GAP program, although Charlie didn't recognise him. He had blonde hair slicked back and a sharp jawline punctuated by five-o-clock shadow.

"Sorry we're late guys," the man smiled as the video feed shuddered and jerked betraying the obvious firing of guns. Then a few seconds afterwards, the part of the ship where Charlie and the Revenge sat, shuddered.

'They're firing at us,' Charlie internalised. But more accurately, they were here to help, and he knew it.

"This is it!" Charlie announced loudly. "Get back to the bridge and fire everything you have, right now!" He didn't take the time to bring the others up to speed and simply assumed they'd do what he said without question.

Stephanie dutifully disappeared along with Mauro and three of the other Ensigns and a few seconds later, the tell-tale hum and wobble that betrayed the engines spinning up rattled through The Revenge. Then the point defence system cannons came online.

The alien security complement and their charges didn't stand a chance. The cannons were designed to fire at and destroy torpedoes and other fast-moving projectiles with hard outer shells and they obliterated everything in the cargo bay around them in a moment, although were not strong enough to breach the internal hull of the battleship. It didn't matter though, the damage had been done and utter chaos caused, until the bay fell back into silence again.

"Uh... where are you?" the voice came from the terminal that Stephanie had left with Charlie.

Charlie smiled. "We're inside the big ass alien ship actually, but don't worry, you just gave us the opportunity we needed. Keep doing what you're doing but try not to blow us all up, OK?"

The face on the terminal turned to speak to someone off-screen. Charlie overheard the man tell whoever it was that he was speaking to, to target the engines and weapons only.

"So I assume you managed to take over your prison ship then?" Charlie asked the terminal.

The man's attention turned back to Charlie. "Yeah, thanks for the heads up. The plan worked perfectly and we got out of the collars with no bother. Those aliens *really* didn't like fighting so taking the crew out wasn't too difficult. Actually we only lost two of our guys, then went around the planet to collect the rest. We have about twelve hundred on board, and I gotta say – some of these cadets are pretty mean."

Charlie's mouth positively hung agape. "You have twelve... hundred on board? How big is your God damned ship?" He had to work to stop his voice going a little *too* high pitched in surprise.

The man smiled. "You can call me Taylor, and it's big." He tapped on his own terminal a few times and his face was replaced by a three dimensional rotating facsimile of his ship. It was just like the battleship that they were currently sitting inside and Charlie felt a little hard done by.

"Damn! I shouldn't have taken the first train out of the station!" he exclaimed.

"Don't worry, we'll come get you after all this is done. Hell, you might even have a real ship of your own by then!"

Charlie wondered though; "how many crew were on your battleship when you took it?"

"There were only about five hundred of them so we had them with even numbers. And like I said, if you just get up in their faces they pretty much just lie down and surrender. It was kind of nice actually."

That gave Charlie an idea of what he might've been dealing with inside his ship, which was always useful information.

"I don't think this is going to take too long though, honestly, it's like these things have never been in a real space battle before," Taylor said. The irony was not lost on Charlie that this was probably the first time that humanity itself had actually been in a space battle, but he kept that to himself.

"I'm sending a live feed of the battle to your terminal so you can see what's happening and if anything particularly special happens, I'll give you a shout," Taylor announced. Charlie thought that he really needed to know how he was able to do all of these things with the terminal so well, but he put a pin in it to revisit at a later date. Right now, he had a job to do.

With the cargo bay clear after their fanfare of point defence fire, Charlie, his team and Cesari led the charge out of the Revenge. Making it to the first door from where the previous aliens had arrived, they took cover at each side.

Distant shudders and dull thuds made the internal lights of the ship flicker and it made Charlie feel good. They had allies, and by his own best estimates, things may have actually started to go quite well for them.

The previous cadets of Camp Rebirth filtered through the first few corridors facing minimal threats. Their overlapping movement techniques ensured that as they moved like a wave through the ship, all avenues, offshoots, corridors and paths were well covered with rifle-fire whenever necessary, though it was seldom an issue. That was until they reached a large, open plan room with terminals all around its perimeter and a pulsating cylinder through the centre. The room was a two-storey affair with metal walkways above which made Charlie think that it was probably the engineering section and he half expected it to smell like oil though nothing particularly new greeted his nostrils. It didn't really matter right now though - what did matter was the fact that the room was practically filled with the blue aliens, each armed with automated laser rifles although looking decidedly unsure of themselves.

The first laser beam missed Charlie by an inch, perhaps even less, and he fell to the ground to minimise himself as a target, and then all hell broke loose.

The humans fired their weapons methodically and sparingly, only pulling the trigger when they had a target in their sights and the gunfire rang out as though a hundred fireworks were going off all at once. The Baccus may as well have been firing into the crowds of human soldiers with their eyes closed for all the good it was doing. Two of the ensigns fell to the ground, hit by the wild fire, then a third – the inaccurate fire hitting them purely through bad luck in their part. The human ranks were definitely dropping in number but that was nothing compared to the losses the enemy were facing. Alien after alien fell to the ground in small clouds of red blood as they were hit systematically and precisely by the bullets of the soldiers of the GAP program, the soldiers that these aliens themselves, had helped to create. There would be no mercy.

Then, clear to both sides, there was an apparent turning point and the aliens knew that there would be no winning. This was not going to end well for any of them and one by one they began to place their weapons on the ground, their hands raised in surrender.

All in all, the humans had lost eight of their number, but the Baccus had lost over fifty, with only ten of them left standing and captured.

Charlie quickly ushered them together into a clump and made them face away from the human soldiers, telling them to walk along the next corridor at their point. There was no time to waste, although he wouldn't kill these creatures in cold blood – humans were not the monsters that the Council portrayed them to be. Honestly though, it felt nice to both have hostages and a human (or alien) shield, though Charlie hoped it wouldn't come to any of that.

The blue aliens led the way towards the bridge, and the explosions and shudders were getting much closer now. All of a sudden, a huge explosion rocked the ship and the lights went out, plunging everyone and everything into complete darkness.

Silence followed before anyone was able to acclimatise to their new situation. Then Charlie heard a sound. It was as loud to him as though he was wearing headphones and it'd been piped directly into his skull. The scraping of a pin being removed. The click of a handle pulling free from its housing. The clang, as the grenade hit the metallic floor.

"GET DOWN!" He cried, though he wasn't sure in that moment if anyone else had heard the sound or even if they would've known where it had come from. Then he was pushed back by the might of a stampeding rhino, away from where the grenade had hit the ground and at the exact same time he saw the bright hot flash of the explosion. The sound of the grenade's detonation was muffled and then again there was silence.

The torches on the ends of the humans' rifles began to click on and illuminate their corridor and Charlie brought himself back to his feet, checking for injuries before following the lights that were pointed at the ground. There, face down, lay his father, Marcus Cesari.

Charlie dropped his rifle immediately and pulled on Cesari's shoulder, turning him over ready to administer CPR. When Cesari lay flat on his back though, it was evident that there was going to be nothing that anyone could do. Where his torso used to be, was a great bloody hole and each of the Ensigns knew what that meant. Marcus Cesari had just given his life to save them all.

"Get Kono! Where the fuck is Kono?" Charlie shouted loudly at nobody in particular. There was no response. They all knew there was nothing to be done.

Charlie closed his eyes shut for a long minute. *'This can't be happening'* he screamed internally, *'Not like this. Not now.'* Then, past the pain and suffering, past the despair and sadness, rage filled his entire being as he remembered the aliens who'd done this. Who'd taken his father.

He raised himself to his feet and retook his weapon, rounding on the closest of the aliens. Charlie took two steps forward and pushed the being with both of his hands as hard as he could. The Baccus collapsed to the ground and started backing away on reverse all fours.

"WHO DID THAT?" Charlie screamed. "I WANT TO KNOW NOW. WHICH ONE OF YOU WAS IT? WAS IT YOU?" He pointed at the terrified Baccus.

The alien's eyes were wide in horror as Charlie's rifle raised so that the creature could see all the way down the barrel. It could see the tip of the bullet right at the back, ready to end his existence, and he accepted it.

Charlie hadn't noticed it before, but the Baccus' eyes were golden. It looked afraid. These weren't beings of war and he felt immediately ashamed at his outburst of rage.

Then his vision started to blur and fade.

'Oh God no, not now,' Charlie thought.

"Where... get... Kono..." he managed to stammer as he dropped his rifle to the ground and he felt two strong arms holding him upright. He fought against it, but his eyes closed against his strong will and his body hung limp between Mauro and Laura.

Charlie didn't know how much time had passed when he opened his eyes again although surprisingly his surroundings didn't look much different to before. Actually, to be precise, he hadn't moved at all. The rest of the Ensigns still stood around in ready waiting, their torches illuminating the surrendered blue aliens. Instinctively, Charlie moved a hand to his face to check if his nose was broken, but stopped halfway there, as before him Laura held in her hand the syringe of pink fluid that Kono had manufactured to calm his tumours whenever they grew.

Laura smiled sadly. "Kono said this might happen. How do you feel?"

Charlie winced at that. It wasn't lost on him that he was supposed to be a soldier, a superman though what good was that if every time he got emotional he was going to pass out. He wondered just what Cesari would've thought about having him as a squadmate back when he was fighting the Scriven – Charlie would've been spider food in no time.

Laura noticed Charlie's attention fall on the broken form of his father but he brought his attention back to her.

"There was nothing anyone could've done. He saved us all and that's what we will remember him for but right now, right now we still have to take this ship."

It did seem to help and Charlie raised himself to his feet and brushed himself off. Stooping down to pick his rifle up from the ground, he smiled weakly. He didn't mean it but he tried his best.

"Better get going then or we might be late for dinner," Charlie said quietly. He noticed Mauro's ear twitch ever so slightly at the mention of food and it made him feel a little better.

Chapter 32

The soldiers of the GAP program progressed through the corridors of the battleship, searching each room and alcove as they went. It was as methodical and surgical as their training had instilled into them and each time they were greeted with an alien presence in a room, they waited before firing to see if the creatures would surrender or fight. If they fought they didn't survive and if they surrendered they were added to the ever-growing collection of hostages the soldiers held.

It wasn't as easy as it had been when the ship had lights, though Taylor had announced through the terminal that the battleship they were currently on board had lost both its weapons systems and engines – so it wasn't going to pose the rest of the humans any further threat. Charlie could barely believe his luck in just how smoothly everything seemed to be going – save for the untimely death of his father of course.

Inevitably, the GAP soldiers made it to the bridge and when the doors opened and their hostages filed into the room, it became apparent that where the Revenge had not exactly fit the bill in terms of the grandeur of the bridge, comparatively this battleship was insane.

The room looked as though it'd been sculpted by a sci-fi writer's wet dream, with neon lights filling the wide-open spaces between island terminals, sweeping ramps and the all too obvious captain's chair. For some reason the power outages that plagued the rest of the ship were not affecting the bridge. Thankfully, save from a few Baccus tapping away on terminals, the room was almost entirely clear. Once the hostages had all been corralled into a corner of the room - there were now over seventy of them and thankfully the soldiers had learned their lesson and searched and removed any explosive devices from them – Charlie took a deliberate seat in the captain's chair. The leather was neither uncomfortably cold nor warm and the seat moulded like a gel to his form as he relaxed his body into it. If he thought about it, this chair was the most comfortable seat he'd ever had the pleasure of sitting in and it made him realise just how much these creatures valued comfort over function.

"Mr Mauro," Charlie announced, to which Mauro saluted over-animatedly in response. "What's for dinner?"

"I'll go see what I can find, Captain Sinclair, SIR!" Mauro replied with a huge grin on his face. The mention of food always seemed to make him happy.

"Laura, please could you remove these creatures from my bridge and place them in holding until we decide what to do with them, and Stephanie, please could you update Earth with our new status. Tell them that there are now two battleships promised to defend the planet at all costs."

He also asked Laura to arrange for teams to sweep the ship for any other aliens that might've been holding out, and for Stephanie to see just how badly the ship was damaged. Laura and Stephanie dutifully disappeared without fanfare though Charlie could see that they were all smiles for the end of the hostilities.

Stephanie took the place of one of the aliens that'd been working on the terminals and immediately announced that they'd done their best to lock her out of the system. Charlie didn't mind though, he knew it would only be a matter of time before she cracked it. Turning his attention back to his smaller portable terminal, he tapped the screen and happily noted that the link between them and Taylor's ship was still active.

"Taylor?" he said confidently to bring his captain counterpart back to attention. "We have the ship."

"Well shit that was fast!" Taylor announced, his face once again filling the screen. "Our scans from here say that there are still aliens on board, though it looks as though they're grouped together. Did you do that?"

"Yep, that was us," Charlie confirmed. "We're sending them off to holding cells to keep them quiet – one of them managed to drop a grenade earlier and… well it wasn't pretty." He could barely bring himself to say the words.

"Shit, much damage?" Taylor asked.

Charlie didn't respond for a long time, though when he did he said flatly : "Not much, just one man down."

"Sorry man," Taylor said earnestly. "They can be tricky but usually once they're caught they just give up, you know?"

Charlie nodded.

"Anyway, your ship is pretty damaged over there but all is not lost, we found out that if we took out the engines the weapons systems would go offline anyway, so if you do manage to repair them you'll basically be fully functional again."

"Well that's some good news at least," Charlie replied. "Any tips on fixing the engines?"

Taylor snorted out a laugh. "Fuck no! This thing was working perfectly well when we got here and it still is, thank you very much."

It didn't matter really, Charlie knew that Stephanie and her team of engineers would be able to figure it out – she always came through when it was something to do with technology.

Then Charlie had an idea. "You know more will be coming, right?" He asked over the terminal. Taylor nodded. "So what we really need to do is get our ship back up and running as quickly as possible right, so that we can defend ourselves?" Charlie paused for a long moment. He needed to be sure that what he was about to say was the right thing. "I think it's time for someone else to take over. We need to go home and let more experienced people handle this, you know?"

A big part of being excessively intelligent, Charlie knew, was knowing when to ask for help and a combination of his actual age, experience and ever-present brain tumours had led him to that, as the only conclusion.

Taylor bit the inside of his cheek and frowned, but eventually nodded. This had gotten way, way out of hand and it was clear to them both that the only way for them to win, was to stop playing.

Charlie switched off his terminal and called Stephanie over.

"Stephanie, I need to speak to someone on Earth. Can you do a lookup or a search or something?" He asked and Stephanie nodded silently.

Charlie asked for the one person that he thought he could talk to in all of this. The one human on Earth that he knew at least knew of him and his situation.

"Please can you try to call a man named Colonel Miles Hardman."

It took a few tries, but Stephanie both found the Colonel and sent the call onto the terminal attached to Charlie's captain's chair. The Colonel was not in uniform and looked tired although Charlie wasn't actually sure what time it was wherever the Colonel was. His face remained unchanged from the last time he'd spoken to him though.

"Who is this?" Hardman said. "And where are you calling from?"

Obviously the Colonel knew that Charlie was calling from 'off world' as he was familiar with the terminal and it's procedures but Charlie had forgotten the fact that he didn't look anything like the boy who the Colonel had spoken to all those months ago.

"Uh Colonel, it's me... Charlie Sinclair. The last time you saw me I was much smaller and in a wheelchair actually."

"No... way..." Hardman replied, slowly placing his hand on the screen as he spoke. "I can see it now... but what's happened to you?" he asked apparently in shock.

Charlie sensed that this was going to be the start of him telling the same story over and over again to a number of different people and he really didn't feel like that was going to be much fun. Nevertheless he brought the Colonel up to speed on everything that'd happened up to this very moment. He left out no details and the Colonel seemed genuinely surprised about most of it. Of course, Charlie didn't mention his PIP level – there were still some secrets that he did want to keep.

"I mean, I knew the cadets had gotten into some trouble out there but, seriously – two battleships – the Council? This is some serious stuff, Charlie," Hardman announced once Charlie had finished speaking.

Of course Stephanie's message had gotten through previously, but it had apparently been somewhat quashed outside of military circles.

"Listen Charlie," the Colonel said eventually after he'd animatedly pulled himself together. "I need you to sit tight and let me run this one up the line, OK? Just give me a couple of hours to see what I can have sorted for you. We'll bring you home, don't you worry."

"Actually, I have a plan for that too," Charlie said with a flat smile. He still wasn't entirely sure that this was the right course of action, but his lack of options had presented no alternative paths.

~

The lifeboats aboard the battleships were so numerous that it only took two trips to replace the entirety of the GAP program with military personnel and civilian scientists. It was explained to Charlie and the others briefly that their first action was going to be to repair Charlie's ship and at the same time compare the systems of that ship with the fully functioning one so that the Earth militaries could learn both how to effect repairs, and how the behemoths operated. In addition, they moved the entire alien crew into temporary housing within a new purpose built facility in the Arizona desert, along with every single member of the GAP program, the instructors and Dr. Kono. They weren't prisoners as the aliens were though, they just weren't allowed to reintegrate with humanity as a whole.

The commandeering of the vessels along with the speed of the rotation of personnel was actually quite astounding and it'd all actually been completed within just ten hours of Charlie's conversation with Colonel Hardman.

Each member of the crew of both ships had been inspected physically and assessed mentally upon their arrival into the Arizona base, though not a single one of them had raised any sort of concern with the experts on either front. For all intents and purposes, each member of the GAP program was a healthy, balanced, level headed twenty-something year old with enhanced physical abilities. If anything, the civilian instructors had caused more concern than any of the soldiers had.

It'd been two weeks since the militaries of Earth had begun their joint venture into the Earth Space Force and by all accounts they'd been acting as though it was their idea all along. The members of the GAP program knew the truth though – without them, the planet wouldn't even have these two gigantic spaceships to play with. They didn't particularly care though. The thoughts that were pretty much universal within the facility were that they'd all done something that would save the planet from destruction, and they didn't particularly care how the military was going to dress it up.

Some of the soldiers had been called upon to help by giving more information to the scientists or tacticians that the military had employed to deconstruct their situation. Specifically Stephanie had been a great help by teaching a group of scientists how both the terminals worked, and how the weapons platform would have carried out its task. Charlie hadn't realised exactly how clever Stephanie had become during her time in the program.

Charlie had been asked about the other races of aliens he'd encountered, his tactics in overpowering them, their tactics, everything down to their general demeanour and speech patterns. He could tell that the military was fishing for information that they could use at a later date, but he didn't begrudge passing any of it on – if it could be helpful in any way, he was going to say it.

Kori had remained mostly quiet since his arrival back on Earth and Charlie theorised that it was because of an internal feeling of abandonment that had returned once he was back on the planet, his cocky bravado simply a front to overcompensate for his personal shortcomings. Charlie didn't push the fact but remained friendly whenever he could.

Mauro and Laura had been spending more time together. It was nice for Charlie to see, though he knew they'd never be anything more than friends. Laura just didn't like Mauro in that way and he presumed that the only love Mauro was ever going to have, would involve food.

It was an odd experience, he and his closest friends had remained close to each other physically, but once they'd arrived back on Earth it seemed as though they all had something more important to do. Kono and Shepherd had all but disappeared though presumably they actually had a lot of work to do, and the rest of the GAP members just seemed to get on with the routine of their lives – training, playing sports, watching the latest TV shows and movies that they'd missed out on in their absence.

However, that was all going to change, due to a single visit from an unexpected and previously unknown person.

"I'm sure you know who I am?" the man said as he walked into the room where Charlie, Stephanie, Laura, Mauro and Kori had been mustered. He wore a smart blue suit with an American flag as a pin, and was accompanied by two larger men wearing earpieces, sporting dark sunglasses and wearing black suits.

"Actually... I have no idea," Charlie replied. "I can take a guess if you like?"

The man cocked his head to the side with a bemused look on his face.

"Well you're not the President of America because everyone knows who that is, even if you want to be. You have two security guards even though you're inside a secure facility with trained and enhanced super soldiers – by the way they really wouldn't stand a chance – and you're wearing a hot looking suit and shiny black leather shoes when coming to a place covered with orange dust and sand. That tells me that you don't belong here. BUT, you arranged for all of us to meet you, so that means you know about the program and probably our specific interactions with some alien beings. My guess is that you're in charge of something to do with alien relations and they've asked you to arrest us and send us off to the Council in exchange for them not blowing the planet into tiny pieces."

The man looked shocked at first, then impressed, and then it seemed that he changed his demeanour purposely to morose.

"That's a very good guess," the man said. "My name is Mr Ainsworth, and I have indeed some knowledge of the program that you have been a part of. In addition, you are somewhat correct in your assumption that we have had communication with the Intergalactic Council, though it is not as dire as you make out. In fact, I have some good news for you. The Council has asked to meet with a congregation of humans that is to include you and your friends, specifically the members of the GAP program that were present on Omnis station during your visit. I understand that Marcus Cesari is sadly no longer with us, so this leaves you and your friends." The man smiled. "I am the head of the IRD - that's the Intergalactic Relations Department with the newly formed Homeworld Security and you, Charlie, are going to be present in the first ever offworld meeting to discuss membership for the human race within the Council."

Charlie frowned and fell deep into thought. Everything he knew about the Council was telling him that this was not a likely situation to find himself within at all. The Council did not walk in grey areas – you were either a threat to be destroyed or an ally to be a part of the group. Human beings, as far as he could tell, were never likely to become allies, and with the failure of the GAP program – the one thing that was keeping them alive by all accounts, their future had seemed so assured.

"So what - now they just want to talk? I don't see how that's very likely," Charlie said quietly, still thinking.

"I know you may have some negativity towards these beings and by all accounts that may be warranted, but what we've been doing over the last few weeks ,Charlie, is nothing short of miraculous and the Council sees that. They see what we are capable of, how resourceful we are and the way we can reverse engineer and replicate technologies. Charlie, we have two fully functional battleships in our fleet and soon there will be a lot more. The weapons systems alone have led to advances in equipment for the militaries of Earth already and the energy transfer systems that the ships used have catapulted our race decades into the future. If the Council thought we were almost ready for membership before, they've certainly sat up and taken notice now."

Unfortunately with this statement, Charlie could both see and hear the grandeur in the man's speech. He knew that he wouldn't hear his counter argument, this man wouldn't believe that the Council would be anything other than impressed by the human race, but Charlie knew better. Everything this Mr. Ainsworth had just said was more of a reason for the Council to be threatened by the human race and would cause them more fear and therefore a refreshed reason to strike out at them again.

"So what are they asking for?" Charlie asked.

"They've got a ship in orbit right now and a transport on its way to this camp right now. That's why I'm here Charlie. We are going to change the fate of the world today."

Charlie almost thought the man sounded deluded, though wondered if it was simply his way to try to get Charlie on board and excited about the situation.

"Have you spoken to the others?" Charlie asked.

"Actually, I was hoping that was something you could do for us," Ainsworth replied. "It might just sound a little better coming from you."

Charlie nodded. It was true, but truth be told he still wasn't fully on board himself. He tried to think through the alternatives, though he knew that if he rejected the proposal he could be putting others at risk. He and his squadmates actually did have the best knowledge of alien beings and the Council, even as diluted as that may have been. He also thought that if things went downhill, he and his squad may have been able to handle things a little better than some of the other soldiers available to the man. If indeed any of this was true, he wanted to ensure that humanity as a whole had the best chance it possibly could at returning with a favourable outcome.

When Charlie met with Laura, Mauro, Kori and Stephanie the group exchanged long hugs and handshakes that were well overdue. With the lack of real time they'd had with each other it was apparent to them all that they'd been missing each other's company terribly, though none of them needed to voice that concern. They all wore the dress uniforms that'd been specifically commissioned for them as their roles as GAP diplomats – a title that was created specifically for these five humans alone. They were not unlike naval dress uniforms, although without the hats, and instead of chevrons denoting rank, on their right shoulder sat a red wreath of knowledge surrounding an embroidered globe. The five actually looked pretty amazing, if Charlie didn't say so himself, the men as polished marines and the women as beautiful as he'd ever seen.

There was no time wasted in getting the squad on board, and within just a few short moments the small transport vessel was departing planet Earth back into the skies and beyond. It was the one place Charlie never thought he was going to have to go again, and he hated it with all of his being.

Chapter 33

On board the ship, the crew had just forty minutes to talk before their arrival on the alien vessel and Charlie didn't want to waste any time in concocting their plan of action. It was just them and Ainsworth on board–along with the alien pilot who was evidently not a sociable creature as he or she didn't leave the safety of the cockpit for even a moment during their departure.

"Why do you think they asked for us?" Stephanie asked in a worried tone. "I was working with a team on the new propulsion systems for our new battleships."

Laura and Mauro glanced at each other but tried to hide it. "We were just..." Mauro started though Laura interrupted him. "We were going through everything we'd learnt on the program with a fine toothed comb," she said. "It's hard to know what we actually learned in Kono's subconscious lessons and they wanted to gauge its effectiveness."

Kori stayed silent. It was clear that being on Earth wasn't actually doing him any good. Ainsworth also remained silent though he was obviously paying attention to their conversation.

"You think they want to put us back in prison?" Charlie asked and he looked at Ainsworth for an answer.

"As I told you, the Council specifically asked for your participation in these talks because they are familiar with you personally. It's just the way things are done in politics," the man replied, though Charlie didn't buy it.

Charlie knew from the way that Ainsworth was speaking, the way that his hands had begun perspiring and the fact that he could see the man's blood pressure and pulse rising by the vein protruding from his neck that he was worried, and in reality he didn't have a clue what these beings wanted them for. For all this man knew, they were all simply going to be killed on sight.

Something still didn't make sense though. Why would the Council ask to see these humans when they were so hell-bent on destroying the planet? It really didn't add up and Charlie turned it over in his mind, removing variables as he searched for an answer.

"I think they…" Charlie said to the room slowly. "… either want to introduce human beings into the Council after all, although on a tight leash, or they want their ships back before they destroy the planet. They don't like to fight so they may want to try to talk them back into the fold," It was a weak idea and he knew it but without more information, he was stumped.

"I hope they plan on feeding us," Mauro said with a smile. "Like, more of that pizza would be nice!"

"Do you mean the pizza that was laced with a sleeping drug that they used to imprison us?" Laura asked with a bemused look on her face.

"Yeah… I could do with a good sleep anyway, and besides, that pizza was great" he kissed the tips of his fingers to sign the international symbol of deliciousness and it made Charlie smile.

"At least we get to wear something half-decent now," Kori said. "Those flight-suits were getting a little tight you know," he held up a bicep and tensed as though to say 'look how big I am'.

Laura snorted. "I'd still take you in an arm wrestle though."

Ainsworth looked on as the pair postured until eventually they did partake in an arm wrestle that seemed to go on without either one of them giving up any ground. In fact, the only reason that the bout came to a halt was because the ship had jerked to a halt as it docked within a cargo bay, presumably belonging to the ship they'd been travelling towards all along.

"Right, here we are," Ainsworth announced as he slapped his thighs and stood up. "Now just make sure you follow my lead then, we don't want to mess anything up now, do we."

Laura raised her eyebrows at him and Kori snorted this time. It was clear that the man's credentials actually meant very little to them as a group – but he was there so there wasn't much any of them could do about it.

Charlie looked out of the small doorway from the transport ship and out into the open space where they'd docked. It was much, much smaller than the cargo bay that'd practically swallowed the Revenge, although their little ship did fit inside comfortably. To his surprise, two of the triangle-eyed security guard aliens came to collect them and passed a kind of scanning wand over them, presumably searching for concealed weapons. Then they led them all to where their meeting was going to be held.

The ship itself was clearly not of Baccus design, if Charlie knew anything about alien architecture, though admittedly his knowledge on the subject was limited. This ship seemed darker and colder than what he had become used to and the metal that was used to construct the interior walls looked very different to the grey-blue metal of the Baccus constructs, being more of a dull brownish colour.

It was almost enough to give Charlie a chill down his spine and the hairs on the back of his neck stood on end as they got closer to their final destination. When they arrived in the small room with a circular table in the centre, he saw exactly why his senses had been telling him that something was off.

On the far side of the table sat The Overseer, Jorell of the Ascara, Callantra of the Scriven, and three more of the triangle-eyed guards, all holding automatic laser rifles. Every single eye in the room was focussed on the humans who'd just entered.

'Hello, Charlie,' Callantra's voice rasped in his head. 'I told you never to cross the Scriven, didn't I?"

Charlie forced the voice out of his head as his mind raced to figure out what was happening. His heart beat out his chest and he blinked quickly to try to will his mind into overdrive, though the only response came that he needed to know more.

"Mr. Ainsworth," Jorell nodded to the human accompanying the squad. "And the humans of the Sinclair Squad. Welcome." Jorell did not smile, and nobody smiled back in response – except for of course, Mr. Ainsworth, who smiled warmly.

"May I say, sir," he started, "that it is an honour to finally meet you, and to be aboard your illustrious ship." He held a hand outstretched towards Jorell, who did not take it.

"I wish to have another conversation with you, Charlie," The Overseer spoke as though he had the full authority to do so. "Is that OK with you?"

Charlie remembered exactly how conversations with The Overseer went, and winced though he did nod in acceptance. The problem was though, that once again there would be no telling any lies to the being.

"Charlie, can you tell me how you escaped from my station?" The Overseer asked as everyone in the room took a seat, except for Callantra and the five armed guards.

"Well.." Charlie stalled to choose his words. "We were knocked out, then when we woke up we were off the station and on a ship actually," he said truthfully.

The Overseer stared at him as though searching for a lie in Charlie's statement.

"Did you arrange for this to happen?" The Overseer continued and it felt to Charlie as though he was being interrogated one-on-one with witnesses.

"No," Charlie replied simply.

The Overseer narrowed his eyes and thought for a moment.

"Did you plan your escape in any way?" he asked.

"No," Charlie repeated.

The Overseer looked to Callantra who didn't take her many eyes off of Charlie.

"How many of the Baccus Council Members' kin have you killed personally, directly and indirectly?" Callantra asked aloud.

Charlie wrinkled his nose as he searched his memory for a moment. "At least a hundred myself if I had to guess," he announced, again truthfully.

Callantra looked at Jorell, who actually seemed a little shocked by the number.

Ainsworth started to speak, but was shushed by a hiss from Callantra.

"As we are all aware, the human race continues to show itself as a threat to the rest of the Council. We must make our judgement to retake the ships from the humans and eradicate them from this galaxy," the spider-creature announced clearly to the room.

'The only reason you are here is because I want you to watch as your planet burns. I want you to see what you have caused because of your belligerence. There would never be any hope of survival. Your fate was sealed the moment human beings joined the wars against the Scriven.'

Charlie turned to the rest of his squad, ignoring the rest of the room. "They took us here to make us watch as they destroy Earth, there was never any diplomacy to be had. The Scriven want revenge for the humans joining the Baccus in their war against them before they were a part of the Council. Presumably they have some plan to deal with the Baccus too." Charlie spoke so quickly that nobody in the room had the forethought to interrupt him, although once he finished he saw Callantra unfold one of her front-most legs and as it reached across the table, he could see that it'd been sharpened to a razor's edge. Before anyone had even had the chance to make a move, Ainsworth's head hit the floor, cleanly detached from his body.

The GAP soldiers all stood up and moved to place their backs against the wall behind them, though it seemed like Callantra had done what she intended to do – there was no need for this man to be with them, her ruse had already succeeded in getting them aboard the ship and at her mercy.

"You are half correct," Callantra rasped. "The human race will face their punishment first, though the Baccus have already begun to feel the pain of their actions. Their only two battleships lie in the hands of your own race – soon to be liberated by the Council itself - and once you divulge how the Baccus helped you to escape from Omnis station, they will be removed from the Council and destroyed like the rabid animals they are."

'The Scriven shall reign supreme once all of this is over and you will be there to watch.'

Charlie looked at Jorell and The Overseer, though neither of them seemed to be moved by what Callantra was saying.

"Oh don't think you can rely on these puppets," she said, noticing Charlie's gaze. "My mental capacities do not simply extend to speaking telepathically, though you five do seem to be somewhat of an anomaly. You see I have the ability to persuade others even to the point of control in some cases..."

Charlie didn't need to hear anything else but as he moved a single foot, all five of the security guards in the room raised their rifles to point them directly at him as though they were all connected together.

Charlie knew that the threat in the room was coming from Callantra herself, especially now that she'd sharpened her legs to razor edges much like her warlike cousins and ancestors, although the rifles were keeping Charlie and his squad pinned in position. There was no cover or any evident weapons he could use nearby, so there was not much they could do but wait and listen.

"You're fucking sick," Laura spat at the Scriven.

"WHAT IS SICK," Callantra almost screamed, then lowered her voice somewhat, "is the fact that you humans thought that you could arrive on a planet that you've never even heard of before, and kill indiscriminately. YOU are the aggressors here. YOU chose to begin this path of war. Do not lecture me on what you think is right or wrong."

There was of course no defence for this, the squad knew that she was right for the most part – if things were the other way around they knew the humans of Earth wouldn't stand for such treachery.

"But you don't have to kill us *all* for those mistakes," Laura objected.

"That may be the case, but what better lesson could there be to the rest of the universe than if you cross the Scriven, it'll be the last thing you do?" Callantra replied. "Now that we know the secrets of the Council, the civilisations that these beings destroyed through fear, it is clear that with the allied might and technology behind the Scriven, we can reshape the universe as we see fit. You are the first to hear these words spoken, but the Scriven will rule where and how *we* decide."

"And you had to kill Mr. Ainsworth for all this to happen? Just leaving his body there separated from its head in some show of ancient ritual where you've sharpened your legs to edges? And keeping us here against our will with armed guards?" Stephanie asked clearly and her statement made Charlie frown. Within a moment he realised just what was happening. The beings had searched for weapons on them, but it didn't seem like they had been looking for anything else – such as terminals or communications devices.

"So you think you can just do what you want, kill who you want and get away with it? Taking over the universe and wiping out civilisations as you go?" Charlie asked loudly and very clearly.

Callantra cocked her large head then looked at The Overseer. It was evident after a few moments that she was giving him some sort of telepathic instruction and she eventually turned to Charlie and his squad, who all still stood with their backs to the wall.

"Charlie," The Overseer announced. "Did you bring any technology on board this ship with you?"

"No," Charlie replied truthfully and The Overseer looked back to Callantra who was apparently intrigued by the situation.

"Are you currently communicating with anybody outside this room?" he asked.

'No' came the flat reply again.

"Did you come to this meeting with any plans other than to speak with us?" The Overseer asked.

Charlie could tell that he was searching for the answer that he already thought he knew, but the issue was that the creature was asking the wrong person. They never even suspected that the subterfuge would be coming from the placid and seemingly worried Stephanie Marsh, once again, just as she'd caught out Matty Henderson what seemed like a lifetime ago. The thought of the deceased soldier brought a pain to Charlie's chest.

He wasn't sure if it was the way that other civilisations or races worked, but Charlie always felt as though he was questioned as the leader, and therefore would have all of the information to hand. It was that simple fact that saved the squad at this very moment, from divulging the fact that Stephanie was broadcasting their entire conversation to the two Earth battleships as it happened. Was it just the way the Council members worked? Their leaders knew everything so they assumed that fact rang true in other races?

One of the security guards promptly left the room, passing by Charlie within a foot and he wondered if he should try to overpower the being, although he knew that if he made his move in that instant, it would mean death for at least some of his squad. They had no weapons or armour and the four other guards remained in the room, their weapons pointed directly at Charlie's friends.

Charlie tried to figure out what was happening in his mind, to fit all of the pieces of the puzzle together so that everything made sense. After a moment of pondering, he simply couldn't help himself.

"So why bring these two now?" Charlie asked. "Why not just bring the Council under your control and destroy us from afar?"

Callantra seemed to smile at the question. "Even my powers have limits. Whilst I am able to control the minds of these... lesser beings at this proximity, the effect wears off over time and it has a tendency to weaken in large groups. It is actually easier to bend truths rather than falsify memories, which is why these two are here. When the time comes, they will remember the decisions they have made and it will be far more palatable for them."

"So you bring them along so they can form some warped memory of our wrongdoing?" Laura asked. "Sounds a bit far fetched to me."

"There are many things you do not and will not ever understand," Callantra hissed with her attention turned to Laura. "But that does not matter. Once you have watched your civilisation burn to the ground, I plan to make you my prized personal servants. I am not worried if whatever gene editing you have gone through prevents my mental manipulations, as if you do not eventually break mentally, you will break physically." The alien sounded calm now, and it made Charlie worried.

Charlie looked at The Overseer and then to Jorell, who both had a very glazed-over look to their eyes. It seemed that they were living and breathing, taking in the conversations as they happened, but they weren't an active part of them. Presumably the security guards were either falling in line the same way or couldn't tell that their real master was under some sort of manipulation. Whatever was going on in the room though, Charlie knew that it was something that he wasn't going to be able to stop.

"So we're supposed to just hand back over the two battleships we liberated, then watch as you destroy the human race?" Laura asked.

"Exactly," Callantra replied. "Though the deal with your officials is that once the ships have been returned to Council control, we will leave and reassess your membership within the Council. It was heavily implied though, that your application would be successful."

"And that was a lie then?" Charlie asked very loudly and very clearly now.

Callantra cocked her head once again.

"I am not sure what you are failing to grasp in such a basic concept, human. Yes, Sinclair, once the ships have been returned to me they will immediately open fire on the most populated areas on your planet. It is not the total annihilation that I wish for, though that will not come far behind."

Charlie waited for a few moments. He knew that would be the final nail in the coffin and he braced himself for the coming impact. Right on queue, the ship rumbled and shook, both The Overseer and Jorell's attention snapping back to the room.

The door flew open and the triangle-eyed security guard that'd previously left ran straight past Charlie and straight up to The Overseer.

"They're attacking us!" The guard announced, and it wasn't lost on Charlie that it was the first time he'd heard one of these beings actually speak. "And we detected a signal being broadcast to their ships but we don't know where it's coming from." The alien seemed both flustered and scared of the words he was saying, though before The Overseer could say a single word, Callantra had cut the guard cleanly in half, his torso, arms and head landing on the ground with a thud before the thinner grey Overseer, who didn't seem to care.

'Which one of you has the transmission device?' Callantra's voice sounded loud in all of the soldiers' heads and Charlie could see the internal fog rolling in once again. He fought it, but could see that the task was difficult for his friends.

More rumbling as weapons fire hit the ship that they were on and rattled the room. Callantra now looked far less assured of herself, though she still persisted in her mental attack. To his left, Charlie could see that Stephanie had fallen to her knees and her hands held her head as though it was going to explode.

Charlie closed his eyes and began to concentrate. He thought about the lives of the people that'd been lost in all of this, of Cesari and even Henderson, the lives of the human race as a whole and the lives of his squadmates and friends right there next to him, right now. He balled it all up into one mental orb and willed it away toward Callantra, down her mental link and across the physical distance between them. He willed her the entire pain of the humankind and in that moment he felt it hit her all at once.

Callantra reeled and screeched an ear piercing cry as the ball of torment hit her and knocked her back off her chair and into the security guards who could do nothing to move out of the way. The Scriven pinned the guards to the wall and the soldiers knew that this was their one single chance to put a stop to the madness. Charlie leapt across the table and bundled The Overseer to the ground whilst Kori was just a moment behind, taking down Jorell. Neither of the aliens seemed to give any resistance to the attack, either stunned by Callantra's scream, or still under the mental control.

Stephanie, Laura and Kori rounded the table on both sides and dove for the dropped rifles of the security guards as Callantra scrambled back to her feet, her senses somewhat returning.

'Never!' Her voice moaned in their minds again. 'I will destroy you all!'

But it had come too late. Stephanie, Laura and Kori had picked up the weapons and were aiming them at the guards who were holding their hands out in surrender and The Overseer and Jorell were unconscious on the floor. All that left, was Charlie and Callantra facing each other in a final showdown that nobody could interfere in.

"You need to get out of here," Charlie said over his shoulder without taking his eyes off of Callantra. "Take the guards, take these two," he nodded at The Overseer and Jorell, and get out. Speak to the battleships, tell them to render this ship fucking useless, then come and get us. Do not let these out of your sight and try to keep our situation under wraps, the less the crew know the better. I'll be OK here, OK?"

Laura opened her mouth to protest but Charlie interrupted her, "OK?"

That was all the group needed to follow the orders that Charlie'd given and within a few short moments only Charlie and Callantra were left in the room. He was worried that they might object and try to stay, although he had the feeling that they were in a slight state of shock at his mental attack that had seemed to throw Callantra across the room.

'You are but a child, there is no hope for you to defeat me!' Callantra's voice filled Charlie's mind but he didn't care. He could hear the weakness in it as well as the fear.

"Your tricks don't work any more, and behind that all you're just a spider." Charlie goaded.

Callantra lunged with a scream.

The muscle tone changed in her front legs as she willed them to shift her size and weight and Charlie saw it. The world around him had slowed to a crawl and he watched as Callantra's expression betrayed her hatred and effort simultaneously bubbling over and before she'd even moved two inches Charlie'd made his dodge. Callantra rolled as she hit nothingness and wheeled to see where her human target had moved to, evidently shocked at the speed of his anticipation and movement.

"Not fast enough," Charlie announced.

Charlie knew that the longer he wasted time for here, the better the chances of his own rescue. He could still feel the rumbles and shudders of weapons fire though wasn't sure how well armed the vessel he was currently aboard was, all he really knew was that his side had two of the massive battleships, and this was only one.

Callantra shifted her weight into her rearmost legs and raised her front pair. Charlie could see just how sharpened they'd been as the light glinted off their razor's edge and he grimaced. The sight was horrific and reminded him of the Brazilian Wandering Spider adopting its 'attack first, no questions asked stance'. That answered his question as to whether the Scriven would play dead when confronted.

Charlie scanned the room in a second and dove to pick up a metallic chair – the one thing in the room that he felt he could wield as an effective weapon. He wondered if he could push the large table across the room but couldn't see if it was bolted down so decided it was best not to make a fool of himself or put himself in a compromising situation.

Callantra launched her attack as Charlie moved, and if he hadn't timed his actions impeccably he was sure the spider's legs would've bisected him. He grabbed a hold of the chair and as Callantra's bladed appendage struck he spun the useful piece of furniture to divert the blow, catching the flat and unsharpened side of the leg between the chair's own, entangling it in the tubes of metal that constituted its stand.

Callantra's leg lie flat on the floor, pinned down under Charlie's unlikely weapon and weight, though he knew there were more where that came from. Using the periphery of his vision and his sense of foreboding he held the chair tightly in his hands and cartwheeled out of the way of the second incoming blow.

Black blood oozing onto the ground punctuated the scream that emanated from Callantra's maw as her leg lie broken, detached on the floor. Charlie had dodged the deadly blow of the second leg and removed one threat to his person.

Callantra had murder in her eyes as the new pain she was in coursed through her body. It was new for her and a part of her wondered if this was how all of her ancestors and cousins had felt as they were injured by the unwieldy humans.

She had few options left now than to press her advantage. She was bigger, stronger and smarter and there was no way that this human could pose her any kind of realistic threat. She brought her front leg up again to strike but her alarm grew as when her leg descended, the human rolled out of the way, entirely unscathed. It was as though he could tell what she was going to do, even before she'd decided on that action. All she could see now though was red, red with the singular purpose to take this being down at all costs.

Charlie watched as Callantra *jumped* into the air, spreading all of her remaining legs wide to fall as a net atop him. Again, his advanced perception slowed the world to a halt and he had all the time he needed to find what he was looking for and plot the proper course.

The Scriven fell atop Charlie and he felt the pain of needle-pointed appendages pin his legs to the ground but he didn't care, the screech that emanated from the spider-being and the blood that began to ooze and stain the floor betrayed the fact that his tactic had been successful. Callantra fell to the side and onto her back, her legs curled up and protruding from her body, her own, previously broken leg sat as the telltale sign that she was truly no more. Callantra's heart, had been pierced by her own, sharpened front leg, just as her ancestors had once used in battle.

Epilogue

Charlie had been collected from the room after again the internals of the ship had fallen dark and quiet. He'd made sure that Callantra was dead just in case she was playing the old spider trick. The battle that'd waged outside in space wasn't as easy a fight as the human battleships had had before, and once he started moving, out of the windows of the ship Charlie could see both human battleships venting atmosphere from hull breaches, orange fires and small explosions erupting over both of the their full lengths. It was clear though from the state of affairs, that humanity had won the day and Charlie and his squad were safe – relatively speaking – even if it looked as though the vessels were set to explode at any minute.

The ship that Charlie and his squad had been on quickly surrendered once it'd been rendered inoperable, and according to Stephanie, once she'd gotten access to the computer system, this particular ship should've been a match for the two battleships currently comprising the human fleet. It would seem that, once again, the tactics of a race of beings who'd long forgotten the ways of war had failed them when pitted against the might of a desperate humanity.

The squad had to remain on the alien vessel for almost a day once the fighting had finished as the three vessels effected their emergency repairs. The human ships had sent over complements of marines to place the alien crew into custody, along with Jorell and The Overseer – though it was quite clear that without the mental manipulation that Callantra had employed, their demeanour was very, very different.

Jorell had eventually explained to Charlie that Callantra had infiltrated the Council as part of the Scriven delegation – a race that really shouldn't have been allowed to join so quickly – and had manipulated her way onto the seat of much of the Council's dealings. It had not been apparent that she was using a telepathic ability at first, though as she crept her way through the members, turning them to her cause, it became clear all too late that anyone standing against her found themselves either missing, a target to be turned, or voted off of the Council entirely. The Scriven had been using the very democratic nature of the Council against itself – for she only ever really needed to bring half of the members to her cause at any given moment to fulfil her goals.

The apologies that The Overseer and Jorell gave did seem genuine to Charlie, though his friends weren't as readily accepting of them, giving them both a wide berth until they could leave the ship.

Once Charlie and his squad were relieved – a transport ship taking them back down to Earth - they were summarily debriefed and had to sadly report the passing of Mr. Ainsworth, who although had tried to carry out his duty with honour, had perished far too soon. It was a senseless death, but one that nobody had seen coming. There hadn't been much explaining required, however, as Stephanie had begun her broadcast almost immediately after entering the room where the aliens had awaited them, and the battleships had relayed everything unabridged to the militaries back on Earth.

The last thing that the military would do for Charlie and his friends though, due to their service, the ordeals that they'd been through at technically such a young age, and the status of Earth in the eyes of the Council, was that they would be discharged to lead the rest of their lives as they would see fit. That was after a few weeks of both physical and mental assessments by instructor Shepherd and Dr. Kono of course, the former very pleased to report no issues whatsoever, and the latter supplying Charlie with both the tumour suppressant he'd concocted, and the formula for more to be synthesised, wherever he chose to lead the rest of his life. Lastly, Kono had told Charlie to keep working hard to increase his PIP level. At passing fifty percent he'd been able to fight off Callantra's mental attacks, but as he grew, the possibilities and feats his body could accomplish would be endless.

All of the cadets of the GAP program been offered a military pension of sorts, to be paid by the Earth Space Corps. They were told that they could leave to live wherever in the world they would like, although some chose to remain with the military to both continue to grow and impart their knowledge onto others. For Charlie there was only one place that he knew he could call home.

~

The Intergalactic Council had received word of the deception of Callantra and the games she'd been playing to further her and the Scriven's own agenda and immediately expelled the race from the Council. They knew that it would almost certainly mean falling into war again, but it was much better to fight an enemy you knew, rather than allow them to integrate themselves covertly within your own ranks. It did however mean that the Council would once again be in need of soldiers willing to fight for their cause, and without the GAP program, things would be difficult for them.

Communicating directly with the leaderships of Earth, the Council eventually offered a new deal to the humans. They would be allowed to join the Council with immediate effect, the GAP program would be restarted at a date and location that suited mankind and the fleet that the humans had so far amassed and would continue to be built would stay within their own hands and command. Needless to say, this was a call to arms, and humanity would answer for the good of the universe.

~

Charlie knocked on the door of the tall townhouse where he knew Mr. and Mrs. Brown lived, the very house where he'd spent so many months trying to regain the use of his broken body with the people that he'd grown to love and who had given up so much of their own lives to care for him.

Charlie waited patiently and his heart rate increased, his palms sweating. He felt anxious but excited to see the Browns again.

The door opened and Mrs. Brown looked Charlie square in the eyes. In that moment, Charlie remembered the fact that he'd aged into a man and that perhaps she wouldn't even recognise him after so many years of artificial ageing.

Mrs. Brown's straight face stared into Charlie's eyes for a long moment, and then melted into a smile as tears filled her eyes and overflowed onto her cheeks.

"You're home Charlie!" she sobbed. "I knew you'd come home."

Charlie couldn't help but wipe tears from his cheeks as they overflowed from his own eyes and he felt the love from the woman wash over him.

"I'm home, mum. And I brought some friends with me." Charlie replied and stepped out of the way to reveal the smiling and waving figures of Stephanie Marsh, Kori Nakamura, Mauro Latori and Laura Giardini.

A Thankyou

Again, your investment of your own time and money is always well appreciated and again, I ask that you **rate** and **review** everything that you read – and not just this book, so that lesser-known authors can grow their audience and gain the credibility that they deserve for their hard work.

Also, check out my website, it's usually kept up to date with current works, reviews and a few extra little bits. You'll find it at:

www.davidlingard.com

Thank you

Printed in Great Britain
by Amazon